CONTEMPORARY AMERICAN FICTION

MERCEDES AND THE HOUSE OF RAINBOWS

Alan Jolis grew up in Paris, went to high school, college, and law school in the United States and now lives in Paris again, where he is writing his second novel.

Mercedes and the House of Rainbows

A NOVEL BY

ALAN JOLIS

PENGUIN BOOKS

PENGUIN BOOKS
Published by the Penguin Group
Viking Penguin, a division of Penguin Books USA Inc.,
40 West 23rd Street, New York, New York 10010, U.S.A.
Penguin Books Ltd, 27 Wrights Lane, London W8 5TZ, England
Penguin Books Australia Ltd, Ringwood, Victoria, Australia
Penguin Books Canada Ltd, 2801 John Street,
Markham, Ontario, Canada L3R 1B4
Penguin Books (N.Z.) Ltd, 182–190 Wairau Road,
Auckland 10, New Zealand

Penguin Books Ltd, Registered Offices:
Harmondsworth, Middlesex, England

First published in the United States of America by
Poseidon Press, a division of Simon & Schuster Inc. 1988
Published in Penguin Books 1989

1 3 5 7 9 10 8 6 4 2

This book is a work of fiction. Names, characters, places, and incidents either are the product of the author's imagination or are used fictitiously. Any resemblance to actual events or locales or persons, living or dead, is entirely coincidental.

LIBRARY OF CONGRESS CATALOGING IN PUBLICATION DATA
Jolis, Alan.
Mercedes and the house of rainbows: a novel/by Alan Jolis.
p. cm.
ISBN 0 14 01.2103 X
I. Title.
PS3560.O43M47 1989
813'.54—dc20 89-32726

Printed in the United States of America

To Maruja, Manolo, Dora, Mercedes,
Oliva, Charo, and Anna-Mari,
who taught me that loyalty to those we love
is all that matters. And, of course, to Cilla.

Contents

"UN AMÉRICAIN QUI PENSE, MAIS C'EST UN PEU COMME UN CHIEN QUI PARLE!"

—*Parisian insult purportedly leveled at Benjamin Franklin*

Mercedes and the House of Rainbows

CHAPTER 1

Kim Novak Is Not a Man and Other Important Discoveries

ON THE WEST side of Paris, by the Sixteenth Arrondissement, where live the elite of the haute bourgeoisie, there is a park of pine, fir, and chestnut trees, landscaped at the turn of the century by le Baron Haussmann. Lovers often go there to rent rowboats and lose themselves in the deep-green confines of the man-made lakes. Away from the main roads and bridle paths, the serene waterways of the Bois de Boulogne cannot fail to evoke feelings of romantic love, especially in one predisposed to have these sentiments.

In one such rowboat, a seventeen-year-old Spanish girl stared longingly into a young boy's eyes. Blue ink spotted his hands and the lobe of his left ear; his fingernails were bitten raw; but he looked at her with such limpid and trusting eyes that she found him irresistible. They were cutting through a glaucous patch of white blooms shining against the moss-green water. A few rose petals fell slowly to the surface of the lake.

"Timoté, in life you must swim like a duck: calm on top, but paddling like furious down below."

After six months in Paris, she spoke French in a deliberate manner, inverting adjectives and getting her tenses mixed up. But she was not shy with Timi—he was perhaps the only other person on earth conversant with her Franco-Hispano-Gypsy dialect.

The boy nodded and watched a family of ducks glide by.

She stared gravely at the lonely condition of the lake. How she loved these charcoal-shaded clouds which sailed by so quickly they seemed to belong in some American movie. She even felt attached to the slurping of the water under the boat and the heavy lichen and weeds that weighed down the oars.

"Timi, last January some *payo* bandits—"

"What's a *payo?*" asked the boy.

"Anyone who is not a *calorró*."

"Why do Gypsies call themselves *calorrós?* No, no. Finish your story first. Go ahead."

"These *payos* in uniforms—our proud Guardia Civil—take our family's tambourines and drums without paying. My papa returns drunk and slaps me so hard, I bite my tongue. My blood splatters all over the horses! He accuses me of being too pretty! 'If you were uglier, the *payos* would not bother us so much,' he says."

She dipped the oars into the water and pulled slowly back, lifting her head to look up at the leaden clouds. If only her love life—which meant her real life—could be as dramatic and all-enveloping as the patchy light in this park! A few drops of rain hit the surface of the lake.

"The last time my father beat me, I remember him lunging, swearing, shouting. Then I faint. When I wake up, I walk straight to Matamoros. It is night. For six hours I lock myself in the public toilet of the train station. At first I think of stealing a horse. But they would be expecting that. Gypsies love horses. It is their favorite method of escape.

"So all black-and-blue and crying, I take the express train north to Bilbao, stealing bread from the station buffets along the way. Gitanos seldom take trains. So I am safe. But I cannot stay in Spain: the brotherhood of *calorró* thieves, street charlatans, and dancers will track me down and return me. From Bilbao I walk to San Sebastián and from there I get a ride on a fishing boat to Saint-Jean-de-Luz, across the border. The voyage is a distance of not more than fifty kilometers, but that sea is embedded in my soul. And with it, the smell of freedom!"

She breathed in now as deep as her lungs would go.

The boy shifted on his seat and looked embarrassed. They

glided quietly. Mercedes dipped three fingers into the reflection of a pink-and-white chestnut blossom and skimmed the water. The rowboat came to a halt, entangled in weeds and water lilies. The drizzle of rain was starting to make a million light pinpricks on the shiny surface of the lake. Mercedes stood up and pushed one of the wooden oars to the bottom.

"Can you taste freedom, Timi, when you breathe in?"

The boy sniffed discreetly.

"Breathe deeply." Her left hand circled under her chin as she inhaled. "More!"

"What are you talking about, Benz?"

"My name is not Benz. I am not a car!" said Mercedes, pushing the boat free.

She sat back now.

"When I arrive in Paris, I wander through the streets without a *carte de séjour.*"

"A what?"

"It is an all-important piece of official blue paper. I do not know how to give the right bribe to the right rat at the right office and so cannot get a work permit, or a resident's visa. Alone, I walk the Métros and the dirty side streets full of bad men trying to pull me into doorways. One day I read with horror a graffito that proclaims "SHOOT THE GYPSIES!" I think of having myself deported. But anything is better than going back to Matamoros. I try working in a hotel, cleaning. But the manager tries to push me into a broom closet and feel me. I break his glasses and pour hot coffee on his arm! Ha-ha! But I lose my job.

"Someday, Timi, I am certain, a man will ride into my life. He will gallop into the Cardozo courtyard, hooves clattering on stone, hair crisp and full of sunlight, and he will shout: 'Mercedes Pilar de los Angeles del Rosario, forgive all the sleazy, slimy males who have importuned you in the past.' He will not say this in words, of course. He will intimate it through his manner. He will kiss my hand, and his eyes will say: 'I understand the load you bear on this caravan of life. I am your soul mate. I cannot draw another breath without offering you the proofs of my love.' " She broke off.

"What are these?" Benz pointed to new cuts on Tim's knees, only partly covered by Band-Aids.

"A fight with Laval and his Republicans," said Timi, lifting his leather schoolbag over his head to protect himself from the rain.

She nodded with satisfaction and bent her lips to one of the Band-Aids. "Remember, Timi, the Gypsies say: 'To the enemy, do not give even water!' Never be afraid to fight. Pay what you owe, but be ready to fight if they come after you."

She wanted her men to be able to defend themselves to the death, even if they were the ones attacking. Mercedes watched several drops drip from the left oar and rejoin their friends, the millions of other drops in this vast expanse of water. Then she continued:

"Without a *carte de séjour*, I am even too scared to go to an employment agency. Marcel, the butcher's son, gives me the lungs, necks, and ovaries of his chickens. Barely enough, but I survive. Then I stumble on the Spanish Church on Rue de la Pompe. 'Too much crying is displeasing to God! Get up, child,' says the priest. He lets me stay at the church.

I do odd jobs, learning not to live scared, waiting day after day for a good *Madame* of Passy to hire me as a domestic. But the Paris *Madames* who come in search of *chachas* never pick Mercedes. They choose the other girls—a fat one from Salamanca who chews gum, a stupid one from Murcia who grunts and smells of bacon. And Mercedes grows very sad."

Thursday afternoon in early April. Around her, within her, everything was mounting, priming her for love. In the dark pine-scented depths of this secluded area of the park, she breathed in the fragrant aroma of wild honeysuckle and sighed. How long, she wondered, would she have to wait? Why did she not ask more of her admirers? Why was she not loved the way she deserved to be, the way Timi loved her? The men she was going out with were fundamentally not good enough for her!

"Benz, it's really starting to rain now!"

She pointed quietly at a vermilion petal shed by a blossoming rose. As it fell, its reflection in the water came up to meet it.

"Timoté, I am seventeen, almost eighteen, and life is passing me by."

"Is seventeen old?"

"Of course! The *gitanos* in Andalucia marry at thirteen or fourteen. At my age, already they have two children! At twenty-one your teeth start falling out of your head, and then it gets worse."

There were not as many hairs on her head as the times she had begged. Her father used to say: "Begged bread tastes best." But as she lay on the caravan floor with all her brothers and sisters, listening to the frogs croaking in nearby ponds and the horses eating their oats, she prayed not to a crucified gentle Christ, who helped the rich unburden themselves of their sin by his shining example—examples did not feed the hungry—but to an Old Testament warrior God who, like Moses, might lead them out of bondage.

"Timi, what the *gorgios* give as charity never fills you. You wake up *jayipí* and you go to bed *jayipí*."

"Benz, continue your story!"

"If you reveal your secrets to the wind, you should not be surprised if the wind reveals them to the trees."

"No, come on. Tell me. You were at the Spanish Church waiting, and then what?"

"Well, I wait. And after almost three months of not being hired, the priest takes me aside and explains that the Passy *Madames* are scared of bringing home a girl as pretty as me for their husbands to pounce on: 'Good *chachas* are usually fat and ugly. So cover your bosom. Do not tell them you are a Gypsy. Do not talk so much. In fact, try not to talk at all. And if they ask you about marriage plans, tell them you do not like or trust men. No one wants to train a girl who will leave or get pregnant in six months.' So Mercedes makes herself as ugly as possible. I wear a black raincoat, put my hair up and smear yellow rice powder on my face. And I wait. My tears are heavy like millstones. The autumnal leaves whisper terrible premonitions to me. But I do not lose heart."

She felt especially tragic today with her jet-black hair waving in the light drizzle and her big tanned legs, just waxed and smooth as silk, under her red-and-white polka-dot dress. It really was ridiculous to get dressed up just for Timoté! Why did she bother?

They exchanged glances. The creaking boat did not advance as quickly with Tim rowing. She lay back gazing at the boy's reflection against a backdrop of passing myosotis: the pink cheeks, the short dark hair with the cowlick in the back, the round horn-rimmed glasses, the cleft chin—these stretched and sank in the water and came back together as Tim pulled on the oars.

"So how did you find *us, Benz?*"

In the waveless blue-gray mirror of the water, the boy looked older, fuller; from the angle where she was seated, his big round lips were like a woman's, and his dark lunetted eyes became mysterious deep orbs. For the moment, the rain seemed to have stopped.

"I tell you too much already. You are only eight!"

"Nine! Well, eight and nine months. Come on, Benz, tell me."

He never tired of the story of how she had run away to Paris, although she had told it to him five or six times before. His pedigreed face looked so noble, smooth, and long in the water. Today, she wanted to unveil the depths of her soul to this boy's reflection, petal after petal, fold after fold, until she was totally naked before him. The problem was that no *payo* could be entirely trusted; nor could Timi, even if he wanted, understand the smell of waking up hungry in an abandoned shed, or of shivering, barefoot, behind a stable door waiting for the police to pass.

"You are a mere baby."

"Tell me or I'll conk you with this oar!"

Mercedes laughed and shouted for help. Couples in two other boats at the far end of the boat basin looked up. She was sorry because her outburst had ruined her inward dreamy state. She quickly sat back and resumed her tale:

"One day in church, this short fat woman with a mustache tells me: 'The priest recommends you very highly, but take that disgusting paste off your face. We are not in some three-dog village. And keep your hands off my husband, Pepe, or I break your face.' Manola, of course, is generous and full of love as all Basques. She asks where I am from. I answer 'Matamoros.' I am embarrassed to answer that I live for years on the *carretera* between Jaén, Seville, and the Sierras, depending on the season and my father's mood. She asks where I have worked. I answer that at home my father lies all day on a cot, smoking or playing cards, while I wash, cook, and scrub. Then she looks at my feet and asks: 'You are not a Gitana, are you?" I shake my head and swear: 'If that is not so, may my two eyes drop in my hat!' I feel like a traitor. But I do not totally lie. My mother, bless her soul, was a *paya*. But still it is a kind of lie. Manola tells me my salary and my vacation days. I try to remain calm, but inwardly I am crazy happy. When I arrive at your house, I kiss her and cry. Then you, Timi—O valiant and spoiled one—enter my life."

Two men had turned their boat around by the statue of Victor Hugo where the swans made their nest and were rowing toward them. Mercedes watched them through her fingers.

"Benz, those North Africans are going to try to talk to you. Please don't answer them!" He gave her a desperate look. "Benz, they're catching up."

One of the men hissed at her like a snake.

"Timoté," she said without acknowledging the presence of the men, "you must protect me!"

She liked the way Tim's eyes lit up behind his round glasses when she cast him in a lead role in her grandiose discussions of love. In the middle of a discourse on her many admirers and her confusing, contradictory desire to be wanted and yet respected and left alone, all at the same time, she would mention Timi's name. Then, as now, he would respond with something akin to panic, and Mercedes found this totally ingratiating and appropriate.

"Benz, they're faster rowers. They're closing in."

"Now, why are you not twenty years older, Timi?"

She knew the men were staring at her legs, but putting on her sunglasses, Mercedes contemptuously trailed the toes of her left foot over the edge of the boat and let the rowing pull her along. The men in the other boat clicked their tongues as if to urge on a horse; but Mercedes was watching a pale pink chestnut blossom, shaped like a little Christmas tree, fall through the honeyed breezes. One day she would fall, in this slow-motion way, into the arms of a man: They would meet just the way this pink flower was falling to meet the water rising to kiss its underside. It would be a perfect juncture. And all the noise, pain, disrespect, and dirt perpetrated on her would disappear, washed away like sin after confession.

"Benz, those men were laughing at you!"

"*Payos* men think I am a little idiot, that I have done nothing in my life. But Timoté, I am a million times more alive, more intelligent and passionate than any of them!"

"What does 'passionate' mean?"

She loved these lazy chatty afternoons with the boy, the endless questions, the arguments about nothing, really. But today, for some reason, her trip on the lake was shot through with memories of Seville.

" 'Passion' is difficult to explain," she said.

"Well, try! How am I going to learn anything if you don't try?"

Mercedes was locked in a strange dream time. There was a humming, a barely audible rush of wind. She stared at the sweeping richness of the trees on the bank. She was not here, she was in the Triana section of Seville, in javelin bolts of sunlight, on rooftops crowded with birds, going from tapas bar to tapas bar, singing for money, with her brothers to protect her from overenthusiastic patrons. When her breasts grew at eleven, dancing became more lucrative than singing or reading palms. And she was on a tabletop now, dancing a *zapateado* in a smoky little dive full of wine-breathing men.

"Timi, passion means to be overpowered or overburdened with feelings."

She helped him pull the unwieldy oars out of the oarlocks as they came alongside the floating pier. The boy steadied the boat and held her handbag as she clambered out.

"The passion of Christ was His suffering as a martyr. Passion means feeling so much that you cannot bear to feel any more."

The boy's shiny brown eyes darted skyward just as thunder

boomed in the east. She and Timi rushed along this Bois de Boulogne footpath, in and out of the dappled patches of shade and zinc-gray skies.

"Timoté, maybe good men when they see me with you, they think I am your mother and am married. So only the bad, shameless ones talk to me?" She had been meaning to bring this up for some time, in a more delicate manner. But she had blurted it out now and felt slightly embarrassed. After a while the boy asked:

"You want us to walk on opposite sidewalks?"

The rain was coming down hard now and they had only one umbrella between them. Benz smiled and laced her arm through his. They splashed through the puddles of this glossy, green park as a tide of cars glided by and riders galloped back to their stables. All the way to the Porte Maillot they ran, then jumped on a Number 73 bus.

And riding home on this rainy spring afternoon, when old concierges hid behind their gauze curtains and Métros roared deep beneath the cobblestones, Mercedes let out a squeak of surprise. The boy had reached up and brushed aside three sets of earrings and was touching her left earlobe.

"You have the softest ears in the world, Benz."

"Thank you," she said, wiping the wet hair from her eyes.

"Benz, why is your skin so dark?"

"Why are you Jewish?" she snapped.

The boy tried to cover up what she was saying with a cough. But Mercedes could be loud when she wanted to be.

"I'm only *half,"* Tim whispered. "Only on my father's side, so it doesn't count."

She knew that he managed to keep his half-Jewishness hidden from his fellow students. Timi attended a Jesuit school where he was the only American. This made him doubly suspect in the eyes of some of his teachers. Mercedes was perhaps triply so: she spoke unintelligible French, was half Gypsy, and had no legal papers—even Spanish ones!

"You and I are in the same position," she said, licking the edge of her handkerchief and rubbing Tim's cheeks to remove some grime. (Why was he always so spotted with blue ink?) "I am only half *gitana*, but they call me a Gypsy nonetheless. You, O spotted one, are half Catholic, but they treat you like an outsider."

The boy nodded slowly.

"You and I are half like the others, but they treat us as if we're different."

She loved it when the boy stared up at her with a mixture of awe and reverence. The bus stopped at the top of Avenue de la Grande Armée and they got off in silence.

"They do not trust us. They call us Gypsies and Jews, but the truth is they do not like us because they are jealous. We are too free for them."

When she spoke to him of the mysterious wanderings of her nomadic people, she saw his eyes light up: her dreary and violent past became somehow translated into a victory march around the world with her golden earrings at full mast, along the highways of Prussia, through Italy, Egypt, Austro-Hungary, and Russia, around Longchamps and Rambouillet and under the Arc de Triomphe. For Timi, being a wanderer put her on a par with Napoleon and all the soldiers who marched past his house and down the Champs-Elysées every Bastille Day. And Mercedes did not mind. But the facts were much different. To be a Gypsy was to beg. Her father had even taught an orangutan to beg. And when the orangutan died, he taught the donkey to beg!

"Timi, do not tell anyone I am half-*calorró*. If they ask you, you say I am very suntan. That will be our secret. *D'accord?*"

Again he nodded. So what, she thought, if this skinny, inky boy with the Band-Aids on his knees and oversized horn-rimmed glasses had never told the truth in his life? He could keep a secret.

TIM looked over his shoulder. The old gate to the first-floor garden was always kept locked, but it had a large rusted keyhole which afforded a quite unobstructed view. He knelt in a bed of impatiens and begonias. Wonderdog whined and scratched himself. Tim shushed him. In the Sixteenth Arrondissement, the center of power and breeding in Paris for at least four generations, one did not peek into other people's lives. If Pepe, the butler, caught him, he'd slap his head into the middle of next week. Tim pressed his eye to the keyhole and held his breath.

Behind the ivy-covered gate, he could smell all the flowers of spring and summer. An ant crawled up his sleeve. His knobby knees sank into the moist earth as he peered into the garden. There were the goldfish pond; the white lattice gazebo, heavy with wisteria and lilac; orange and pink tulips perky among the yet-to-bloom hortensia and rhododendron. And now Tim saw her, on the wooden bench, surrounded by a pale rainbow of flowers not more than 10 meters away. There was no longer any doubt—Kim Novak was not a man!

When Aunt Phoebe had read his dad's most recent letter, announcing the arrival of a new movie star, no one in the household—even Benz, who read all the movie magazines available—could say whether "Kim" was a man's or a woman's name. Endless arguments had ensued.

Something large, perhaps a dragonfly, buzzed around Tim's head. He again held his breath and, brushing aside the ivy that tickled his nose, peered through the keyhole. Kim was dressed like an Algerian: ripped T-shirt, cut-off jeans, wraparound sunglasses. Her hair was in a bun with a black knitting needle stuck through it. Tim felt an enormous sadness for this international star, blond like his mother, who sat by herself in this jewel of a garden. She was walled off from the rest of the avenue, picking at something on her thigh.

Sitting in her flowered dream kingdom, Kim Novak gave off a smell unlike anything Tim had ever encountered before. It was a smell all her own. What, he wondered, could cause this starlet with the unpainted lips and uncombed hair to dress like the poorest *clochard* on the street?

Wonderdog stirred in the *plate-bande* of begonias and licked himself. Tim yanked on the leash to make him stop. The studio sent actors here who needed quiet and rest. They arrived at night like exotic migratory birds, in flamboyant colors with a loud flapping of suitcases, sometimes stalked by photographers, autograph seekers, and gawkers. But when the heavy front portals shut behind them, all was silence. If Tim passed them in the driveway or on the staircase, he was supposed to pretend not to notice them.

He changed eyes now. Swallows swooped overhead. It was getting too dark to see. Wonderdog wrapped his front legs around Tim's left arm and began his own peculiar form of canine sexual activity. Master Tim jumped up, brushed off his dirty knees, and yanked the dog toward the elevator.

How different this pale, long-fingered blonde was from his nanny! Benz was a splash of neon-bright Techni-color in a gray city. The first thing she'd said to him on the first day she came to pick him up at school was "I like *gorgio* men who wear glasses. It makes them look vulnerable."

Tim would never forget how he had self-consciously pushed his glasses up the bridge of his nose. Mercifully for him, she had pronounced vulnerable "boulnerabel," and his classmates waiting at the Number 52 bus stop had been so blinded by her flashing blood-red lipstick and gold-and-coral earrings that they had not paid much attention to her half-Spanish French.

"Are you a Royalist?" he had asked her that first day.

Tim's class was divided between Royalists and Republicans. The distinction was extremely important and determined whether you sat in the front, with the kiss-asses, or in the back, where the spitballs and paper clips flew so thick, it sometimes looked like a snowstorm.

Tim had repeated the question in Spanish, but still there was no answer. This open defiance by his nanny set a bad example for his troops.

"Hey, are you deaf or something?" he whispered, slamming an elbow into her ribs.

Without moving her eyes from a billboard advertisement for colored tights, Mercedes instinctively slapped him up the side of the head and sent him spinning. He drifted slowly skyward, his head buzzing like a deflating balloon. This woman with the booster-rocket hands was unlike any nanny he had had before.

There were snickers in the bus queue, but he managed to hold on to her arm.

When the Number 52 bus arrived, they sat on the rear banquette. Tim decided to make peace by offering her his *goûter*. From her expression, he could tell she did not understand the offer. For the first time in his life, Timothy felt that the delicious buttered quarter-baguette with hard dark chocolate stuck through it was somehow inadequate.

"No, really it's very good. I'm serious. Everyone eats *goûter* at four o'clock."

Tim wiped his nose dry with his sleeve and watched Benz take her first bite. She chewed and nodded slowly, staring out the bus window. How could she not know what a *goûter* was? thought Tim incredulously. For a time they rode without a word. Then she took three more quick bites.

MERCEDES was collecting all the clothes in her hamper. Her room was small, stuffy, damp, and squeezed under the mansard roof. She stood by one of her small windows known as *chiens-assis* that protruded from the sloping gray slate roof and looked out at the Paris rooftops. When the sun was bright, these round dollhouse windows became tunnels of silver-and-white haze. When it rained, she could make out the Tour Eiffel as a faint scribble in the distant smoggy sky, and leading up to it row upon row of black chimneys in a field of dazzling shiny gray slates. Her room was on the sixth floor, reachable only by a narrow spiral service staircase. There were other maids' rooms at that level, but Manola and Pepe lived on the fourth floor with the Aunties in case of emergency. So Mercedes had this eagle's nest all to herself.

What attracted her most about this giant ship of a house at Number 10½ Avenue Foch was the confidence it exuded. The neoclassical window ornaments, the turn-of-the-century wrought-iron balconies and heavy white satin curtains proclaimed sturdiness and comfort. They seemed to say, "Everything that was is, everything that is will be." Mercedes sensed in these walls a total lack of ambiguity, and though she had lived in this house only a year, she was more loyal to this palatial *hôtel particulier* than to any caravan or campsite she had known in Andalusia.

Benz stopped and felt the silk slip Auntie Agatha had given her. How soft it was; it smelled, damp and faint, like scallions in the rain.

Now she carried the wicker basket of wash down to the fifth floor. She knew there was no laundry here on this empty floor, but she felt she owed it to the house to visit the majestic private apartments of Alphonse and Cascasia Cardozo. These eerie giant rooms were shut off for months from the outside world, the furniture protected by dust covers, awaiting the return of Monsieur and Madame. In their absence, the house was run by Mrs. Cardozo's blue-haired dowager aunts: Agatha, who was blind, and Phoebe, who, though she could see, was forever misplacing her glasses. Both ladies had perfected ameba-travel; this was a technique whereby they glided along in their slippers with one hand extended in front of them until stopped by some natural obstacle, such as a chair or a door.

The Aunties insisted on doing their own wash. And so, on the fourth floor, Mercedes walked through Phoebe and Agatha's amber-amethyst-and-rose-painted rooms, as soft and muted as the Aunties themselves, to Manola and Pepe's room, collected the couple's dirty clothes, and proceeded to the third floor.

Mercedes swept down the central staircase singing to herself a timid version of "Funiculì-Funiculà," trying, with little success, to imitate Mrs. Cardozo on her phonograph records. She remembered a time when she would peer, barefoot, into houses just like this one, catching a forbidden glimpse of the same giant cream-colored grand piano painted with multicolored Venetian birds and the elegant guests flashing sequins and jewelry. And her mother pushing her into the crowd, shouting: "Come away from that nice lady. Don't bother the dear woman. *Manga chavorí, manguela!*"—which in *caló* meant, "Beg, girl, beg!"

Mercedes had no use for *payo* money or ostentation. But

this house had a soul! Even in Madame's absence, her presence was everywhere, imprinted on the draperies and furniture. Even the small gold cherubs on the walls seemed to sing out Madame's favorite *bel canto* arias.

In Timi's room, on the third floor, Mercedes carefully picked out the boy's dirty clothes. In addition to the omnipresent blue ink stains, she noted a hole in his sleeve, at the elbow, that needed mending. His dirty shirts always had their own aroma: not acrid—sweet, actually; smelling faintly of old chocolate, schoolbooks, and much-used handkerchiefs.

She walked to the second floor to a grand ballroom with a million-crystaled chandelier that used to take her three days to clean, until Timoté had earned his way into Gypsy heaven by suggesting she place newspaper on the floor, dip each crystal in Miracle-Clean and let them all drip dry onto the paper. Mercedes twirled flamenco-style in the center of the room. One day she would lead her own troupe through the capitals of Europe. Her name would flash in lights on the marquees. She would wear Greta Garbo sunglasses, chew nervously on long white cigarettes, refuse interviews and, of course, men.

She entered the laundry room and began to separate a load of whites. For a moment, she listened to a floorboard creaking somewhere; then she leaned over to switch on the washing machine. Two hands grabbed her hips from behind. She jumped; it was Pepe. Every month or so, he tried this. And now as she turned to push him away, she remembered the first time Pepe had grabbed her, that day when she'd first arrived at the Cardozos' and stood in the bathroom by the kitchen; she had cried and cried, convinced Manola would throw her out. Now she looked back on her innocence with nostalgia: how they pass, she thought, the passing years!

"Mercedes, *que buena eres!* You are so ripe, so hot!" said Pepe, trying to kiss her neck.

"You are hurting me! Stop it! Stop!"

Pepe's fingers were as hard as meat hooks and would leave bruise marks on her arms. She struggled to push him off. She knew that for Pepe this was not love—not even an approximation—but rather a habit he was powerless to break. He was like an insomniac who gets up to check that his door is locked in the middle of the night, although he has already checked it a dozen times before.

"You have the best *derrière* in all of Paris!" said Pepe, nibbling on her left ear and tightening his grip.

Pepe was sixty-seven and married to Manola. He was everything a Spanish male should be: irascible, generous, petty, chauvinistic, and bullying. He was "large" in the small things of life and "small" in the large things: He farted at the kitchen table; he spoke of women as if they were oxen. He never worked, but complained all day long about his work hours. He was so rude to the Aunties the few times they suggested he repaint a door or mend a fuse box that they had stopped asking him to do anything at all. And yet when he played the guitar, he could make the notes dance by themselves, thousands of them cascading out of the shiny rosewood instrument. And for this, Mercedes forgave Pepe his many sins.

"Pepe, stop! If Manola catches you, she will kill us both!"

Pepe stopped. There was someone in the room. Mercedes felt his presence before she actually saw him. A tall stranger stood in the doorway, staring at them. Mercedes caught her breath. He had thick wavy hair, the color of wild strawberries. With what dazzling irises he looked at her, taking her all in! Mercedes had excellent intuition. This man was special. She had never in her seventeen years felt such immediate attraction to someone. The man said something which neither she nor Pepe understood. He must be British or American. She felt faint.

"Can you help me? I seem to be lost," repeated the man.

Mercedes remembered that she was wearing no makeup of any kind. Without paint on her face, she looked, as Timi said, like a boiled egg—tiny eyes disappearing in a big moon face. And to make things worse, she had a dish towel wrapped around her head. Despair engulfed her: she had probably never looked uglier in her entire life!

"Non, non. Tout va très bien," muttered Pepe, who understood even less English than Mercedes.

She tried to smile and put her right hand up to the back of her head as Katharine Hepburn usually did when she did not know what else to do with her hands. The man was about to leave. She had to say something, but what?

"Excuse me," she blurted out in her best movie English. "Are you looking for someone, Monsieur? Are you a guest?"

"No, no. My name is Sean O'Kelley. I work at the Irish Embassy next door. I just took a wrong turn somewhere. Went left instead of right, I think."

His ruby lips were water-licked and curved at the corners. His reddish hair was neatly combed down the middle, and his blue eyes smiled in a slightly lost way. When she approached him to show him the way back to the embassy, she moved to the left in order to get by him and then to the right. At the same time, he moved to the right and then to the left, blocking her way. Blushing now and touching her elbow, he excused himself, but his fingers rested on her dark skin a moment longer than they needed to. The acorn, thought Mercedes, does not fall very far from the oak. First impressions were crucial to her. She indicated the way back to the embassy and, as she did so, noticed how Sean's hair curled behind his ear. This was important: when she embraced a man, she planned on gazing at that part of him a good deal.

"And what is your name, Mademoiselle?" said the man with smiling eyes.

"I am Señorita de los Angeles," she murmured.

He bent to kiss her hand.

The red-haired stranger in his pin-striped diplomatic gray pants and Bordeaux cummerbund seemed to move in slow motion.

"And you work for the Cardozos?"

"Oui."

Her face was aflame. This Irishman was assassinating her with his eyes. He was flooding her with his fragrance, as if her soul were the central repository of all things noble and straight in the world. Her intuition told her she was ripe for a man; getting overripe! Soon, if she was not careful, she'd be rotting.

• • •

THEY were sitting on the Number 52 bus, returning from school. Mercedes was reading a copy of *Paris-Unveiled.* Now, there was a headline worth pondering:

SNAKE ARRESTED CHEZ MAXIM!

"Why do you do that to men, Benz?" said Tim.

"Do what?" she asked.

"Make them talk bad to you and whistle like that?" He looked accusingly at her new polka-dot dress and spike heels.

"I do nothing! I disdain them! They are savages, and this is not my fault. Timoté, you must not listen to them. You must guess at what they are *not* saying."

"But when I go out with Manola, strange men never stop to talk to her. The savages let her alone."

"Manola has a mustache and a hairy wart on her neck. And her hands smell of ammonia and javel. Do you want me to be ugly—is that what you want, Timi?"

It was true, thought Tim. When Manola pressed Timi to her bosom, he could always tell what they were going to eat that evening. He looked over Mercedes' shoulder:

HOW I MATED WITH AN EXTRATERRESTRIAL!

Mercedes was not paying attention to the article. What she hated most about her past was the selective *gitano* morality that condoned, in fact almost required, that sons lift the skirts of any female tourist, according to the "law of the lettuce," but forced daughters to remain virgins until they married. Women were supposed to carry the Honor of the Gypsies not on their backs, but in the other place! They had drummed it into her head before she could decide not to respect their stupid Honor Code. So she had little choice in the matter. She turned a page of *Paris-Unveiled*:

PARIS SEWERS TO BE CHECKED FOR ESCAPED CONVICT.

The day in the Cardozo laundry room when she had first met Sean, she had felt an overwhelming desire to love and be loved. Sweeping through her was such a need for adoration that unknowingly, she groaned out loud. Yes, she would have him! So what if she carried the weight of All Spain's Honor firmly and unfairly implanted between her legs? Let the men carry their *own* Honor, if they think it is so important! She went on to the next headline:

NUN FINDS GIRL IN FREEZER!

Would he too, the boy sitting next to her, this nail-bitten, ink-stained Master Timoté, who loved her absolutely and unquestioningly, end up like most of the men she had met—crude, insensitive, selfish? Would he too think, as her father used to, that if you lift up girls' skirts over their heads, they all look like lettuces? ("Don't waste your time with the leaves on the outside; go right for the heart of the matter," he would say.)

Mercedes let out a sigh, looked up from her newspaper, and ran her fingers through the boy's brown hair:

"Timi, men are stupid because they do not see like we do that longing is the very core of our *drom*—I mean of our road, of our existence. They think we exaggerate, that we are too emotional. But that is life! Everything else is nonsense."

"WHO is this 'M. de los Angeles'?"

"The woman who looks after me."

"Is she related?"

"No."

"So, she is your nanny."

"Yes."

"Why does she sign your weekly report card?"

Tim shrugged his shoulders and looked down at a raw cuticle on his left thumb. There was a strand of Benz's black hair on his sleeve. It was almost a meter long. Just one of the many one would need to tie, end to end, to climb out of a dungeon tower on a moonless night when one's horse is waiting by the castle moat below.

"Why do your parents not sign?"

"Because they're away."

"Away where?"

"I don't know."

Tim felt no desire to elaborate. He sat there, listening intently to the radiator's bang in the hallway outside. At the moment, he was not a military genius or an emperor; he was a boy sitting in an unlit principal's office waiting while Claude Monet, S.J., leafed through his report-card booklet.

"So, she is your nanny . . ."

Tim fidgeted. He was desperately needed outside. The battle would be a complete shambles by the time he returned.

"Cardozo, you will notice that we have assessed you a fine of ten thousand francs for damaging school property."

His Marshals Gerbi and Leclerc were good. They could carry out orders; but they could not be trusted to make decisions. By the time he got back to the courtyard, his troops would probably be dispersed and hiding in the side streets.

"Well, do you have anything to say about the fine, Cardozo?"

"It wasn't me."

"Who else would carve your name on your desktop?"

"It wasn't me, sir."

"In letters eight centimeters high?"

"You should see Gerbi's desk."

"We are not discussing Gerbi."

His army's left flank had no artillery. His right wing had so much light horse it was probably swinging the whole battle around in circles. "Send the infantry in first," Napoleon had said; "horses cost money. Save the horses until last!" But unlike Napoleon, Tim had the luxury of an all-cavalry army; he could afford to be wasteful.

"No one has a desk as filthy as yours, Cardozo."

"Gerbi does."

"Cardozo, do not compound your offense by refusing to accept responsibility."

"It's true. Gerbi has naked women and a caricature of de Gaulle carved on his desk."

The school church bell rang. Father Monet joined his hands in prayer over his nose and looked right through Tim, into each nook and cranny of his mortal soul. The Principal had a handsome face, with wide eyes, and an odd thin beard running along his jawline. Outside the gray window, a blooming lilac bush shook and the low clouds of early May began to dissolve like aquarelles. Monet turned to the window as the rain began to fall.

"You pick on me . . . because I am American."

"We don't pick on anyone. We punish those we catch."

"You *catch* me because I am American."

There was silence. Other than Gerbi, an Algerian, Tim was the only non-French boy in the school. Behind the Principal, a long dark crucifix hung on the wall. Piled in the corners were song sheets, Bibles, and missals wrapped in the yellow-and-purple of the Jesuits of Saint-Philippe de Passy.

"Cardozo, we will no longer accept the signature of your Spanish nanny on your report card."

"Why not?"

"Because she is not your legal guardian."

"She takes care of me! You think she's ignorant, but she's very smart. She can read and write. How do you think she keeps all the shopping accounts?" He bristled at the hint that Benz was not fit to be his guardian.

"I am sure Mademoiselle de los Angeles is a good woman. But our policy is that only a parent or guardian may sign a report card."

Another silence. The wooden chair began to hurt Tim's bony backside. He shifted uncomfortably. Monet's big eyes looked down at him like two windows from a castle tower. Rain continued to fall in diagonal streaks. Tim wiped his glasses on his cotton shirt.

"I would like to meet with your parents, Cardozo."

"They're not here, sir."

Timothy felt embarrassed and stupid.

"When will they be coming back?"

He shrugged. All he knew about his father was that he was a movie producer who traveled often and rented the first floor of their house to famous actors. He regularly sent Tim rocks for his collection of semiprecious stones and photographs of movie stars. On one, Victor Mature had signed: *"For Little Corporal Timothy, love from Victor."* On another, Ava Gardner had written: *"To the Gallic shrimp, with love, Ava!"*

"Are your parents always away, Cardozo?"

"Yes."

"Oh,come, come. Don't exaggerate."

Father Monet ran his fingers over his clean, smooth desktop. His Adam's apple jutted out over his stiff white collar.

"They cannot always be away! You are not, after all, an abandoned child, are you?"

That was a typical reaction. Tim didn't bother to explain. The smell of incense and old leather bindings had begun to sicken him.

"When do you see them, Cardozo?"

Tim thought for a moment. Every six months or so, at the outside, his mother returned from an opera tour, sat in her bubble bath, and then spent hours at her large mirrored desk, thick with appointment books, laughing into the telephone. Until the age of six, Tim did not realize that his mother and the telephone were two separate entities.

"I've said nothing to make you cry, have I, Cardozo?"

Tim shook his head. He felt sorry, not for himself, but for Benz, who suddenly seemed to need his protection.

"Good; then stop."

Father Monet slowly reexamined Tim's weekly grades with a pained look on his face.

Who in that sun-filled house, thought Tim, was qualified to sign for him? That big mule-head of a butler, Pepe, when he was sober and could be torn away from his Longchamps racing sheets? His Great Aunties, Phoebe and Agatha, who ran Number 10½ Avenue Foch by judicious means of letters from his mother concerning everything from how much to give to the Red Cross volunteers who rang at the door to when Tim should stop wearing short pants? Who else was there in that enormous six-story house where a boy of eight could live for days without running into anyone except his toy soldiers and XKE, his white mouse?

"Here, blow in this."

Father Monet wiped the boy's tears with his white pocket handkerchief, then held it to his nose. Tim's eyes orbited the room as he breathed in the soft linen's aroma, a mixture of hair lotion, shaving cream, and cologne. Then he blew his nose vigorously and repeatedly.

"Cardozo, you *must* have a *legal* guardian."

Tim would call his father's studio and have them send over Charlton Heston and Rita Hayworth for some publicity shots. He'd sashay in one day with Chuck and Rita and their bodyguards, press agents, and script girls, and say, "Father M., here's my pa and ma. They're shooting *The New Testament* at the Boulogne Billancourt studios, so make it quick, will ya?" Monet would be down on his knees so fast with his hand out for unwed mothers and *pied-noir* children it would make his head spin!

"Cardozo, don't pick your nose when I'm talking. And try to look me in the eye. That's better."

The Principal leaned back. His long fingers tapped one against the other like two black widow spiders doing battle in midair.

"Cardozo, your classroom behavior is improving slightly—your teacher no longer has to tie you to your chair. But he still complains of your 'silent insolence'—meaning, I suppose, that even when you have done nothing wrong, it is clear that you are still thinking it."

Tim looked down at his lace-up shoes, shined to perfection by Mercedes. His thoughts were a great menagerie of airborne dragons. He couldn't wait to grow up and be able to lean across this desk, tweak Monet's nose, and pull selected hairs from his perfectly groomed beard.

"Does it speak to you?"

Noticing that Tim was staring at the crucifix on the wall, Monet had changed his tone of voice:

"Do you know, Cardozo, that when I behold the Brunelleschi crucifix, I commit the sin of envy." The Principal stopped and leaned slowly forward. "See how anguished is the expression of the face, the parted lips, the eyes? If you feel lonely, just try to imagine how lonely our Saviour felt."

Tim stared blindly at the crucifix. He didn't feel lonely at all. He never felt lonely living with Benz, Manola, Pepe, the Aunties, Wonderdog, and XKE. And what business was it of Monet's what he felt, anyway? Tim, the most talkative boy in all of Saint Philippe de Passy—all the teachers complained about him—had become a deaf mute.

"Don't forget to ask your parents—or your guardian—for this week's donation."

Father Monet pushed forward the preprinted envelope. Dazed and numb, Tim took it and waited. Outside, the rain was giving way to spirals of coiling mist. If Mercedes was good enough to handle the donation, why could she not sign his report card? The total unfairness of the world suddenly choked him.

"You may go now, Cardozo."

Master Tim walked back down the long dark hallway, covered in peeling paint and graffiti. Outside, it was still drizzling. He could see his troops huddled under the chestnut trees at the far end of the courtyard, some shooting marbles, others dribbling a soccer ball. So this was what happened when he left them alone: they declared peace! They couldn't be trusted to continue fighting by themselves for ten minutes! As he reached the gold-and-white marble panels listing all the Saint Philippe alumni who had fallen for France in World War I, he made up his mind to sign up for one of Professor Feng's accredited Judo, Jujitsu, or Tai-Chi classes:

Enables even the MOST COWARDLY
to destroy an opponent
THREE TIMES his own size!

Have people RESPECT AND LIKE YOU!
With Dr. Feng's patented
martial-art techniques,
get your hands registered with Interpol
as ENGINES OF WAR!

MERCEDES did not go to church very often; but this was All Saints' Day, and she was quite superstitious. The holy card she drew from the basket being passed down the pew was that of Saint Agatha. The saint was pictured with tears in her eyes, holding her martyr's breasts, shaped like loaves of bread, on a silver platter.

"Legend has it," read the note on the reverse side,

> that Saint Agatha of Catania, Sicily (third century), was a poor girl of great beauty who was pursued by a Roman Consul named Quintan. When she rejected his amorous advances, he tried in vain to corrupt her by entrusting her to a woman of bad morals. She was tortured in various ways, but each time Saint Peter intervened to save her. Finally, Quintan had her breasts cut off, and she is represented in Christian iconography carrying them shorn off with tongs as Angels deliver a crown. Because her breasts often resemble loaves of bread, her feast day is commemorated by the blessing of bread in church. Bell founders have adopted her as their patron saint and show her breasts to be bell-shaped.

Mercedes now recalled two Gypsy sayings. The first was "Out of guts make heart." Through all the lonely months when her father beat her, this had become a favorite saying of hers. She knew that there was a reason why she had received this Saint Agatha card. Perhaps Sean would be her Quintan, her reckless torturer? Perhaps her suffering was not over, but had only begun? As she folded the holy card and put it in her pocket, she felt her nipples go cold and taut. They ached so much that she put a hand at each armpit and held her breasts, as if ordered by the saint to do so. The second Gypsy saying had been a favorite of her father's, though she had never really understood it, and did not know why this particular wisdom should come to mind now: "When you throw a stone to the wolves, the one you hit screams."

Mercedes was an autodidact of love. She had spent most of her adult waking hours studying men—how to avoid them, attract them, control them. And she concluded that men and women lived in basically different worlds. Men (and by this she really meant men like her father) had no charm, almost no sense of self, little style, and no guilt. For all the hot hours of pinch and bite that she had allowed herself since arriving in Paris and for all her reading of pulp romances, she had never let anyone enter the Honor of Spain. Before running away, she had never had an unchaperoned date; she had not kissed the intended groom her father had selected for her when she reached fourteen, although her family had exchanged rings with his. Her four older brothers, who were less honorable in other respects, had been most vigilant. Now, at seventeen, she considered it a question of personal honor and taste. She did not like drinking, hitting, or spitting. She also did not like men who had large pores, fat ankles, big derrières—or, for that matter, skinny men, macho men, egotists, dummies, name-droppers, money-scroungers, misers, pretty boys, bookworms, athletes, or men who combed their hair up from the back or the sides in order to hide their bald spots. And that left very few men up to her standards.

Her admirers had been a rather odd assortment. They included Trifouilli, an Algerian brick-and-window man from La Porte des Lilas who had fixed some plumbing on the second floor; René de la Baleine, a student from the Rue Quincampoix who read Jean-Paul Sartre books, mouthing the words silently, on the same park bench she often used; and, of course, Marcel the butcher's son, a frantic swivel-head from the Place des Ternes. But all these men added up to what? A group of infinitesimal piss-ants! Perhaps she had not spent enough time or effort on the search for the appropriate male. She knew these things took time.

As she tried to recall what these other men had meant to her, the Irishman from the embassy next door shone impressionistically throughout her thoughts. He did not move—he danced and sparkled with sunlight. Mercedes' endless sniffing in front of bakeries, her love of morning dew and breezes, the isolated tower of her life, these all brought her back to Sean. Perhaps there had never really been anyone before him, either physically or mentally.

The service long over, she walked to the vestry and knocked on the door.

"*Padre,* here is this month's envelope."

"I will make sure it reaches your family," intoned the Spanish priest, taking her letter with the name of her siblings scribbled across it in big round letters. It contained one-half of her monthly salary.

ON a Sunday afternoon, Mercedes and Master Tim walked in dappled sunlight through the Jardin d'Acclimatation. She brought the boy here almost every weekend, sometimes on Thursday afternoons as well. Even though Tim knew every inch of the amusement park by heart, he never seemed to grow tired of it. For her it was a ritual, like visiting an old friend whose entire conversational repertoire had long ago been memorized; but Mercedes enjoyed being out in the fresh air.

They had gotten off the wooden train that runs from the Porte Maillot through the Bois. Now they were passing the flowered clock, the curved mirrors, the monkeys with the red backsides, the flying saucer in which Tim had pedaled so hard his little Algerian friend, Gerbi, had gotten motion sickness and vomited out the porthole. They stopped and bought an ice cream. Mercedes asked the fortune-teller who doubled at the duck-fishing pond, replacing prizes which had been fished out:

"How many husbands will I have?"

"Eight!" shouted the Corsican machine-gun man next door,

whose three-legged dog was snoring on the counter. In the background, they could hear the bumper cars playing Elvis Presley music.

"Get out of here before I call the cops," said the fortune-teller. "And don't start any trouble. I'm warning you!"

Benz sneered at the little stand with the painted outline of two hands on the sign and the large, very plastic crystal ball. Mercedes' mother, though born a *paya,* could read the dregs of coffee cups, the shape of broken twigs, clouds, beans scattered on a handkerchief, cards, stones, palms, egg yolks, pupils, pigeon droppings. She was not like these fancy cosmopolitan clairvoyants, who needed cheat cards stapled to their side of the table.

The boy pulled her away, toward the Fratellini circus.

FOR his ninth-birthday party, Master Tim invited his entire class: forty children, including Delacroix, Paoli, Leclerc, Bouigues, Dhont, Forrestier, Gerbi (the Algerian boy who ate his own snot); granddaughters of friends of his Aunties'; and even Laval, who had been his most trusted general before bolting over to the Republicans in the middle of a battle. Aunt Agatha held that even the greatest generals must learn the art of diplomacy and had insisted Tim invite the entire rival Republican gang.

It was a costume party, and Tim was especially proud of his Napoleon outfit, complete with gold epaulets ("gold earrings for the shoulders" Mercedes called them), a tricolored bicorne hat, and field glasses.

"Benz, how do I look?"

"If you must have the body of a male," she said, "then at least have the brains of a woman. You'll be smarter."

She poured tumblers of chocolate milk and passed out party favors, while Tim tried to understand what she had meant, if anything, by that last sentence.

"Hey, Benz, I have a good one for you: How do Spanish ladies tease their hair?"

Tim smiled, lifted one arm, played with his hairless underarm, and sang: "Nia-nia-nia-nia-nia . . ." He stopped. "Don't you get it?"

Instead of laughing, Mercedes grimaced and slammed his Napoleonic bicorne down over Tim's eyes and ears. He tried to push it back up, but it was stuck.

"Hey, wait! Someone's turned off the lights!"

His classmates had started singing "Happy Birthday." Above the whistling and clapping that followed, Tim shouted:

"Benz, you great big ox, that was only a joke! You never understand anything!"

Napoleon was beginning to suffocate inside his hat. Aunt Agatha, the blind one, told him to blow out the candles and make a wish. He tried to pry the hat off his head and managed only to rip out its tricolored feathers. He couldn't spend his entire birthday stuck in the dark like this!

"Benz, you're really nuts, you know that?"

Mercedes now held his head still and, using a pair of kitchen scissors, cut two small holes in his hat at eye level. For a moment, the room was silent. Tim bent over the pink candles and made a wish. He wished for Benz to get a bigger brain. He wished for another white mouse so he could have races with XKE. And he wished for more victories over the Republicans.

Mercedes clapped her hands above her head and started singing *"La Cucaracha."* Almost immediately a human chain formed behind her. Linked hands-to-waist, hands-to-waist, they danced around the dining room table singing and thrusting their hips out with every "CHA!" Most of them just shouted without knowing the words. Tim tried to taste some cake, but his bicorne was stuffed too snugly around his face to allow a fork into his mouth.

"Hey, guys, I'm the masked Prisoner of Zenda! Yahooo!"

He now joined the chaotic dancing snake that bobbed up and down as it careened by. Through the house they went, kicking out their legs, laughing, pushing their hips to the left—

LA CU-CA-RA- - - -*CHA!*

—knocking over chairs, and then hips to the right, banging into lamps, out onto the balcony and up to the Aunties' boudoir on the fourth floor and into Tim's father's study on the fifth floor, a room of red and gold with the head of a lion shot in Kenya, a zebra skin, books in ancient Greek, a gold statuette from Hollywood inscribed with his father's name—

LA CU-CA-RA- - - -*CHA!*

—down to the second floor, the unused ballroom where all the furniture was covered in white bed sheets and at last, huffing and puffing, back up to the dining room on the third floor, where the whooping and singing human chain broke into pieces.

Mercedes felt happy and rich, leading these children like so many ducklings behind the mother duck. She wore her billowing orange-and-green fiesta dress. If only Sean could walk in now and see her, so elegant in these fluffy leg-of-mutton sleeves and five layers of petticoats, leading this garland of shrill-voiced skinny arms and legs kicking, from left to right and back again, in rhythmic unison like the shameless Folies Bergères leg ladies.

"Y que canten, niños! Sí, cantar, hombrecitos!"

Sean had said "Yes, yes," he would come, and so she had slaved to fix herself perfectly to compensate for her having looked so awful in the *lavanderie.* But now, clapping and singing in her expensive *sevillana* fiesta dress, she knew he would not come. It was just as well, she thought, feeling the knot in her stomach loosen. And she sang:

Those eyes of yours I cannot bear.
They are as big as the sky
And have the color of the sea.
Do not look at me,
Or you will make me fall in love.

In this gray candid light, Mercedes relaxed. Her eyes flashed not so tense. The Angelus struck somewhere deep in her memory. This dress brought a hundred images swelling through her bosom, just as if she had opened Madame's box of potpourri on a rainy day. When she put on this dress, she also donned the sunlight on the red-tiled roof of the Barrio Santa Teresa, the Gypsy children in multicolored socks, smoke from tall stacks waving in the distance like a white handkerchief. How nostalgic she was for the henna-matted hair, the charcoal-painted eyes, the 25-peseta sprigs of oregano that were guaranteed to cure baldness, infidelity, and impotence. She missed it all; even the begging. Even her father.

Tim stopped. The evening sun was striking the living-room chandelier and lighting the walls. Wherever he looked, there were bright mauve, violet, orange, yellow, green, and blue patches.

"Come on, Cardozo, move!"

"Hey, wait. Look—the House of Rainbows!"

The others kept dancing like whirligigs, but Tim stood in the center of the red Persian rug, speechless, staring at the magic rectangular bands of light that were climbing up the living-room walls. The late-afternoon sun barely cleared the Paris rooftops, but as the angle of sunlight striking the crystals changed, the rainbows moved up the wall, splashing bright, multicolored light in all directions. There were rainbows in the fireplace, on the ceiling, on the Picasso. The room was alive!

"Hey, guys, look at my birthday present!"

But one by one, or perhaps all at once, as Pepe could be heard yelling in the distance, "Stop pissing off the balcony," the rainbows went out and the sparkling chandelier returned to its usual transparent state, unnoticed. The idiots were banging their rubber hammers on each other's heads and a segment of the human centipede danced on, shouting Cha-cha-cha, some of its legs performing the Bossa Nova, others the dance of Saint Vitus, most just running to catch up.

"So you are Anatole Gerbi?" said Aunt Phoebe leaning over to shake the boy's hand, but holding back when she noticed it was covered with chocolate frosting.

Gerbi did not answer, for he was in the process of stuffing

another slice of cake into his trouser pockets. Aunt Phoebe continued:

"You should know, young man, that we—The Ladies of the Passy Literary, Knitting, and Opera Society—have fought quite long and hard with the Jesuits of Saint-Philippe to encourage them to accept you and other Algerian children as boarders. I do trust that you are not letting us down."

Mercedes had noticed a lighted window across the courtyard. She leaned out and stared at what looked like Sean pouring himself a drink. Mercedes the dark deliberated with Mercedes the saucy beguiler as to whether Mercedes the *chavorí* should throw something at the first-floor window—perhaps a slice of bread or cake—to attract his attention. Or was it better just to let him see her staring up, full of yearning, at the gray Paris sky? Framed in that giant candlelit embassy window, in his Bordeaux smoking jacket, the Irishman looked magnificent. For a moment, she was swallowed up in a vast, misty sea. But abruptly, the man turned and she saw, with disgust, that it was Ambassador McLuck. He waved, opened the great French window, and called out in a voice rich with drink:

"*Soubrette, venez me visiter!*"

Mercedes quickly closed her window and turned her back to the old goat as he shouted:

"Do not think I have not noticed you staring at me from time to time, *ma chérie!*"

CHAPTER 2

Love Is All, Said Benz, Looking over Her Shoulder

WHEN MERCEDES WENT to bed, she often, before falling asleep, listened to her heartbeats travel down through the mattress to the center of the earth. At the age of five, she was already so lonely that she would often walk out alone onto the main road between Matamoros and Fuente de Cantos and would press her cheek against the sun-warmed macadam, believing that somewhere far away, perhaps at the center of the earth, was a soul who understood and loved her. Her mother had earned money the *paya* way, taking in wash under the aptly named statue of the Virgen de los Dolores de Olivares. But the Guardia Civil did not jail pregnant women for pickpocketing, and it paid much better. When Benz was fourteen, her mother contracted pneumonia and died, shortly after her third miscarriage. Overcome with grief and bitterness, her father had taken a knife with him into the mountains. The children, fearing suicide, had run after him and found him drunk, holding the heavens personally responsible, and threatening the Almighty.

Now she turned on her stomach and counted her heartbeats. Sean had not called on her once since they had met that day in the *lavanderie*. Of course, there had been chance meetings in the courtyard, once returning from shopping and another time on her way to a movie. For two months now, she had been replaying the same first meeting with Sean over and over again in her head—she holding one hand up to the towel around her head, shifting nervously from one leg to the other like a colt; he staring, stroking her body with his lilac-blue eyes.

THE café-au-lait was spilling into the saucer as Timothy rushed up the stairs with a red rose in his mouth. Every Sunday he served Benz breakfast in bed. This ritual required his braving the crocodiles that Manola said inhabited the cellar (and by extension the service staircase), then climbing the steep spiral stairs without dropping the breakfast tray. This rose was a first. Would Benz like it? Would she notice it on her own, or would he have to point it out to her? He ran in and out of the thin slices of gray light that knifed through the narrow air shafts in the service staircase.

At the top, he stopped to catch his breath and to press the timer switch for the light. He carefully poured the contents of the saucer back into the cup and, holding his breath, pushed open Benz's door. She was still asleep. He sat down on the edge of her bed.

Mercedes loved this Sunday-morning moment when Timi shook her by the shoulder and whispered "Psssst . . . psssst." She peeked now through one eye; Timoté was tasting the coffee to make sure it was not cold. She could not restrain herself any longer. She wrapped her arms eel-like around him, spilling the coffee.

"Hey, watch it!"

Tim ran cold water on a washcloth and wiped the coffee from her blue blanket.

"Timi, you will not believe what happened last night!"

She sat up, wide awake, and gnawed on a piece of toast the boy had brought.

"Yesterday, I was at the Spanish dance hall on Avenue Wagram, and he was there!"

"Who?"

"Sean."

"Who's Sean?"

"At first, we just sit on either end of this sofa. It has a broken leg, so we keep seesawing back and forth. Very symbolic, don't you think? Then we dance. Sean is especially good at waltzes."

She had to tell him every single detail, exactly as it had happened. She jumped out of bed; her white nightgown, the one with the little boats around the hemline, covered her to the ankles. She held a broom up to her chest and danced around the room. He watched her turn and turn on her tiptoes and not stop.

"Sean who?"

"He is Irish. Timoté, what do you know about Ireland?"

"Nothing."

"He is *roux*. Do you like redheads?" she asked, still turning.

Tim began to answer that Laval was also red-haired, but she cut him off with a laugh.

"It was not what the French call the hour between dog and wolf, but the hour between man and angel."

The azure light over the rooftops, the subtle perfume of this unbearably blue, almost pink-blue morning gave her a sense of oneness with this city. All that Mercedes loved rushed out over Paris in the fleeting moment that she opened her window. She was engulfed by these mansard roofs, the two salmon-colored clouds, the texture of the gray neoclassical buildings. Paris was a place inside her soul; it started where the trees and avenues ended.

"Benz, Manola says we have crocodiles in our cellar."

"Oh, Timi, what I am to do? When I think of Sean, I cannot think of anything else. I cannot work!"

"I'm serious! Manola says they have enormous red eyes. They might at this very moment be dragging their wet carcasses up that polished staircase."

"Timi, this Sean is not like the others. You will like him very much. I know you will, Timi!"

"Benz, you think Manola is crazy. But why should she lie? And what if she is telling the truth—then what?"

He bent her little pinkie back as far as it would go. He did not want to hurt her, but at this very moment, giant hungry lizards escaped from the banks of the Upper Nile might be feeding on his Aunties while they lay in bed.

"*Estúpido,* are you *loco?*"

Mercedes slapped him on the head and held her wounded little finger up to her lips. Good—now he was quiet, she thought. Let him pout. She leaned out her small window and breathed in the rich morning air. All of nature seemed to share in her love this morning, even the pigeons cooing in the giant chestnut tree.

Having danced all night in Sean's arms, she no longer found the Cardozo house a series of cavernous rooms where she spent her days cleaning; it was her château, and this was her own personal rooftop esplanade. Leaning out her window—with a view of Napoleon's Arc de Triomphe to the east, the Bois de Boulogne to the west and the curving arm of the Seine—she was a replica of all those great movie heroines whose fates are inextricable from their castlelike houses. From here, with Sean's love, she could reach out and touch all the expensive boutiques of Avenue Victor Hugo and Rue de la Pompe, and beyond that, the sleek, gold-statued Trocadéro with its vista across the Seine to the Tour Eiffel.

"Is this new guy as ugly as René de la Baleine?" asked Tim, sitting on her bed and eating one of her croissants.

Mercedes realized it was a tactical mistake: why had she bothered to tell the boy? The problem was that she could not *not* discuss her love life with Timoté. No matter how shallow or off the mark his comments, she needed to confess all to his clean, lineless face. Within limits, she did not really care what Tim said. Or that he said anything at all.

"Timoté, 'a girl cannot whistle and have flour in her mouth at the same time,' " she said, trying to confuse him so he would not start asking about Sean.

The boy nodded. But he was thinking of the inhabitants of the Gallo-Roman well that had been built in their cellar, according to Aunt Phoebe, by Marcus Aurelius, as a first way station for fresh water on the road between Lutèce and Rouen. The Aunties believed theirs was mountain spring water draining down from the Juras and often asserted that if properly bottled and marketed, it could outsell Evian, Vichy, or Badoit. Tim imagined the crocodiles sipping their cure of fresh mineral water like his Aunties' rich friends who returned from their fat farms ever fat, but talking a blue streak about the weather at the thermal baths.

"Timoté, everyone does the big things," Mercedes said, turning from the window. "Everyone wears clothes and says 'thank you' and 'please.' So you must judge on the small things in life. You must judge according to how the sunlight strikes the curve of a man's lips."

"Benz, why don't you go down there to the wine cellar and look for yourself?"

"Timi, when you become old, it is not just a membrane that gets ripped, it is the whole world in your head that gets ripped . . ."

She slid back under the heavy blankets. He crawled in next to her, took off his glasses, and laid his head on her pillow. She sniffed at Tim's hair. His ears were terribly waxy. No wonder the boy never listened to her.

"Timi, I worry about you."

"Why?" He stared up at her green ceiling.

She felt his cold, clammy feet under the heavy bedding.

"You are so subdued. You are all shadows and sensitivity. I live at a thousand kilometers an hour. And what will happen to you without me?"

Her Sunday-morning confidences were always like this: complicated, unending, and so different from one week to the next that he never knew what she was going to say. But her bed always smelled warm and moist, like a hot hibernating animal. In fact, her room was more of a bear cave, really. She hugged him so hard he could barely breathe.

"Timi, perhaps you are too feminine."

"Huh?"

This was a new one. He stared at Benz's deep, thick scalp. Her black mane entered her forehead with such strength—it never ceased to amaze him how powerful her hair was.

"Did you bring me that, Timi?"

She pointed to the long-stemmed rose in a glass of water by her washbasin.

"*Oui.*"

"No one has ever brought me a fresh rose before, Timi."

"I stole it from the front garden."

She fell back on her bed and sighed.

"Oh, Timi, Timi, Timi, I would be a much better man than you! And you would be a much better woman, I think, than me. Does it upset you I say this?"

He shook his head.

She squeezed him. Tim did not understand, but he held on to the gaze of her green eyes like a fragile mooring line on the end of which he drifted. Then he snuggled warm and cozy in the crook of her big arm.

"Timi, I think men are like cigarettes: The first time, you try one out of curiosity. And later it becomes a habit . . ."

"But Benz, I hate it when you smoke!"

Sometimes the boy was so stupid, so unaware of her moods, she could scream! How did these *payó* children survive, so innocent and so ignorant of what was going on around them? At his age, she had already worked as a tambourine maker, a monkey trainer (with her father), and a knife grinder. She had sold needles, glass, bangles, fake gold, astrology charts. She had been a spoon maker, a wool dealer, a merry-go-round operator.

"You don't like that I smoke?"

"No, I don't."

"Well, you are an ignorant fool."

"GERBI, will the O.A.S. invade tonight?"

"Vloop, zing."

"Gerbi, you're from Algeria. You should know."

"Splotch, dling."

"Gerbi, if you don't start talking normal, we're going to rip off your ears! You think de Gaulle can stop them?"

In the back row of the class, Gerbi laughed and pointed one of his eyes south and the other one north. Tim was very proud to have recruited Gerbi into the Monarchist camp. He had taken a big risk. At first no one knew what to make of this *pied-noir* who insisted he was not a *pied-noir* at all but a real Arab, from a town in northwest Algeria; and the more the enemy knew him, the more fear and awe he inspired. In addition, he was their one direct link to the war hysteria that was sweeping through Paris. The newspapers were full of rumors of invasions and putsches. The political issues, the actual events, and exactly which French generals in Algeria wanted to keep that colony French were rather fuzzy here at Saint-Philippe de Passy—especially as most of their hard information came via Gerbi.

Just then Gerbi removed his glass eye and cleaned it on his ink-stained green sweater. His neighbors stared in disbelief. Father Brouette continued to read from Caesar's *Commentaries.*

"Gerbi, you're not going to put that back in your head, are you?"

"Dling!"

"Use my handkerchief. It's clean."

"Vloop. Splotch!"

Gerbi licked his eye clean and popped it back into its socket. Then he smiled and jammed his pinkie into his left ear.

"Gerbi, you're absolutely disgusting!"

"Dling!"

"Why do you talk like that?"

"Boing. Splotch!"

"Is it Algerian?"

"Vloop, vloop!"

When Tim first arrived, he had been a skinny stick, running his tail off to no purpose. But slowly his courtyard powers had increased. He had begun to hold mysterious sway over his classmates. Not all, of course, but many of the ten-year-olds, perhaps even the majority, galloped behind him and followed his orders, no matter how ruthless or unreasonable.

One day when he tried to split up his troops and catch the Republicans in a swift pincer movement, he ordered some of his troops to ride with his first deputy, but they had refused. This was a revelation: they wanted to stay with him! Tim could not say exactly how he got this ability to control others. He was always scared, in the back of his mind, that one day the balance of power would mysteriously shift away from him. Tim's military success was perhaps due to little more than the fact that he firmly believed that Napoleon was "the greatest man in the world." Everything he had read or heard confirmed him in this belief. The curtains of his bedroom window had prints of Napoleon dashing across the Pont D'Arcole and accepting the spoils of victory at Valmy. His father had given him a bronze statuette of Napoleon on a rearing horse. He had seen the movie *Austerlitz* four times. And Tim's idea of re-creating Napoleon's empire at Saint-Philippe de Passy captivated most of his classmates.

The more studious brown-nosers were not Monarchists, but Republicans. They wasted time trying to elect Constituent Assemblies and making peace treaties. But Tim and his followers —Gerbi, Leclerc, Paoli, Dhont, Gâche, Bouighes, Forrestier— would accept nothing from their sworn enemies short of unconditional surrender. Even this was suspect in Tim's eyes. There was a knock on the door. Father Brouette interrupted his Latin. As soon as he stepped into the hallway, combat broke out on all fronts in the classroom. Gâche and Laval hit each other with rulers. Paoli drew Kennedy and Khrushchev on the blackboard. Dhont pushed Father B's desk to the edge of the dais, where the slightest jolt would make it fall off. Rubber bands and paper clips sliced through the room toward the Republican kiss-asses, who, well forewarned, were crouching below their desks. Bonaparte shouted to his Chief of Police:

"I need broad boulevards for my artillery."

But Gerbi was not listening. He was busy perfecting his famous bill-swallowing trick. This consisted of taking a 500-franc Pasteur, folding it, swallowing it, and after several nervous minutes of burping and pounding his chest, making it come back up intact!

Desks slammed shut. Entire regiments hid behind piles of notebooks. Father Brouette was back. The priest stood at the podium with his hand on the neck of a tall mulatto boy. Gerbi adjusted his false eye. Paoli let out a long whistle. The others stared in silence.

"Class, this is Roland Lapatte. He is from the Caribbean— the place we studied last semester. Now, I'm afraid the only seat left for you, Roland, is next to Cardozo, our other American friend."

Father B walked the boy down the row of students. He sidestepped a puddle of a urinelike substance and folded back his black cassock sleeves to protect them from open inkwells.

"The entire back row is quite primitive, so let me know if they cause you trouble."

From under his cleanly pressed, short-sleeved blue shirt, this strong café-au-lait boy extended two long polished forearms that reminded Tim of Benz's skin. He gave off a sweet fragrance unlike anything Tim had ever smelled on a boy. His brown-violet eyes were so meek and mild—if Benz thought Tim looked feminine, what would she say about Roland? For the rest of the class hour, Tim smiled nervously once or twice at his exotic new deskmate, but could think of nothing to say.

During recess, Monarchists and Republicans alike crowded around Roland, shoving from all directions. He was clearly embarrassed by all the attention he was getting:

"Does your color wash off?"

"Is it *Ta*-hiti? Or *Ha*-iti?"

"I just want to touch you—okay?"

Tim pushed Laval and the others away from Roland. He could not allow this gentle giant to fraternize with the enemy. It wasn't Roland's crystal gaze or the alfresco sun-drenched skin that he wanted, but his large native fists. He escorted the Haitian to his throne room in the back of the courtyard and offered him his *goûter*—that all-purpose bribe and loosener of tongues.

"Roland, your goose bumps! Don't you have a sweater? Or a shirt with long sleeves?"

"No."

"Roland, you'll die out here. They say it's going to snow today!"

"Joséphine was a mulatto, like me—did you know that?" said Roland, smiling enigmatically and pulling on his nose.

"Napoleon's first and greatest love was café-au-lait?" said Tim in disbelief.

"Yes. She was a quarter Martiniquaise. I am one-half. Ask anyone."

"Benz is one-half also," said Tim, who did not want to appear ignorant or left out of the conversation, but did not yet trust Roland enough to divulge his own status.

Rubbing his arms, Roland spoke of his distant island, full of nighttime executions, palm fronds, sharks, Voodoo priestesses and children so hungry they ate dirt. "The Tontons Macoutes burned down a neighbor's house. . . . Coming out of school one day, I saw a dead man in the streets of Port-au-Prince with a red hole in his forehead like a chrysanthemum petal. . . . Carnival dancers disappeared and became zombies. . . . And now my family is in political exile."

Tim listened entranced, his chin in his hands. Roland's wet brown eyes reminded him of that other exile standing on the cliffs of St. Helena, staring at the deep and hungry sea. Tim felt a lump in his throat: why couldn't he be a political exile too?

In the distance, he saw Gerbi being made a prisoner. There was no time to waste.

"Cardozo, why do you play Monarchists and Republicans? Why not Cowboys and Indians?" asked Roland.

"I don't know."

"Do your battle lines reflect political distinctions?"

Tim had never thought of this before. He remembered that the love of Aunt Agatha's life had been a certain Marquis de Prévost, a printing-press genius and inventor of unsuccessful alternative-energy machines who had died many years before, but in whose honor Agatha still hung a chamber pot from their balcony on Bastille Day, rather than a flag. But the Cardozos had never thought of themselves as *aristos*.

"Hey, hey, let's go!"

This was no time to philosophize. Paoli was being defenestrated. The Imperial troops were in full retreat. Tim jumped onto his faithful horse, Pamplemousse, pulled Roland up on the saddle behind him, and galloped across the courtyard. "*Pour une dent, toute la gueule,*" shouted Tim, which according to Pepe was the war motto of the French Foreign Legion. It went further than the biblical "tooth for a tooth" concept, and asserted that for one tooth, you took the other man's entire face.

Using Roland's deep suntan as a new weapon, they broke

through the front line of defenders. The Republicans had Gerbi down on his knees, his hands tied behind his back, and were hammering a nail into his head.

"Hey, you guys crazy?" shouted Tim. "Hey, *merde,* stop it! He's bleeding!"

Gerbi had a 5-centimeter nail sticking out of his skull. Blood flowed down onto the neck of his shirt. Tim went straight for Laval and chased him to the outdoor toilets, where the coward locked himself in a stall. It was starting to snow lightly.

"Laval, right to left or left to right, your name spells the same thing: coward and traitor!"

"Cardozo, you do much worse to us" came the muffled response.

Gâche and d'Harcourt were bandaging Gerbi's head in a gym towel. Paoli went to the dispensary to fetch Mademoiselle Savonex, the nurse.

Tim took Roland aside. "Would you like to replace Gerbi as my aide-de-camp? Gerbi needs a rest; I'm appointing him Chief of Protocol. Roland, what are you looking at?"

Roland was smiling at something extremely distant, not of this courtyard, perhaps not even of this world.

"Come on, Roland, you stand over here."

Tim called his generals to witness the giving of the Imperial Oath. They stood very quietly. The café-au-lait boy repeated his oath of undying allegiance, staring at the million deliberate cotton-white flakes that fell gracefully all around him in the gray courtyard and that melted in his outstretched hand.

Tim bestowed on Gerbi the supreme honor of being allowed to sit on the Emperor's throne. He was proud of his North African Marshal, who presided, dazed and happy, with his good eye pointing east and the glass one heading south. So what if he ate his own snot? Gerbi had enough Almighty Allah in his muscles, enough crazy Bedouin coursing through his veins to scare those Republican mamma's boys silly! Tim never went so far as to defend Gerbi in class openly, because Gerbi's reputation for ignorance was too well entrenched for Tim to risk his own status and position. But when Laval accused Gerbi of "stinking like shit," Tim reminded his classmates that Louis XIV, *le Roi Soleil, "avait une odeur particulière." Le grand Louis* washed "max-max" (as Gerbi would say) two times in his entire life: once for his baptism, which did not really count, and again twenty years later for his wedding ceremony.

Recess was almost over. Gerbi's brains were still leaking out of his head, and he did not really have much of them to spare.

"You all right, Gerbi?"

"Vloop, zip."

Tim speeded up the swearing-in ceremony, but it was interrupted by Gerbi shouting, deliriously, that the bandage around his head make him look like Lawrence of Arabia. Tim ordered his bodyguards to carry his new Chief of Protocol to the dispensary.

He was proud, too, of Roland, who had landed some magnificent fists on these Passy millionaire *merde*-for-brains and their delicate olfactories. His latest recruit had lashed out on all sides, under these falling gray and amber skies, without asking too many questions as to how or why. How strange he looked, shivering in short sleeves in the center of a circle of generals, his mouth wide open, staring up at the sky.

"Roland, haven't you ever seen snow before?"

SEAN did not call her every day. Sometimes weeks would go by without news from him. Mercedes began to suspect the worst: perhaps he was married, or he had other *Mademoiselles*. He certainly did not appreciate how wonderful she was; perhaps the man was simply deranged. Benz continued to see other men, but she did so more out of principle than out of desire.

Then one wet morning, as she was reaching for one of Madame's silver cigarette cases, which had fallen behind the gold-and-white sofa of the third-floor salon, Sean suddenly appeared at her side. He was immaculate, in his Bordeaux-and-gray livery with a starched white collar and a garter on each arm. He had never looked handsomer. Would Señorita de los Angeles like to go on a date this Saturday night? She nodded, forgetting to ask what time, where they would go, or what she should wear. Benz was suddenly like that small Venetian toy Madame Cardozo had given her which when turned upside down caused all the snowflakes to swirl and swirl around the winged lion of San Marco. "PAX TIBI—MARCUS EVANGELISTA MEUS," said the golden book at the bottom of the toy where the lion rested his right paw.

Saturday night, after applying makeup and redoing her nails, she remembered she had forgotten to walk the dog. This was what she hated: waiting for weeks and suddenly being in a mad, crazy rush and having to do everything at once. With five minutes to spare, she ran out with Wonderdog tugging on his leash. The dog sniffed at the tire of a parked limousine. Mercedes could swear that when she was in a hurry, he deliberately slowed down his miniature apparatus so as to deposit just one drop here and another there. Tonight she had no time for his endless sniffing and pawing.

"*Mais oui! Mais oui!* You are so clean," said Helga, enveloping the dog in the reek of her cheap perfume.

When properly washed, this West Highland terrier looked as fluffy and pure as a spool of white wool. The leg ladies who worked the *contre-allée* at the corner of Avenue Foch and Rue Rude—Nicole, Helga, and Monique—always made a terrible fuss over Wonderdog,

Mercedes looked up at the Cardozo house. On the fifth floor, Monsieur and Madame's windows were sealed tight like a snail that has pulled its horns in to die. Below, on the fourth floor, Auntie Agatha appeared at her window, sucking on the end of a goose-quill pen. She floated up there with her pale eyes and ear horn like some bathrobed ghost doing its insouciant housegliding. Despite the hour, Mercedes could not help but stare up at the frail figure with the marble-colored hair caught, as always, in a chignon. How beautiful she was, this blind, gentle woman. Mercedes' love for the Cardozos and for this giant house now mixed with her memory of the martyred third-century saint who was Agatha's namesake, and she unthinkingly crossed her arms over her breasts.

"How is my favrrrite little Gypsy tonight? Up to no good again?"

Ambassador McLuck had climbed out of his chauffeured limousine and was pinching Mercedes' left cheek. She usually chatted flirtatiously with him when she walked the dog. His shock of white hair, florid complexion, fatherly paunch, and jovial thick accent were often quite charming; but tonight she had no time for such nonsense. Wonderdog was sniffing His Excellency's pant leg, and Helga was pacing up and down, marking out her territory, muttering about how foreigners were taking good jobs away from honest hardworking Frenchmen.

"You must come over for a drink, my dear. I am quite lonely with the missus away," said the Ambassador. Mercedes excused herself and pulled on the leash. On the way out, walking the dog was like a Ben-Hur chariot race. But going home was the opposite scenario: she had to drag him, skidding on all fours, past limos with blinking lights double-parked in front of the embassy, past the majestic old chestnut trees lining the avenue, back to the private driveway of Number 10½.

"Hi, there."

Sean was standing under the heavy wooden portals, smoking a cigarette. Evidently he had been there for some time. His eyes glistened in the shadows.

"Oh, sorry," she mumbled. "I will be right back. I must to put the dog away first."

Mercedes ran to the elevator, which, according to Manola, had been built "in the Year One." As usual, it was not working. She rushed up the lavender-waxed staircase, thinking who was this man who appeared and disappeared in her life, so unannounced? Pepe claimed he was only a lowly butler at the Irish Embassy. But because of the late hours he kept and the many trips he took out of Paris, Mercedes liked to think of him as a diplomat of some stature. Walking back slowly down the stairs, she could feel her love right there, flopping in her chest like some big beached fish. Sometimes it scared her how strongly she felt this need to give herself to a man.

• • •

They walked. In the quiet after-rain, Sean took her to a café, where he had a beer and she a coffee. Afterward, they lingered by the Quai de l'Alma, staring at the *bateaux-mouches* and the reflections in the Seine. They sat on a bench and talked. Sean said he came from a very old, noble family and would one day take her to his ancestral home. He showed her a photograph of three large rocks piled one on top of another on a green hill and explained that this had been the family's domain when they ruled all of Western Ireland. It was not much, just three silly rocks—but breathing in the smell of his cologne, Mercedes imagined it in its glorious heyday, full of laughter and waiters and steaming white sauces, very much like the Cardozo house when Monsieur or Madame returned and threw a party.

She was wearing one of the strapless black silk gowns from a Spring/Summer Collection of three years ago that Madame Cardozo had given her for Christmas. She felt overdressed; surely the shoes were wrong. She had tried on twenty or so different pairs and, in a manic rush, had settled on these red high-heels open at the toe only because Manola insisted they looked right.

For a while they sat on the bench in silence. He put his arm around her shoulders. She did not think of the strength it had taken to leave her family and friends behind. She did not think of the loneliness she had found in Paris, where a Spaniard without a *carte de séjour* was treated almost like an Algerian, which was to say like a stray dog. She did not think of the money she sent by certified money order to her brothers and sisters in Matamoros. She did not think of her father at night expertly flicking a leather whip around the neck of a chicken so quietly the farmer never woke up. Nor did she think of the courage it had taken all these years to believe in love when one is not loved in return. For tonight, sitting next to Sean under the passing full moon, all was possible.

She could spend the whole week like this, her head resting on his shoulder, the streetlights reflecting like long sticks of gold in the black Seine waters, his arms around her like an enchanted forest. She tried to fix in her memory his smells—musk and just-washed dog, mixed with the aroma of red wine, enveloped in cigarette smoke—for she saw herself already, alone in the sleepless nights to come, trying to evoke the man's many scents.

A plume of red and gold lit up the sky. Someone was shooting fireworks across the river on the Champs de Mars. It was a long time from Bastille Day, but Mercedes did not stop to question why the sky was glowing. She felt she had known this man, who resembled Gary Cooper, for many years, and so falling in love with him was like falling in love with him for the second time. Now and then a pink or green anemone of fireworks bloomed behind the Tour Eiffel and melted into the night. If Timoté were to ask her then what Napoleon's last words had been, she would have answered: ". . . Ah, Paris . . ." (She would remember to tell him that.) They strolled to the Quai des Tuileries. Her gaze glided swanlike over the pristine medieval architecture of the Left Bank, the Conciergerie, the National Assembly, the Mint—when God was in a good mood, He created Paris!

"Come on, let's break into one of these *bateaux-mouches*," she said.

Sean did not answer.

"Come on! What are you scared of?"

She imagined how they might hoist themselves down onto the rear banquette of one of these boats and sit together there like two Americans, quietly, in a kingdom of floating glass, staring up at the moon. And she would let him. Why not? The Honor of the Tsigani would go to this tall, restrained, slightly shy Irishman whose patrimony consisted of three handsome rocks on a hill and a strong dislike for England. Mercedes had carried her albatross of do's and don'ts long enough. She would take this great gawky man's silence inside her. She would send him into the world reborn from her loins. She could almost taste the vibrations of his boots on the banquette, as quiet phantom ships passed up and down the river. His pounding would make endless little ripples on this glasslike Seine, and those ripples would continue all the way to the estuary at Rouen and would join the other great waves of the sea made by countless other lovers.

She let him kiss her neck. Staring up at the full moon, an aureole of silver-white above Sean's head, she decided that he could have her absolutely right here, on the quai, and the *flics* and the late-night tourists be damned! She saw herself sipping white wine with Sean and making love to him repeatedly in a boat off some deserted continent.

"Come on. Let's go home," said Sean.

On the way back, he told her how the Aunties had rented one half of Number 10½ to the Irish Embassy back in 1940 in exchange for diplomatic immunity during the Occupation. And how the Aunties had danced with General von Stülpnagel, whose headquarters was at Number 50 Avenue Foch, the old Palais Rose, originally built for Anna Gould, while the cellar had been used as a place of concealment for various Resistance activities of Alphonse Cardozo and his friends. According to Sean, Ambassador McLuck called Neville Chamberlain "*Neville J'aime-Berlin.*" She did not understand this joke, but it did not matter. What mattered to her was that the embassy was next door.

"There are hundreds of ways to slip from the embassy over to the Cardozos' and back," said Sean. "Around the central courtyard, through the common wine cellar, along the gutters and drainpipes, behind the *trompe-l'oeil* bookcase."

"Oh, good," she said, imagining herself in bed, listening to the creaking of the floorboards, awaiting his light knock on her door in the middle of the night, and the unbuttoning of his high wing collar after a diplomatic evening.

It was strange how sated she felt walking home through the deserted streets, arm in arm with him.

"Girl, you'd be wise not to get too attached to me. I have other duties to my country—well, to my cause: the Irish Republican Army. I am in great personal danger."

At the word "danger," her arms floated up to his neck. Immediately a silence took hold. His blue eyes looked vulnerable in this half-light. She tasted his lips.

"Sean, I want to give myself like I never have given myself before. Do you understand me?"

Her words were overflowing from her lips into his mouth.

And she found herself saying truths which she did not recognize as such until she saw them reflected in his eyes.

In the courtyard, as he kissed her good-night, she was a different woman from what she had been before she had left on this date. She felt much older and calmer. They had not broken into the *bateau-mouche.* They had not done anything, really. But Benz no longer felt like a virgin. Pausing at the bottom of the six flights of stairs, she could still taste Sean's lips and the sweetness of his breath. She dug her fingers into her forearms to keep from shouting out loud.

And yet, on this quiet night of nights, as she climbed the stairs, virginity ambled home with her, with all its fears and frustrations, insistent as ever.

THE Fratellini circus was set up near the back of the Jardin d'Acclimatation, next to the miniature-golf course. Tim pulled Benz by the arm into the little candy-striped tent just as the afternoon show was beginning. They sat down in the third row. The drums rolled; pencil beams of light from two projectors circled the ring like robbers in an empty house. Two Fratellini brothers came out. The one with blue eyebrows and orange hair began sawing the left side of an imaginary log; suddenly the right side fell off!

"Hahahahahaha."

These clowns were stupid, but the boy couldn't help laughing at the same gag every time he saw it. Mercedes opened her newspaper:

MOTHER FALLS OFF DELIVERY TABLE—KILLS SELF AND CHILD!

"Hey, stop reading! Benz, you're missing the best part!"

The band started to play. The audience clapped rhythmically. A large dappled horse now pranced around the ring while a woman in fishnet stockings sat on its back. What Mercedes loved was not the shining trombones in the blue light, the candy-striped music stands, or the smell of horse dung. What she cared for most was Timi's ooh-aahing, his donkey brayings of laughter, and his grabbing her arm tightly when the trapeze lady twisted and turned, sailed and dipped at the top of the tent like a fly on the ceiling. She turned the page of *Paris-Unveiled:*

SLAIN BEAUTY QUEEN FOUND
WEARING CHASTITY BELT!

"Benz, come on! Pay attention! This is important!"

The Fratellinis were sitting down at an imaginary table, pulling imaginary chairs out from under each other and falling on the ground with a loud thud on the bass drum. Tim clapped along with the others while Mercedes read her stupid paper:

SAILOR WATCHES HIS ENTIRE FAMILY DEVOURED BY GIANT SQUID
STRICKEN MAN TELLS OF HIGH SEAS TERROR!

Tim watched Mercedes get that glazed look on her face and bite her lower lip as she always did when she read about some particularly grisly murder. He imagined a giant squid walking up the Champs-Elysées swallowing up carloads and movie theaters full of families.

"Benz, why do you worry so much about death?"

"Because it waits for us under our pillows. Death hopes we will forget to wake up in the morning."

"I'll wake you up. Don't worry."

"Some *calorrós* say: 'If your companion's beard starts to burn, put yours in water.' "

"Why do Gypsies say so many stupid things, Benz?"

"You are the stupid one, *estúpido*."

"No, come on. What does that mean? If your companion's beard starts to burn, put yours in—"

"It means we must to be extremely vigilant. Because the real danger is to die without having loved. Timi, do not ever show your palm like that! That is how you cast an evil spell. You must always be waving with the palm of your hand toward your own face, like this."

She raised the blue devil's eye she wore around her neck to ward off curses and pressed it to his lips.

"Do not show anyone your palm, unless they do it to you first. Then, of course, you must defend yourself."

The boy could be so attentive sometimes; it made up for all the other times, she thought, going back to her newspaper:

GERMAN SHEPHERD DOG EATS BABY
WHILE MOTHER AWAY SHOPPING!

Tim practiced this new method of hand waving, but was suddenly quiet, staring at her forearms: they were covered with black-and-blues:

"Benz, what happened? Who did this to you?"

She looked up and quickly covered her arms with her red-flowered woolen shawl.

"Benz, everyone loves you! Who could possibly want to harm you? Monsieur Henri? Marcel, the butcher's son?"

"It is nothing," she said sharply, turning to another page of *Paris-Unveiled.*

"Was it the Irish Ambassador? Or Jujule, the artichoke salesman? He always likes to joke with you! Tell me, was it Jujule?"

"I fell down the stairs, *borracha.*"

"No, you almost never drink. Come on, tell the truth, Benz. Did Pepe grab you or something? Did Manola?

"You ask so many stupid questions, you give me a headache!"

For the first time in his ten-year-and-three-month life, Tim considered the possibility that men had touched or would be touching his Madonna. He thought of the stench of their fat pores, the filth of their bruising hands, the lies of their tongues. How many men had already caressed her beautiful cheeks—a dozen? A hundred? Would her lips reek of men when she came to kiss him good-night? Tim felt disgusted.

He stared at Benz's black-lashed eyes. In the shadows, she was reading, or trying to read, the newspaper. He wanted to squirm and plead with her to tell the truth, but he knew she would not.

A human pyramid rose six humans high. In the red harlequin light, he saw Benz wink at him with both eyes. But Tim was angry and did not wink back. An overwhelming sadness was taking hold of him.

FROM a distance, the great open-air Saturday marketplace sounded like a symphony tuning up; but once in the Place des Ternes, the roar became deafening—an orchestra with no conductor, each merchant playing his own tune at his own tempo:

"PORTUGUESE SARDINES FROM MALAYSIA VIA THE BALLEARES AND NOVA SCOTIA! LADIES-LADIES, GET THEM WHILE THEY LAST!"

The trombone voices blared. The kettle drums struck repeatedly in a flurry of arpeggios as rough hands threw kilo weights on the copper scales. Mercedes loved these triangular piles of oranges, tomatoes, lemons, and red beets; no one was *jayipí*—starving—here! Ripe chèvre and blue cheese tugged at her nostrils and drew her down the narrow crowded street. A fishmonger with a white apron tied over one shoulder threw a bucket of dirty water on the sidewalk:

"DON'T TOUCH, HONEY, DON'T TOUCH!" said the leek salesman.

"Benz, I really think we have crocodiles in our cellar! I mean I haven't actually seen one, but there are things moving around in the well water—definitely alive," said Tim as he grasped a firm hold of her blue overcoat.

"Leave me alone with that nonsense, Timoté!"

"I'm serious! Have you been to the cellar lately?"

"FRESH SOLE: 3.90 FRANCS A HALF KILO! 5.50 FOR ONE!"

Master Tim loved coming here every weekend, towed behind Benz like another little food wagon. This controlled hysteria reminded him of his school battles. He especially liked the different types of people all pushing to buy: women lining up for fresh baguettes, Algerians ripping open crates with crowbars, boys piling salads up to the sky, fishmongers, in their black rubber boots, dumping tons of ice on blind-eyed fish and octopus. He was always fascinated by the endless nonsense the vendors screamed, especially as no one seemed to pay attention to it, not even those doing the shouting:

"FIVE FRANCS FOR THREE. FOUR FOR FOUR. FIVE AND YESSIREE, WE GIVE YOU THE CAPTAIN OF THE BOAT FOR FREE!"

What Mercedes most admired was the huge butchers in their white coveralls, carrying half-steers tight to their chests like sailors dancing with recalcitrant partners. The men were not necessarily handsome, but in their big faces and bright bloody aprons she saw a hint of martyrdom: the suffering of the innocents that fed this hungry city. These men, who danced with a combination of strength and grace, who turned on their heels before coming to rest by a freezer or a meat hook, commanded her respect. They were definitely more seductive than the leek or cabbage salesmen.

Jujule, the artichoke man, suddenly leaned over and licked Mercedes' face. She screamed and wiped her cheek.

"What are you, crazy?"

Jujule tried to lick her again! She slapped him, her nostrils flaring, like those of one of Monsieur Cardozo's racehorses after a race. The oyster-shucker intervened and explained to Mercedes that ever since his wife had left him, Jujule had taken to drinking and acting *fou*. The man did indeed look deranged. Mercedes left, pulling the food cart and Timi behind her.

"You see what it is to be a woman, Timoté?"

"What?"

"We are too vulnerable. They want us to be victims and not act unladylike or scream. But a *gitana* knows how to defend herself from the wolves!"

"What did Jujule want, Benz?"

"To show his masculine ego. To have power over a woman—just like my father. They are *loco*!"

"What is ego, Benz?"

"Timoté, *por Dios,* do not start with me, not here!"

He could tell when she was angry. And now was no time to get on her nerves. Above Tim's head there towered piles of artichokes, endives, black radishes, cabbages. What he wouldn't give to dive head first into these mounds of red, yellow, and purple! Behind a small glass partition he saw trays of sheep's heads, brains, kidneys. Naked rabbits dangled from their hindquarters along with other bunnies who managed to keep their gray fur coats intact.

"Benz, don't get angry, okay? But just tell my why you don't want to discuss the crocodiles in our cellar."

"Because I do not know what you are talking about! Okay? *Basta!* Why can't you leave me alone for a second?"

"But I've just told you a million times. You never listen. And this could be really serious!"

"Timi, I am in love. Understand? In love!"

"So?"

"So, to be in love is to be in a kind of craziness. Like that Jujule. Sometimes I dust your room and then I wake up and I am lying on a couch in the second-floor ballroom. And I do not know how I got there. It is like a drug. Sometimes, I wake and find that Mercedes is talking to you. Understand?"

Metal doors slammed. A short-haired dog barked from inside a woman's handbag. A cashier with a pince-nez sat at her booth looking exactly like the neon horse profile outside the horse-meat store.

"Timi, this man, Sean is for me forever!"

"How do you know?"

"Because I know."

A cheese man cut a small slice of Bonbel for Mercedes to taste and she handed it to the boy.

"But you haven't known him that long."

"Some things take only an instant."

"But how do you really know he is not a 'savage' or a 'wolf,' like all the others?"

"I just know it."

Mercedes was in her food-buying trance: caressing a clump of fresh white asparagus with a slow, long admiring hand, popping a white mushroom into her mouth, and examining a multipronged gadget that for 10 francs promised to cut-slice-dice-dip-start-open-turn-shape-sharpen-and-that's-not-all!

CHICKEN LIVERS: SIX FRANCS THE KILO, ELEVEN FOR TWO, SIXTEEN FOR THREE! HURRY, HURRY, HURRRRRRRYYY!"

"Well, Benz, if those aren't crocodiles in the cellar, just what do you think they are?"

"I don't know."

"But I asked you what you *think,* not what you know!"

She was hovering over a pile of unblanched Valencia peanuts. Tim hated it when she buzzed around food like this and paid no attention to him. And he was in no mood for Marcel, who loved to show off his stupid magic tricks. From her fake laughter, he could tell that Benz didn't really enjoy the butcher's son's dismal tricks either. But now she giggled stupidly as Marcel made a long string of blood sausage disappear behind his left ear. An old woman pressed her thumb deep in the red of a rump steak to test its freshness. The hot-chestnut vendor stirred his coals. Marcel's dad chopped away at a pile of ribs, muttering: "One day I'll miss and I'll have nothing to pick my nose with!"

"ESCARGOTS—TWENTY A DOZEN, SIX A PAIR, THREE FOR A SONG, FIVE AND WE CALL IT QUITS. LADIES, LADIES, LAAAAAADIES!"

On this gray Saturday morning, with one of Tim's knee socks slipping down to his ankle, thyme and rosemary wafting into the butcher shop, and a Trini López song in the air, Mercedes took out her old red Moroccan leather wallet as Marcel counted out twelve slices of the leanest *filet de boeuf.* She went to stand in line in front of the cashier. This was always the hardest—seeing an ex-boyfriend and trying to act as if nothing were the matter. She had dodged all his calls, through Manola's good services, and had skirted this store for several months. How could she ever have thought enough of Marcel to give him her phone number? If she didn't have her head so in the clouds today with constant thoughts of Sean, she would surely have remembered not to shop here. Standing with her back to Marcel's counter, she wondered what she might say to him when she picked up the meat.

"Marcel, baby, real life is nothing but a huge approximation. At best we settle for something resembling or very much like or almost akin. Get used to it. Treat the next woman like gold, even if she is not twenty-four-karat. Or if you have the patience of a saint, hold out like I did for the real thing to come along.

And do not even touch the *presque,* the almost, the *casi,* the sixty or seventy percent, until you are sure it is a hundred percent what you want. Now do you understand why I have not been returning your calls?"

The truth was she had nothing to say to Marcel, and not enough feeling toward him even to want to invent lies. Especially not in front of the boy and the customers.

Tim looked up at the dead rabbits dangling in midair, their gray coats on, delicate oregano leaves in their mouths. The lurid gleam in the bunny eyes seemed to await a predetermined signal to turn and run out of the store. Riveted by this sudden insight, Tim was ready, more than ready, to assist in the mass getaway of all these animals that hung upside down, including the wild boar with blood on his dangling brown tongue and the guinea fowl with their beautiful red-gold-and-green plumes so regal and warm in this gray light. Tim innocuously shuffled sawdust on the white marble floor and considered how best to help the rabbits in their great escape.

"TRAAAIIIIIIIPE! NORMANDY-FRESH CHAROLAIS TRAAIIIIIIIIPE!

Marcel took Benz by the arm and whispered:

"*Ne me quitte pas, Mercedes!*"

She loved the Jacques Brel song title he had used, but she worried that one of the neighbors' maids would overhear this and it would get back to Pepe, who would tease her mercilessly. Worse yet, it would get back to Sean!

"*Mercedes, je t'en supplie!*"

What had she ever seen in this crude young butcher's son with a cowlick at the back of his head? (He was handsome, but there were limits.) Marcel tightened his grip and twisted her wrists. She did not want Marcel. She wanted only Sean; his ruined castle on the green hill; his healthy children, all eight of them, speaking Irish and playing with cats and dogs. She wanted to be independent, but since true love was slavery, she did not mind being chained by the leg to his bed or his kitchen. She didn't mind if a man told her when to get up in the morning and when to go to sleep, as long as that man was Sean.

"*Mercedes, ne sois pas vache. Ecoute-moi au moins.*"

Marcel pulled her behind the far counter and pushed her

toward the meat freezer. Mercedes did not want to create a scandal, but when she saw the half-cows and whole sheep hanging there, smoking-cold in purple-and-white splendor on the other side of the small glass window, she kneed Marcel in the groin. He twisted her left arm behind her back so tightly that tears came to her eyes. Benz grabbed the edge of the counter and the freezer door, clawing and wrenching quietly from side to side. She knew that once inside the cold-storage room, she would have no chance.

"Mercedes! J'ai mal."

Well, good, she thought. A little pain would help Marcel immensely. He was giving *mal* to her wrists. They were equal. If she had been a *paya,* she might have lied, even perhaps kissed Marcel just to get free of him; but her only thought now was that once and for all, she was going to stop taking to men the way cloud shadows passing over fields and hills take on different shapes. She would be a rock, unchanging and permanent, in the flood of Sean's love.

"Mercedes . . ."

"Fiche-moi la paix!"

Marcel tried to shove his tongue between her clenched teeth. The freezer door felt clammy like a dog's runny nose.

"Je t'adore, chérie."

"You *estúpido,* let me go!"

She tried to bite his arm. Her grip on the edge of the doorjamb started to slip. If only she had a *churi* to cut him with! Lifting her up, Marcel pushed her into the hanging beef shanks. She felt her hair sticking to a mass of wet tendons and deep purple meat.

"Timoté! Ayúdame, niño!" she screamed as the freezer door closed behind her.

Deep in conversation with his dead rabbits, Tim heard a muffled shout and turned to look. Benz's cart was in the middle of the store unattended. The sun had disappeared behind a cloud, and the market was cast into nebulous late-winter mist, full of green and brown woolen overcoats and lined boots. Where was Benz?

"PIGS' KNUCKLES CHEEEEEEEEAP, VERY CHEEEEEAP! LIKE THE BIRD WHO ALL HE COULD SING WAS CHEEP—CHEEEP-CHEEEEEEP!"

Tim spied a blue coat walking down the street and turning the corner. He ran toward it shouting Benz's name. She was so impulsive and unpredictable! When he caught up with her and pulled on her arm, a Frenchwoman with a face like a crab turned around and scowled at him. He said, *"Pardon, Madame,"* and rushed back to the butcher shop.

She couldn't just disappear like this. Where was Marcel? He asked the cashier, but got no answer. Benz's *filet de boeuf* lay wrapped on the counter. Marcel's papa was calling for more rump cuts. New customers were filing in. Tim turned and saw some movement in the small windowpane of the meat-storage freezer. He stood up on his toes and peered in, wiping the condensation of his breath off the glass. He could make out the massive white-aproned Marcel holding Benz up by the wrists and kissing her neck. So Marcel was the one causing the ugly bruises on his nanny's arms! Tim felt an overwhelming desire to bite a hole in Marcel's throat and rip off those disgusting liver-colored lips.

"GIVE HIM KNUCKLES TONIGHT, KNUCKLES, LADIES, KNUCKLES!"

Tim yanked on the handle of the heavy freezer door. It would not open. He saw Benz spit in Marcel's face as she strained and struggled to get away. Pulling down with all his weight, Tim finally clicked the door and swung it open.

"Benz!"

He rushed in, his breath billowing in front of his face, and gave Marcel a mighty Dr. Feng–patented roundhouse special kick meant to break the enemy's ribs, but which landed on Marcel's left kneecap. *"Oh, putain!"* grunted the butcher in surprise as Benz ran out. On his back in a crate of lamb chops, Marcel held his left leg and swore like a sailor. Quickly, Tim leaned against the heavy lead-and-wood door until it clicked shut. Nobody in the store seemed to have noticed the scuffle. By the time Marcel's father found him tomorrow, he would be frozen *steak tartare*.

Without stopping to wipe her hair that was tinged red from

the beef flanks, Benz rebuttoned her coat and packed up the filet. She grabbed the boy's hand and the two sped up the crowded sidewalk, stopping at the Place des Ternes so that Benz could switch hands. Her wagon was overflowing with meats and fruits, and Avenue Carnot was quite a steep climb back.

"Thank you, Timoté. You are my hero!"

"How could you let him touch you, Benz?"

Her nose twitched impatiently.

"Is he your boyfriend?"

Wiping away the tears in the corners of her eyes, she gave a nervous laugh which, although it was clearly phony, did not mean either yes or no.

"Is he?"

"Sometimes I wish I were ugly so they would all leave me alone!"

"Just tell me. Is he?"

"What do you think I am? *Estúpido,* you know very well I have only one man. Now be quiet and do not ask so many ignorant questions!"

The clouds were zooming low over the Arc de Triomphe. Mercedes stopped to check her makeup in the reflection of a café window. She gave a scream and quickly pulled out a handkerchief to wipe the cow blood from her neck and hair.

"What is the matter with you, Timoté? You let me walk like this in the street? You crazy!"

She pinned her greasy hair up in a bun and felt nauseous. Behind the glass she could see a giant silver espresso machine and Algerians eating their lunch at the *zinc.* One of them, swarthy and dirty, lifted his wineglass to her. She gave him the hand-in-the-crook-of-the-arm sign and walked away.

"You men are all the same!"

"What do you mean?"

"Timoté, my mother taught me to love with all my soul and to leave the rest to fate. But she did not teach me that you must trust absolutely no one. Not even yourself at times!"

Tim helped her pull the cart up the last two blocks. Helga stood at her post on the corner of Rue Rude, smoking one of her long Turkish-blend cigarettes. The policeman guarding the Irish Embassy smiled at Mercedes and tipped his *képi* as they passed. As always, Tim admired the gold harp hanging on a purple escutcheon over the entrance to the chancery and the curious Gaelic words: AMBASSAID NA HEIREANN.

"Timoté, did you notice that Marcel has thin lips?"

"No."

"Parisians are a thin-lipped race! They have not the milk of human kindness."

She threw back her head with a fierce note of contempt. Her lush blue-black hair came undone and fell down both sides of her long face.

"Frenchmen are cheap! They count out their affection in centimes. They give their love coin by coin! I am poor, but I refuse to be a miser of the soul. And you must be the same way, Timoté—generous in everything!"

Mercedes stared at him with a smile forming on her face as if it were the first time she had ever laid eyes on him.

"You really cracked Marcel a good one," she said, squeezing his hand.

At first Tim thought she might be crying, because her chest was shaking so violently. But she was hiccuping and could not stop laughing.

"Benz, are you having an attack?"

"Timoté, Marcel is a fool, but at least he showed his emotions. That is exactly as it should be. Good for Marcel!"

"I don't understand, Benz."

The wind played in her long hair. It scared him how unpredictable she could be.

"Timi, you think playing Napoleon is exciting? Imagine how much more important are the games lovers play! Oh, why are you only ten?"

Master Tim pulled up his right knee sock, which had slipped down to his ankle.

"*Gitanos* say, 'Better to die than to lose one's life.' "

"Better to die than to lose one's life? That makes absolutely no sense, Benz."

"It means that if you do not have passion, you do not live!

Marcel gave us some passion today! Did he not? Ha! And you were so brilliant. I will never forget you swooping down like an eagle to save me. Thank you, Timi."

They climbed into the Elevator from the Year One, which was working for a change.

"Benz, what are we going to do about those lizards or crocodiles in the cellar?"

She slapped the back of his head and pulled the food wagon, on its creaky wheels, noisily into the house.

CHAPTER 3

Tim Turns Eleven, Benz Twenty

MERCEDES SLOWLY CLOSED his door and sat down in the dark on the edge of the boy's bed. Manola and Pepe were fighting again. Their yelling was so loud, it cut through the meter-thick masonry.

How, she wondered, was he expected to wake up refreshed and smart for school after a night of Manola screaming at her husband for betting on the horses? The room was pitch-black, but she could hear XKE stirring in his cage. The familiar smell of dog, ink, chocolate, and musty soccer equipment invaded her nostrils. The boy had his head under the pillows. Was he sleeping? She nudged him.

"Timoté, can you lend me some money?"

He sat up on one elbow. He must have some *calorró* blood in him, thought Mercedes, for only Gypsies had such quick brown squirrel eyes.

"Now?"

"Yes, I'm sorry to wake you up."

The boy turned on his brass Napoleon lamp, got out of bed, padded groggily over to his dresser, and took out the Junior G-Man–Al Capone Savings Bank that his father had given him for Christmas two years before.

"How much do you need?"

That was what she most admired about the boy—his unthinking, unhesitating devotion; his absolute, unconditional loyalty. She could run in here anytime and announce to the boy that she had just murdered the President and Tim would hide her in his closet, no questions asked.

"Whatever you can spare, *chéri.*"

Every Christmas and birthday, the Aunties gave the boy shiny new bank notes (1,000-franc Corneilles and 500-franc Pasteurs), which he collected in this little safe that he kept hidden in his sock drawer.

"What do you need this for, anyway?"

"Two may keep a secret, if one of them is dead."

"You're not going on vacation, are you?"

Tim could never remember if it was double thirteen to the left, then eighteen to the right, or vice versa. Mercedes glanced impatiently out the window.

"Benz, if something is wrong, just tell me."

She tried to think of a Gypsy proverb that might be an appropriate nonanswer. At last the metal box swung open. Master Tim gave her all the bills left inside and replaced it in its hiding place behind his socks. Tears came to her eyes—the boy had not counted, or given her half, or two-thirds; no, he had instinctively made the noblest gesture!

"I will not forget this great kindness, Timoté."

"But you wouldn't go on vacation without me, would you? I mean if you go, you'll take me with you, right?"

Tim pulled at a thread on his pajamas.

She nodded, counting the bills. He repeated his question. Instead of answering, she fluttered her eyes like night moths flying out of a dark closet and bent to give him a kiss. Tim ran back to his bed. If she was going to kiss him, he wanted her to do it the way she always did: leaning over his pillow, her black hair cascading down on top of him, engulfing him in her many and luxurious smells.

She sat down on his bed now. Tim wrapped his arms around her neck. How beautiful she was—deep emerald eyes, shiny thick hair parted down the middle like two mirrors, sculpted mouth with its blood-red lipstick and her long flared nostrils. During the day, in her black outfit with the white lace collar and cuffs, Benz wore her hair neatly tucked in a bun. But when she got dressed for a date, she let her hair down and wore clothes that were either too tight or too skimpy. So this evening, she appeared bigger, full of skin and curves, round and rich on all sides, unlike anything she was in the daytime.

"Como se pinta!" Manola would say, shaking her head.

Benz indeed did "paint herself." Tim would watch her for hours as she sat on the bidet with a little brush and a mirror, applying an entire rainbow of colors to her face: a black line around the lips, a base of rouge, silver under the eyes, blue, purple, or even mauve for the eyebrows, gold and red coral earrings, a tortoiseshell comb on the side and a red rose behind the opposite ear—no one else in this gray city gave off as much color as Benz when she wanted to light up the night! And she smelled pungent: all the oranges and lemons of Seville, all the wisteria and honeysuckle of Matamoros followed her when she stepped out of Number 10½.

She finished counting the bills and stuffed them inside her bra.

"Timi, you will go to *charó* for being so good to me."

"I'll go to heaven only if you come with me, Benz."

She dug her fingernails into his scalp and stuffed her face into the crook of his little neck. Tonight, she felt his love for her to be a palpable intense longing, a struggle for survival, almost like a barnacle clinging to a ship. Too bad men could not stay as sweet as this after they discovered they had a penis between their legs.

"Benz, don't go out tonight. Stay with me."

"No, Mercedes is already late. Tonight is very important!"

"Benz, stay and teach me flamenco."

She had broken a fingernail and had spent most of the evening filing the others to equal length. And now she was late. Sean was probably on his fifth cigarette, waiting in the courtyard, puffing mad.

"Darling, Mercedes has to go."

"Stay and knit me a scarf with my school colors: purple and yellow. Just like the sweater you made for me last year."

Unclasping Timi's hands from the nape of her neck, she gave him one last kiss on the forehead, her mass of tangled hair falling across his face. Would tonight, she wondered, be like all the other nights with that excessively polite Irishman? A good-night kiss at the door and *c'est tout?* How ironic that she had spent most of her life keeping men out of her bed, and now that she at last found one she wanted in it, he left her with the Honor of All Spain still intact! Would she have to lead him by the organ like that vet in Morón de la Frontera whose job it was to lead bulls into cows? *Me vuelven loca, estos hombres!* thought Benz.

"Why can't I meet this Sean?"

"I do not trust you."

"Huh?"

"You could ruin my whole life without even trying! It is too risky for me."

He looked at her with a mixture of shock and despair on his face.

"I trust you. But men are strange. And you are a little man, and, and I must run now."

"BEEEENZ!!!"

"Shhh! If Manola and Pepe hear you, they will bite my head off for keeping you up so late!"

"Good! I'll wake up the Aunties too! Now just explain to me why I cannot meet Sean."

"Because you can't, and that is that! Now good night!"

She switched off the overhead light that also controlled his bedside lamp. He called out her name in the dark and waited for an answer. From the hallway, she whispered:

"Timi, I'm late. If you have any feelings for me at all, go to sleep!"

"Benz, you promise you are not going on vacation without me?"

There was no answer. Tim got out of bed and walked slowly to his door. In the hallway, he heard the back service door click shut. XKE squeaked inside his treadmill. Tim did not turn on the lights; instead, he parted the Napoleon-motif curtains and opened his window. The damp April air crept under his cotton pajamas. Tim could make out the red tip of a man's cigarette down in the courtyard. He held his breath and leaned over his balcony railing into the darkness. He could not make out the man's face or even his size. But he heard Benz's characteristic high-heeled clip-clop echoing as she crossed the courtyard.

"Is that all you brought?" the man asked Benz.

Tim heard money change hands—most likely his own money; then:

"I'm sorry, but the boy detained me."

"The boy, the boy! That's all you ever talk about! Dammit, we're going to be late!"

The man rushed out of the courtyard, pulling her by the arm. Tim ran to the salon, on the other side of the house. From there he would be able to see them walk out the driveway, perhaps even discover who this man was and where they were going. But when he got to the front balcony, the driveway below was deserted. They had vanished. He waited, shivering, tapping his bare feet on the cold stone. What a liar she was! Benz was leaving on vacation—why else would she need such a large suitcase? She was the biggest liar in the entire world! He would punch her on the nose when she returned. His hands clutched the wrought-iron railing.

"BEEEEEEEEEEEEEEEEENNNNNZ!"

There was no answer, not even an echo. Nothing out there but secret-service "leg ladies," as Pepe called them, and cars in the night. The wind blew through his pajamas, chilling his groin and sweeping down to his ankles. What were they going to do with his money? Would the man kill her? Tim saw her beaten, lassoed, tied to the bottom of a well, throttled, blown up, buried alive, shot.

"BEEEEEEENNNNNZ . . ."

He felt stupid out there on the balcony in his bare feet, shouting. He sneezed and listened. Very faintly at first, he heard the clip-clop of Benz's heels rushing up his veins and down his soul. Yes, she was hurrying away from Passy, from Wagram and the Place des Ternes, where Spanish maids congregate on their days off to go dancing; louder now, she was running down deserted boulevards of the Rive Gauche, past empty paddy wagons and Algerian pickpockets, past the Porte de Clichy and the Porte de Vanves, along tiny side streets in Picpus and Villejuif, to the *périphérique* and all the highways and byways that lead out of the city, past all the truck stops and unlit garages where men strangle maidens by the dozen and leave them in shallow graves for *Paris-Unveiled* to photograph and run on its front page.

Tim returned to his bed with death in his soul.

BY the time Benz had extricated herself from the boy's clutches, Sean had smoked half a pack of Caporals and was in as foul a mood as she had ever seen him. They missed their train, but caught another. The Saint-Plomb Express snorted and whooshed and started to pull out of the Gare de Lyon as they ran with their suitcases down Track 18. It was movie-perfect, how they jumped on at the last possible moment, with the passengers leaning out the compartment windows to watch them defy the irate conductor. Benz had never ridden in first class before. Nor did she understand why, if Sean was truly a pauper and they were using Timi's little savings, they should not travel in third class or even in the baggage compartment. Sean never fully explained himself on this point except to say cryptically that "Money is something I never worry about."

When the steward came to prepare their *couchettes,* she realized that a whole era of her life was mercifully coming to an end. That night, as the train sped south, she relinquished gratefully, though not without some residual guilt, the Honor of her people. Afterward, as she lay on her back with goose bumps on her arms, staring up at the little triangle of white by the Emergency Stop that appeared and disappeared with each passing street light, it was hard to remember exactly what had been so horrible about having to carry that Honor for twenty years.

As a teenager, Mercedes had thought that if she ever allowed herself premarital relations, she would probably enjoy sex so much she would become a hopeless nymphomaniac. But that first night, she discovered that her desires were not uncontrollable, even as she gave way to them. Though Sean lay snoring on top of her, his enormous bulk was wonderfully light, almost weightless. She was twenty and she had her first lover. The train blew its whistle and jolted them from side to side. The triangle of passing lights flashed on and off overhead. He was an Irish diplomat whose family castle consisted of three stones, one atop another, on a beautiful rolling green hill. Even if Sean was only a butler, as Pepe insisted, he would do admirably for her purposes. Lying under him in a bunk, she was as happy as a potato under a tree.

"I am scared that the sky here in Paris is going to fall on my head," said Roland.

They stopped for a red light. Roland stared into the distance, listening to the thud of pétanque balls on the crisp gravel. Master Tim was not going to give his mulatto friend the satisfaction of asking him what in God's name he was talking about. The sky falling on his head? He had said this without any trace of irony. When Benz made such statements, Tim automatically discounted them. But when Roland said equally outrageous things, he reserved judgment. After all, in Port-au-Prince, Roland had seen zombies; and only yesterday, he had asked Father Brouette, S.J., in front of the whole class:

"If God is omnipotent, can He create something that is too heavy for Him to lift?

How did Roland come up with this stuff? Behind that mysterious, imperturbable smile, what was the mechanism of Roland's mind? He understood things no one else in the class had ever thought of.

"I don't mean 'the sky will fall on my head' literally. I mean it figuratively."

Roland did not explain the word "figuratively." It lay between them like a gauntlet. American tourists were taking pictures of the Arc de Triomphe. It always depressed Tim enormously to run into his fellow countrymen. You could recognize Americans a kilometer away: They wore ill-tailored, too-short pants, glasses with pointy Cadillac fins, and checkered, vomit-red shirts. Their accents were so unnatural, they could peel paint off walls. And Americans in groups were infinitely worse than one at a time.

"Roland, how can such morons expect to beat the Russians to the moon? You think Yuri Gagarin walks around in a clown outfit like that? Of course not!"

"My dad says you Americans are responsible for the Tontons Macoutes putting electrodes on his balls."

"What are electrodes?" asked Tim.

"Your Marines train our secret police to torture prisoners."

"That's not true!" said Tim. He was not going to allow anyone else to criticize the United States, and this accusation required absolute denial. They walked up Avenue Victor Hugo.

"Your country taught our Macoutes how to put military electric plugs on prisoners' *zizis* to make them talk."

"That's a lie!"

"No, it isn't."

"Yes, it is."

"My dad couldn't sit down for six months when he came back from the Tontons. There were burn marks all over his scrotum."

Perhaps it was electrodes that made Roland's *zizi* so purple and so much longer than anyone else's in class. Tim thought for a while, then pretended to have a fainting spell. Roland caught him as he fell. Tim jumped up, pummeled his friend in the kidneys, tried to kick him in the backside, and ran for cover, as Roland shouted:

"Tim, your attention span is getting closer and closer to nil! What about our blood-brother ceremony?"

As agreed earlier, they raced all the way to the driveway of Number 10½ Avenue Foch. Huffing and puffing, they stood under the shadow of a linden tree. There, Tim pulled out his Swiss Army knife. Slowly they cut little gouges into their wrists and pressed them together. It didn't hurt very much. By the ivy-covered wall of the garden, eye to eye, wrist to wrist, they stood as their bloods mixed.

Master Tim was no longer a half-Jew, second to last in class, like Churchill and Napoleon and other misunderstood geniuses destined to rule the world (he thanked God for Gerbi or he would have been last); now he was one-tenth black as well. He was everything Roland connoted: he was part wildcat, iguana, jaguar, Andean condor, greased gazelle, Tonton Macoute, Voodoo priestess, chrysanthemum spot of blood on a dead man's face, and houses burning in the night! Negroid gods did the breaststroke through his arteries. Drop by drop, Tim felt his blood brother's soft and gentle nature seep into his veins and gain his consciousness. Pumping through him were Roland's mulatto dreams, the blood bones of his ancestors, his *Gioconda* smile, and even the would-be electrodes that made his *bibi fricotin* so purplish. Tom-toms beat in his temples. He felt himself growing a permanent suntan.

From the fourth-floor balcony, Aunt Phoebe could just make out the silhouette of Master Tim and his little mulatto friend in the driveway below. How skinny they both looked! She hurried to the kitchen to tell Manola to prepare an extra-large dinner for them. She would sneak a raw egg into Tim's hot cocoa, a drop or two of cod-liver oil, and some raw marrowbone as well. He would never notice. After all, she did not want her grandnephew to remain a runt all his life.

IT was the off season, a rain-soaked blue-gray April afternoon in Cannes. The resort was practically empty, except for locals clustered in a café and men fixing the sidewalk. The major hotels were closed, but a few remained open, manned with skeleton staffs. Benz insisted they go for a walk, and Sean grudgingly agreed. They huddled together under her little beige umbrella and headed up the wide empty beach, into the wind. For a long time, she was quiet. They stopped to look at the million rain-drops spraying the sea. Benz looked with old mariner eyes, eyes that had been here before. The sight of this slate-gray Mediterranean with its waves foaming onto the neutral-colored sand made everything she had stored inside her well up. Working in Paris, she had no time to feel this surge of peace, but here the soft pounding of the sud-foaming sea harmonized with the pounding in her chest, and reaffirmed her dreams.

"We better go back," said Sean as wet sand seeped into his shoes. Only a dimwit, he thought, would want to stroll along the beach on a day such as this.

Mercedes did not answer. How dramatic she felt on this deserted and immense beach! Gray-and-white squall clouds moved overhead, racing with the distant thunder out toward Morocco and places south.

"Look, dear, I have an important meeting and I do not want to miss it," said Sean, surveying the empty, endless sea.

The rain was getting worse. But Mercedes insisted they walk to the lighthouse at the end of the bay. The night ride south on the train had taken on mythic proportions now in the pantheon of Mercedes' memories. She loved the passive-active combination of staring through the window at all of France floating by, the frantic clickety-clack of the wheels on the track, the humming of the wind. And she recalled every moment rocking gently in that *couchette*.

"Furrrrrrchrrrrrisake, let's go back inside!"

"No, please. Just a little bit more."

"It's pouring! This is really stupid. My feet are soaking!"

He grimaced, but to Mercedes, caught up in this romantic walk, even a downpour seemed like a permanent river of sunlight.

"I'm going back to the hotel," said Sean, disgusted.

"Isn't it magnificent?" she said, pointing to the breakers and deeply breathing in the salt-sea air.

He pulled his arm out of hers and turned back. Mercedes started to cry, It was involuntary, but the drama of separation suited the day. She wanted him, busy and preoccupied as he was, to turn and see her "bleeding from the eyes" because of him. And he did! (What control she could exert over events when she put her mind to it!) He rushed back and hugged her.

"Darling, I have to get back. I am getting my drop today."

The more he kissed her, the more she cried.

"If I don't get this drop, we won't be able to pay for the hotel. And you can't fool around with the I.R.A."

She did not understand what a "drop" meant. But what she clearly saw was that for all his breeding and gentlemanly manners, Sean did not dream half as much as she. When they slept together, for instance, she stayed awake, losing herself in endless thoughts, feeling the soft, fine red hairs on his forearm, while he snored next to her with one hand tucked under his pillow.

"Don't cry. I'll see you back at the room," he said, and left.

Mercedes stopped crying and watched him grow smaller and smaller. In Matamoros, there was a saying that "the difference between zero and one is infinity." Now she understood what this meant: The distance between having no man and having one was infinite. By comparison, the difference between one man and all men was no difference at all. In fact, man number one to man number one million were all more or less alike.

Walking by herself now, she clutched the little umbrella. The wind buffeted it around and turned it inside out. If Sean was in trouble with the Irish Salvation Army, she would make love to him so often and so well that he would be too exhausted to get himself into mischief. They would be poor and surrounded by children. She would slave for upper-class women who spent their stupid lives on sofas fanning themselves, with green feather boas draped over their negligees.

She felt such an affinity for this violent weather! Rain made one curl up into one's intimate thoughts. It triggered humility and self-appraisal. A sunny day, on the other hand, brought out the worst in humans. It made them cocky and godless. Sunshine made men strut and preen and go whoring!

The rain was letting up. She returned to the hotel. At first they had stayed at the Negresco. Then, when Timi's savings ran out, they had moved to La Pension Rififi, one of the few bed-and-breakfast places that stayed open during the off season. But Sean insisted on keeping the shutters drawn and their door locked, as if they were criminals. With their last 10 francs they had bought a bottle of Evian, a baguette, and some *pâté de campagne*. Mercedes hungrily recalled the lavish *goûter* sandwiches she would prepare for Timi.

When she got back, soaked and shivering, their hotel-room door was locked. She knocked and called out Sean's name. No answer. The keyhole was blocked, but she could not tell if it was by the key or from someone standing on the inside. She heard whispering. When the door at last opened, a silent mustachioed man in a raincoat brushed past her, adjusting a rain hat over his eyes. Sean pulled her into the room and locked the door behind her. Slivers of daylight through the closed shutters cut zebra swaths of pearl-white in the dark room. He reached under the bed and pulled out a mysterious leather suitcase she had not seen before. It was full of brand-new 1,000-franc notes. He had either won the National Lottery or robbed a bank. She questioned him closely to find out which.

"Mercedes, these funds are not mine. They will help political prisoners escape from Belfast to make their way to a safe haven. You know what the I.R.A. is, don't you?"

"Of course."

Sean was in some sort of danger. If she were not in love, she would have been able to discuss this rationally and analyze the problem. But she recalled a certain type of poisonous Andalusian frog which, when placed in a pot of water, does not notice the rise in temperature. When the water begins to boil, it feels no pain; and well-cooked, it is excellent to eat. Benz felt like that frog now: She did not care how hot it got around Sean. As long as he wore the Saint Catherine medal she had given him, she did not care what hidden purpose of the Irish Salvation Army he served.

SATURDAY afternoon. The blood brothers were on their way to Gerbi's birthday party. As they walked around the Etoile to the nearest Métro stop, Master Tim showed Roland all he was bringing to surprise Gerbi: itching powder, a dribble glass, soap that turns the skin black, a hand-buzzer, a whoopee cushion, a plastic turd, a spoon that melts in the soup, multicolored candles that could not be blown out. Tim stuffed some of these back into a plastic bag and some into his pockets. Their friend would go nuts! On the Métro map, they located Gerbi's address on the other side of town: at the Stalingrad station on the Number 2 line—farther east than Tim had ever traveled in Paris before.

Tim looked over at the headline of a passenger's *France-Soir.*

ALGERIAN GENERALS' ATTEMPTED PUTSCH FOILED!
EVIAN TREATY GIVES FULL INDEPENDENCE FOR ALGERIA.

Tim didn't understand why the generals didn't drop their parachutists on the Champs-Elysées. One plastic bomb here, another there—that was no way to run a war. He had waited up night after night, hoping to see the white chutes arc gracefully over the city, thousands of them invading the capital like a World War II movie. And now, all he had to show for this secret war was deep circles under his eyes. He yawned. Roland fingered his second-class ticket as the DU, DUBON, DUBONNET signs of the black cat with red eyes went whizzing by in the dark Métro tunnels. Clickety-clack, clickety-clack.

COURCELLES, MONCEAU, VILLIERS, ROME, CLICHY, the Métro station zipped by. Gerbi had announced they were going to put the Métros on Michelin tires. Tim was dubious, but anything would be better than this spine-rattling clickety-clack. Tim looked down and noticed that both his knee socks had slipped to his ankles. Usually it was only the right—things were getting worse.

"I bet you don't know why the poor live on the east side of Paris," said Roland, looking at the map of the Number 2 line.

Tim shrugged. Why couldn't the Aunties buy him socks that stayed up?

"Because the invasion route is from the east," said Roland with a beguiling smile spreading over his Silly Putty face. "The Germans came from the east in 1870, in 1914, and again in 1940. Well, northeast. So the rich moved to the west side and put the workers to the east as a buffer."

"Who told you that?"

"Nobody. I just thought of it now."

At times like these, Tim simply basked in wonder at his friend's intelligence.

BLANCHE, PIGALLE, ANVERS, BARBÈS-ROCHECHOUART, LA CHAPELLE. The farther they went, the dingier the faces and the shabbier the clothes: Street cleaners in blue coveralls with vacant gray eyes. Factory workers with broken or black teeth. Algerians. Cripples. This was *La Cour des Miracles* at Lourdes —the last refuge for the hopeless cases of this earth.

"The Germans can take the east back as far as I'm concerned," whispered Tim.

He wished they had cheated and ridden in first class. They sat in their car like two minnows in a shark-hungry sea, obvious bait in their blue blazers and striped ties. Beatniks with death's-head tattoos on their biceps stared at them. So did cleaning ladies with hair sprouting on their legs. The reek of underarms made him gag. Tim could feel Arab cooties jumping off the construction workers' heads onto his. He could almost see twelve-legged ones lining up to jump into his better-bred scalp. He began to scratch all over. Perhaps it was the itching powder spilling out of its little box in his jacket pocket—his whole left side was stinging! Finally, STALINGRAD. The passengers stood up. When the doors opened, Tim grabbed Roland and they rushed out of the Métro as fast as they could.

"I wonder who else Gerbi's invited."

"He's got no friends, really, except us."

"He'll probably have camels in his house! And sand dunes!"

They stopped at a grocer's and bought two artichokes. With his Swiss Army knife, Tim dug a hole in the bottom of each one and inserted a small red firecracker. These artichoke hand grenades had worked miracles against Laval. If lobbed at night from a balcony, with one's arm straight à la Steve McQueen, the grenades arced high and wide and, just as they were about to land, exploded in bright red-and-blue tracers and left the terrified enemy covered in vegetable debris. It almost seemed worthwhile to move to Brittany, where artichokes grew and where Tim could imagine great trench warfare filling the sky with flames and showers of green leaves.

They found Gerbi's house above a small florist's. The building smelled of sewage, and there was no elevator. They walked up the lopsided stairs to the fourth floor and waited in the dark. Tim readied his hand-buzzer and the whoopee cushion. They listened for music or laughter coming from inside, but everything was quiet. Maybe they had the wrong address? At long last the door opened.

"Happy Birthday, idiot!" screamed Tim as he stomped on Gerbi's foot, then stopped.

In the doorway, under the glare of a naked light bulb, stood a little man in a gray tie, gray suit, and slippers.

"Entrez, entrez. Je suis Mohammed, le papa Gerbi," said the little man, bending at the waist and extending his hand politely.

Roland and Tim looked at each other. Tim pretended he was incapable of extricating his hand from his pocket, equipped as it was with a super-whiz 8-volt Capitaine Haddock hand-buzzer. They followed Gerbi's dad through a narrow hall piled high with old newspapers to a small kitchen where light streamed in through threadbare curtains. Gerbi was sitting at a minuscule round kitchen table along with a man wearing a brown suit and a white shirt buttoned at the neck without a tie. He was quite dapper, with a goatee, but covered with cat hairs. There was a strained silence, then the rumbling of an elevated Métro arriving into the Stalingrad station.

They each took a stool and accepted a glass of *citron pressé.* Tim tasted a slice of stale brioche and tried to give his seat to Gerbi's dad, but papa insisted on standing by the sink as he sipped a bowl of steamed milk. Gerbi sat there rolling a green booger between the thumb and forefinger of his right hand. Another awkward silence followed. Roland handed Gerbi his present: a beautiful red leather schoolbag, finely crafted, with his initials on the front. Roland's mom must have bought it *chez* Hermès, thought Tim as he tried to hide the brown paper bag containing his explosive artichokes. Gerbi's father and the other man resumed their interrupted conversation:

"Mohammed, okay, we have our independence now. Or soon will. But the Anarcho-Syndicalists in Algiers have nothing in common with the Trotskyite wing of the Party."

"Moscow wants you to believe that, Ismäel, but they work hand in glove. And what are we to do?"

Tim watched horrified as Gerbi's dad opened the brown paper bag, showed his son the artichokes, thanked him, and before Tim could say anything, put them in the icebox. Tim quickly rehearsed every excuse, denial, lie, pettifogging explanation, obfuscation, misrepresentation, and muddling bamboozle he could think of.

"Mohammed, de Gaulle hangs over the consciousness of France like an enormous lead cloud. He paralyzes us all with that great nose of his!"

Roland was resting his chin on the palm of his right hand and staring out into the colorless courtyard where bed sheets flapped in the sun. Tim had never known anyone who could stare into space for hours the way his friend could. When Roland was pensive, he had an absolute disinclination to move or to emit any sign of life at all. It was infuriating. Tim knew that Roland was now orbiting through galaxies of ideas and could no longer be reached by conventional means.

"This is no time to stand on formalities: Maoists and Trotskyites must unite!"

Tim's mouth dropped open. The man with the cat hairs on his brown suit had picked up the trick dribble glass and was filling it at the faucet. Tim watched him drink. The water dripped down the man's goatee and onto his shirt. After a pause in the conversation caused by one Métro arriving and another departing, Ismaël slammed his glass on the table:

"Dammit, when were those Stakhanovite intellectuals last able to organize a demonstration? Mohammed, if the Party snaps its fingers, three hundred thousand people take to the boulevards."

Master Tim envisioned legions of street cleaners with hammers and sickles marching on his lovely tree-lined Avenue to murder his blue-haired Aunties and Wonderdog in their sleep. He recalled his father saying the Russians would one day take over all of Europe. Gerbi was busy caressing the soft beige inside of his leather *cartable*, not listening to the conversation. Roland was off in intellectual orbit. So it was only Tim, his pocket crammed with itching powder, who turned his head, first left and then right, to listen politely to this heated debate being carried on in Arab-French political jargon. It could have been Swahili or Javanese for all Tim knew. Or cared. How strange, these gray-faced little men who argued the day away sitting in a kitchen and did not notice the nonchalant dripping from a dribble glass.

"Ismaël, we are Cartesian hair-splitters! The syndicalist movement ought not be hostage to ideological infighting when the class enemy still controls the means of production!"

Tim nodded his polite agreement to Gerbi's father and tried to catch Roland's eye to indicate that they should leave now. But Roland was off, staring at the thin white trail of a jet in the cloudless sky and methodically rubbing the white cotton of his shirt against his forearm.

He couldn't just give Gerbi two loaded artichokes, not after Roland had given him a leather satchel! Tim suddenly remembered he had a rose-and-aquamarine 25-franc mint-condition 1957 Monaco stamp, commemorating the first supersonic transatlantic flight. He felt his inside blazer pocket, pulled out the clear plastic envelope, and slipped it across the table toward Gerbi.

"Here—this is your real present."

Anatole Gerbi smiled, searching for something to say. As the Monte Carlo stamp lay amid the brioche crumbs and glasses of *citron pressé,* he whispered:

"Not as crowded as your birthday, is it, Cardozo?"

"Oh, no, it's really great, Gerbi! Sorry we were late."

Tim felt like taking his stamp back. (It was a philatelic gem; he had hunted it for weeks.) The man with the cat hairs now slammed his fist on the stamp as if to break the table and shouted:

"Mohammed, since when does Moscow dictate to us?"

He repeated the question, staring at Tim as if he expected an answer from him. Métros came and went. Tim scratched his left elbow and right ankle. The itching powder he had bought was badly packaged. He pointed to his watch with its cracked crystal and reminded Roland that they had to get back to study their Latin. Roland the Wise, Roland the Distant, Roland the Maddeningly Inscrutable deigned to float down to earth long enough to ask Tim to repeat what he had said. Tim motioned toward the door. Still scratching himself, he shook hands with Monsieur Gerbi and his friend Ismaël.

"Thanks. Great party. We really had a great time!"

"Yeah, really great, Gerbi."

They shuffled toward the door. Tim did not try to retrieve the dribble glass, which had been tossed, wordlessly and without humor, into the garbage. As they hurried out, Gerbi's dad started to scratch his neck and behind his ears.

And on this gray overcast day, as they ran down the graffiti-covered streets where garbage was accumulating on the side-walks, Tim felt sad for his Algerian friend, and guilty for trying to cover up for the artichokes by bribing him with a prize Monaco stamp when he knew full well that Gerbi did not collect stamps. What if the roles had been reversed and Gerbi had handed the Aunties some highly explosive grenade-vegetables? On a grimy wall, painted in big red letters, Tim read:

STOP COCA-COLONIZATION! YANKEE GO HOME!

Tim *was* going—he was *running* home! Where was the damned Métro entrance? He hoped Gerbi had the presence of mind to take the artichokes out of the icebox and put them in the trash underneath the eggshells, empty yogurt cups, and brioche crumbs, where his papa was not likely to find them. (They didn't have a telephone, so Tim would have to wait until school on Monday to warn Gerbi.) Roland and he jogged toward Jaurès, where, they had learned, the 1870 Communards were shot down like rabbits and buried in mass graves. And back to the speeding, itchy, lard-smelling Métro.

"Roland, did you notice the cat hairs and stains on their suits?"

"Those are intellectuals, Tim. They live for ideas. They don't care about bourgeois comforts."

The train clickety-clacked back to the rich people's section of Paris. Tim did not feel like talking. He compared the pyramids of dirty plates and crystal piled up in the kitchen of Number 10½ after his own birthday with the few measly items left at the bottom of Gerbi's sink: two chipped bread plates and three water glasses! Surely this was all being recorded in some Great Book somewhere.

"The German invasion route is still from the east," said Roland, pointing across the way to where a group of German tourists were sitting.

Tim noted with satisfaction that the Germans had even wider electrode-stuffed backsides than the Americans.

"Roland, what exactly is Coca-Colonization?"

"Communist propaganda."

"How do you know?"

"Because the French are too smart to let themselves be colonized by anyone—unless they want to be, of course."

Tim did not understand exactly what Roland meant, but as an *Amerloque,* this made him feel somehow less guilty.

"Roland, if you had paid attention to me, we could have left Gerbi's an hour earlier. But no, you just sat there comatose, staring out the window!"

Roland turned his island-soft, purple-shot eyes and, waking from his reverie, said:

"When you visit Port-au-Prince, Timothy, you will see the difference immediately. Where I come from there are no clouds, just miles and miles of blue. There you never have to worry about the sky falling on your head."

ON the train ride back to Paris, Sean snored. Mercedes floated under him, weightless now that the ball and chain of *gitano* Honor had forever been removed form her. In the scented darkness of the *wagon-couchette* hurtling north, she breathed Sean's unmistakable musky aroma—at times, he smelled so strong! (She remembered something Tim had read to her from a book of Napoleon's correspondence: After the Battle of Austerlitz, the Emperor had written to Josephine: "*Chérie,* I shall be back at Malmaison in four days. Please do not wash until then.") Napoleon was right. One's desire depended on the "bouquet" of a person's odors. Sean's underarms made her think of Manhood tramping barefoot through fields of freshly mown hay. She promised herself not to wash her sheets when

Sean was out of town—that way, she would never really be alone.

The taxi from the train station circled the Porte Dauphine and stopped at a red light. Mercedes gave a little scream.

"It's flying away!" she said, pointing ahead.

Sean looked down the oily black arm of the wet cobblestoned avenue. The Irish Embassy in the distance, at the top of the avenue, was pale white in the approaching dusk. Streaks of watercolor pink were beginning to shoot over the rooftops, but he noticed nothing peculiar or special, except that the building stood in stark contrast to the others that had not yet been cleaned.

"Sean, let's get out here and walk! Come on, pay!"

"Don't listen to her," said Sean to the taxi driver. "Girl, we have bags to carry."

"Sean, do not argue! The house is floating away like a cloud! Cannot you see? Come on, quickly. Get out!"

Sean followed her out of the taxi. The facade of the Cardozo house and the embassy next to it had recently been sandblasted and washed, but this was the first time Mercedes had seen it from a distance. The heavy turn-of-the-century sandstone building appeared feathery soft and weightless, like a giant bird rising through the charcoal of the black wet trees. The house was so light-colored, it hovered in midair. As they walked up on the opposite side of the broad avenue, the house began, chameleonlike, to disappear. It took on the pale, streaked color of the evening sky above the gauzy nimbus of the recently lit streetlights. Mercedes stood quietly savoring the moment. It was impossible to tell where the floating house stopped and the sky began.

"Qué belleza!" whispered Mercedes, her mouth feeling dry. The Aunties had had the house sandblasted as a pilot project for their friend André Malraux, the new Minister of Culture, who was thinking of ordering the whole city washed, clean and sparkling. Algerians in yellow slickers had erected scaffolding and blasted away for days at the soot-encrusted sandstone facade with high-velocity steam and water hoses.

"Yeah, very nice," said Sean. "Come on, it's getting dark."

Mercedes had always lived for escape—escaping her father, escaping a life without love, escaping *gitano* rules. But today, rushing back to the Cardozo house, she felt she was returning to a place where she belonged.

Alone at the top of the avenue, the Irish Embassy and the Cardozo house circled the Arc de Triomphe once and flew west with the last of the light blue tinges in the sky. There was nothing left at Number 10½ but a smudge of evening beige and on either side, dark, unwashed, weighty old buildings. Benz hurried home, dragging her suitcase.

"SO that's all you did—went down for a weekend and came back."

She lay on her stomach and felt Tim's hands run up and down her back. He was a terrible masseur. He was not lazy, but he had such a short attention span that she had to shout at him continually to pay attention. Mercedes had grown up with cats, dogs, brothers, and sisters in her bed, and she missed the feeling of other bodies crowding hers. She stared at her café-au-lait, steaming in the Sunday-morning sunlight.

What thick calves she has, thought Tim, comparing them to her thin ankles. And what were these? Hipbones? He examined the beauty spots dotting her strong back. Giving Benz back rubs was like taking an aerial geography lesson. Sometimes he visited the enormous snow-veined peaks of her bosoms and the timbered dark enormities under her arms. Today he was cataloguing the system of relentless hair follicles, the flat savanna interrupted in the rib area by arid stretches of desert skin. He could never have imagined her physical reality merely by seeing her in her uniform. There was so much more to Benz than just her proud nostrils, green eyes, and high-arched feet.

"I'm bored with this, Benz."

"Okay, just lie down on my back. There's a good boy."

The boy lay on top of her so lightly that at any moment, she felt, he might pull her up like a balloon. She turned her head and, over one shoulder, put her nose up to his; when he exhaled, she inhaled and took into her chest the taste of his little breath with all its dreams.

"How do you know Sean wants to marry you?"

"Because I know."

"Have you asked him?"

"Do not be *estúpido!*"

"Well, then, you don't know."

"Oh, leave me alone!"

"Has he actually said he would? I mean, what were his exact words?"

Master Tim had tried to get details, but she had evaded all his questions. Finally, he said:

"Benz, he's not going to marry you. 'Why buy the cow if you already have free milk,' huh?"

She jumped up.

"Who teach you that expression?"

"You did, Benz."

"No, no. *Never!* I never speak like that."

"Yes, you've said it to me several times."

Tim had tried this odd expression on Pepe and the results had been excellent! Pepe had burped, slapped his knee, coughed up his red wine, clapped Timi on the back, and repeated *"Mierda"* several times. So Tim knew that it had to be a good one.

"I tell you that, Timi?"

He nodded. Her green eyes narrowed, and the heavy eyebrows formed two peaked windows.

"Timoté, I talk too much to you. I pour my heart out to you. You are my only ally and I forget you are only eleven. Since Sean, I do not know what I am saying or doing! But please, do not repeat what I say, okay?"

She made the sign of the cross and kissed him on the lips.

MERCEDES checked her watch. The ticket taker eyed her, as did several daytime patrons. This was the last time she would rely on Sean to keep an appointment. To go to the movies alone was one thing—she often came to the MacMahon alone; in fact, sometimes she considered this tiny *cinémathèque,* which catered mostly to Americans, her own private viewing room—but to wait like this for twenty minutes, first standing by the cashier, then coming and going like a leg lady waiting for a customer, then ordering a cappuccino at the bistro next door, was absolutely degrading. Sean was always late! She could have invited Fufa or Esperanza (after all, she was not someone who had no friends). Giving up on Sean, she finally paid and entered the theater by herself. The movie was *Bell, Book and Candle,* starring Kim Novak and James Stewart.

It was an original-version film with subtitles. The Cardozos often gave her passes to first-run movies, but these were usually dubbed in French and shown in crowded theaters. She much preferred to go to a half-empty neighborhood *cinémathèque* and let the original dialogue waft over her in great Anglo-Saxon waves. This allowed her to give her own interpretation to what the actors were saying and so rewrite the movie several times in her head. But today, Benz plotted exclusively how to handle Sean. He was forever forsaking her with no explanation, no forewarning. On Monday at 9 P.M., he appeared in her room merely to kiss her on the cheek and place a heavy suitcase in her closet; on Tuesday at midnight, he came to borrow 2,500 francs she had hidden under the floorboards by the bidet and then disappeared; on Wednesday, he slept over, but left at sunrise. She had heard him rummaging around in a duffel bag he left under her bed. On Thursday, when they had dinner together, she let him talk politics for an hour—she was completely willing to ignore his past behavior, for calling attention to it would only ruin the evening—but on Friday, she didn't hear from him; and tonight he had broken a date.

A man who wants to keep a woman has to take care of her, thought Mercedes, because all she has to do to find a replacement is walk out of the house. Perhaps she had been too good to him, allowing him to make telephone calls during their dates, letting him store suitcases in her closet. Her father was right when he said, "Part of every favor you do is receiving insults from the person you've helped for putting him in your debt."

The movie was not great, but she was impressed by the easy way in which Kim Novak could manipulate James Stewart, almost willing her passion into her leading man with a flick of her cat eyes.

Returning to her room after the movie, Mercedes found Sean asleep in her bed, snoring. Conventional words would be of no use. She was fed up with this man who could not see in front of his face. Benz took her movies very personally and had identified perhaps more than the makers of *Bell, Book and Candle* had intended with Kim Novak's role as a witch. Feeling violent and reckless, she pulled Sean's bag from under the bed and forced it open. Inside was a mass of wires, electric plugs, timers, and what she thought, on the basis of knowledge acquired at an Edward G. Robinson *film noir,* was a detonator. She did not care what Sean's motives were, or what lies he might use to explain away his behavior. Nor did she want to hear another political tirade from him that would betray her naiveté. No, she intended to force it into Sean's thick skull that their relationship overshadowed anything else he thought mattered.

She leaned over her man. Using a technique she had seen her mother use several times, she grabbed his groin as hard as she could.

"Hey, what the hell?" said Sean, jerking upright in bed.

Pushing her face right up to his, Mercedes now raced through her litany, all the while squeezing his scrotum:

"The problem with you, Sean, is that you have lost the roots and cling to the treetops, to hot air and nonsense. Oh, Sara the Black, Mother of Andalusia! Sean, your seed will shrivel up and die—you will never have progeny! You do not realize everything we have. You have no respect for this relationship, or for me. Oh, yes, you are very nice now and then, when you want to be. But you have no time, always rushing around, always late, always making telephone calls and going to meetings!"

He tried to push her hand away. But her grasp was too tight. Benz knew that even the least superstitious were susceptible to doubt. If a Gypsy's threats were sufficiently rapid-fire and foretold enough natural disasters, a man would be a fool not to listen. She saw him hesitate—and that was all she needed, that split-second of doubt, to create real fear.

"Benz, stop it."

She redoubled her efforts, rattling off invocations and squeezing his testicles.

"Sean, you say you love me, but let me tell you, you will die unloved, unwanted in a gutter—bald, impotent, and cuckolded. Thirty minutes I waited for you in front of the movie! You forget everything! I don't know why you need a woman. I am sick and tired of being left alone, of being paid no attention to. I need a man who cares and does things for me! The war you should be fighting is with me, on my battlefield! I swear, I am going to leave you!"

Maybe she lacked practice. Maybe she had not watched her mother carefully enough. (Her mother could move *payos* the way a puppeteer manipulates her marionettes.) And she was a far cry from the Kim Novak witch, for no matter how wild her imprecations became, she was losing her grasp on Sean's imagination.

Sean managed to turn her over on the bed and to hold her arms down. As she continued a steady stream of insults and threats, he kissed her mouth and throat passionately. Slowly she stopped talking and put her hands on his hips.

TIMOTHY stood in the third-floor kitchen with his lips pressed to the thin gauze fabric that veiled the windowpane. He watched the guests walk through the courtyard, and gradually became aware of the cold of the glass through the gauze. The front doorbell was ringing. He galloped up the hallway to the foyer and back to the kitchen.

Normally, when Alphonse Cardozo returned to Paris and threw a party in the grand ballroom on the second floor, Benz's job was to open the door for the guests and take their top hats and thick chinchilla coats. But tonight she did not feel well.

Manola's chicken consommé was coming up again. She ran to the bathroom. Tim pushed open the toilet door and asked if she was all right.

She slammed it shut and locked it. Thank God, she thought, her mind racing, that Manola was making so much noise, banging pots together and shouting orders to the young waiters sent over by Monsieur Cardozo's film studio, that no one could hear her silent agony in the small yellow toilet. The nausea subsided now. She stood up, steadied herself, looked in the mirror. She pinched her cheeks, wet her lips, and wiped a trace of lipstick from her two front teeth. Outside the bathroom, by the sideboard, she could hear Pepe grumbling to himself:

"It's against all union rules! The C.G.T. will hear about this! Eighty guests with no forewarning! This is intolerable! 'Pepe, you look like a good loyal sort. Bend over. This won't hurt one bit!' No, nonono. What do they take us for—indentured slaves?"

Mercedes waited until Pepe's footsteps receded down the hallway and then came out of the bathroom, straightening her black uniform with the high lace collar, the one she reserved for special occasions. The front doorbell rang again. Young waiters with sparkling faces and gold buttons on their white jackets swooped down the long corridor from the kitchen, down the main staircase, to the ballroom. Their heavy silver serving trays were loaded down with plates of cheese-and-salmon-covered crackers, olives, and poached oysters.

Mercedes walked slowly back to the kitchen, sat down at the small round table, and continued stabbing plastic toothpicks into baby Viennese sausages.

"Eyes of my life," said Manola, "tell me the truth."

Manola leaned away from the smoke of the oven, wiped her face with her apron and repeated:

"Tell me, beats of my heart, breath of my days, who is the father?"

Mercedes did not want the Aunties to know or worry. And she knew from experience that confiding anything to Manola or Pepe was like placing an advertisement in *France-Soir*.

"*Princesa,* there is nothing bad about raising a child by yourself. Why can you not tell me?"

White sauces on steaming fish, slices of beef with dill and diced truffles were carried down to the guests. The milk was boiling over. Manola gave Master Tim a spoonful of béchamel; he had ingratiated himself some time ago into the honored role of master taster and guinea pig.

"Benz, are you sick?" asked the boy.

"I am fine," she said, looking pea-green. But in fact, she was anxious, worried about what Sean would say, and above all full of wild hormonal changes.

"Yahooooh!" shouted Timi, running out of the kitchen. Pepe entered, shaking his head:

"I've done my eight hours a day for thirty-three years! Regulations are regulations!"

"Shut up!" snapped Manola, stacking clean dishes.

"They seem to forget that the Bastille was burned down a long time ago. *Oui, Monsieur!* 'Pepe, you dumb peasant, you don't mind giving us a hand tonight, do you?' 'No, of course not, sir! I'm only too pleased to lick your boots! And thank you for my overtime, O generous master!' "

Pepe looked over at Mercedes, who was staring out the window.

"Hey, you! Why don't you work for a change?"

"Leave my princess alone," said Manola pushing Pepe out of the kitchen.

Mercedes stood and picked up the tray. The sight of all this food revolted her.

"*Princesita,* tell me: it is Ambassador McLuck from next door, is it not?" said Manola, holding her by the arm.

"Let me pass. This is very heavy," said Mercedes, turning her head away.

"Blood of my veins, sun of my days, do not trust the ambassador. I have seen him with streetwalkers! Yes, with Nicole and Helga. Really! O roundness of my ribs, I so worry for you!"

Mercedes made her way down the long hallway. Usually she felt excited when the house was aflame with people and noise like this, but now she just stared at the canapés. The boy galloped after her, skidding on the waxed parquet.

"What's the matter? Are you sick?"

"Do not start with me, Timi. And stop shaking me; I will drop everything on your head!"

The chandelier pendants in the main staircase emitted a delicate tinkling sound. Mercedes looked in the mirror and was pleasantly surprised to find that the face she had so carefully painted carried no trace of her recent nausea, and that her hair remained in an impeccable beehive.

Time to sail in now, to pass the expertly toothpick-stabbed sausages and caviared eggs, to maneuver like a dancer in and out among the penguin-outfitted big shots in order to get close to Sean, who was out on the balcony serving drinks. All right, so he was a butler, not a diplomat—she absolutely did not care. He carried himself like royalty, and that was all that mattered to Mercedes. Tonight, the Aunties looked so elegant, their blue hair sparkling and their hearing aids turned to maximum volume. Agatha wore a hat with cherries on it and Phoebe one with lilacs. Year-round, the ballroom was so quiet; only Mercedes entered it to clean. It pleased her to see it tonight full of expensive-looking men and their tall women, and the promise of more guests arriving every minute.

A man in a smoking jacket with a tall rich lady bathed in perfume was asking Timoté:

"And how old might you be, then?"

"Eleven."

Tim did not like his house to be invaded by strangers. He felt highly vulnerable, almost naked, when strange men with strange faces filled the high-ceilinged rooms with cigarette smoke, turning them into giant cargo ships, destroying his hiding places, opening up the concealed staircases and the trapdoors of his mind. But he saw his father so seldom that he had to forgive this intrusion upon his territory. His father was a mythical figure with a black patch over one eye. He saw him now in the ceiling-high mirror that made everyone look as skinny as rails, a glass in his hand, saying to an American guest:

"The term '*pied-noir*' derives from the last great wave of

emigration to Algeria. After 1870, Alsatians fleeing territory annexed by the Germans arrived in Algiers wearing lace-up black boots. So the natives dubbed them 'black-feet.' Now, a hundred years later, they are returning shoeless."

Mercedes' tray was empty. She put it down on the kitchen table and wiped her forehead with a dish towel. She was so tired, she felt she could sleep for a year and not wake up. Manola looked up from the oven.

"*Princesita*, sap of my loins, beauty of my days, tell me the truth: it is not Pepe, is it?"

"Manola, why do you insult me like this?" shouted Mercedes, half hysterical, shaking herself free of Manola's greasy hands. "It is your cooking, that is all! That is why I am sick! Now leave me alone!"

Manola washed her hands under the faucet and whispered half to Mercedes, half to Wonderdog, who followed her every movement in the hope of scraps:

"If it is Pepe, I will kill that pig! If he has defiled or so much as touched an innocent like you! No, no-no, it cannot be true. Tell me, *por favor*, that it is not true!"

"Manola, I swear I never let Pepe into my room, no matter how many times he comes to knock at night."

Her ducks with green olives were sizzling.

"He knocks? On *your door, at night???*"

"No, I mean . . . Oh, Manola you do not understand!"

Mercedes grabbed the butcher knife out of Manola's hand and stood defiantly, arms crossed, mascara running, blocking Manola's access to the other knives.

"Do not be hysterical, please, Manola. It was nothing."

"The saints help me to breathe!" said Manola, sitting down at the kitchen table and starting to hyperventilate.

Benz fanned a dish towel in front of Manola's face like a manager trying to revive a boxer and explained that Pepe's flirts were totally innocent. But Manola just sat there repeating to herself:

"Oh, I am going to kill that man."

Tim careened into the kitchen, looking for something to nibble on. Sean followed him with an empty silver ice bucket.

Mercedes forced herself not to look at him. She had not found the time or the courage to tell Sean about her situation. As soon as the kitchen was empty again, Manola asked:

"Who is it, sweetness? Tell me! Sooner or later I find out. So tell me! It is not the Baron Roastchild? No, it cannot be. He is seventy-five at least, older than Pepe even! No, darling, tell me at least it is not he."

Mercedes was exhausted with Manola's prying, with life, with everything in general. She sat down and picked up the bag of knitting she had left in the drawer with her shopping lists. She felt too tired to make another pass with a silver tray, at least for the moment. She counted the stitches in the last row of the 2-meter-long purple-and-yellow scarf she was knitting for Timi. But Manola would not change the subject:

"Every time Roastchild comes here, he pinches your cheek and looks at you as if you were a small dumpling for him to eat. Yes, yes, do not blush. It is true! I see him!"

Mercedes put away her knitting. Even if her swollen ankles were killing her, it was better to be serving guests than to sit through Manola's interrogations. She walked down the long hallway carrying a tray of clean crystal glasses, collecting and reviewing all her memories of Sean: his bare arm indolently extended on her bed as far as it would go, the turquoise-veined underside turned up for her lips to kiss; his palm open, revealing the thin white texture of his upper-class origins; her waking up in the middle of the night, as the direct descendant of the ex-rulers of Western Ireland snored; and her being comforted by the strong, steady fullness of his breathing. These images danced around her like the blue dots left after a photographer's flashbulb. And always when he was not next to her, she felt a longing for the touch of his soft hands.

"Ratatatatatatouille!" shouted Timi, as he ran back to the kitchen—when he learned a new word that he liked, he became impossible. Mercedes already rued the day Tim would finally master the art of whistling.

Auntie Phoebe was saying to her good friend the Comtesse Louisa de Beaulieu, née Rodienko von Shtad (the "cadaver lady" to Timoté):

"Yes, 'precocious' comes from Latin—*'prae-coquere,'* meaning 'precooked.' Our Timothy is a precooked child, don't you agree?" Phoebe laughed. "That would explain why he is so smart for his age: he has already been cooked before! We are only reheating him."

Mercedes passed around another tray of goat-cheese and smoked-herring canapés. She worked the guests half in a daze. The past few weeks had gone by in a fog. Each morning after morning sickness, she would go out for some fresh air; Andalusians believe that 'Life is in the streets, and one's home is merely complementary.' The housecleaning definitely suffered. Sometimes she would wake up in an empty room, the duster and mop across her lap, and Wonderdog whining to be taken out. Then after half an hour's work, she would awaken on Tim's bed, staring at the model planes he hung from his ceiling.

The cadaver lady was repeating to a heavily diademed guest by the balcony:

"Yes, *'ricotta'* in Italian means 'twice-cooked.' Just like the French *'biscuit'* or the German *'zwieback.'* "

Mercedes lingered by the windows looking out over the broad Avenue at the aqueous green shadows of the chestnut trees. "Twenty," she thought despondently. "I am twenty already and what do I have to show for myself?" The plane trees were bare, but the horse chestnuts' branches were laden with nuts that hung like black earrings. Ammunition for Timi and his little friends, thought Mercedes, for the chestnut wars.

"Are you sure you're okay, Benz?" asked Timoté.

She looked down.

"Can't you tell me what's bothering you?" said the boy.

"I am between the cabbage and the goat and I cannot tell you because I cannot tell you, *voilà!*"

"What does that mean, you're 'between the cabbage and the goat'? "

"Oh, leave me alone."

It made her angry when her one true friend in the world did not instinctively understand her moods. Was Tim her soul mate, or was he just a spoiled upper-class twit, lifeless like the rest of these blue-blood guests? Could he ever learn to put himself in her shoes?

"You are very beautiful, Mademoiselle," said the Baron Isidore de Rothschild, helping himself to a second smoked-salmon toast from her tray. The Baron complimented her on her perfume. She could find nothing to answer. She sensed that Sean was looking at her from across the room.

Yesterday, too sick to walk all the way to the Spanish Church on Rue de la Pompe, she'd taken two sturdy hairpins and forced them into the lock of the private chapel on the fourth floor of the Irish Embassy. And slumping to her knees, she had prayed with all her heart. Her chest rose and fell like the wave on which the fishing boat rose and fell when she had sailed from Spain into France more than four years ago. She prayed for a quick wedding. But then she remembered her mother's admonition:

"My child, do not presume to pray for anything specific. La Virgén de la Macarena knows better than you what is good for you. Maybe something you think you do not want is, in the long run, exactly what you need."

So Mercedes had prayed only for generalities. She'd prayed until her knees grew stiff. She'd prayed for life to be no longer a mere approximation, a distant foggy image of what it should or might be, but to declare itself bright and glorious like a cherry tree when it blooms in spring. Her mother used to say:

"Pray once and then leave it alone. It's heard the first time. Don't go bothering God over and over again. Just put it in His hands and let things happen. Otherwise you will make yourself a nuisance."

Alphonse Cardozo was saying to a group of guests:

"Come and kiss him good-night. The boy loves movie actors."

As soon as Tim overheard this, he galloped back up to the kitchen, which was next to his small bedroom. He was about to warn Manola that the big moment had arrived, his father was coming, but stopped with his mouth open: Pepe was kissing her on the lips! Manola had her fat red hands turned out so she would not dirty her husband's clean, starch-white jacket. It came as a shock to Tim that a couple who fought so much could have moments like this.

"Get ready! Papa is coming back here," he said at last.

Manola pushed Pepe away, wiped her lips, and rescued a smoking pan.

"What are you looking at?" growled Pepe, as Manola threw some dirty pots into the sink.

Timi ran to his bed, slipped between the sheets with his bathrobe still on, switched off his bedside light, and pretended to sleep. His heart raced so fast he was sure his father would hear it as he walked by to the kitchen. Tim imagined Manola wiping her hands on her apron and growing red in the face from all the compliments they were showering on her. Twenty years in Paris and she still couldn't put together a sentence of French. But she could understand compliments about her cooking in any language. Tomorrow she would repeat the English, German, or Russian words phonetically to Tim and shoeshine each one as she placed them in her memory bank.

Tim waited in bed, staring at the shadows of his Spitfires and Messerschmitts under the ceiling, their MM-109 rockets blazing silently in the night, their desert camouflage useless in these northern latitudes. His door opened.

"Timothy, I have brought you some visitors."

He pretended to wake up. His father should have been a movie actor. He was clearly the handsomest man in the world, with his salt-and-pepper hair sleeked straight back over his scalp, a black patch over his right eye and the thick smell of Scotch on his rosy cheeks. How proud Timi was of his important papa! He did not want to share him tonight with anyone, not even with famous actors.

Diamond-tiaraed ladies in evening gowns took turns kissing Tim on the cheek. These were quite different from Manola's *soupe du jour* kisses, or even Benz's, which were bouquets of Nivea and Cri du Coeur. An old man with a monocle, identified by his father as the Baron de Rothschild, played with one of Tim's hand-painted lead soldiers. Why didn't they all just leave him alone with his father? The Comtesse Louisa de Beaulieu poked her cadaverous ring-laden finger into XKE's treadmill.

Ambassador McLuck, with a florid, almost shining red face, asked Tim if there was any trouble at school with the influx of *pied-noir* refugees. Tim shook his head. How safe he felt now, standing in his father's arms, wrapped in the new yet familiar protective smells.

A woman in a strapless black satin gown flashed her sky-blue eyes at Tim. She was fingering one of his gold Napoleon busts and asked him where he had gotten it. Tim explained:

"I won it at Monsieur Henri's steam-engine raceway at the Jardin d'Acclimatation."

He suppressed a fart. Gas usually built up inside him when he was nervous, and this woman terrified him. She was almost as tall as he standing on his bed. Her magnificent cheeks were soft like highways of gold. He could not say where he had seen her before, but her good-night kiss was so graceful and grand that he imagined her living on a huge ocean liner, like the one in the postcard on Benz's mirror, and he could not stop staring at her.

"Kim, I do believe you have another admirer here!"

Tim blushed and hid his face in his father's neck.

"Dad, is that Kim Novak, the actress?" he whispered.

"Yes. Why?"

Tim could not believe that this ethereal, weightless blond creature with the aquamarine sea-bottle eyes was the same woman he'd caught sight of munching on a baguette, alone in the garden, two years before.

"Papa, there are a lot of things I have to tell you—I haven't seen you in so long! You wouldn't believe the things that have been going on here." Tim caught his breath. "We have sea monsters in the cellar. Mercedes is paying off some strange man, I don't know who—maybe Marcel, the butcher's son. And Manola and Pepe get into such terrible fights, sometimes they keep me up all night. And Roland's dad had U.S. electrodes attached to his *pipi* . . ."

His father nodded and listened gravely. The cadaver lady was telling the Baron that the Cardozo Aunties had tried to have the name of "The Ladies of Passy Literary, Knitting and Opera

Society" changed, but that this name went back to Madame de Montespan, Louis XIV's mistress, and was therefore sacrosanct.

"We French respect everything old—even the bad taste of a tawdry concubine at a time when Passy was nothing but cow fields, far from Paris."

His father pinched his cheek and whispered:

"Let me get rid of these guests and I'll be right back to read you a story. Then you can tell me all about your terrible problems. All right?"

Tim nodded. The glittering grown-ups waved goodbye. Kim Novak blew him a kiss. His father switched off the light and closed the door. Tim was alone again. He had so much to tell his father! He absolutely must have him appoint Mercedes his "legal guardian."

He lay there counting the waiters' footsteps as they carried heavy trays past his room and down the stairs to the ballroom. He could still smell his father's after-shave and Scotch. Curtain shadows moved, drawing Kim Novak's face in swirls of sepia and bronze on the ceiling in place of horses and moray eels. How beautiful she was tonight!

His father would be back. He would sit on Tim's bed and extend two giant hands that would give his chest a formidable squeeze-squeeze-squeeze until Tim begged for mercy. Then he would read him a bedtime story until his voice got bleary and he couldn't see the words anymore. Tim lay under the covers farting to his heart's content. He thought with what terrific energy his dad would press his fist against Tim's puffed-up cheek and force him to blow out all the air in little jolts. And after the good-night kiss, and the closing of the shutters, the world would swell with salvos of "Papa, Papa, come earlier tomorrow so you can read longer." And the Messerschmitts and Spitfires—the red ones, the blues, and the tricky desert-camouflaged ones—would shoot through the night, firing at the gold Napoleon figurines. Napoleon was the only grown-up, other than Benz and maybe his dad, who understood Tim. How generous of him to have built just at the end of the block, inscribed with the names of all his victories, his very own Arc de Triomphe, lit up at night like a giant chocolate cake from which radiated twelve broad avenues—Foch, Grande Armée, Carnot, MacMahon, Wagram, Hoche, Friedland, Champs-Elysées, Marceau, Iéna, Kléber, and Victor Hugo—and which for Tim was the center and starting point of all the roads of Europe and, of course, of the greater universe as well.

CHAPTER 4

Husband-Hunting on Avenue Wagram

"BENZ, ROLAND'S DAD says that in America they make blacks sit in the back of buses. Is that true?"

"No—only Algerians."

She said this with absolute conviction. Tim nodded and went back to his studying.

MASTER Tim opened one eye. His curtains were still drawn shut. Eight A.M.—*Hé, sapristi!* Where is my hot cocoa? I'll be late for school! No wonder I get zeroes for conduct and attendance: no one bothers to wake me up anymore! thought Tim, as he jumped out of bed and put on his bathrobe. It can't continue like this. When the only grown-ups around are doddering blue-haired Aunties, the hired help start taking enormous liberties. "When the cat is away, the mice dance!" Where's my pressed shirt, my knee socks, my stupid gray flannel shorts?

It was another dreary morning. The rain knocked a series of dots and dashes against the window. The kitchen was empty. So were the pantry and the *lavanderie.* Tim climbed up to Benz's room, two steps at a time, just in case the beasts from the basement were on the prowl. When he reached the sixth-floor landing, the light-switch timer automatically clicked off and threw him into darkness. His palms felt their way down the greasy walls. He tentacled slowly forward in the dark like Aunt Agatha. Benz's door was not locked, and he entered without knocking. She was lying on her bed with deep circles under her eyes, grinding her teeth.

"Hey, what's the matter with you?"

Her face paints had turned to ugly drunken reds and bloated blues.

"Benz, get up! I'm going to be late for school!"

She did not move.

"What's the matter? Are you sick, Benz?"

Through the two small windows, oblique lines of silver rain smudged the contours of the slanting rooftops. Across the Avenue, the chimneys, which usually looked like overturned flowerpots, were mere blobs of orange. The black metal smoke pipes were only crooked sticks. Far in the distance, awkward like a child's drawing, stood the Tour Eiffel.

"Benz, are you okay or what?"

Still no answer. He sat down on the edge of her bed, waiting for her to move. Her strong shoulders were quivering and felt hot. Maybe she was faking?

"Benz, I've learned a new flamenco step. Look!"

He spun around, thumped his heels, let out a deep moan, broken by a cracked toothache-type wailing, twirled his hands above his head and twisted his wrists as far as they would go.

"Benz, am I doing it right?"

For Christmas she had given him a pair of castanets painted with charging bulls. She had shown him how to use them, arching her arms above her head like a swan's neck, spinning arabesques all up and down her back, then crossing her hands in front of her face while looking violently to one side.

"Timi, for the hands, it is very easy," she had explained. "Just imagine you take a pear from an imaginary tree, you bite it, and then you throw it away. *Voilà tout!*"

Usually she could not resist laughing at his terrible technique, but today she paid no attention to him. To make her laugh, Tim took a plastic rose from above the washbasin and tucked it behind one ear. Then he let out a gutteral "Rrrr" and ended it with a heel-clicking *zapateado* hard enough to loosen the silver crucifix on the green wall above Benz's head. He repeated the pear-eating exercise seven times while mimicking the sound of a guitar.

Tired, he lowered his arms and caught his breath. In the semidarkness, her beautiful Madonna face did not seem even to have moved. Was she crying? He sat back on the edge of her bed. The reds and blues on her cheeks came off in gobs on his fingers. She opened her mouth but made no sound. The entire left side of the pillow was drenched. He knew instinctively that these tears were connected with Sean.

"Hey, Benz, get up. This is enough now . . . I'm bored!"

His left hand felt sticky. Looking down, he saw the sheets were red with blood!

"Benz!"

He grabbed her by the shoulders and tried to shake her awake. She whimpered the name of Saint Agatha, but kept her eyes closed.

"Benz, should I call Manola? You want a doctor? Benz, tell me what to do!"

"I am dirty," she said in a low somnambulist voice that Tim had never heard before.

"No, you're not! You look great!" said Tim.

"Wash me, Sean."

"Sean isn't here!"

He rushed to the washbasin. With shaking hands and tears blurring his vision, he moistened a sponge. And in the graying light of dawn, as a cold November rain tapped on the windows, as all his little friends assembled in class, Tim wiped his nanny's face clean. Boulder-size tears rolled continuously down her high cheekbones, each one more unbearable for Tim than the last. A dark blue vein throbbing at her temple stood out like a flooded river that split into a pale blue delta at the base of her thick mane of hair.

"B-Benz, *te juro que no eres sucia, de veras,*" said Tim, not knowing what else to say.

"Where is Sean?" she asked in the same monotone.

He pulled the washcloth around her massive collarbone and over the freckles on her neck. Her bronze skin was shiny with sweat. She was boiling! She was going to explode! Tim tried to give her a massage. Where was the blood coming from? She was never sick. Maybe it wasn't hers? Perhaps Marcel, the butcher's son, had visited and forgotten to take off his apron?

There was no sign of any wound. The smell of stale sweat welled up from the sheets as he tried to move her. He worked quickly, thinking that to do otherwise might prove fatal to Benz. She lay spread-eagled on her bed. Her breathing was slower, more even now. But he could not get her to turn over on her stomach. Oh, my God, thought Tim as her breasts fell to either side, limp and heavy, these are the breasts of a dead woman! Their tips were mauve in the center, beige on the edges. Tim knew little about these except that Pepe called them "the grapefruit of emperors." He felt her heart knocking like an angry man at the door, and he had a terrible premonition.

"Benz! Can you hear me, Benz?"

No answer, but he could see her chest slowly rise and fall. The rain was still coming down behind the Napoleon curtains made with material left over from Tim's room. He ran the sponge between her legs.

"Benz, are you dying?"

He wanted her to be full of sunlight and songs. He wanted her to be the way she always was, talking a mile a minute about *gitano* cat-o'-nine-tails, burnishing the silver candelabra, spouting stupid proverbs that meant absolutely nothing, and discussing her many admirers and would-be lovers in a mixture of French, Andaluz, *Caló,* and English that not even the devil himself could unravel. He wanted her to stand up now like Lazarus and practice her *paso doble,* with her hair pulled back by a dozen hairpins and her gold-and-coral earrings tinkling. He wanted her to sing "Poor Bartolo had a flute with only one hole," her voice breaking with a rich, powerful sorrow—a sorrow so strong it gave you hope, not this quiet, whimpering kind of sorrow. And he wanted her to throw her arms around him.

Benz let out a wail. Tim snapped his head back. Her eyes were open, fluttering as if from an enormous distance, sad and gentle. She lifted her palms to her face and said:

"Oh, no, the boy is here!"

Benz pushed her white nightgown down below her belly, where Tim was wiping her with the sponge, and turned her face to the wall.

"It's all right, Benz. I'll take care of you."

"Timoté, you are the only man who ever loved me!"

"Shhhhh. . . . Don't move."

Wiping her tears with her sleeve, she fumbled for a lacquered box by the bed. Tim helped her search through the photos: of Luis Mariano, the singer; of Gypsies standing in a field—tall, dark men in sombreros and white shirts; of Benz as a little girl of seven with a middle tooth missing. At last she found her beloved licorice sticks.

"Timi, the proofs of love are more important than love itself. You understand? You are here and Sean is not!"

The Irishman had promised to give the child his name. She was sure she had not dreamed it. But where was he? Outside, a weary drizzle wrapped Paris in mists. Sobs racked her chest; Benz thrashed from side to side in her bed.

"Timi, I am *estúpida*—empty and *estúpida*. I deserve nothing."

"Lie still, Benz."

Oh, how she wanted to be back among the olive groves of Cádiz! Give me back, she prayed, the rebels, saints, martyrs, heroes, drunkards, and picadores of Jaén! Who could live in these tiny maid's rooms, waiting for the greatest disappearing artist since the Invisible Man to slip over at night from the Irish Embassy to tell her that he could not live without her and ask if he might please spend the night? To hell with you, Sean, and may a car run over your face!

"Timi, loyalty is everything. Everything, Timi! When you grow up, fall in love with a dog, one that is always there to lick your hand."

"Benz, I am loyal!"

She turned over on her side and felt her heartbeats travel down through the mattress, in search of the rich red earth of Andalucia. Give me Matamoros, she thought. Give me puffs of locomotive steam, guitar notes pouring out of a doorway and geraniums cascading from the balconies of a walled city. She was not alone in this lumpy wet bed. She was surrounded by all the choirboys, palm readers, cowherds, bulls, and green-and-white Andaluz flags of her youth. Her room was crowded with men in broad-brimmed hats, *ganaderos* in leather pants transacting millions of pesetas' worth of business on a handshake with tattoos on their biceps and farms as big as provinces.

"Benz, if you die, I'll die too. And it'll be your fault! I'm late for school. Help me get dressed! Come on!"

She opened her mouth for more: Tim was squeezing a sponge over her face. How soothing these cool drops felt on her burning, chapped lips! What redemption in this cloth wiping lightly over her eyebrows. She licked the cold drizzle of tap water that splashed down on her aching eyes.

"Timi, promise you will never lie to me!"

"Benz, why are you bleeding?"

"In matters of love, Timi, there is nothing worse than breaking trust. You can do anything to a woman, but never lie."

He wiped the sweat from her upper lip.

"And Timi, a Gypsy can always smell a Jew. Do not try to hide your Jewishness."

"I don't hide it," said Tim, untwisting her fingers from the brass bedstead.

"Timi, *Gypsies* love children. At my age a *gitana* might have seven or eight children. But here it is a scandal if I have even one! *Payo* values are shit, Timi! And I am a coward."

He caressed the side of her head where the veins were throbbing and bloated. She blew her nose in a tissue.

"And Timi, do not let one sock always slip down to your ankle. It is difficult to respect a man who has one sock up and the other one down."

He wanted her to conserve her strength, but she was talking so fast he could not interrupt.

"While my mother was alive, life was almost normal. But after she died and my father started drinking, it was terrible. I apply for an apartment for the family in one of the government resettlements. When he finds out, he explodes: 'You want us to live horseless? Wanderless? You *estúpida*, you are not your father's daughter!' I try to explain to him that I want a steaming breakfast every morning with fat cups of coffee and jam and butter. But he answers, 'To be *jayipí* is to be free! Those bureaucrats say they want us to assimilate. But I know what they want: they want to enslave us.' "

The stuffy room reeked of Suchard chocolates, pastilles Valdas, and apple peels. Tim pushed aside a pile of *Ciné-revue* magazines and opened a window.

"Timi, you know why Jews and Gypsies have survived so long? Because for centuries we have had strong rules against marrying outside our own race. If we intermarry, we disappear. Oh, I am so stupid to go out with Sean!"

Tim wanted to encourage that sentiment, but suddenly Manola and Pepe appeared in the room—she making the sign of the cross, and he muttering: "*Mierda,* this is all we needed!"

They picked Benz up, one under each of her arms, and carried her down the stairs. Tim followed them to the landing but then returned to the room to fetch her bathrobe and slippers. Behind him, in the stairwell, he could hear Pepe's oaths and Manola's prayers to La Virgén de Badajoz. Master Tim grabbed whatever Benz might need—her makeup case, some magazines. Something caught his eye: on the floor by a pile of crumpled-up Suchard chocolate wrappings stood a green plastic basin. The blood inside it was still warm, but hardening, turning brown. Slender iridescent shadows moved as he dipped his index finger into the thick, layered mass of her blood. He knew she was dying. Benz was like those delicate lilac blossoms that start to wither as soon as they are cut and put in a vase.

He imagined Benz standing behind him, about to speak, winking, slipping off her black flats to rub her left instep against her right calf. She was always scratching something somewhere, leaning against a door or chair. He looked up. But the room was empty. Manola screamed from the courtyard for him to get dressed and go to school. Tim flew down the staircase, four steps at a time. He didn't bother to wash his face or brush his teeth before jumping into yesterday's clothes. Who could eat a croissant or drink hot cocoa at such a time as this?

Pepe rushed into the kitchen with blood-smeared towels.

"These peasant wenches think they can do everything with

old maids' remedies. But these operations are against the law. And against nature. Serves her right! Now get to school, you're late!"

"I'm staying with Benz!" said Tim as firmly as he could.

Pepe eyed him with a trace of humor.

"Is Benz going to die?" asked Tim in a whisper.

"No," sneered Pepe, as though she deserved to. "Now get out of here, quick!"

Tim wrapped the purple-and-yellow wool scarf that Benz had knitted for him twice around his neck. He had worn it and chewed on it so often as he walked to school, reviewing his life's many problems, that it was already coming apart in the middle. He hid his face in it now as he sloshed through the soggy dead leaves. The sounds of car horns, buses, and rain striking pavement were faraway, as if blurred by some gauzy heavy mist. Tim tried not to attract attention as he boiled over with tears.

TIMI was at school. Manola had gone to do the shopping. Pepe was placing bets on the Longchamps Sunday races at the P.M.U. on Avenue de la Grande Armée. That left only the Aunties to answer the doorbell, and they were more than a little deaf. Someone very insistent was at the front door now. Mercedes slowly got up and steadied herself. She was tired of lying in bed with nothing to do. (Manola had insisted she stay downstairs with them since her return from the hospital.) She tied the belt on her bathrobe and walked slowly down the hall, every muscle in her body aching, her joints stiff, her stomach raw and bloated with water. She looked through the front door peephole. Before her was a tall man with a thin neck beard, wearing a priest's collar.

"Oui, qui est-ce que c'est?"

The man did not answer. But noting how neatly pressed and clean were his black robes, she slowly opened the door.

"Bonjour, Mademoiselle. I am Father Claude Monet, the Principal of Timothy Cardozo's school. Is either of his parents at home?"

She shook her head. She knew something about Jesuits. They were among the very few creatures in the world that had made her father shake and tremble, and accordingly, she had come to hold them in awe, almost in reverence. It was just like them to sneak up and appear unannounced at your door like this.

"Do you know when they will be back?"

"*Non.*"

"Timothy tells me they are not home very often."

Benz viewed all official visits—by priests or anyone else—as exercises in duplicity. She would divulge as little as possible about anything.

"You are not, by any chance, Mademoiselle de Los Angeles who signs Timothy's weekly report card, are you?"

"No, I am not."

He smiled and looked around the foyer. Mercedes made a movement to close the door. Strangers were always prying into the lives of the Cardozos, attracted perhaps by the possibility of a movie star's autograph.

Monet, S.J., now did something wholly unexpected. He touched Mercedes' cheek and gently tilted her head. She pulled back quickly, but the Principal had about him a natural authority, and Benz continued to hold the door wide open. Timi had told her about this man's terrifying power at school, but in the house today she saw only a handsome face with big, deep-circled eyes, not in the least frightening.

"Excuse me," said the Principal, "but you look so much like Mary Magdalene. This high forehead, this wonderful olive skin —I can tell you have suffered a great deal."

He was looking deep into her eyes. It was more like a doctor or a dentist examining a patient than a man looking at a woman. There was nothing lascivious about his actions; in a way, they were even reassuring. She let him take her chin now and feel her bone structure.

"Last night I had a dream, my child."

"What kind of dream, Father?"

"I dreamt of Saint Simeon Stylites, who lived in the fifth century and spent the last thirty years of his life sitting on top of a pillar twenty meters high. He said he would send me a messenger. I thought perhaps it was you."

If anyone else had said this to her, she would have doubted the man's sanity, or been concerned with the obvious phallic connotations of Saint Simeon's pillar. But she felt safe with this priest. His words commanded respect.

"In renouncing the world, Simeon was trying to escape temptations of the flesh. But did not God command us to love our neighbors, as well as Him?"

Mercedes noticed that there was not even a tinge of embarrassment or unease about the man as he caressed her forehead. Monet spoke as if she were a statue or some archeological find, and did not seem to be really aware of her as a woman.

"Your suffering, child, is the *'imitatio Christi.'* We all need redemptive sacrifice; we too need stigmata."

Her necklaces jingled. He glanced at her medallion of the Virgen de la Macarena and at her blue devil's eye to ward off the spirits. Then he fell silent.

With her neutral, police-at-the-door voice, Mercedes said:

"When Monsieur and Madame return, I will tell them that you wish to speak with them."

Claude Monet thanked her and walked slowly backward into the courtyard.

"Child, if you ever want to change your father confessor, please feel free to come to me."

"Merci, mon père."

She smiled back at his generous and intelligent face. The door, when it closed, seemed to sever tiny litle gold threads that linked his eyes to hers. I must ask Timoté about him, she thought, as she crept, bloated and sore, back to bed.

THE twelve-year-olds of the Saint-Philippe de Passy School shuffled, one by one, down the dark corridor for their annual medical checkup. Tim felt absolutely no connection with the naked boys around him, most of whom covered their privates with one hand in case of sneak attack. He trudged along next to Roland, thinking only of his sickly, vulnerable nanny.

"Trunk to tail, trunk to tail," chanted Gerbi.

Last year for the same occasion, when the doctor had asked them to cough, Gerbi had made scientific history at Saint Philippe by hacking so loud his glass eye had popped out of his head!

The nurse called for silence. Master Tim felt small in his stockinged feet. Delbrel, Duval, Gâche, Dhont, and the others had all shot up past him, even Gerbi. Tim was not embarrassingly short, but he seemed to be growing shorter every year. This posed discipline problems for a commander in chief. Napoleon had been only 1.52 meters tall, but he was on horseback most of the time.

"Cardozo, Lapatte, et Gerbi," Mademoiselle Savonex called out. They walked together into the large dispensary. The nurse handed them each a paper cup. Behind in the hallway, Tim's troops were lunging at the Republicans, pinching their privates and raising gales of laughter. The central heating thudded and creaked. These autumn checkups were a good barometer of physical development. They revealed to the whole class one's pubic hair, or lack thereof, muscle tone, height, and other key indicia. Tim stared down at his legs; they were toothpicks compared with Gerbi's massive tree trunks. Becoming Roland's blood brother had not noticeably improved his physique. Tim's parents were both tall, but month after month he continued to hover at Pepe's and Mercedes' height, and this worried him.

In the bathroom, he turned to Roland:

"Give me some of yours; I just peed."

Roland doled out half the contents of his plastic cup into Tim's.

"It's not mine. It's Gerbi's. I always get too nervous at these things. When it's over, I piss like a racehorse."

"You think Gerbi has a disease?"

They looked dubiously into their cups. Tim's was frothing white like draft beer. Roland spat into his repeatedly.

"At least the spit is mine—that'll add some of my own chromosomes."

"Some what?"

"Some of my human-cell nuclei. I don't want my dossier saying I'm part Algerian."

Tim also spat copiously into his cup—to be a half-Jew in a Jesuit school was bad enough. The nurse took their cups and marked them carefully so as not to get them confused.

"Can't you put that on a leash?" Roland asked Gerbi.

Gerbi's penis was wagging back and forth like a giant metronome. Tim stared in disbelief. It wasn't a worm, it was a policeman's baton, almost a *demi-baguette*, covered in long wispy hair! Mademoiselle Savonex pretended not to notice.

"Would you three please bend over and hold your ankles? This won't hurt at all. The doctor only wants to have a look."

Upside down now, Roland's cafe-au-lait cheeks grew red as blood rushed to his head. Tim stared at the green paint chipping on the wall. It embarrassed him to show his knobby knees and little white biceps to his soldiers. Even his torso felt scrawny and thin like a chicken neck. When would his dainty body start to grow? *Merde!* He must get Manola to pray for height, as well as brains, when she went to church.

The doctor entered the room, inserted a long thin coil into each one and shined a tiny flashlamp in the eyepiece. Gerbi winked at Tim with his good eye. The doctor paused over Gerbi's rear end and, pointing, asked the nurse:

"Mademoiselle, what do you make of this?"

"I don't know, doctor. It looks like . . . an eyeball!!!"

Savonex screamed and ran out of the dispensary. Gerbi jumped up, laughing, displaying the eye proudly to his friends:

"So that's where it went! I was looking all over for it!"

Pandemonium broke out in the hallway. The Royalists cheered wildly. They stomped their stockinged feet on the old varnished wood floors and clawed at undefended gonads. A spitball sailed down the hallway toward the Republicans, followed by a vast migratory flight of epithets.

"Bravo, Gerbi!"

"Encore, Gerbi!"

The kiss-asses retreated, and the doctor rushed to telephone the Principal: Gerbi must be disciplined once and for all or expelled, no matter how much scholarship money the good Ladies of the Passy Literary, Knitting and Opera Society donated for helping North Africans. Gerbi, eyeball in hand, took deep reverential bows, clearly enjoying his moment of genius in the sun. Father Claude Monet, S.J., appearing in person, dragged Gerbi down the dark hallway by the ear—like a gangly gray hawkmoth wriggling between a lepidopterist's fingers. D'Harcourt, also half-naked, ran to catch up with the howling Gerbi and handed him his smelly pants, the ones reputed to be infested with tiny Saharan *pied-noir* lice not visible to the naked eye.

Gerbi tried to wave goodbye to his cheering classmates, but the pinching of his left ear, the obligatory boot in the backside, and the Jesuitical abuse kept him walking fast-forward on tippy-toes, one eye open, one eye closed. Monet was pulling Gerbi's ear up so high, the boy seemed to be skimming three inches off the ground.

"Roland, what if his ear becomes deformed?" asked Tim. "Like those native Ubangi women who wear coins in their ear-lobes?"

"Don't be stupid."

Tim did not argue with Roland, but his father had photographs of such women in his study. Suddenly Tim had a brilliant idea: if it was ripped off, Gerbi could get a replacement ear, as well as a fake eye and limbs. The Republicans could hammer nails into him all day long and he could just unscrew his robot hand or leg and walk away. If the system was ever perfected, Gerbi could remove all his limbs until the enemy was left with only his pants and shirt. They would stockpile extra limbs before every attack. The possibilities were endless!

"Cardozo, when are you and your friends going to grow up?"

"Doctor, I don't know. But I seem to be falling way behind. In fact, I'm becoming a real shrimp."

The doctor made Tim say "aaahhh" and peered down his throat.

Making certain his troops in the hallway could not overhear him, Tim said: "Doctor, look at my armpits: there's absolutely nothing there. Laval's are like a forest!"

The doctor stepped back and took an overview of his patient's physique. Mademoiselle Savonex returned from the ladies' room, recovered but still looking peaked. She picked up the eyeball, which was rolling on the floor like a marble, and wiped it, with obvious disgust, between two layers of white tissue paper.

"Do you exercise, Cardozo?"

"Of course."

"I hope you do exercise better than you clean your ears; they look like public *pissoirs.*"

"Oh, I'm a purple belt in Dr. Feng's Jujitsu class. I took first prize in the falling-down competition. Roland and I practice twice a week."

"Is life at home all right?"

"Sure."

"Any fights with your parents? Any special worries?"

How could he explain what Benz had gone through? He was not even certain himself, except that Pepe insisted she was a murderer.

"My Aunt Phoebe says I don't eat enough marrowbone sandwiches and cod-liver oil," said Tim to change the subject.

Mademoiselle Savonex scraped something off the eyeball with her long painted thumbnail, then washed it in the sink. Tim returned to the changing room with Gerbi's hazel-brown glass eye, on the back of which was etched "MADE IN LUXEMBOURG." It was shinier and brighter than ever before, clean of its traces of ball-point pen and green slime. Tim examined the intricate little thing with its minute red veins and the delicate coloring of the iris; he imagined the master craftsman leaning over his worktable late at night, mixing the pigmentation, adding a touch of cream here and black to the pupil so as to catch Gerbi's peculiar sallow complexion and not make this eye noticeably more beautiful than his real one.

Timothy C. is skinny and nervous and suffers from anxious neurasthenia. He is in need of a calm and serious regimen, plenty of fresh air and food. Recommend exercise and rest at home.

In the hallway, Tim tore up the doctor's report. This would be just one more excuse for Pepe to persuade his Aunties to send him off to boarding school. He climbed on Pamplemousse, his winged steed, and, making clicking sounds with his tongue like those of a horse galloping, went in search of his one-eyed friend.

THE chestnut and plane leaves were falling in marmalade colors. Benz was outside for the first time since the abortion. It did her good to be on Avenue Victor Hugo, painted with all the colors she had not used in four weeks, with the boy on her arm. For once, Tim had refrained from asking a thousand questions about what had happened to her. She wondered whether he was not finally growing out of that maddening question-asking phase; or perhaps he was becoming more sensitive than he let on?

As they passed a beauty salon, where Parisiennes were being waxed, pulled, straightened, and tucked, Mercedes told Tim that she was thinking of getting her hair cut short—perhaps bobbed straight across the back, or in a pageboy style so they could be twins. The boy begged her not to. She smiled and brushed the hair out of his eyes with an open palm. He always knew exactly what to say.

Suddenly a ray of sunlight struck the pavement where they were standing. She grabbed the boy's hand and pointed.

"What, Benz?"

"We have the sun for the first time in three weeks!"

He watched her laugh and do a little dance. Then she stopped and peered at him.

"Timi, is the blue on my eyebrows balanced?" She closed both eyes. Tim studied the two blue butterflies alighting in front of his face and tried, in vain, to compare them.

"You're fine, Benz."

She should know better than to expect an objective answer from him! So down the beautiful avenue with the expensive storefronts they sashayed. What would she do if Sean happened to cross her path? Forgive him again—as she always did when he returned unexpectedly to her bedside with incredible tales of hidden cash and bombs? Live totally at his mercy and be powerless to hurt him back? She had not seen him since before the hospital. "Sean, you waste my time, you waste my life, you don't know what is important. You make phone calls, you hide things under my bed, you disappear. Well, go, go, and may the mosquitoes bite you! I am twenty-one, and the blood of Gypsy kings flows through my veins." From now on, she would be—or at least, act—brave, like those little Andalusian lizards which, when threatened, puff up to twice their size and scare off predators.

Gold bars of light were shooting across the city. And the many sandblasted buildings (now that Malraux had ordered them all cleaned) breathed fragrant and fresh. She stopped in front of an *haute couture* shop's windows and offered her patented laugh, like a trumpet out of a clear sky, as a critique of what passed for *la mode* these days: and what about the morals of the girls who would wear such things?

"Timi, would you light my cigarette?"

"Me?"

"Yes. I show you how."

"But Benz, I've never done that before."

"Here, try."

The boy held a box of matches and struck the phosphorus tip against its side, sparking an ignition. He held up the flame, with shaking hands, to his nanny's filterless Gitane. Total success! Tim saw himself becoming an expert lighter of cigarettes, called upon for his services by royalty and jet-setters. There was nothing to it! He could light his mother's cigarette when she gave a recital in Australia and fly back to light all the filterless Camels, Gitanes, and exclusive Turkish blends of his father's guests in Paris. He would wow the pants off them with his incandescent powers: "Timothy, I brought some friends to kiss you good-night." Oh, yeah? He'd jump out of bed and wave the old dukes and counts into his room, all with their thousand-dollar cigars; starlets in ball gowns would turn their unlit meerschaum cigarette holders toward him, waiting. "Hey, no pushing at the back! The line forms at the right." And snapping his incendiary fingers, he would baptize them all with the gift of fire!

"Timoté, why do you not take me dancing?"

"I, I don't know how to dance!"

"I will teach you!"

"Hey, what's the rush? Slow down!"

She had not had the courage to go back to the Wagram dance hall since the abortion, for fear Sean might be there. But now, with the boy as protector, why not? Mercedes stopped to look at herself in a café window. This morning, she had found a little piece of handwritten paper slipped under her door. When she saw that it was from Sean, asking her to meet him at the Wagram dance hall, she had to lie down before she could reread it.

"They won't let me in there. I'm only twelve. Hey, wait, Benz! Where you going? Hey, answer me!"

She was rushing down Rue de Presbourg and over to Avenue Carnot. Her tight red dress that she had hemmed at the knee was alive with white flowers. Mercedes was so full of longing, she had to bestow it on someone. In Matamoros, when a Gypsy girl was ripe for picking, her father would say, "That one is so hot, not even death could cool her off!"

"Benz, we have to go home now. It's almost *goûter* time! Anyway, you're still sick. Pepe said so!"

Mercedes charged forward. She was discovering that desire could store itself in the marrow of her bones and then one day, without warning, flood out in huge, unstoppable waves. Why am I spending all my nights alone in that garret apartment, where the wind whistles like a faint violin, when there is an amorous and glorious city out here that is waiting to give me supreme happiness and good fortune?

"Benz, you have to be eighteen, maybe even twenty-one, to get into those places. Would you please stop and listen to me?"

There was much trombone honking from the traffic as Benz

ran, Tim in tow, to the other side of Avenue MacMahon. She raced along the crowded street. She was sick and tired of allowing men to make her decisions for her. With Sean she had always tried to keep her opinions to herself and let him take the lead. She would not make the same mistake with Timi.

"And I have a lot of schoolwork to do," said Tim, running to catch up with her, fear creeping up his spine.

"Timoté, I promise you will love dancing."

"How do you know? And what if I don't?" He tightened his grip on her arm.

"Trust me. If you do not like it, we will leave."

They waited for a light. Her memories of Sean were becoming orphans. She recalled the rhythm of his late-night breathing and the taste of his red licked-lollipop lips. She pictured his half-parted mouth kissing her quivering breast. She wanted her bed shaking and vibrating once more to the rhythm of the world. She wanted his big Irish hands on her buttocks and his tongue probing her mouth. She wanted him again planted in her, through her, with the permanence of a tree rooted in the ground. What was her pride but a mere flyspeck on the light bulb of reality?

"Benz, I'm going to look really ridiculous in there in my short pants!"

Tim straightened his clip-on bow tie. "People at Wagram study dance all their lives. Gavotte, rondeau, *valse grand chic* and . . . And I don't feel well."

Suddenly a juicy red leaf falling from a tree slapped Mercedes across the face. She slowly peeled it off her eyes. What sign or omen was this? A *chunanjañi* or a good *penar a baji* could study this leaf and foretell the names of her children! She put the leaf in her handbag and silently cursed the imprescient city.

Slipping out of Tim's grip, Benz sailed down Avenue de Wagram. She hated it when the boy pulled on her arm. She had been too sweet with Sean, and he had left her; she would not make the same mistake twice!

Tim watched Benz rushing away from him. He imagined the headlines in the following week's edition of *Paris-Unveiled:*

IDIOT DANCERS RIDICULE THEMSELVES:
MAID AND BOY FUNNIEST ACT
SINCE LAUREL AND HARDY. FIREMEN SPEND HOURS
REMOVING LAUGHING MEN FROM HYSTERICAL DANCE HALL

He ran and grabbed her from behind.

"Do not ever surprise me like that, Timi! You could give a person a heart attack," said Mercedes, who was pretending to apply rouge, but had actually stopped only to give the boy time to catch up with her.

"Benz, why this sudden urge to go dancing? We can do flamenco at home if you want. Please . . . Hey, I can show you this neat new step I've been working on."

She pretended not to hear him and continued down Wagram, fixing her hair. Halfway to the Place des Ternes, she stopped and read a large billboard:

TODAY AT 1600 HOURS:
LUIS MARIANO AND HIS INTERNATIONAL RHYTHM BAND!
LOVE SONGS, ZARZUELAS, FANDANGOS,
PRIZES, EXCITEMENT AND MORE!
TICKETS 30—40 FRANCS. LADIES HALF-PRICE!

Every Spanish and Portuguese maid in Paris was in the lobby of the theater, shoving to get to the ticket window. Benz waded in, waving money, and broke through the crowd. The press of dingy coats and elbows on all sides prevented Tim from following her. He found himself back on the sidewalk, where Algerians were hawking discount dresses and contraband watches. Dark-skinned men with brilliantine slipping from their curly locks smoked cigarettes in doorways and crowded around pinball machines. He watched Benz push and fight her way up to the ticket counter. She was really much stronger and braver than almost anyone he knew. Maybe Benz was right, he thought: maybe she would have made a better man than he! She emerged from the crowd and grabbed him by one arm.

"Quick, Timi, follow me!"

The cavernous auditorium was dark. Music was playing on a phonograph. He fumbled his way, aided only by Benz's firm grip. As his eyes grew accustomed to the dim red light, he noticed a group of thugs standing by the bar, smoking, drinking cheap wine, eyeing Mercedes, and puffing out their chests like pigeons in spring.

"Benz, if I want to go home, even if it's only after ten minutes, we'll go—right?"

"The cow may be black, but the milk comes out white," whispered Mercedes, giving the men at the bar her broadest, lushest smile. Even from this distance, she could see the bulging blue veins of their wrists and smell their fresh Aqua Velva cologne. One man she could handle, but many, lined up in a row like this, made her feel giddy.

"What does that mean, 'the black cow gives white milk'? Huh?"

She smiled and stood by the dance floor at the back of the theater, admiring the lineup as she would a stall full of fresh vegetables.

"Timi, 'things were much better when they were worse.' *Non?*"

Tim lost himself in thought: How could things be better when they were worse? What a perfectly bizarre motto that could be for his Monarchists! Laval and his Republican satraps were beginning to question Tim's political aims and philosophy; it would take them months to figure what that saying meant!

"Benz, why don't we go sit down in our seats?"

She dug her fingers into his shoulder and stood on her toes to catch someone's eye in the distance. The record skipped. Dancers waited for the needle to be pushed along.

"Timi, does my face need more powder?"

He examined her cheeks, thick and sticky with makeup, and the bright carmine swath on her lips. When they were alone at night, the paint looked beautiful because it was offered only to him. In this gray, drizzly city, she was his sunburst of rich color. But in this dance hall, she gave her face to each of the cardboard-haired men who used bargain-basement turpentine to clean their arms and necks, and he wanted her to look hideous for them.

"Oh, you need a lot more powder!" he whispered.

"Más . . . de veras?"

Tim nodded. Let the bright turquoises and purples disappear behind a wall of white. Let her look like an apprentice Fratellini clown. The needle was again jerked across the record grooves.

"Still more, Timoté?"

He nodded vigorously.

"More powder? No, it is not possible!"

"Benz, I don't like it here. Let's go."

"Pay attention, *niño,* this is important."

"Benz, you tricked me into coming here. And now you won't take me home. You lied!"

"We will go home. But not just yet! Now be good to your Mercedes. Are you sure I do not have *too much* powder now? It feels like Pancake."

Couples sliced across the dance floor in a stylish *tango inverso.* It was almost five months since Benz had last seen Sean. No flowers, no messages, no rings, no love poems, no delicate squeezing of the hand, none of that golden clairvoyant feeling when one's lover appears unexpectedly at the door. His silence had forced her back among the everyday gray-faced legions who muddle through life, passionless.

"Benz, how long are we going to stand here like two boobs?"

"Timoté, I hate it when you become like this."

"Well, I hate when you become like this, too!"

Timi, Timi, thought Mercedes. What can I tell you of sadness on this road? The problem in life is not what to do, but how to love. And if I can teach you that, you will owe me a lot! My mother was the death and turmoil of many men, but she ended up marrying a drunken horse-trader because it was better than being alone. My bed up on the sixth floor is so full of sighs, even my walls are impregnated with loneliness. This morning, for no apparent reason, he leaves a message under my door asking me to meet him here this afternoon. Why today? Where has he been for the last five months? I think I prefer animals to men.

"Timi, I should get a cat. My room needs a happy cat to fill it with dreams again, don't you think?"

"Benz, if you don't take me home this instant, I am going to tell the Aunties you loiter in dance halls!"

"It is none of their business where I go!"

"Oh yeah? You think they'll really appreciate your coming here when you should be doing the silverware?"

"This is my day off! Now leave me alone!"

"I'll tell them you forced me to come here."

"Oh, you are so impossible sometimes, Timi, I could wring your skinny neck!"

It would be a cold day in hell, she thought, on the last day of never, when she let Sean lie on her pillow again with both eyes shut. Mercedes was no call-twice-a-month slut! She had decided not to let him stare at her misty-eyed and speak to her of love ever again. And yet, here she was this afternoon as the handwritten message had requested.

"Benz, why don't we go sit down, at least? You know we have seats!"

"Shhh. I am looking for someone. Now be quiet."

"Who? Tell me! Who are you looking for, Benz?"

"Shut up!"

A *paso doble* boomed out across the dance floor. Half of her wanted to kill Sean. The other half wanted to kill Timoté, that terrible brat! She walked around the bar as the amber lights changed to blue, and then to a deep hot red.

"Yoohoo, Earth to Benz! Earth to Benz! Tell me, who?"

"Who what?"

"Who are you looking for?"

"I do not know," she lied.

"How can you not know?"

She turned and stared the boy down. Why was she wasting her life on a child who could be such an ungrateful little shit, a child who was not even her own?

"Benz, just think for a second: how can you be looking for someone if you don't know who he is?"

Couples swept back and forth in perfect step, their shadows gliding along behind them like pools of ink.

"I am hunting," she said, enunciating slowly and clearly. "I am husband-hunting."

Tim started to laugh.

"Do not smirk, *estúpido!* I am telling the truth. I am getting old. I am twenty-one. I want a husband!"

Tim gazed around the room and cringed at the idea that these greasy, thick-necked guys, each one more repellent than the last, were prospective husbands for Benz. These weren't even butlers; they looked like garage mechanics or fried-fish salesmen, with dirt under their fingernails.

"Benz, are you serious?"

He would rather die than let one of these wine-burping, glassy-eyed escaped convicts dance with Benz.

"Benz, these guys aren't fit to lick your boots!"

Over to one side, a gaggle of maids fluttered as the men hissed insults at their backsides.

"These men are the salt of the earth," said Mercedes, whose right hand was itching to smack the boy. "Upper-class men have water in their veins. They are boring! Money isn't everything, Timi. In fact, it is nothing."

"But these men aren't interested in you," mumbled Tim.

That wasn't true. The sharks were circling ever closer. And Tim noticed the usual danger signs: Benz's palms had begun to sweat and her eyes were fluttering nonstop.

Mercedes stared at a dancer who had his back to her. The curl of hair behind the man's left ear looked almost exactly like Sean's. (Once, acting on the same clue, she had pursued a man for three blocks only to discover it was someone else.) This too was a false alarm. She wiped off the perspiration from her upper lip.

"Dance with me, Timi."

Before he could argue, she had pressed him to her chest and was jerking him around the dance floor.

I am tired of living in dreams and yearnings, she thought. Give me palpable realities: eight children; a large dog snoring by the fireplace; deep, foamy waves going thud-thud on a beach all night like an ancient washing machine outside my window. I refuse to be dependent on a stranger who never calls, never writes, never proves his love in any way. And this time, for once, I will not equivocate!

"Timi, one step to the right, one to the left. Do you not have any sense of rhythm?"

She had watched her father teach a bear to dance; circus trainers could teach elephants to repeat the same step four or five times, if set to music. But Timoté was a lug with two left feet. She could not get him to follow her effortless spinning. The boy kept grunting and slipping off balance; other couples slammed into them mercilessly.

"Timoté, a *valse* is very easy. Just follow me. One, two, three! One, two, three! Never stop turning! Why do you stop? One, two, three—why are you not following?"

She felt a queasy despair: Was the boy doing this on purpose to embarrass her in public?

Tim's clip-on bow tie was choking him. He felt totally out of place in his short pants. His knees looked even knobbier here than they had at the last medical checkup. And as if that were not embarrassing enough, Benz's idea of ballroom dancing was attracting more than its share of guffaws: she would turn twice in front of an available male, then trip, skid, slide over to the next eligible drunk, where the process was repeated. Tim never knew which man she was aiming for next, and consequently, he was forever being pulled off-balance in a musically unwarranted direction.

"Benz, you said we would go as soon as I wanted to. You're a liar!"

The cigarette smoke was so thick he could not stop coughing —no need for his incendiary talents here! The music changed to a tango, and almost immediately, whatever semblance of grace Tim and Mercedes' dancing had had now completely broke down. He felt like punching her in the nose.

"Benz, it takes years and years to find a husband!"

"Yes, Timi, gold is heavy, but it rises to the top."

"It's not like going to the Ternes open-air market and buying a ripe apple! Benz, this can't be how you find a man."

"Then you show me how."

"I don't know. I'm not a specialist, Benz."

"Well, neither am I."

"Benz, the Aunties never married, and they're happy. Maybe not *everyone* is supposed to marry?"

She boxed Timoté's ears.

"You little *merde.* You mean I am supposed to become an old maid?"

"No, Benz."

"You insinuate I cannot find a husband? Is that what you think?"

"No, Benz. But maybe you are better off without one."

Whenever Mercedes thought of Auntie Agatha and her stormy love affair with the Marquis de Prévost, the printing-press genius who had been run over by a train, she became quiet and dreamy. Agatha did not smoke or even tolerate tobacco in her room. Yet alone at night, she often lit a Players filterless and left it to burn by itself in the ashtray. Benz had caught her several times, staring out the window, reveling in the scent of the Marquis's favorite brand of cigarette. The sight of the long, virgin ash in the porcelain ashtray always brought tears to Benz's eyes.

A dark-haired man was looking at her. Mercedes blushed, lowered her eyes, and played nervously with Timi's hair.

"I will have to marry *you*, Timoté. That is the only solution!" she said, smiling her phony, *angoissé,* finger-caught-in-the-door smile that Tim knew was directed not at him but at the man across the room.

"Timi, why is it always the ones I don't want who want me?"

"Stop staring at him."

"I'm not. He's staring at me."

"Come on, let's go home."

The lights went out. The crowd started screaming. Luis Mariano appeared on stage, sitting on a white cardboard horse, the silver spangles of his suit reflecting off his gleaming teeth.

Benz grabbed Tim's hand and rushed forward to their mezzanine seats. It was pitch-black down the center aisle. Mercedes swore in Spanish as she ran ahead. Tim tripped on a step. *"Assis! Assis!"* hissed a lady as she poked him in the ribs with her umbrella. Benz let go of his hand. Tim was now navigating in the dark through a melee of angry patrons. HEY, THAT'S MY FOOT! Excuse me, sir. *Pardon, Madame. DIOS,* ARE YOU DRUNK? He called Benz's name and reached out for her in the dark, by mistake grabbing a man's nose. WHAT THE HELL? He edged forward ever so slowly. GET OUT OF THE SIGHTLINES! He was dragging someone's coat along. *ESPECE D'ANIMAL,* YOU'RE BLOCKING THE VIEW! He bent over like a clamshell, trying not to trip over anyone's legs. He heard Benz calling his name above the loud shushing of several aficionados. *ON NE VOIT RIEN!* This was their row. Now for a dignified, discreet sit-down. YOU'RE STEPPING ON MY CORNS, IDIOTA! He squeezed in. Not only was the theater filled to capacity, but the producers had lengthened the rows to augment the seating. Excuse me, Madame. *Pardonnez-moi,* I have to pull my other leg in now. . . . *Merci.* He crabbed along sideways. An elbow caught him in the eye. He fell back. A woman pushed him off her lap. *Pardon, madame.* He was bumping the knees of those in back and rearranging the hairdos of those in front. *ASSEYEZ-VOUS!* No matter how lightly he put his feet down, they crunched some sensitive anatomical part. *AH, NON! ENCORE CE ZYGOTO!* At last, he saw Benz's eyes. He quickly sat down and tried to disappear into the dark padding of his chair. His ribs ached from all the pummeling.

Benz sat on the edge of her seat, entranced, singing along and clutching Timi every time Luis Mariano approached their side of the stage:

"LOVE ME FOREVER AND MAKE ALL MY DREAMS COME TRUUUUE!"

Benz had grown up surrounded by music and dance. Her mother, during her many pregnancies, had never stopped flamencoing. She claimed that all her children "came out dancing!" Benz had learned *zapateado* at the age of one and a half, her mother holding her arms and making her stamp one foot, then the other.

"You dance better than Saint Vitus," men used to tell her. "One day, you will design flamenco dresses and lead your very own zarzuela group around the capitals of Europe!"

All around Tim, maids from Passy sobbed hysterically and blew kisses at the big, sparkling phony up on stage. Tim thought he heard the scratch of a record needle, and wondered whether Luis was not mouthing the words to the song. Luis was probably a deaf mute who could not even speak in B flat, much less sing in it!

"LOVE ME FOOOOOORRREEEEEEEEEEEVVVEEEEEEEEERRR!"

Mercedes sensed Sean's presence. She did not know how the knowledge came to her, but searching through the crowd, she caught sight of him standing behind a column. She was never timid, but now such contradictory feelings swept through her that she could hardly sit still. She was tempted to forgive this man for letting her almost die in that stinking, humid room alone.

"AND MAKE ALL MY DREAMS COOOOME TRUUUUUE!"

She was tempted to forget everything; but temptation is more powerful sometimes than an action itself. When she turned her head and saw him, Sean was looking straight at her. This *payo* bastard was imposing his will on her—all over again! She jumped up.

"Hey, Benz, wait! Where are you going now?"

Again Tim was stepping over women's laps, tripping on their handbags, staggering over piles of coats and, at last, rolling out into the aisle. Luis Mariano at last closed his mouth, thereby bringing his song to an end. The audience broke into a delirium of clapping.

"Benz, will you please tell me why we're leaving?"

"I saw Pepe," she lied.

Tim glanced over his shoulder. No one was following them. No one was so much as watching them; the audience was giving Luis Mariano a standing ovation.

"Pray to God, child, but keep rowing to shore," said Mercedes.

They ran over to Carnot, past Le Veau d'Or, where the Aunties had listened to Edith Piaf in the Thirties. For the first time in her whole life, Mercedes felt she was in control of her own destiny.

"Why are you so scared of Pepe? What has he done to you?"

"Timoté, this is my forward escape."

"Your what?"

In the past, whenever she had been with Sean, her power to say "no" had rather insultingly refused to function. But today she was saying "no," and *"basta,"* in a big way! She was not his *femme-objet.* If they met again, it would be on her terms, at a time she selected.

"Today, Timi, I am running forward so fast, the past will never catch up with me. It is an escape, but it is an escape forward."

Helga was on duty across from the Irish Embassy, wearing her usual leather miniskirt and black boots. A policeman standing guard in front of the entrance to the chancery whistled through his teeth as Mercedes walked by. Tim yanked her arm to get her to stop. She was doing the Countess of Wiggle-Waggle, which consisted of sashaying along as if her shoes were three sizes too small for her.

"Benz, my dad could talk to Gregory Peck; he was downstairs last week. He'd make an excellent husband for you! Did you ever see *To Kill a Mockingbird?"*

They climbed into the elevator from the Year One, which had recently been overhauled, greased, and checked by the Roux Combaluzier people.

"If Pepe or Manola asks you, tell them you have been playing with your friend Roland. *De acuerdo?"*

She pushed the third-floor button, and the elevator slowly responded.

"Benz, just promise me you won't go husband-hunting on Wagram ever again—no matter how desperate you get!"

"All right; but Timi, you must find me a suitable admirer."

The elevator, tired from its effort, groaned to a halt just shy of the second-floor landing. Tim had to slip out through the half-open door and help Benz climb out after him. As she lifted her skirt to squeeze out of the exasperating contraption, she wondered how she would react the next time she ran into Sean. They were bound to meet at the end of some dark passageway, late at night, in the Paris mists. Or perhaps they would meet when she was doing a load of wash. What would she say to him, face to face? This forward escape was no escape at all. It was only a play for time so she could think of what to say to him.

As she forced the elevator door shut to prevent the Aunties from hurting themselves, Tim grabbed her elbow and whispered:

"Benz, if you really want to marry me, just wait six years until I am eighteen. You could clean my house and I could light your cigarettes. What d'ya think?"

CHAPTER 5

When We Love, We Love Too Much

TIM RAN TOWARD Monsieur Henri's steam-engine speedsters. This had always been his favorite ride in all of the Jardin d'Acclimatation. He knew each skid mark on the bean-shaped racing track like the back of his hand. The best speedster was a blue Number 7 modified Jaguar XK-150, and it happened to be free now. He strapped himself in while Monsieur Henri, the all-purpose engineer and maintenance man for these cars, squatted by the cockpit. His arms were black with grease up to the elbows.

"Where's your nanny?" asked Monsieur Henri. "How come she never comes with you anymore?"

"You mean Benz? Well, I'm twelve now. She hasn't been accompanying me here for a long time."

"She's a beautiful woman," said Monsieur Henri, his eyes deep in the shadow of his visored hat. "You ever seen her undress?"

"Sure I have."

Tim followed the man's gaze. He was staring at the empty bench by the ticket window where Benz used to sit and wait for Tim to finish his racing laps.

"She's probably the prettiest woman I've ever seen in my whole life," said the usually quiet man.

Tim nodded. It was important to stay on Monsieur Henri's good side if you wanted him to let you take extra laps and to provide inside tips on how the speedsters were performing that day. Monsieur Henri licked his lower lip.

"When she walked her body seemed to cry out loud: 'Come here. I need you. I am lonely!' " He winced. "And she used to read that stupid newspaper. I remember one of her favorite headlines was MAN BLOWS UP ON OPERATING TABLE! MEDICAL WORLD SHOCKED!"

Tim didn't know what more to say. He revved his engine, checked his pressure gauge, and adjusted his goggles. Monsieur Henri gave him the thumbs-up sign to indicate the track was clear.

Tim floored the accelerator and became Sterling Moss, Fangio, and Ines Ireland all in one. He leaned into a turn and gritted his teeth as the two rear wheels began to skid. What did these men find so beautiful about Benz? She was large, top-heavy, exotic with her gold and technicolor makeup, but Tim had never thought of her as especially pretty.

He remembered almost six months ago riding back with Benz from the Jardin d'Acclimatation on the wooden train that chugs through the Bois de Boulogne. Her warm bear-cave and underarm smells, the blue Number 7 speedster, and the Fratellini clowns, all swirling inside his head. Tim had asked:

"Benz, are you going to marry Monsieur Henri?"

"Do not be silly, Timi; when I marry, the world will shake. The cards have predicted that I will elope on a white charger."

"What cards?"

"Why should I tell you all my secrets?"

"Monsieur Henri really likes you."

"Timi, I drew the Ace of Spades and the Queen of Hearts. That means fire and blood. When I marry, war will break out on all sides."

Tim had leaned his head on her shoulder; he was too tired to ask questions. And he was easily embarrassed when she talked of her grandiose, labyrinthian projects, half-dream/half-wish, fueled by Andaluz soothsayers who claimed she would be a world-class dancer and appear with Luis Mariano on stage. She was gullible, and the readers knew it.

• • •

THERE was a gunshot, or maybe a car had backfired in the distance. Then another. A woman screamed in the courtyard. A third shot rang out. Tim jumped out of bed, pulled on his cotton bathrobe, and ran to his balcony. Benz's screams filled the night. She was shouting from a sixth-floor hallway window:

"I will kill you, *bastardo!*"

This was it: Benz had flipped! Now she would be taken away in a straightjacket for sure, thought Tim. She was quite beautiful up there in a little cocoon of light, waving a gun, her emerald eyes flashing like stars. She fired another shot. A window shattered in the Irish Embassy, the pale silk curtains of the Ambassador's residence floating out like magnificent scarves in the night.

"Benz, don't shoot; it's me, Timi!"

On the other side of the courtyard, framed in a second-floor window of the Irish Embassy, Ambassador McLuck raised his glass to the night:

"Is it Bastille Day again?"

Benz fired another shot, this time striking the champagne glass in McLuck's hand. The Ambassador wiped his fingers with his handkerchief:

"Wonderful marksmanship, *ma belle*. Didn't even scratch me!"

The Aunties' bedroom window opened. Blinking in the bright light from the embassy chandeliers, Aunt Phoebe, whose hearing was better than Agatha's, said:

"Oh, my, I do hope the Germans are not invading again!"

Mercedes reloaded her pistol. Manola's bedroom light went on, as did those of many neighbors. There was a clattering of footsteps in the service staircase. Sean appeared at the foot of the stairs, out of breath, missing one shoe and with his shirt unbuttoned. Tim had a chance to see him very clearly for an instant.

"You do not respect me! You pig! And for me, respect is *all-important!*" shouted Benz as she fired again.

"She's frigging crazy," Tim heard the Irish Embassy butler mutter as he ran through the shadows to the driveway, a bullet ricocheting off the garage wall.

"Please stop!" shouted Tim, his face pressed against the stone floor of his balcony.

"Sean, your father is a scorpion who mated with a lizard!" screamed Mercedes.

Manola put on her bathrobe and said to Pepe:

"My beautiful Mauser! The only memento I manage to save from the Battle of Madrid! Benz was supposed to clean it for me."

The Aunties huddled together. Agatha waved her white handkerchief of surrender out the window. McLuck rocked gently on his heels and shouted:

"That's what I like in a woman: spunk! Stand up for your rights, girl!"

By now almost all the windows in the neighborhood were lit up. Timi heard a couple say: "*Elle est vraiment folle, celle-là!*" Wonderdog barked from under the dining-room table, where he had taken refuge. Manola raced out into the courtyard, her bathrobe flapping open like great wings:

"Poor Benz. What did they do to her this time?"

"Always taking her side," said Pepe, lumbering after his wife and switching on the light in the back staircase.

"Wait . . . hey, wait. You don't know how to talk to her," shouted Tim, racing up the service stairs after them. "Hey, wait for me. Let me talk to her."

They arrived at Benz's room, panting and shouting to each other to be allowed to speak first. Wheezing for breath, Pepe tried unsuccessfully to break open the locked and barricaded door. Manola pleaded with her Princesita, saying Auntie Phoebe was good friends with the Minister of Justice, and that if she surrendered now, they might find her not guilty by reason of insanity, or some other technicality.

Inside her room, Mercedes sat on her bed, her head in her hands. Sean hadn't knocked. He had made his bold, dramatic entry by crawling out onto the drainpipe and tapping on her window. It had been easy to run away from him at the Spanish theater on Avenue Wagram. But tonight this handsome man with the pale high temples and the straight nose looked so helpless out there against the blackness! She could not leave him dangling on the narrow crooked gutter, clinging to the slanting gray mansard slates, a duffel bag slung over one shoulder. He had risked his life for her!

She had opened her bedroom window and plucked him from the stars. And she had swooned at his sweeping, wide-lipped Clark Gable kiss, as if the whole world were finally stuffing its tongue down her throat. How handsome he was in his uniform, extracting from the duffel bag two bottles of champagne, fresh bread, chèvre cheese, prosciutto, and *pâté de campagne.* Love was all she knew and all she wanted to know on this night of nights, when her Sean had finally knelt before her and asked:

"Señorita de los Angeles, will you marry me?"

She fully intended to answer *"Oui."* She dug her fingers deep into his thick, curly red hair, smelling the whiskey on his breath, admiring the blue stand-out veins on his forearms, and was about to add some suitably dramatic touch, such as fainting to the floor; but instead she found her hand slapping his face and her mouth saying:

"Where have you been for six months, *especia de salop?* Who do you think you are that you can appear like this after so many weeks of sleepless nights and just run your hands all over me? No, never! *Jamais de la vie! Jamás!* Honor is everything, and you have none."

"Darling, I love you," said Sean. "Forgive me—I've been underground, hiding from the police. I'm sorry. Someday when I can, I will tell you the whole story."

He had not even prepared a suitable lie in advance! For half a year she had been saving herself for this moment. She ached to throw herself into his strong arms. He was irresistible, yes; but she could be more resistant than a mule when she put her mind to it. And now that he was actually before her, in her room, the drug of absentee love had worn off. "Chase away your true nature, and it will come galloping back," her mother had said. She could not and would not let a man use her and get away with it, even if she loved him, even if he were the Lord of all Western Ireland and Prince of County Mayonnaise, which he insisted on calling "Mayo."

She sat down on the bed and tried to control her temper. She could not just laugh this off, make love to him and let him slip away without an explanation, the way she had a hundred times before.

"And why do you leave your damn suitcase in my closet, and that crap under my bed? Are you using me? Is that all I am, a baggage depot to check your stuff when you're in trouble?"

"Girl, I am going absolutely clean. I promise you."

"You are a liar. The Salvation Army never bombs anyone!"

Slowly, Sean explained the difference between the I.R.A. and the Salvation Army:

"Remember the Spanish Civil War? Well, we have the same thing in my country now. Except that instead of Moroccan troops on our soil, we have English occupation forces in the North. I am not violent, but we have to defend ourselves. Mostly what I do is provide fake I.D. papers for escaping political prisoners."

She did not believe a word of all his lies, but what choice did she have? Even if he were telling the truth, she knew that for Sean a promise never to fight for the cause again would be like an alcoholic promising never to take another drink. Even if Sean were the most faithful husband in the world, he might on any given night feel the patriotic itch. A telephone call would pluck him from her bedside (as had happened in the past) and extend to him the far more glorious opportunity of offering his life for the cause. Oh, how generous these men were in giving away lives that really did not belong to them anymore! She would stay pregnant for ten years; she would pile so many family responsibilities on him that he would have no time to think of the I.R.A.

In a moment of roguish Don Juanism, Sean had smiled at her. She thought she had seen a tinge of condescension, a tinge of "I am a man, dear; you are only a woman," and suddenly she found herself fishing in the closet for Manola's Civil War Mauser. Its weight in her hand was tremendously reassuring. Oh, these rabbit-footed lovers! They were so sluggish to propose marriage, but how they raced like hares in the middle of the night, when they'd worn out God's welcome and revenge was in season!

"Benz, Manola and Pepe are gone now," whispered Tim. "You can let me in. It's only me. They've all gone now."

She did not regret the shooting at all! She'd be arrested, but so what? *("Al enemigo, ni agua!")* She could hear the Ambassador and Aunt Phoebe talking in the courtyard. Blue and white flashing police lights splashed across her ceiling. She wanted at least to smell nice for her first day in jail, so she busily spread Nivea cream on her arms.

"Benz, don't worry, you can come out now. Aunt Phoebe sent me back up to tell you she telephoned Martin Duchesne, the Minister of Justice. Everything's going to be okay."

She looked in the mirror above her washbasin and leaned forward until her eyelashes almost touched their reflection. I am getting old, she thought, spotting two gray hairs. Death is everywhere, and I cannot find a good man because my longing is too loud; it scares men away.

"The Minister's wife is on the Board of Directors of The Ladies of the Passy Literary, Knitting and Opera Society. Things will be all right for you. The inspector won't take you away. He just wants to ask a few questions. He's waiting in the Aunties' living room. Look, if I say you don't want to come down, they're just going to come up and get you."

In an aromatic cloud of Nivea, she descended quietly with her black handbag and coat. She expected to be shoved into a police van and taken away; but Timi had told the truth: Phoebe was entertaining an inspector, and Manola was serving them tea and liqueurs. They were whispering as if there were a sick man in the house. Mercedes, with her eyes downcast, sat on the couch and answered questions. Extreme conduct, you say, concerning my personal affairs? Oh, no, Your Honor, I did not make threatening telephone calls, or write abusive letters, or put arsenic in the anonymous box of chocolates like one reads about in *Paris-Unveiled.* No, I acted calmly and rationally. As Gypsies say, "What counts is not only what the net catches, but what escapes through the meshes."

The inspector examined the gun.

"A family heirloom," explained Phoebe, lying. "Our nephew, Alphonse, has a whole collection on the fifth floor."

Agatha coughed uncomfortably.

"And did you know your assailant, Mademoiselle?"

"No," said Benz, without raising her eyes.

"Have you any idea who he might be? Or why he did this?"

"No."

"Think carefully, now."

"Monsieur l'inspecteur, I've given up trying to understand men. The sheep never knows the face of the wolf."

The Aunties nodded their full agreement, and Phoebe passed the inspector a plate of Crêpes Dentelles cookies.

TIM'S Royalist forces were still by and large intact. But in recent months, the Republican armies had dwindled away rapidly, and without a decent enemy, what fun was war? Courtyard politics were changing. The old Republicans were becoming Socialists, Communists, even Anarcho-Syndicalists—talkers, all of them!

One day a boy told Tim that the Americans should not get involved in Vietnam, as if Tim were personally in charge of the situation. He paid no attention to this new insult, and continued galloping. Another day, a boy two grades ahead of him shook his hand:

"It must be really hard on you, Cardozo. No?"

The crisp autumn day flooded the schoolyard with zinc-gray light. Dead leaves and horse chestnuts covered the courtyard of Saint-Philippe de Passy. Father Picabia offered his condolences. Tim made certain no one had pinned a cut-out paper donkey to his back and that his fly was zipped.

"I'm really sorry, terribly sorry," said Gâche.

Tim began to worry that something had happened at home that he was not aware of. Even his imaginary horse, Pamplemousse, was catching diabetes from these sugar-coated phonies! He took Roland aside and asked him what this was all about.

"You don't know?"

"No. Tell me."

"Your President was shot."

"De Gaulle?"

"No, idiot, Kennedy!"

"Who?"

Because Tim was the only American in Saint-Philippe, they wanted him to provide more details. Had he ever met Kennedy? Or Lee Oswald? With so much public interest, Tim hedged his answers. After all, Kennedy and he were both Americans. And there were other affinities as well. His dad had mentioned giving money to someone for an election campaign. Tim was not sure who, but his father had sent a telegram and contributed to some president or other. Once. If he had not in fact given it to Kennedy, it was merely an oversight. Roland took him aside:

"Tim, you have your nose pressed up so close to everything, you never know what's going on! How can you exist in such a fog?"

"My Aunties don't allow television in the house. They say it makes you stupid. They don't read anything published after the seventeenth century."

"That's no excuse. You are a sentient being."

A what? Tim let this expression go by. The truth was that the only newspapers in the house he ever looked at were Pepe's Longchamps racing sheets and Benz's *Paris-Unveiled*.

"Tim, you have to hear and understand all things at all times and be cognizant!"

Tim imagined Roland's brain as a giant cocoon of a million tiny synapses pulsating, invisible silk threads interconnecting his brilliant thoughts all at once. He could feel a zillion voltages clicking on and off in his friend's throbbing cranium. He felt abysmally ignorant.

• • •

BENZ opened her eyes. Countless drops of moisture hung from the bathroom ceiling. It was a large, gloomy room, eminently bourgeois and moldy. She lay in the warm bathtub water, fighting for breath and sighing like an old man climbing a hill. Since Sean had left, she had felt an anvil pressing down on her chest. When we Gypsies love, we love too much, she reflected. Nothing but cold, slow, empty death stretched in front of her. She would see a doctor, ask him to knife out her heart and feed it to the sparrows. She would donate her smile and laugh muscles to science. Her road had come to an end; in this morning light of autumn, she knew she was dying.

"Benz, I have your café-au-lait. Open up! It's me, Timi."

She hardly heard his voice or the knocking on the bathroom door. She hadn't eaten in two days and had no appetite. The weaker she got, the purer the air became, the more indirect the light, the shorter the days. She was ascending into heaven by way of hell.

"Benz, open up before I spill it all."

"Go away!"

"Hey, come on, don't make me beg!"

"Leave me. I have a raging fever."

She raised herself from the bottom of the tub and felt the warm suck of water against her, as if she were pulling her foot out of a deep mudbank.

"Benz, you're fine. You haven't eaten, that's all. Hey, this coffee is burning my fingers!"

A yellow plastic duck floated gently by. She turned to the wall and felt her burning forehead. The whiteness of the walls bothered her. (White is for mourning, the *gitanos* said. Life needs color!) She lay helpless, in a zebra swath of light that cut through her metal shutters, thinking: Benz, your tides are abandoning you; so are your many hummingbirds. You hardly exist anymore, except as a potato peel exists, cut off from its support system and waiting in the garbage to become dust.

"Benz, you always say, 'Men are like buses. Another one always comes along.' Now, open up!"

Her dry mouth tasted of the chocolates she had been eating all night. The anvil on her lungs was growing heavier. It was a boulder; it was becoming the cover of her pine coffin.

"Benz, promise me you will never date that creep Raoul."

"Who?"

She thought of the other girls she knew, who when asked could assemble a respectable number of happy moments, like pearls on a necklace. But Mercedes really had very few. She choked with self-pity.

"He's the policeman in front of the Irish Embassy who winks at you when we go shopping. He came around the other day asking if you lived here. I said you didn't."

Tears hammered up her throat and down her nose. She kept thinking of everything she had lost, her plans for the future: Sean's Irish hunting dogs with floppy ears full of thistles snoring by the fireplace, their eight fat children seated around the kitchen table screaming, the translucent green fields dotted with sheep. All that Sean had promised her now became a faint blur against the black.

"Benz, I'll leave the tray out here on the landing. I brought you coffee, the English strawberry jam you like, toast, a soft-boiled egg, an apple, and this week's *Paris-Unveiled.* The front page says: 'MOTHER SUPERIOR RETURNS FROM INTERGALACTIC VOYAGE WITH MARTIAN!' And the police called to say they have no leads in their investigation. Really, it's safe. You can come out now."

She was not a clairvoyant, but she knew something of how to use palms, beans, and the bones of sheep to foretell her future. She knew the basics of the grand art of *penar a baji.* Her mother had read the future with an egg in a glass of water. As soon as the boy had left, she got out of her bath, brought the breakfast tray in, and got back into the tub. She added more hot water and tried to remember her mother's lessons. A pet dove and a flute would have helped, but she had to make do with what was at hand. First, she pressed the egg to her teeth, hair, and face. *"Naclé, dani, bal, chichi,"* she said. It was all flooding back—the taste of food seasoned with hunger. Her father cutting a pear in half with a silver knife while cursing a man who then was found dead in a ditch. As the yellow of her egg dipped down into the glass, she muttered what she used to hear her mother say:

"You were born lucky in some things, but not all."

The egg dipped and slipped to the side. She thought she sensed footsteps (Timi's?) outside the door, but continued:

"You have a friend who isn't a friend—beware. You've helped others who wouldn't help you. . . . By asking and asking again, you finally arrive at the truth."

There were many men in the glass of water. Too many. All of them aloof and enigmatic like Sean. Nose, teeth, hair, face—*naclé, dani, bal, chichi!* What Mercedes wanted to see in her fortune in this steamy bathroom was a man in all respects like Timoté, one who would know instinctively when to be quiet, and when to hold her tightly in his arms overlooking a honeysuckle-scented bay. But the trail of the yolk indicated a handsome, black-eyed man, with thick, sensuous lips, wearing a woman's robe! Could that be Pepe disguised as la Comtesse? No, something was wrong. It was not Pepe. The man had delicate hands, teeth like jewels, arms as hard as trees, a heart as big as a province, and a smile as beautiful as a near-autumn sky.

"BE extremely careful!" said Aunt Agatha.

"Oh, yes, be very careful," said Aunt Phoebe.

"And remember, pigeons do their business out there."

"Here, take my gold whistle in case anything happens."

"Phoebe! That's solid gold!"

"So what? Don't you trust Timi?"

The Aunties debated the issue. At last, the hand-finished 24-karat signed, dated Cartier gold whistle was added to Tim and Roland's survival pack. This consisted of a rope, a flashlight, a newspaper, a can of Mace, a jug of milk, pillows, sleeping bags, Himalayan permafrost yak-wool socks, mittens, lighter fluid, a yellow Nova Scotia fog hat, all the *petits beurres* in the house, two chocolate éclairs, two *mille-feuilles,* a brand-new BB-pellet air gun that Tim had won at the Jardin d'Acclimatation, a slingshot, Jaffa oranges, an Hermès pin-striped umbrella, three *Lucky Luke* comic books, and excerpts from Maurice Herzog's *Annapurna* with easy-to-read diagrams. So equipped, Master Tim and Roland ventured out onto the balcony of the third floor of Number 10½ and bedded down for the night.

At first it was not easy to get used to the cooing of pigeons or the motorbikes that sped toward the Bois de Boulogne, their tiny engines tearing the night wide open. Car after car turned down the side street and stopped at the corner of the Rue Rude; there the secret-service ladies smoked and flashed their long, silken legs. Peering through the wrought-iron balcony, Tim could see their lipstick, bright red like vampire blood in the headlights. Just a stone's throw away, the Arc de Triomphe, with the giant tricolored flag between its arches, loomed up like some mythical ship ready to set sail.

Roland counted the *petits beurres* in their overnight survival pack. The floodlights of the Arc de Triomphe went out. Must be eleven o'clock, thought Tim as he jotted down the weather conditions in his Benz diary. If he did not confront her with the written evidence of when she got home and with whom, she would deny everything.

"Tim, did you ever wonder why the verb 'to keep' in French is '*garder*'? In English, no one would ever 'guard' anything in their pockets."

Tim gazed up at the low, luminous clouds. This was nothing compared with Herzog—the great alpinist had managed to survive frostbite, amputation of all ten toes, snow-blindness, elevation sickness, 50-mile-an-hour winds and the loss of all his equipment to the crevasse of a glacier!

"The French 'demand' questions and 'guard' their possessions. Is it that the Americans are dreamers, or that the French are cynics? Or both?"

Tim did not answer. When Roland got onto his vocabulary tangents, it was best to keep quiet.

"But the French do have some finesse. Just take the expression *'il me manque.'* Anglo-Saxons do not have that sophistication when it comes to missing people!"

Master Tim scanned the side streets, feeling wise and quiet, like an old sailor, waiting for Benz to appear, clip-clopping on her spike heels. Leaves tore off the chestnut trees and swept across the avenue in great swirls. Streetlights glowed feathery under the trees, each one shrouded in darkness. Tim extracted a chocolate éclair from his survival pack.

Roland was collecting his things and opening the apartment window.

"Hey, you can't go inside now! You won't be able to see who walks Benz home tonight! Isn't that important? You traitor, Roland! This is excellent training, you scaredy-cat! You deserter!"

Tim would have to go it alone tonight. He lay back wounded but determined, his arms crossed over his chest. Sometimes Roland made him so angry! A Mobylette engine could be heard winding down like a distant mechanical toy. October was colder than usual this year. He tossed and turned in his sleeping bag. His Himalayan yak-wool socks were cutting off his circulation below the knees. The Jaffa oranges and *mille-feuilles* were starting to decompose into a wet lump soaked with lighter fluid at the bottom of the knapsack. Benz had better return from her date before he caught TB or beriberi! What would Tim do in case of fire? He had forgotten to bring a fire extinguisher. Herzog said the secret of success was to be prepared for anything. Oh, no! Where was the little gold whistle the Aunties had entrusted to him? Tim farted nervously as he searched the depths of his sleeping bag. Pigeons cooed eerily from inside their warm chimneys. The last of the secret-service ladies got into a car and was whisked away. Roland walked out onto the balcony:

"There's someone ringing at the front door, Tim."

"At this hour?"

The cold night air made him sneeze. He checked his watch: it was a quarter past midnight.

"She's a countess or something."

Tim hopped in his sleeping bag down the three flights of steps and to the front door, where Wonderdog was sniffing. Roland followed, the two potato-sack racers arriving at about the same time. Above the shrill ringing of the bell, a woman was screaming in a falsetto:

"Laissez-moi entrer! Ceci est intolérable!"

Roland boosted Tim up, minus his sleeping bag, so he could look through the peephole. Timothy saw a white cotton glove, a large plumed black hat, and a veil.

"Madame Cardozo sent me. Open up, *vite!*"

"Oh my God, I think it's the cadaver lady!"

How had this woman gotten past the front gate that Pepe so carefully locked every evening? Why had Tim not noticed her walking up the driveway?

"Madame Cardozo isn't here. We do not know when she is due back," said Tim through the keyhole.

"But you simply must let me in! I am La Contessa Louisa de Beaulieu et Gouligouza, née Rodienko von Shtad."

The incessant bellringing was followed by pounding.

"Is Cascasia's darling son, Timoté, in? The one who is so handsome?"

"Now we know she's crazy," whispered Roland.

"What should we do?"

Roland shrugged and took his turn staring through the peephole. After further deliberation, they opened the massive steel-and-oak door.

"Well, it's about time," said La Contessa, extending her white-gloved hand for Tim to kiss and sweeping in. She was sweating profusely and carried a parasol.

"I'm Tim. This is my friend Roland. And you are?"

"Oh, we have met many times. My latest husband's name is 'de Gouligouza,' but actually it's pronounced like a cough and a snort—like 'Haw-Haw-Haw.' Just as if you were losing your dentures. Now, tell me—I don't have much time—are you the one who is to be devirginized tonight?"

Masters Tim and Roland stared at each other with round eyes. La Contessa was clearly tired from her long trip, for she kept slipping off her high-heel shoes. Something about her reminded him of Pepe.

"Oh, do not worry! I have devirginized the leading nobodies of my time! The Tsarevitch's cousin Vladimir. And even Lord Mountbatten's homosexual nephew on whom everyone had given up hope!"

"She's nuts," whispered Roland into Tim's ear.

La Contessa spoke with a part Spanish, part Russian accent that sounded familiar to Tim. But she kept twirling the white parasol so it covered half of her veiled face.

"Before I begin, I must have a large Dick-Dick."

"A what?" said Tim, zipping himself back up in his sleeping bag.

"I'll show you."

The Contessa lunged past them up the stairs and into the living room, where she turned on the light. She obviously knew exactly where the bar was located, even the glasses. Tim and Roland shuffled behind, their bedding still wrapped around them.

"I met a Countess of Gouligouza something-or-other at one of my dad's parties," whispered Tim to Roland. "In the movie business they're all crazy like this."

Where the hell was Benz, he wondered, when he needed her most? Tim and Roland watched silently as this mountain of sweating woman poured out a full glass of twelve-year-old Scotch. Her perfume was a mixture of cheap cologne, vinegar, and bad breath. When she had finished gargling with the Scotch and when it was polite to interrupt, Tim said:

"Madame, I think there has been some mistake."

"How old are you, my little *ouistiti?*"

"Thirteen."

"Do not lie. You are twelve and a half. At that age, you should not be sleeping with other boys! Your mother was right to fly me here from Siberia."

La Contessa's left breast had slipped down. She pushed it back up to its normal position and looked around the gold-and-red living room, kicking off her high heels.

"But, my darlings, I am famished. Would one of you angels prepare me a collation? A *pavé d'agneau,* asparagus vinaigrette, and hand-peeled grapes from Macedon? Oh, and my feet, my feet! Timoté, your nanny tells me you give divine foot massages. Would you wash and then rub mine, *chéri?*"

She had such a peremptory voice and such a deep, throaty laugh that Tim found himself obeying. He and Roland were filling up a plastic basin with hot water and bath oil. His mother was the same way: she got people to do the most incredible things for her, just by assuming that they would not say no. The only person he had ever heard successfully say no to her was Pepe, and that was only when he was drunk.

"Let's kick her out," said Roland.

"We can't do that," said Tim.

"Why not? What are you afraid of?"

When they returned from the kitchen, La Contessa de Gouligouza, née Rodienko von Shtad, was pouring herself another Scotch.

"Timoté, please understand: I am a *mademoiselle* in quotes, like that slut Mercedes. I am a liar, yes, but only on weekends and also during the week. I am a defrocker of priests, a starter of arguments. And I worry so about the approaching end of love and of history!"

"That's not a real countess," whispered Roland to Tim. "She's a fake—I'm sure of it!"

Enormous biceps rippled under the woman's full-length white gloves. Roland elbowed him, and Tim saw that her right breast had slipped below the left one. She was looking worse and worse by the minute. Up close, you could see chin hairs poking through the white makeup.

"You are Pepe, aren't you?" shouted Tim.

La Contessa de Hawhaw quickly opened her lacquered fan and began agitating it in front of her face.

Manola appeared from behind a door, laughing, lunging at the Contessa and grabbing her false breasts. An orange slipped to the floor. Pepe managed to hold on to his other orange and the wig as he dashed off, with Wonderdog barking at him. Manola slapped the armrest of the couch repeatedly and pressed her knees together as she dissolved in laughter:

"Oh, Pepe, Pepe! I am going to pee in my pants. . . . Timi, hold me!"

MERCEDES was in the Pharmacie de l'Etoile, reading the personal ads at the back of *Ciné Revue.* At first, she had read the ads placed by men, but eventually she had found them too cut-and-dried, too simplistic. It was not the whole woman that attracted men, but an ass or a particular chest. A woman, on the other hand, fantasized about a man's whole personality; her companion needed to have charm, humor, kindness, loyalty, brains, integrity. She could identify with the classifieds placed by women.

Honesty and financial security were the two qualities most in demand by single women in Paris these days. Yet Benz found it odd that no one ever referred to "passion" or "love," and she wondered what the recurrent search for "fun-loving" was supposed to mean. She moved forward in line. The more personal ads she read, the more she realized the entire city was confusedly and desperately alone, and this somehow reassured her. Only one more customer and she would be at the front of the line.

> Young Catholic woman seeks older, thoughtful, kind, honest, financially secure gentleman . . .

The old ones were no doubt more charming and gentlemanly than the young ones, but Benz could not imagine running her fingers over a balding scalp.

"Oui, Mademoiselle?"

Mercedes handed the salesgirl her prescription. She had never taken the Pill before. She hoped not so much that it would prevent pregnancy—the rhythm method could do that—as that it would give her an "I'm available" glow which eligible bachelors all over Paris would be able to sense even in their sleep. Of course, she was not entirely "available": she was rather hermetically sealed to everyone except Sean; but what better way of getting him back than to make him jealous?

Two gray-haired ladies, standing in line behind her, were talking, carrying laxatives and packets of suppositories. Mercedes distinctly heard one say to the other:

"Yes, and a Catholic, too! Isn't it a shame how these girls lose their morals as soon as they come to Paris?"

Benz tried not to pay attention to these neighborhood busy-bodies who had nothing better to do. But the old gray-haired witches behind her in the Pharmacie de l'Etoile kept talking just loud enough in their scrapy little Mother Goose voices for everyone in the store to hear:

"It shouldn't be permitted! It's disgusting, really. For shame!"

Mercedes knew she should control herself, but already she had wheeled around and was saying:

"Keep your big trap shut, you old sow!"

The ladies were not at all intimidated. On the contrary, Benz's comment seemed to spur them on:

"What image does that give our neighborhood, to buy contraceptives here? If they want to be sluts, they should go to Pigalle!"

Benz slapped the woman across the face. The slap was perhaps harder than it needed to be, and the little woman fell to the floor, pinned there like a moth. But spread-eagled on the black and white tiles, she was at least quiet and behaving herself. For a moment, Benz thought of smacking the other old hag, who was screaming: *"Cette gitane est folle!"* But the pharmacist and his assistant were rushing from the back room.

"She's crazy! She's the one who fired those gunshots several months ago; remember that scandal?"

Mercedes ran out without waiting for her pills. She fully expected to be followed and arrested. But perhaps the pharmacist and his assistant saw the justice of her case—she clearly had been provoked.

When Benz got back to her room, she took off her clothes, put on her bathrobe, and ran the water in her tub. Parisians were so smug, petty, and judgmental she could scream.

There was a knock on the door. Had they come already to

question her about the incident? So soon? She turned off the water faucet slowly and remained very still.

"Gendarmerie!"

Another knock.

"Police. Ouvrez, s'il vous plaît."

"No comprendo," she whispered.

"Open up, please."

"Perdón, personne est là. La Madame est sortie."

Her doorknob turned slowly. She froze. It was Raoul Delbosc, the policeman from the Rue Rude.

"Oui?"

"I hope I am not disturbing you, Mademoiselle," he said with his *képi* in hand.

"Well, you are, actually. You certainly are," said Benz, closing the top of her bathrobe.

"My eight hours of duty in front of the embassy are over, so I came by to say hello."

For months now, Raoul had made small talk with her. It had started as a tip of his *képi* when she passed in front of the Irish Embassy and had progressed to questions about what sort of provisions she had bought at the market. He was a melancholy boy with short hair and a mustache who looked somewhat lost in his policeman's uniform. His presence was quite forgettable, and Benz usually paid little attention to him.

Today, showing a newfound boldness (she had not told him where she lived), Raoul had found her room.

"No more assailants in the middle of the night? No more break-ins?"

"No, it's been quiet. Thank you." She knew very well this was not why Raoul had come.

"Just wanted to make sure," said Raoul, nodding and retreating doorward.

He was shy and quiet; not intelligent, perhaps, but she could see he had never deceived anyone, and that was a welcome change after Sean. Staring down at his hands, he blurted out:

"I don't imagine you would want to go out Saturday evening, would you?"

Mercedes saw good tactical reasons why it might be useful, for a time, to have a policeman for a friend, and she agreed.

•

MERCEDES gave the squeeze bottle another shake and with a plastic-gloved hand, applied more of its contents to the roots of her hair.

"Benz, what are you doing? What is that you're pouring on your head?"

"Timi, leave me alone. I am busy."

Doesn't the lock on my door ever stop anyone? she thought, still bent over the washbasin. My room offers about as much privacy as the Gare Saint-Lazare at rush hour!

"I didn't know you colored your hair, Benz."

"I don't. This is just a rinse."

She picked up a comb and wiped her forehead with the back of her hand. She knew it was hopeless to ask the boy to leave; that would only make him want to stay. Timothy had developed a telepathic ability to appear at her door when she least wanted him there.

"But it says here, 'DEEP, LASTING COLORING.' Look."

Timi was holding up the bottle for her to read, but she kept her eyes closed, trying to avoid the hundred questions which this assault on her few gray hairs would bring on.

"*Chéri*, it is just for highlights. It is nothing," said Mercedes, tugging the comb through her hair.

"But it says 'BLUE-BLACK, SUPER EXTRA-GUARANTEED FORMULA."

"It is nothing, I tell you. Now be quiet!"

Tim spread some of the viscous ink-black substance on his fingers and stained his shirt.

"Benz, will this stuff wash out, do you think?"

"Leave me alone, *idiota!* I am sick of you! Napoleon is dead and you are only a snot-nose! Pretend this door is triple-locked, barred, and chained!"

With her elbows, she pushed him out of the room, and with her knees she wedged the bed against the door.

• • •

FOR their first date, Raoul was taking her to visit the apartment where he lived with his mother and his little cat, Pierre, in Sartrouville.

"It's three train changes. But in the morning, I start before rush hour, so the commute isn't so bad," explained Raoul.

Mercedes nodded. They were standing at the Etoile Métro stop waiting for a train. Across the platform, waiting on the Direction de Neuilly side, stood Sean. She knew it was Sean before even seeing his face, by the red hairs sprouting on his freckled hands. She sensed him, the way Wonderdog might lift his ears and become motionless at some barely perceptible signal. He was wearing a dark raincoat.

The signs of his recent drinking were etched on his face: his eyes were veined with red and there were dark circles under them. Good! She was happy. At least she had made him suffer, taste a little of what she had experienced! Perhaps he had not suffered as much as she, but he had that wild look on his face. Maybe he was not thinking of her at all, but of his beloved I.R.A.

"It would be better, I think," said Raoul, "if you did not mention to my mother that you intend one day to become a professional *danseuse de cabaret.*"

Mercedes nodded while staring clinically at Sean. There was nothing so special about him, really. He was a rogue with curly red hair. She put her hand on Raoul's arm. When she compared the two men, face to face like this, Raoul did not appear such a bad alternative. She let Sean stare her in the eye.

"Mercedes, I feel like a millionaire, just standing here next to you waiting for this Métro," said Raoul.

Sean's moist mouth, his undershirt smells, his night tastes were beckoning her. How many times would Fate knock on her door? And if I send Fate away this time, thought Benz, would she ever come knocking again? Should I mumble my apologies to Raoul and rush over the tracks after Sean? Would I be rushing after him all my life? The train was pulling into the station. It was a momentous decision, but she did not scream out Sean's name; instead, she grabbed Raoul and kissed him violently on the lips, until she was certain the train carrying Sean pulled away.

Raoul wiped his lips with the back of his hand and stared longingly into her eyes.

Once seated in the second-class compartment, Mercedes turned to him and snapped:

"I do not want to be a *danseuse de cabaret*, but a flamenco artist, imbecile! There is a huge difference! Your mother would tear her eyes out for a chance to see me dance."

Raoul fidgeted uncomfortably.

"And Pepe has probably already told you that I have a history of mental instability. He tells everyone that. So don't get me angry!"

"HAVE a seat, Cardozo."

Tim closed the heavy oak door and sat down on the straight-backed chair, the one with the pale velvet cushion and the carved lion's head on the armrests. High on the wall behind the Principal hung the Brunelleschi Christ with its long contorted face, expressing such pain and sadness that Tim could almost not bear to look at it.

"How old are you, Cardozo?"

"Twelve."

There was a silence.

"Cardozo, you are not our best student. But you do show a certain intellectual perseverance which is remarkable in one of your generation."

Was this meant as a compliment? You could never really tell with the Jesuits. When they were nice to you they were most likely to slap you down harder than ever. Tim stared out the window.

"I see that you are first in Religious Instruction."

Monet flipped through Tim's *carnet scolaire*, then rubbed his hands together as if to wash them: Pontius Pilate, thought Tim, staring at the peeling paint. Monet's office was even dingier than he remembered it. Outside in the hallway, footsteps echoed like the metronome on Aunt Phoebe's piano, then gradually faded.

"Why, Cardozo?"

"Why what, sir?"

"Why are you first in Religious Instruction?"

Tim shrugged his shoulders. When would he get to wear long pants to cover these ridiculously bony knees of his? No one else in class wore short pants anymore—was it any surprise that he was losing his troops?

"Isn't it amazing that this should happen to one who is consistently in the bottom half of his class in every other subject?"

"I didn't cheat. I swear it!" said Tim, jumping to his feet and looking instinctively at the crucifix for support.

Father Monet leaned over his desk and peered into Tim's eyes, down his trachea, lower intestines and into the blood vessels in the soles of his feet.

"We appreciate your zeal for the New Testament, Cardozo. But if this is the way you feel, why not try to persuade your parents to have you baptized? Otherwise your religious studies will be an empty intellectual pursuit. As you know, your class is coming up for First Communion this spring."

Tim sat back. He didn't know what to say. His Aunties had already selected the white cotton robe he would wear at the ceremony. Manola was sewing a new dress to wear for the occasion. Gerbi, Roland, and his other Monarchists had planned to sit together in the last row of pews.

"You are half Jewish?"

"On my father's side, the side the Jews say doesn't count," said Tim, digging his nails into the wooden lions on the armrests.

"Look, my friend, I know what you're going through. I commend you for finishing first in Religion. But we cannot allow you to participate in the First Communion exercises without a formal conversion on your part. It would set a bad example."

Tim's hands were shaking. He stared at the priest, who with his narrow beard and big round eyes looked like one of the El Greco saints he had seen when his mother had taken him to the Louvre. Would it do any good explain to Monet, of the Society of Jesus, that his Aunties were half gaga and went to the Protestant church on Sundays only because that was where The Ladies of Passy Literary, Knitting and Opera Society met? And that Tim went along only because he did not want to show then any disrespect?

"How about Gerbi? He's a Moslem, but you let him participate."

"Well, he is different. He's a scholarship student. His parents have appointed us his legal guardians. Cardozo, do not misunderstand. We want you in the Church. Conversion for you must be the first of the sacraments. Without it, it makes no sense to proceed with the others."

Monet tapped a fingernail on the top of his shiny desk. Roland would get dressed in white robes, and so would Gerbi, Gâche, Dhont, Bouigues. Not to mention D'Harcourt, Forrestier, Laval, Paoli! Tim, who was losing his Republican enemies as well as his own troops to Socialism, Syndicalism, and God knew what other "isms," was now going to have Christ taken away from him as well?

"Cardozo, try to understand me. Make an effort. It is too easy for a boy your age to think: 'My teachers are all stupid.' "

Tim felt like one of those deaf mutes who Benz said collected under the clock tower in Matamoros at five every afternoon.

"Cardozo, you are learning what it means to grow up. You are learning that there is much more to all this than just getting out of bed in the morning, playing with your little friends in the courtyard, and going to sleep at night. . . . Are you listening to me?"

"I don't want to kick a soccer ball all by myself," said Tim hoarsely, "while the others are inside taking their Catechism. Especially with those white Communion robes!"

The Brunelleschi crucifix had clear empty eyes like the windows of Tim's soul. Its mouth was so finely carved, so fragile, it seemed to drip with pain. Tim would tell his mother about this. She would return from wherever she was, singing her head off, would put on her gaudiest diamond necklace, flash her billion-franc smile, waltz into Monet's office, and make him dance to a different tune!

"Cardozo, don't look at me with such insolence! Have you ever heard a single word I said?"

MERCEDES was again lost in her private mists. Her absent-mindedness was becoming worse. She would lift up her head and find herself rinsing out her hair, measuring out a cup of the deepest dye. Timi would be standing there next to her, with his big expressive eyes. The next time she came to, she'd be massaging lotion into Madame's hands in the pink bathroom. Then she would gain consciousness supine on the floor of her room staring up at the ceiling. And when she did happen to look at herself in the mirror, the circles under her eyes reminded her of deep saucers with rings of dirty café-au-lait at the bottom. One day when Madame had returned from New York and was between two singing engagements, she asked Mercedes if she was sick.

"No, Madame, I am depressed."

"My poor darling! You do not dress properly, that is why!"

Cascasia clapped for her accompanist, Signor Cinquemani, to continue practicing by himself, sent away her hairstylist, asked Pepe to bring her another espresso, and rushed to her closet of operatic costumes, where she started pushing and pulling her way through a forest of velvet and taffeta gowns.

"Benz, you should go out and have a good time. Live a little!"

In the back of the closet, Cascasia found a white lace veil and a long ruffled gown she had last worn in the ball scene of *La Traviata*. The metal hoops were twisted out of shape, but Mercedes found the gown beautiful.

"Phoebe tells me that a guard from the Irish Embassy is taking you out. Well, *comment ça va*?"

"I don't know, Madame. Maybe I am too difficult. Maybe I was never meant to find anyone. I have such a terrible temper."

"Nonsense," said Madame. "Mine is much worse than yours."

Even if Mercedes were never to wear it (and she wasn't likely to, being a good two sizes larger than Madame), it was a mark of distinction just to have such a gown in her closet. Cascasia opened a hatbox and pulled out a long, sparkling silver feather boa.

"You look marvelous," said Cascasia, making her turn in the antique full-length mirror.

"Madame, I do not love Raoul."

"Here—try this," said Cascasia, putting a long sable hat on Mercedes that she had last worn in La Scala's production of *Tosca.*

"Benz, it is always better to be the one who is more loved than loving. That gives you some measure of control. God knows we women need all the power we can get."

"Yes, Madame, I can control him without problem. But I worry: what if after we marry I happen to meet someone else for whom I feel real passion?"

"Oh, Benz, that is really stunning!" Cascasia dug into the back of her closet for more hatboxes. "You will grow to love him with time. And who needs passion anyway? What is important is security, the pleasure of being desired, the gratification of a household. Now, can this Raoul fellow provide you with all this?"

Cascasia stopped to look at her little Spanish maid.

"Manola tells me my son is becoming quite a good dancer, thanks to your teaching."

"*Sí,* his hand arabesques are not bad. But he lacks the sacred fire, Madame. To be a good *flamencero,* you have to dance like blood is dripping from the walls and the carpet is in flames. Timi does not have sufficient pain for that."

"Oh, my," said Cascasia. "Thank God for small favors."

The high heels from *La Traviata* were like stilts. Mercedes was scared of falling off and twisting her ankles, but the white *I Puritani* cape made her feel chaste and Madonna-like.

"Benz, how old are you now—eighteen?"

"Almost twenty-two, Madame."

"Well, I know the boy worships you. We *all* love you very much. But he really does not need a nanny anymore. Have you thought of what you really want to do in life?"

Mercedes took off the heavy cape and the *Don Carlo* gold earrings. She felt her lower lip begin to tremble. Cascasia pulled out an old mink and draped it over Benz's shoulders.

"Don't get me wrong, we would love to keep you here forever. But you have so many other abilities."

Mercedes dug her face into the mink and cried. Madame felt her forehead.

"There, there, my baby," said Cascasia. "Oh, what big tears you have today."

Benz's soul was as flat and waveless as a frozen lake in a December dusk. Earlier in the day, she had been on the point of telling Madame of her plans for getting back into dance—either to study somewhere, or to get part-time work at a Spanish restaurant like La Venta or Chez Gorkin. But to be invited to leave—that was different.

"Benz, you cannot stay here forever. Timi will be leaving too, one day, to go to university."

Payos were all the same, sooner or later, thought Benz. They respected you only if you told them to go to hell, or if you were an internationally famous star, like Manitas de Plata. Did Madame think that she relished the thought of being a *chacha* in this gothic nightmare of a house? She didn't need anyone's charity to get a *carte de séjour.* And she would not wear this slave's uniform one more minute than was absolutely necessary.

"Now, stop those tears or you will ruin your beautiful gown."

Crying came easily to Benz and left her feeling refreshed and happy. But today, confronting the schism between her life with and without Timoté, she felt anxious and desperate. She wanted to bury her soul in this house, among these Renaissance halls full of sunlight and love. In school, when her friends had asked about her father's job, she had always been ashamed that he had none. But maybe he was right. In the work force, the unscrupulous took advantage of *gitanos,* especially if you were a woman. Alone, she and Timi were easy prey. But together, ah—he with his little squirrel brain, she with the muscle and will—they formed more than a whole person!

Already she carried the memory of the boy as if it were a diamond in her pocket. Already she missed the amoeba ladies leaving faint trails of eau-de-cologne as they bumped along the hallways; the leg ladies; the cadaver ladies; Manola's six-course meals; the daylong pyramid of dishes after Monsieur threw a party; the black-chimneyed rooftops; Pepe's guitar strumming; the rainbow prisms at dusk when she and Tim would wait for the setting sun to strike the living-room chandelier. Mercedes closed her eyes and cried.

HE lay down on his mother's bed and watched quietly. There was no possible doubt in his mind that she was the most beautiful woman in the world. Surrounded by her pianist, Signor Cinquemani, a manicurist, and a personal secretary, she was the Queen. When she returned like this, the house's daily routine collapsed. Benz, Manola, Pepe, even Wonderdog rushed around like mad insects. No one was fed, or went to bed, on time. It was a glorious chaos, a maelstrom of high C's and panic. Tall, rich, beloved, followed by extras wherever she went, his mother was an epic movie! How many years of training were needed to perfect his mother's *arpeggio-allegro* laugh? And who, with a voice like hers, needed a telephone? If she just leaned off the balcony, her arias would probably reach Australia without the aid of any cables or satellites.

Tim felt quiet in her presence. He could stare at her Romanesque nose and distant golden eyes for hours. She looked up at him from behind her desk. The stream of "love-bun"s, "daahling"s and "I love you"s gasped into the telephone speeded up to a *rapido-vivace* thumping in Tim's chest. He was not used to being stared at by the Queen. She shifted the telephone over to her other ear and said:

"Timi, you are becoming so handsome. Now, if we could only make you tall like your father."

Everything she said was so dramatic that Tim never knew

whether she was talking to him or to some movie director standing behind him operating a hidden camera. She embarked on yet another *molto-prestissimo* transatlantic conversation, her voice darting around the room like wild clarinet notes looking to be set free. Tim played with the gondolier hat she had brought him, and with the ball-point pen with the Tower of Pisa that slipped up and down its plastic cap.

Everything about her spelled success, friends, life. He walked over to her. The last time, about five months ago, her scent had been woodsy, like peat moss and pines. Today, she was more like ripe apples softening in an orchard, or fields of wind-ruffled wheat speckled with red poppies. He touched her hair.

She cradled the telephone receiver on her left shoulder and patted his triangular face as it lay in her lap, bending to smother him with perfume and kisses, but without breaking off her call.

"Tell me all your deep, darkest secrets," she whispered to him.

Tim's heart was as full and heavy as one of her traveling steamer trunks. He quickly recapitulated how Mercedes had shot the lights out in the Irish Embassy. He told her about Gerbi hiding his glass eyeball in his backside. And most important of all, he confided that when he finally grew up, he and Benz would go live together in the Bois de Boulogne: he would work for Monsieur Henri, repairing the steam-engine speedsters, and Benz would sell tickets and change the Elvis Presley records.

His mother laughed and laughed. Kissing Timi on the forehead, she interrupted the person on the other end:

"You won't believe what my son has just announced to me!"

Tim listened, horrified, betrayed, ridiculed, as she repeated his long-range plans over the phone to a stranger. He wanted to kill her!

"Yes, with the maid . . . Isn't it priceless? Just absolutely divine!"

Who was she babbling to at the other end of those thousands of kilometers of copper wires zinging and twanging across international boundaries? Some millionaire cigar-chewing producer? A famous slick-haired Italian set designer? He tried to snatch the receiver away from her. But she shouted for her pedicurist, begged Tim to fetch her something for her throat, and continued laughing into the phone.

Tim fled with the dog to the kitchen. Benz was right: if you reveal your secrets to the wind, the wind will reveal them to the trees and the trees, with their incessantly chattering leaves, will call Hollywood. How could his mother treat his confidences as just another source of gossip? Everything to her was material for chitchat. No wonder everyone she spoke to was a "daahling" and a "love-bun"—she couldn't remember their names! She was such a phony! Tim could just imagine her awaiting the guillotine: after being sentenced, she'd probably sing a little crowd-pleaser, sign autographs, and comment on the weather.

CHAPTER 6

Barbeji Nastis Jalar con Breca (or, Beauty Cannot Be Eaten with a Spoon)

SHE POINTED TO the screen, but Raoul was asleep. He did not like movies. Mercedes adored them. They had gone to the MacMahon to see *Austerlitz,* directed by Abel Gance with Pierre Mondy as Napoleon. She really should have brought Timi! Here was the Emperor in all his glory—brooding, laughing, hectoring, dictating twelve letters at the same time; here he was walking around the campfires late at night, disguised as one of his men, listening to his beloved Grenadiers and Dragoons discussing the next day's battle. Short like Timi, Napoleon had the same darting squirrel eyes.

And here was Michel Simon, playing a grizzled and wizened old sergeant. This actor had a wonderful, fold-out face, more like ancient parchment, really, than skin. In one scene Napoleon reaches up to pull Michel Simon's right earlobe. "Sorry, sir, that one I lost at Wagram." The Emperor, nodding, now reaches up to pull Simon's other ear. "Sorry, sir, that one I lost at Valmy."

Mercedes could hardly sit in her seat. The first day she had brought Timi home, in that Number 52 bus, when she'd first tasted his *goûter,* he had reached up and touched each of her earlobes. How perfect that Timi and his mythical hero should practice the same gesture of affection! Raoul grunted and shifted in his sleep. Mercedes decided not to wake him.

• • •

MASTER Tim and his two friends clattered down the spiral service staircase to the basement. The air was musty and cold. The layers of masonry grew dark and dingy as they descended to the bowels of the house.

"Cardozo, it stinks down here."

Tim stopped and flicked on the light switch. A naked bulb gave off a weary, dim light. They advanced toward rows of empty wine bottles, glistening green beneath a series of musty low arches. In a corner, the furnace growled like some mythological giant. Sparks flew from its orange mouth, throwing red and black shadows on the ceiling. Mysterious concentric circles of fear widened in the semidarkness.

Masters Tim, Gerbi, and Roland inched closer together. The bones of the early Christians buried here splintered underfoot and crunched into dust. Tim swept his flashlight into side galleries where nude alabaster bones were collected in big eerie piles. The tombs themselves were like drawers, one on top of another, on either side of narrow passageways. Tim kicked a tibia and a jaw out of the way. The rest of the cellar was crowded with statues of Romans without pupils in their eyes, opaque glass cupboards, moth-eaten plumed hats, a jungle of faded opera costumes and ostrich feathers. Tim threw a piece of coal into the furnace. It growled and flared like a hungry dog. They heard a drop of water *plop-plop* in the distance. Steamer trunks appeared in the recesses of the cellar, as well as ancient family portraits, trays of rat poison, Nazi uniforms stolen at the end of the war, and a medieval suit of armor that once had graced the foyer.

"People have come down here and *never* been seen again," whispered Tim. "Manola says this is an evil place."

Roland pulled a string on an old harp. Its twang echoed plaintive and gloomy through the eerie landscape. Gerbi sneezed. "*Whoosh whoosh*" went the furnace.

"See these little green mushrooms on the wall? At night, they open red eyes and grow tiny legs, and they start crawling—

hundreds of thousands of them. They get into the pipes. When you're sleeping, they climb out of the faucets and into your ears!"

"You're lying," said Gerbi without much assurance.

"When you wake up in the morning, they've eaten all your brains! You don't even remember your own name! All you have left is mushrooms rattling around inside your head like dice!"

Tim ran to the stairs screaming, then stopped and laughed. Neither of the others had moved. Roland was studying the innocuous green lichen that covered the moist wall. Tim coughed and wiped his sweaty palms on his shirt. Little feet scurried in the coal bins. They stood very still.

"Hey, something just fell on my head," said Gerbi.

Tim cupped his hands over his ears to block the entry of the hungry mushrooms. What had started off as a joke became—amidst this mass of Grand Cru bottles, brass bedposts, and steamer trunks—spooky and easy to believe. There was a silence. The solitary confinement of these low cellar rooms, the dust, the dingy mausoleum smells drew tightly around them. Roland tripped and fell.

"Hey, you all right? Roland, where are you?"

His friend had banged his head on something that resounded with a dull metallic thud. Tim shined his flashlight. It was a shovel partly covered in fresh dirt. He helped Roland climb out of the hole into which he had slipped. Who could possibly be digging down here, and for what purpose? Gerbi, with teeth chattering, suggested they go back upstairs.

There was a hole not far from the first which, according to Roland, was a meter wide and 50 centimeters deep. Crawling, he found another hole beyond that. Holes were sprouting all over. It was like Swiss cheese down here—A terrible hole epidemic had broken out in the Cardozo cellar!

The vapor of Gerbi's breath dissipated in the damp shadows. Aunt Agatha had once told Tim that "the City of Paris has ten floors below the ground for every floor above." He was starting to realize she was right. Roland tapped his Emperor on the shoulder and pointed to the surface of the fresh water well.

"Is that where you say you have crocodiles?"

"Well, I've never seen any myself. But Manola says *she* has, several times!"

The vapor of his breath curled into the beam of his flashlight. Tim and his two friends slipped past a pile of dusty bones that lay in spider-infested moisture. A mouse scurried along the wall. The part-American led the part-African and the one-eye through the low-ceilinged, vast system of underground galleries. Leopard spots of orange flashed from the cast-iron furnace. Shadows danced on the stone walls and across Roland's soft face. Gerbi, pointing his good eye toward one of the mysterious holes that glistened luminous and wet in the dark, shouted:

"Hey, if this digging continues, your house is going to cave in!"

Roland slowly knelt, picked up some moist cellar earth, and smelled it. Tim and Gerbi waited for his Holmesian deduction. Roland stood up at last, his eyes clean and purplish in this glowing half-light.

"On my island, we have zombies . . ."

"What are zombies?"

"The living dead. They come out at night. I've seen a couple from a distance. They used to work in the fields."

Tim felt something crawl across the back of his neck. Peering into the darkness, he could see Gerbi plucking one of the green mushrooms from the wall and biting into it.

"What do you mean 'living dead'?"

"In Haiti, our Legal Code says that anyone who revives the dead for the purpose of making them do compulsory work is guilty of murder. The peasants near our summer house are so scared of being dug up that they bury their loved ones under the macadam of the roads. That's to make it more difficult for the Voodoo priests to find them." Roland raised a knowing eyebrow.

"If you ask me," said Gerbi, swallowing the rest of the mushroom, "this is the work of Algerians—tunneling the hell out of France with their bare hands because they are too poor to pay their passage home."

A silverfish crawled along the damp wall not far from Tim's

head. The shiny breastplate of a suit of armor loomed out of the darkness as he swept his flashlight in all directions. Water plop-plopped in the nebulous depths of various unlit passageways.

"I thought I heard someone rummaging around," said Roland.

A current of helplessness wafted through Tim. The living dead? That was all they needed! He imagined the scene down here at midnight, when the suit of armor stirred, bowed low, and danced with his mother's emerald, sapphire, and ruby costume jewelry hanging there on the moth-eaten baldachin bed. A magnificent black-and-gold creature—half bee, half lizard—flew through the beam of his flashlight. He shivered.

"Gerbi, will you stop eating those filthy mushrooms!"

Gerbi's donkey-brayings of laughter echoed along the catacomb walls.

"If zombies do live down here, there's enough rat poison on the floor and frozen meat in the large freezer there to feed them for years," said Roland.

Tim gasped: What if these piles of bones were brought back to life and joined the zombies? It would be more crowded down here than in the Châtelet Métro station at rush hour! They could drink from the century-old vats of port, resplendent with mold and dust. They would never need to go to a store.

"Could it be Wonderdog digging these holes?" asked Gerbi.

"No, he's gotten so lazy in his old age, he hardly raises his leg to pee anymore."

Master Tim uncovered two copper electrical wires. He tried to follow where they led, but both disappeared into a hole in the wall at the end of the furnace room. He squashed a bug that was crawling on his cheek and decided to twist the copper filaments together. This seemed the appropriate thing to do with wires. His fingers worked quickly. Roland was busy examining a small pale blue fresco above one of the catacomb graves.

Seven floors above them, Mercedes leaned out her window. It was a soft, warm, odorous morning. For the first time in weeks, Paris was bathed in sunshine. She garlanded her arms around herself and stretched. She remembered the suitcase that

Sean had left in her closet—the last, ugly vestige of that worthless man. How extremely symbolic to someone as superstitious as Mercedes, to throw it and all her memories of him away at the same time. She emptied out its contents, including the Edward G. Robinson detonator, and with a sense of finality, stamped down upon them with her high heels as she piled Sean's leavings into the garbage. And don't you dare come back, you *salopard!*

There was a jolt of electricity through Tim's fingers. He let go. A tremendous explosion shook the house.

"Nice going!" laughed Gerbi, picking himself up off the ground.

"Hey, I didn't do a thing; I swear I didn't!" shouted Tim, as they half-ran, half-stumbled back up the spiral staircase to the courtyard.

Mercedes could hear shouts in the street. Black smoke coiled out of the Ambassador's residence like a great airborne dragon. She looked with horror at the detonator lying on its side, then ran down the service stairs, using the banister to leap five steps at a time. The Cardozo house was relatively unscathed. However, the fuse plugs had blown out, and the entire house was dark. She felt her way until she got to the driveway. The iron bars on the windows of the Irish Embassy were twisted back and bent like pretzels. Shreds of heavy gold velvet drapery floated out through the shattered windows on the second floor. The metal harp on the blue escutcheon below the flagpole was lying a block away in the middle of Rue Rude, a mere cinder. Ambassador McLuck, in his shirt sleeves, was pacing up and down in front of the entrance, chewing on an unlit pipe and shouting at his staff. They stood around him in a semicircle of striped livery.

"Holy shit, hell, piss!"

Raoul Delbosc had suffered some minor facial wounds. He was talking to the Chief Inspector now. Mercedes heard him explaining that he had seen nothing suspicious and that he had not been asleep at the time. Above the sirens and police radios and the flashing blue and white lights, she could hear McLuck's booming voice repeating:

"Holy shit! Christ!"

Timoté grabbed her:

"Benz, why are you dressed like a countess?"

Today, just for fun, she had put on her *Traviata* gown with Violetta's gold high heels and Madame's silver boa. As the initial shock of what had happened receded, she squatted with Tim behind a car and kissed him on the neck and arms.

"Timi," whispered Mercedes. "I did this!"

"No, Benz, I did it! I tied two wires together. It is all my fault!"

"But I push a handle down. I should never have touched that black box."

They stared at each other for a second with the same wild and panicky eyes. Quickly, an unspoken secret spread between them that defied explanation. It was impossible to know whether they were scared, or happy, or both.

"Shit, shit, shit, shit!!!" continued the Ambassador.

The yellow and red fire-truck lights filled the morning with a wild, flashing carnival energy. News photographers and passersby clustered behind the police barriers that were being erected around the embassy. Neighbors looked down from their balconies. Benz could imagine what they'd be whispering about her now, dressed as she was with four layers of petticoats and a silver boa at eleven in the morning!

TIMI, Roland, and Gerbi were washing their hands at the kitchen sink, using Manola's strong soap that smelled of lye. As they dried their hands, Tim asked as nonchalantly as he could:

"Pepe, are you digging holes down in the cellar?"

"No," said Pepe, without looking up from his Longchamps racing sheets.

Tim examined the man: his fingernails and shoes showed no trace of mud. Would Pepe, who had such a thorough aversion to any kind of work-related activity, lie about digging holes in the cellar?

"Here's a horse called 'Petit Derrière.' Think I should bet on him, Timi?"

Pepe didn't expect answers to such questions. And Tim returned to his room with his friends.

"You couldn't have crocodiles down there," said Roland. "Crocos are land animals. They'd have to surface for air every so often."

SHE bent to kiss him good-night. After five years of this nightly ritual, she knew by rote the meaning of his silences. Tonight it was the You're-not-going-to-get-engaged-to-Raoul pout. ("Benz, I know it's not going to work! Have I ever led you wrong before?") He was so perfectly eatable. She bit into his cheek.

" '*Barbeji nastis jalar con breca.*' Timi, in *caló* that maxim means 'Beauty cannot be eaten with a spoon.' "

"Yeah, only with a fork."

"No, it means beauty must be prized. Timi, you are becoming so handsome! You are growing into your face."

In the freezer she had found a candle broken in two and wrapped in tinfoil. The boy must have put it there (maybe she had once taught him this curse), so that Raoul's feelings for her would grow cold. How pale he became when he was depressed! And how different the good-night kiss had become, now that he was thirteen; it was like kissing a young gentleman.

"Benz, why Raoul? It makes no sense."

Mercedes pulled the skin of his temples back on both sides until she gave him cat's eyes.

"Okay, let me go. Raoul gets jealous when I spend too much time kissing you good-night."

"Good!"

She got up to leave. The boy sat up on one elbow.

"If you marry him you will never become a flamenco dancer—he won't let you! Is that what you want, to be a fat housewife for a flatfoot?"

She closed his door and tried not to listen to what the boy shouted through the wall. She ran to the kitchen, selected a bottle of Pepe's Beaujolais de Campagne and two glasses, and turning off the lights so as not to awaken Pepe or Manola, returned in the dark. She sat down at Tim's bedside and lit a small candle. For once the boy did not ask any questions. He just watched her quietly pour the two of them a drink.

"I am going to break off with that sweet, but slightly *estúpido* Raoul! Tomorrow, or maybe on the weekend, I will tell him."

Tim knew that the more Benz spoke, the more real her plans would become. She was testing them on him, and he wanted to do nothing to change her mind. She could easily decide one thing and later do the very opposite, without necessarily noticing any inconsistency.

"*Chéri,* Benz cannot work in your house forever. One day I will leave. You know I came out of my mother dancing. So I will take my skills out of the attic and dust them off. I will work night after night like a dog. And those *bastardos* who say I will not succeed as a professional dancer can all go to hell."

She poured him another glass of wine. He didn't like the taste of Beaujolais, but it was a small price to pay for hearing Benz talk, breathless, of her future, her eyes reflecting the candlelight.

"I will need money and courage. I will need you, Timi, to give me strength."

I too, swore Tim to himself as she spoke, shall become a *gitano* and a Spaniard. I shall wear brilliantine in my hair and smoke filterless Gitanes that will turn my fingers yellow and leave clouds of blue smoke behind me wherever I go. I will learn to play the guitar like Pepe so that a gadzillion rapid notes cascade from my hands. I will ride a white horse like all good *gitanos*. And when I meet a priest in the street, I will bow and kiss his ring. But after he's gone, I will spit in the gutter and invoke the memory of the Partido Obrero de Unificación Marxista, Manola's beloved POUM. And I will curse Negrín and his henchmen La Pasionaria and Jesús Hernández who sold the Republic to Moscow and murdered the gentle Andrés Nin and thousands of other anti-Fascist Loyalists. Whenever I get drunk I will raise my clenched-fist salute. And like every Spaniard I have ever met, if a stranger asks me for the shirt off my back, I will gladly give it. If Monet questions why I have suddenly become a Gypsy, I will answer: "You ignorant *payo,* why do *you* not have the *gitano* blood of El Cid and Miura bulls, San Fermín and Teresa de Avila coursing through your veins? Get a *chunanjañi* to teach you *caló* and to change you quick into a *calorró*, before it's too late!"

"So, *chéri,* I will need all the capital you can spare," said Benz. "I will sew all the clothes myself. It will save money. I will pay you back, every centime, I promise!"

Tim felt in direct contact with Benz's struggle against the narrow-minded fates. Why was her life always so full of crises? Did she attract disaster or have a certain propensity for it, the way others had a facility for languages? In her candlelit eyes, he saw ships laden with hope and hurricanes of fear and despair and bloody heroes screaming for help. He gave her what money he had, even his pocket money and the money for the mouse's food; but by the way she re-counted it, he knew it was not enough.

"Don't worry, Benz. I'll sell the best stamps in my collection. I'm bored with stamps now, anyway. I can have a hundred thousand francs for you in a month. Just trust me. You shouldn't skimp on your flamenco costumes."

MERCEDES took the Number 52 bus up Avenue Victor Hugo. When she arrived at Saint-Philippe de Passy, she found Father Monet in the library. Forgetting that there were students and other priests in the reading room, she said to him:

"Father, they say that 'the Gypsy's church was built with bacon and the dogs ate it.' But that is not true. I care very much what the Church says. Please help me."

There were various throat-clearings from other Jesuits. Monet raised Mercedes to her feet and took her out into the hallway.

"Father, these letters were all returned 'addressee unknown.' "

Monet fingered the batch of old airmail envelopes held together with a rubber band.

"Every month, through the Spanish Church, I send money to my family. But today my letters return to me in the mail! Do you think they are dead? What has happened to my brothers and sisters? Could you perhaps send them money through the Jesuits? Everyone says you are the smartest, most organized of the orders."

Monet began counting the bills in each envelope; after opening three, he closed them up and returned them to Mercedes:

"Child, keep this money. You need it more than they do."

"Oh, no, they are starving! I can afford it."

"A thousand eight hundred francs a month?"

Tears welled in her eyes.

"Child, I will put a notice in our paper, offering a reward. I will ask them to write to you giving information. Will that help you?"

Benz knelt and kissed his ring. She had meant to kiss him on the lips, but remembered he was a priest. To calm her nerves she played with her strand of imitation pearls and pulled so hard that they broke and sprinkled along the parquet floor, rolling down the hallway, disappearing into dusty cracks and niches. She and Monet crawled on their knees to gather them. She could not understand why Timoté hated this soft-petaled, flowerlike man. He was not a disciplinarian at all; he was understanding and compassionate:

"Mercedes, you have suffered enough, child. God wants you to be happy. No one says you have to be a saint to be a good Catholic."

"Father, I so want to start my flamenco career! I have already started making outfits for me and my accompanist."

Father Brouette was coming down the hall. They stood up and waited quietly for him to pass.

"My friend Raoul says that only harlots dance in cabarets."

"Then he is an ignorant man. King David had dancers. And so did wise Solomon. Dance is the loftiest, the most moving, the most beautiful of the arts."

"Look under every stone, lest a fool bite you," she agreed.

"Exactly." Monet laughed. "Look twice."

She felt strong with this priest standing next to her. He treated her as an equal and was seasoned enough to appreciate her wisdoms.

SATURDAY afternoon. The plane trees were wreathed in mid-spring fog. The horse chestnut blooms waved like miniature pink-and-white pine trees among the baby green leaves. Under a gray drizzling sky, with sparrows hopping after bread crumbs under the café-terrace awnings and with queues forming outside the fashionable movie houses, Masters Tim and Roland walked down the Champs-Elysées toward le Rond Point. Tim carried his All Nations black morocco-bound stamp album tightly under his arm. It contained the *crème de la crème* of his collection and he was scared of losing it.

Most of the philatelists at the Marché aux Timbres were old codgers with bad breath who had spent the whole of their adult lives staring through a magnifying lens. They could spot tiny imperfections in the width of perforations or in the watermark of paper a kilometer away. He had come here because Mercedes needed money; but now, standing on the edge of the open-air stamp market, Tim was panicking. He had never tried to sell anything to anyone before. In spite of the "WE BUY" signs on the stalls, he knew he was breaking some unwritten rule. The young either exchanged or purchased, but only the semisenile dealers, who had been buying stamps night and day since the War, had earned the right to sell. And Tim knew this attempted transgression would be remembered every Thursday and Saturday afternoon for the rest of his life.

Their best chance was Auguste H. Javrekian, the most kind-hearted and gaga of the old-timers. "Toutpourmoi," as he was known, was an Armenian who spent most of his time sleeping in his stall like a fat boar. Over the years, Tim, and now Roland, had purchased a small fortune from him. Often Tim had slipped one or two extra stamps into the glassine envelope without the old man noticing. Roland nudged his friend forward.

"Don't be scared."

"Roland, I don't feel particularly well today."

It was true. He needed a long drink of Vichy water to settle his stomach.

"Our forefathers were businessmen, Tim! It's in our blood. In our genes. We have a leg up on everyone else."

Tim let himself be nudged forward as far as Le Breton's display of mint 1965 French Heroes of the Resistance. From here, he could just make out Toutpourmoi's shiny bald pate and the white hairs sprouting from the end of his nose, as the man dozed with his arms over his stomach.

"Roland, have you ever really done this before?"

"No."

"But you said you had!"

"Genetically, I have. My forefathers were all traders. Anyway, buying and selling are essentially the same thing."

Tim felt vomitous.

"Hey, you have absolutely nothing to worry about, Tim! There's been a devaluation of the franc. We're in an inflationary spiral. Toutpourmoi will thank you for offering him the chance to buy back stamps. He needs to renew his stock."

"Roland, let's do this some other day."

He let Roland push him forward out of the rain and into the small booth. Toutpourmoi was snoring lightly. Each time, it seemed to Tim as if the liver-colored birthmark on Auguste's cheek—which matched the color of his veins and ran down his neck and into his shirt—had gotten bigger.

Tim tried to speak, but nothing came out. The stamp dealer stirred as Roland opened Tim's album. Stretching, Toutpourmoi smiled a beatific smile, and waved them in:

"Ah, my good, good frrrriends. I have missed you terrrribly! Look what I have just rrreceived forrr you: a mint set of big cats from Upperrr Volta!"

The stamps in question showed lions and leopards with little red mirrors for eyes. Roland took out his finest pair of tweezers and slung his pocket loupe around his neck.

"And these Rrrras-al-Khaima three-D stamps that shine in the darrrk? Perrrrfect, *non*?"

Roland cleared his throat and slipped the most expensive

stamp Tim owned from the book, a 10-franc sepia-and-ultramarine Napoleon III, and presented it to Auguste.

"My friend here has laryngitis, but he would like to know what you think of this specimen. Not that he desires to sell, of course. But we want your professional opinion."

Auguste H. took the stamp, switched on his deskside lamp, and bent over his magnifying glass. This was his most familiar pose—a halo of white silky hair around a bald cranium and a baggy brown suit that disappeared into the darkness at the back of the stall.

"Rrrripped!" said Auguste emphatically.

Tim shrieked and jerked forward to examine his prized stamp. Even with his 50× loupe, Tim could hardly see the tiny tear in the glue on the back that Auguste H. pointed to.

"You sold it to me that way last year!" said Tim, shaking.

There was a strained silence as Auguste replaced the stamp in Tim's book. Roland quickly selected Tim's second-oldest stamp, a British Penny Black, and set it on the table.

"I haven't touched that Napoleon the Third ultramarine-and-sepia since you sold it to me. Not even to brush off the dust!"

Roland stepped on Tim's foot.

"Not even to measure the perforations!"

Roland directed Toutpourmoi to the 1845 indigo-and-black U.K. stamp, filigrane offset with 13-millimeter teeth.

"Quote us a price."

"Rrreally boys, I would like to help you. I am sorrrry."

"Just look at it!" pleaded Roland.

Auguste handed back the stamp without even examining it under the magnifying glass. Another customer entered the tent. Auguste swatted a fly away from his face, shifted his weight, and tried to ignore the two boys.

"Are you perhaps interested in a new butterrrfly serrrries from Poland?" he asked the new walk-in.

But Roland continued undaunted, his voice growing louder and louder.

"How about this mint 1870 German locomotive series?"

"Not unique enough forrrr me," said Toutpourmoi.

What a thief, thought Tim, as he watched the rain slide hypnotically down the clear plastic awning. Other philatelists began to crowd into the little booth, interested in the controversy. He tried pulling his buddy aside, but Roland would not be put off. His lean, strong brown fingers continued to flip the pages of Tim's book as he extolled the virtues of perfect pre–World War II imperforate surcharged stamps from San Marino and Ifni. Old-timers smiled as Auguste shook his head.

"How about South America? What is that worth to you?"

"Not one rrradish, my friend! Not one cucumberrr."

"You haven't even looked at them!"

More rib-poking and smirking in the peanut gallery as Auguste announced he had just received a shipment from Uruguay and if the boys were not interested they should not bother him further. Old men in berets and wire-rimmed glasses leaned over Roland's shoulders to get a better view. Tim felt air bubbles forming inside him as his stomach constricted. Then Toutpourmoi did something unprecedented: he actually stood up behind his counter! For the first time in the six years Tim had been coming here, Auguste had unglued his backside from his chair, and his giant Perrier-bottle shape now towered over them. Philatelists and colleagues came running to witness this *événement*. Roland pressed his attack with a Singapore, British military occupation precancelled war-bonds series. The stall was thick with the grinning teeth of men who had nothing better to do that day. Toutpourmoi navigated toward other customers. Tim vainly pulled on Roland's arm.

"How about this 1937 Spanish Republican mini stamp?" said Roland, grabbing the old man's hand. "It was cancelled by La Pasionaria herself! Is that rare enough for you? And look at this Sons of Liberty from the U.S.! It still has traces of Jefferson's spit where he licked it! Here, feel the moisture. It was hand-carried to Paris by the Marquis de Lafayette on a billet-doux for a mulatto chambermaid Jefferson fell in love with when writing the Declaration of Independence. You can't possibly have this stamp—I know because she was my great-great-grandmother on my father's side. You can't imagine how many offers we've turned down for this one!"

Tim had never seen Roland like this before. Roland's coffee, sisal, and cotton instincts acquired from his millionaire Haitian robber-baron uncles were aflame! The usually somnolent denizens of the Marché aux Timbres were buzzing with excitement. Toutpourmoi started telling an endless war story to a man with a yellow cigarette butt stuck to his lower lip. Pushed beyond all endurance, Roland slammed Tim's morocco-covered book shut and wrenched his way out of the crowded stall.

Laughter built up behind them as they walked away. Tim wanted to hide for a week between his mattress and box springs as he heard one of them shout "Troublemakers!" But Roland would not give up. They walked from stamp booth to stamp booth offering the prize gems of Tim's collection at one-half or two-thirds off the catalogue price. For the first time in his life, Master Tim looked at his 10-franc sepia-and-ultramarine Napoleon III not as the crowning jewel of his collection, but as a square of colored paper.

"The market's tight today," said Roland an hour later. "We should wait until demand picks up. You never want to sacrifice-sell."

"What are you talking about? We couldn't *give* these stamps away!"

Exhausted, the blood brothers walked back up the Champs-Elysées. The rain had now stopped, but the sky was still overcast. The stamp market appeared only as a wrinkle of white awnings at the end of the gray avenue. The café terraces were full of Americans in their high-water pants. The Algerians who clustered around the tourists hawking rugs and ebony statuettes seemed to be having much better luck than Tim.

"It's all supply and demand," insisted Roland. "Don't you know anything about economics?"

Tim shook his head. What money would he give Benz now?

They stopped at Le Drugstore and ordered mocha-chip banana sundaes. Slowly the redness in Tim's face drained away. Never again! Or as Benz put it: "*Jamás, jamais, nunca,* never." This was the end of his business career. No matter what his gene pool contained, he would rather go hungry than suffer this embarrassment again. As he swallowed a spoonful of fresh cream, Tim decided his future: He would learn to dance flamenco with Benz. They would perform in the corridors of the Métro for coins. Or they would join the Communist Party, like Gerbi's dad. Anything was better than a career in business. Tim offered Roland the cherry from his sundae.

"Next time, you'll see—it'll be different, Tim," said Roland, who hated cherries.

Tim felt relieved: he had decided what *not* to do in life. Surely that was as important as knowing what you wanted to do.

"You know, Benz is in real financial trouble."

"Don't worry, your Mercedes likes to self-dramatize."

"What do you mean, Roland?"

"She loves crises. That is her nature. You have to accept it. She is a semihysteric."

Tim was silent, for he had heard these words before from Pepe.

THE Cardozo Aunties were in the habit of examining Timothy's school books and notebooks from time to time. It did not take expert psychiatric skills to decipher the airplane and Napoleonic doodlings in the margins and reach certain conclusions as to how the boy was progressing and how much of his mind was on his studies.

This particular day, Agatha and Phoebe were in violent disagreement about what to make of their most recent discovery concerning their grandnephew's marginal notes. Phoebe was for immediately calling the boy's father in Hollywood. Agatha, who generally took a less drastic view of the world (except when it concerned pigeons and the washing of dirty buildings), was for calling in the Principal of Tim's school and discussing the matter with him over a nice cup of tea. They decided to compromise by calling Mercedes in and confronting her with the evidence. They rang the silver bell.

Mercedes knew something was wrong. When she entered their room, the Aunties did not smile, nor did they look her in the eye. She waited for Phoebe to speak.

"Now, you know, child, we never pry into your personal affairs. And we do not care how you spend your free time."

What had the silly boy done now? Told them about Sean's bomb? Mercedes sighed and poured the tea that had spilled into Agatha's saucer back into her cup.

"The most efficient way we know of keeping tabs on Timothy is through his doodlings."

Mercedes leaned over the desk and recognized Tim's history notebook. Phoebe flipped through the front pages, and pointed at Tim's blue Spitfires and red Messerschmitts. A few pages farther on, he had drawn a Brunelleschi crucifix. Then toward the middle, she stopped at a page titled:

POSSIBLE HUSBANDS FOR MERCEDES

Mercedes did not bother to read the entire list, which started with Monsieur Henri, Ambassador McLuck, Raoul.

"We realize the boy loves you very much, child. But what bothers us is that beneath all the names, beneath Rothschild and Gregory Peck, he has added his own to this list and underlined it twice."

Mercedes blushed.

"Oh, I am twenty-two," she said nervously. "Timoté is only thirteen. When I was his age, I dreamed of marrying my brothers. Most of my *calorró* girlfriends and cousins were married by thirteen."

There was a silence. She had a feeling she had not said the right thing.

"Mercedes, if you are looking for a husband, we would be happy to help you find one."

"Oh, no. Thank you. I am fine. These doodlings of Timi are not serious, I promise you. He has a hyperactive imagination, that is all."

Agatha got up out of bed and took a long sip from her weak Lapsang souchong tea.

"There, Phoebe, now you have caused enough trouble. Let the poor darling get back to work. Mercedes, don't worry your little head about this anymore."

Mercedes left the Aunties arguing with each other. When she put her ear to the keyhole of their door, she heard Phoebe say:

"I just do not want this to go unaddressed, Agatha. Timothy is at the age where these things become questions in his mind."

Pepe was lumbering down the hallway; Mercedes quickly stood up and disappeared in the opposite direction.

MERCEDES let Tim lead her along the pebbled path of the Bagatelle polo grounds, where Mr. Cardozo owned a stable and kept several Arabian ponies. The light, though trembling with falling leaves, was still warm. She loved the smell of leather and polish. They did not visit often, once a year at most, but she felt at home here, happy among the riders' silk jerseys—royal blue, mauve, yellow, turquoise, black, red, and orange—hanging up to dry. Mercedes loved to watch this grooming ritual and would often stand in the doorway to some stable, staring at the noble animals in their stalls, their hindquarters ripe and shiny like oversized Anjou pears. Today, as trainers carted about bridles and leggings, she stopped and looked at her reflection in a water trough.

"Come on, Benz, you're beautiful."

"Oh, no, my nose is too big! I should buy one of those nose straps to make it smaller."

"Leave it alone, Benz. Your nose is just fine."

"Oh, Timi, God gave pants to those who have no backsides."

"What is that supposed to mean?"

Benz sniffed at the fresh October air full of horse smells.

"Timi, I cannot explain why, but for Gypsies, the horse is very special, almost a sacred animal. We reserve our greatest affection for *gratés*. Not only are they smart, but they permit us to travel lightly and to escape. They symbolize freedom."

Gerbi worked part time in the Cardozo stables, shoveling manure, but he was not here today. How she loved this expanse of polo green with the upright goalposts so white and crisp, this leisurely promenade through the endless rose gardens of Bagatelle. They watched an old painter apply shades of red to a small canvas with a one-hair brush. That was the way Mercedes wanted to paint her soul, centimeter by centimeter, as if painting a single rose.

"Benz, what does that mean, 'God gave pants to those with no backsides'? Does it mean God is nuts?"

"No, it means that if you are in a desert and need water, you will find pearls instead. You always get what you do not need."

She selected two white lounge chairs by the clubhouse, and they sat down. Dazzling white clouds hung over the manicured carrot-green field. A waiter appeared with a folded napkin over one arm. Mercedes ordered two *menthes à l'eau*. Tim lit a match. She wanted to tell Timi he should wait until she pulled out a cigarette first, but he was such a little gentleman when he did this that she chose not to hurt his feelings.

"Benz, there are lots of classy men at this club. This is where you should husband-hunt, not on Wagram!"

Mercedes was not certain of the etiquette required among these blasé sophisticates. She watched a red-haired man out of the corner of her eye. Upon closer inspection, he was definitely not Sean, but it was amazing how many men looked like him of late.

Riders took to the green. Beautiful black and dappled stallions pranced and tugged at their bridles. Mercedes felt like one of those horses, eager and straining to start the race. She was primed, she was ready. For years she had been preparing for just such a sun-shot day when a horseman with a sure hand would get on her back and tame her, one who would still love her and want her and depend on her after the race.

"Benz, do you still love Sean?"

"Of course not," she lied.

She removed the floppy white hat that she had made for this occasion out of the cup of a bra (size 95), sheer gauze, and a brim of muslin. She did not feel out of place or shy, but fortunate to be among these moneyed couples who strolled by, discussing Antibes. What poetic justice it would be to return one day to Matamoros with a husband whose car was so long it would not fit on the main street. How the *payos*, the ones who spat on Gypsies in the street, would grovel then! An elderly gentleman smiled at her. Mercedes returned his compliment, raising her eyebrows and trying not to show the gold teeth in the back of her mouth. Men are April when they woo and December when they wed, she told herself.

"Benz, see anyone here you like?"

"No, not really."

The man who had smiled at her passed by, tipping his hat. She did her best to ignore him this time.

"Timi, men are like toilets: Either they are occupied or they are full of *merde*."

"Benz, I never know when you're being serious."

"Neither do I."

"Are you still hunting for a husband? Or what?"

"In summertime, one should not forget winter."

She looked over the group of seemingly unattached men lounging around the club, waiting for the polo match to start. How to go about meeting them? Would they judge her on the basis of her substatus of servant? She was not what she wanted to be, not yet. And she was not interested in the sort of man who would typically be attracted to a common maid.

"*Bonjour, Mademoiselle.*"

She suddenly recognized the gentleman who had passed and tipped his hat to her. He was the Baron Isidore de Rothschild, who in March, at Monsieur's dinner party, had pinched her cheek when she had stood in the foyer taking his coat. How flattering that he should now bow politely and seat himself at a nearby table. She breathed in deeply and rotated her right hand in front of her bust as if to indicate that she was filling her chest with the horse-rich air of this Saturday afternoon. How nervous she was! Men noticed that sort of thing. Timoté certainly did:

"Benz, are you all right?"

She continued her breathing exercises and, so as not to be overheard by the Baron, quickly signaled to Tim with her left index finger. Tim leaned over to see where she was pointing. He saw no one of any importance—only a fossil chewing on his dentures and staring at Benz through a myopic lopsided grimace caused in part by a monocle in his right eye.

"That old skeleton, Benz?"

"Oh, yes, the air is so invigorating!" said Benz loudly. Then, as she coughed, she whispered the Baron's name and that of his bank. Tim was unimpressed:

"Benz, that chowderhead could be your grandfather! He looks like something left over from the Ice Age."

"Oh Timoté, do not be so narrow-minded!"

"Better to be narrow-minded than to have no mind at all!"

"You wanted me to find someone with *categoría, non*?"

"But the Baron's not going to marry you."

"How do you know? Ever see *My Fair Lady*? I am much prettier than Audrey Hepburn. At the end Eliza turns out to be *une grande dame*. And her accent was ten times worse than mine!"

"That was a movie, Benz! This is real life."

"You are always jealous of anyone I become interested in."

"Benz, the Baron has one foot in the grave!"

"When you reach puberty, we shall discuss this again."

"Well, how is your dear father?" asked Isidore, digging himself out of his lounge chair and trying to start a conversation with Mercedes through the boy's intermediary. Tim pretended not to hear the question.

"Answer him, you fool," whispered Benz. The snotty boy was so contrary when he wanted to be!

With his pearl tiepin, two-tone spats, and top hat, the Baron was not just a man, he was a vanishing way of life! She loved the turn-of-the-century affluence exuding from his pink boutonnière. Gypsies accorded enormous prestige to old age. A plaintive "*Soy puri, soy pureta,*" meaning "I am old, I am ancient," aroused nothing but respect in Matamoros. No Gypsy dared laugh at the infirmities or disabilities of old age. Mercedes knew that if Tim continued, a curse from the Baron might bring him seven years' bad luck.

"Timi, *por Dios,* do not be a snot-nose or I shall slap you."

What topic of conversation should she broach? Benz kept windmilling her right hand in front of her face. Yes, he was old, but he was a gentleman in the best sense of the word. If she squinted, he fit quite nicely into the pattern she had established for the perfect male: gentle, smart, tall, dignified, honorable. (And he was probably a devil in bed.) But was he trustworthy and loyal? Would he know when to look deeply into her eyes and hold her, just hold her, as dusk grew into night?

"How is your lovely mother? As beautiful as ever?"

She knew the boy had heard the question and was only pretending to stare at the horses in the distance. She also knew that the Baron could repeat himself fifty times and Tim would still not acknowledge his presence or that of his chauffeur. The latter was also quite handsome. He stood behind Isidore wearing goggles atop his black leather cap; a double-breasted tweed overcoat swept down to his ankles.

"Madame Cardozo is more beautiful than ever!" said Mercedes, surprised by how well she could imitate Madame's swan-necked telephone voice.

"Cardozo, what a beautiful nanny you have," said the Baron.

The boy blew his cheeks out. He pretended to whistle, but he did not know how; Benz knew that he did this to indicate his total lack of interest in the conversation. She was sick of this charade. If the Baron would not talk to her directly, she would talk to him! And so, fanning herself with her bra-cup hat (which to her great pleasure was attracting jealous stares from many of the *Madames*) and checking the pins in her hair, she risked everything on one unservantlike comment:

"Baron, they say that God created Eve out of Adam's rib so that he would not have such *ennui*. A lot has gone wrong since then, but at least no one has had *ennui*!"

The Baron laughed, nodded gallantly, and ordered them another round of drinks. She had won the first skirmish. Why did she not speak plainly for once in her life? Why not just tell this banker of her plans and ask him to finance her flamenco troupe? She would sign over her maid's soul and *chacha* life as collateral for the loan. And then, like a cherry tree that blossoms in spring, she could at long last declare herself.

Mercedes was happy: the thud of hooves on the crisp turf, the ladies in their deck chairs sipping tea, the swift charges of horses up and down the field, the waiters' gold buttons polished mirror-bright, the white mallets swinging at the bouncing ball, the nostrils snorting in mid-gallop. How easily she could get used to this life! She giggled at something the Baron said. The only problem with being happy was that happiness was written in disappearing ink. She did not really listen to Isidore or remember what he said; she just indulged herself in the moment. The boy pulled at her elbow. He was standing at her side.

"What is it, Timoté?"

"We're late. We have to go now."

"No, no. We're not late," said Mercedes to the Baron with a broad smile. "Don't listen to him." Then, as she pretended to clear her throat, she whispered, "Sit down, you little fool. You're going to ruin everything!"

But the boy would not sit down. He nodded toward the exit.

"Dinner'll be waiting for us. I don't want you to get in trouble for keeping me out so late."

"I really do not know what he is talking about," said Mercedes, giggling. "It is only six o'clock. We never eat before seven-thirty. Sometimes eight!"

"But it's a long way home. There's a lot of traffic. And we have to wash up and change," insisted the boy, in a loud voice.

Would he never shut up? Mercedes lifted her drink to indicate that she had to finish it before they would be ready to leave. Turning away from the Baron, she whispered:

"You *consentido* brat. I will rip your vocal cords out when we get home."

When she put her mind to not drinking a drink, she could be as slow as a sloth tasting arsenic. She clutched this 25-centime glass of tap water and mint concentrate with its two ice cubes as if it were her lifeline. She could tell Timi was itching to make a scene here. She shot him the most brittle and terrifying wild-horse eyes she had in her repertoire of stares.

"My limousine can take you," said the Baron, motioning for his chauffeur to pay their bill.

What could she do now to recapture their easy flirtatious laughter? She gripped her glass tightly to keep from breaking it against the boy's head. He was so selfish! How many times would she have the luxury of enjoying this inspired swish-swish of silk gowns and new-fashioned hats (none of which was as eye-catching as her own)? Only thirteen and already the boy was such a martinet! Would she ever have sufficient saintliness and *paciencia* to teach him how to be civilized, if not charitable?

"Oh, we don't need your car. We've already called a taxi," lied Timoté.

This was the last straw. She felt as if she had just swallowed a liter of black coffee, enough to jump out of her socks and strangle the boy! The Baron helped her on with her coat. She selected the biggest smile she could find as he bent to kiss her hand. And out of Bagatelle they fled, Adam and Eve chased from the garden. The only original sin in this case was that she put up with Timoté's outrageous behavior, she thought, hurrying through the parking lot.

"I am not your possession, your—your chattel! You traitor! The minute I have fun, you ruin it for me!"

"Benz, the Rothschilds are Jewish."

"So what? It is absolutely none of your business! You are not my father! You are only a cross I have to bear for a short while —an increasingly short while, believe me."

"You're Catholic, Benz. He would never marry you."

"That is not up to you to decide! I am a big woman. Bigger than you!"

"Benz, you deserve better, that's all."

"Oh, that much is for certain!"

She tapped her long red fingernails against her black handbag. Yelling at him was never as effective as the silent treatment. She would give him two hours of silence; no, two days! He would die—it served him right! She watched the boy wave at passing taxis.

"Benz, I want to find you a movie star with a house full of hummingbirds, thousand-nozzled sprinklers going in all directions, one who really cares for you."

"Yes, Rothschild does not own enough hummingbirds for me. Thank you, Timi. Thank you." Too disgusted to talk to the boy, she applied fresh lipstick.

"Benz, I only did it for your own good."

"You say no male is good enough for me. But why? What

you want is for me not ever to find anyone! That is what you want—to, to, to make certain that you have me all to yourself!" Tears welled up in her eyes. "I cannot stand your jealousy, Timi. You are worse than any grown man I know!"

A bus stopped and she reluctantly followed Tim onto it.

"Benz, I'm sorry. I didn't mean it."

"But you do it all the time! And then to say no to his offer of a ride home! That was spiteful! Oh, I hate you!"

A group of American tourists climbed onto the bus. They wore the regulation white socks, checked double-knit pants, and Cadillac-winged glasses that Tim always ridiculed. For once, Mercedes ignored them. Was it too late to jump into a taxi, go back to the club, and take the Baron up on the offer of his limousine?

"I spend my whole life looking after you. And the minute I start thinking about my own miserable existence, you do not allow me! Timoté, I am not just a *chacha*! I have a soul! You are an egomaniac and you are never going to become a great man if you cannot understand how I feel right now!"

What about my newfound Baron? thought Mercedes. Was he, at this very moment, sitting in his leather-padded kingdom on wheels, alone, smelling the lingering fragrance of the red rose she had plucked for him just as they were saying goodbye? Love is more a matter of the imagination than anything else. And she coined her first saying out loud:

"Imagination colors and perfects love's reality."

"What did you say, Benz?"

"Nothing."

"Benz, the Baron can have any woman he wants! He's a multigazillionaire with a girlfriend in every city. Why would he want you?"

"Because his wife just died. Because he thinks I am beautiful. Because he needs someone to take care of him in his old age. Because I am intelligent—too intelligent to be wasting my life with you. Don't touch me."

"He wants to *use* you, that's all."

"Where did you hear that expression? Huh? You know nothing! I *want* him to *use* me. That is exactly what I want—for him to use me as I like, and not to *mis*use or *ab*use me, like you do!"

"I abuse you?"

"Yes. All the time! Now be quiet. I have a raging headache, and I am not ready to forgive you yet. Maybe in several years."

CHAPTER 7

Flamenco Dancing and the Art of Saying What You Don't Mean

MERCEDES STRAIGHTENED HER black uniform and went to answer the door. It was Father Monet. He had shaved off his beard and looked younger, with full, sensuous lips and the same dark intellectual pouches under his eyes. Monet smiled broadly and asked:

"Child, why have you not come to confess yourself to me?"

"Because, Father, I am without sin," she said, winking at him with both eyes.

She knew the Aunties had their hearing aids turned to maximum volume, so she took his raincoat with lowered eyes and ushered him to the salon, where the Aunties were awaiting him. She watched Monet stare at the sumptuous *trompe-l'oeil* Renaissance bookcases. How quiet and awed newcomers always were when they first entered this house!

Later, when Mercedes brought in the silver tea service, she noticed that the Aunties had Timoté's history notebook open to the page where the boy had made a list of prospective husbands for her. She blushed. Father Monet was in mid-sentence:

"Oh, no, I would love a chance to talk to Timothy. He is, quite frankly, an enigma for me. I have the feeling he resents my authority and, for that reason, is not overly fond of me. But I would consider it an honor to act as his legal guardian. Provided, of course, that the boy accepts. He is quite strong-minded, you know."

Mercedes paused by the piano, pretending to dust the keys. But out of the corner of her eye, she saw Raoul walking down the hall with his police notepad open, making his daily security rounds. She had assiduously avoided him for weeks now ("Raoul, we are 'together, but not scrambled,' as they say in Andalusia"), and so she hurried back to the kitchen.

When Father Monet left, Mercedes rushed to help him on with his raincoat. As he had the first day he met her, he touched her cheek gently:

"You have such expressive, Mary Magdalene eyes, child."

Her father used to say that Jesuits were so crooked, they used a corkscrew for a ruler, but Monet's tone of voice was reassuring, not flirtatious at all. She did not flinch when he looked deep into her soul. This was what Mercedes wanted from a man: to be inspired! If he was in love with Mary Magdalene, then she would gladly be his Mary, and she would look as saintly-innocent or as wild and sluttish as he needed her to be. There was something protective and reassuring about this man of God. And yet, she thought, a man in a hurry to get into heaven would not stand here staring at me so long.

"We shall try to keep Timi on the right path," said Monet, flipping through the pages of the boy's blue notebook.

"Oh, he is an excellent child! You will find none better in all the world!" said Mercedes, her bosom rising as immense as Saint Peter's dome.

Claude Monet of the Society of Jesus nodded and walked toward the Elevator from the Year One.

"The boy is terrible with his accents. Have you noticed he gets his *aigus* and *graves* forever mistaken."

"So do I," snapped Mercedes, who did not allow even the slightest criticism of Tim. "I tell him to just put all the accents in a little matchbox and sprinkle them over his compositions here and there like salt on a roast, *non?*"

The elevator strained mightily and began to carry the Principal down. She saw him smile and bow to her, then disappear.

• • •

HOW many times had Master Tim made this labyrinthian trip before? He trudged down to the courtyard, across the cement soccer field, around the basketball hoops at the far end, down the dingy hallway. This time, he could think of nothing he had done wrong. He opened Monet's heavy door. The familiar Brunelleschi crucifix welcomed him with open arms.

"Cardozo, pull up a chair."

Tim did as he was told and stared out the window at the courtyard he had once ruled. It was hard to fire his imagination with the smell of gunpowder and the sound of thousands of boots marching when only three followers were left to him. This was his Elba, his Saint Helena.

"Cardozo, when you sing our hymns, you show me a face that is so pure, a high voice so incapable of sin, that I ask myself, Where have we gone wrong? Why doesn't this boy trust us?"

The only thing Tim could really still count on at Saint-Philippe was Pamplemousse, his winged horse. With an ageless steed like that, all was possible: he could jump out Monet's window and leap into the gray light, with the fragments of shattering glass flying silver and gold all over the courtyard; land in the saddle; and gallop hellbent-for-leather across the plains of Central Europe.

"Jesus was more concerned with the one lamb that strayed than with the ninety-nine others who remained in the flock. Cardozo, you identify too much with Napoleon. What would happen if you were to direct all your energy and imagination into the worship of the Emperor Christ?"

The boy shrugged.

Brunelleschi's Christ would never have said anything so ignorant. First, Bonaparte was the only man who had done anything right in France. Europe had come of age in 1804 with his coronation. That was why Tim, like most Frenchmen, had a nineteenth-century soul. The twentieth century belonged to the Americans. And with their loud high-water pants and electrodes bulging in their crotches, they were welcome to it. Second, Tim did not think he identified too much with Napoleon; he thought he identified with him too little! The chestnut wars had essentially come to an end. No one called him "Emperor" anymore, unless it was with a smirk. He had no bodyguards, no throne room; no more Chief of Protocol, bowing to announce the visit of some foreign ambassador.

"Your great-aunts have asked me to act as your surrogate legal guardian in your parents' absence. If you are agreeable to this suggestion, your wishes concerning First Communion and the other sacraments can now be fulfilled—under my supervision, of course."

Tim looked at his palms. Monet was expecting some spontaneous cry of joy on his part. But the Aunties had gotten everything wrong. The time for First Communion had been a year ago, when Roland and the others dressed in their clean white robes with the lovely hoods and trooped off two by two to the chapel, while Tim stood there like a heathen and watched, hands deep in his pockets. What was the point of going through the mumbo jumbo litany now by himself?

As Tim sat staring up at the tortured face of the crucified Galilean, all he could think about was the fact that although almost fourteen, he was still not allowed to wear long pants. Being denied TV and chewing gum by the Aunties was nothing in comparison with not having long pants (even though Forrestier said that if you chewed gum hard enough, your jaw would become as square and strong as Terry's in *Terry and the Pirates)*. What were the Aunties waiting for—for him to die of old age?

"Cardozo, your generation and mine are like two trains going in opposite directions. We're allowed a moment or two, if we're lucky, when the passengers can get out and chat to each other, a sort of way station of the soul. But it is all too brief. I do not want to miss this opportunity to get to know you."

Claude waited for an answer. Tim stood up. It was time now. Time to be quiet and walk slowly to the door. Time to put one's hand silently on the heavy brass handle and wait for Monet to say:

"Cardozo, there's something else. I must also ask you to exclude that Spanish girl, Mercedes, from your intimate thoughts. It is not good for a boy your age to concern himself too much with persons of the opposite sex. I say this for your own good. Remember, we are all quite alone without God."

The Principal handed Tim back his history notebook. He did not have to mention the list of Benz's husband candidates; it was all the more devastating if he kept quiet. Saint Ignatius of Loyola, founder of the Society of Jesus, had said: "Give me a child until he's seven and he's mine." Tim was already twice that age.

"Don't take her into your confidence. I mean, it's touching that you care for her so much, but she has her own life to lead. Act as if she means nothing to you and you nothing to her. It will be better for both of you."

A light private smile floated over the wooden crucifix' mouth. That Brunelleschi sculpture was no doubt hung behind Monet for the express purpose of belying everything the Principal said. It made perfect, twisted Jesuitical sense. How many guilty, semi-innocent, wrongly persecuted, or simply frightened boys had spoken to the mute Christ and received a private answer from those clenched fingers and bitter lips? Tim walked out into the hallway with his throat cramped and dry.

MEN and women live in different time zones, thought Benz, counting the stitches in her knitting. The Baron had not called since that fateful day of husband-hunting at Bagatelle. To Benz, "Call you soon" meant "tomorrow," if for some reason it couldn't be today. But to a man, especially to Isidore, it could mean six months, if she was lucky.

"He's not a baron, he's a goat," said Pepe, who sat in the kitchen poring over his racing sheets.

"But they say an old goat needs a young pasture with fresh grass," said Manola, scrubbing a pot.

Benz grew depressed and irritated at the public debate concerning the Baron's behavior. Raoul entered the kitchen, unannounced. Since the explosion at the embassy, the police had tightened security considerably.

"Sorry to interrupt, but I have to check all *cartes de séjour*," he said opening his daybook and wetting the end of his pencil.

There was a strained silence. Manola experienced a little fainting spell and went to lie down. Pepe downed his glass of Médoc and said he had to fetch medicine for his wife. This left only Mercedes, busily knitting yet another sweater for Timoté.

"You know I have to report you," said Raoul.

"No comprendo francés," said Mercedes, lying with big angelic green eyes.

"Last year you spoke perfectly good French! And even though you treated me extremely badly, I am going to be as impartial as I can with you. You're illegal in France and I must do my duty. I have no choice."

Mercedes poured him a glass of red wine and considered methods of escape. The Aunties would die! *Quel scandale!* She had laundry waiting to be dried in the first-floor *lavanderie,* but Raoul made her sit down. His pencil point broke. She fetched him another pencil from the kitchen cabinet where she kept her shopping accounts. When in doubt, give men wine; it confuses them and slows them down. She poured him another glass.

"Do you want to make a statement?" asked Raoul, brushing back his mustache. "Anything you say, of course, will be written down and used against you."

Her attempted smile was not overly successful. Outside, a low ceiling of misty clouds threatened rain. Across the inner courtyard, above the Irish Embassy—sandblasted and shiny—the tip of the Tour Eiffel disappeared in fog. Mercedes was honey-tongued only with her arms and legs. Her dancing could speak directly to men's groins and souls as her words could not. Staring Raoul in the eye, challenging him to watch, she started a hard staccato hand-clapping.

"What are you doing? S-s-stop that!"

Mercedes closed her eyes and began to swivel slowly on her heel, tapping her left toe as rapidly as she could. Her body movement was at first imperceptible. For lack of a long-stemmed rose, she bit her 18-karat gold chain.

"Do you hear me? I said for you to stop!"

She let out a deep-bellied groan, pulled a green-and-red dish towel off the stove door handle, and wrapped it around Raoul's neck in the Gypsy nuptial fashion. This quieted him. With each rhythmic stamping of her heel, she felt more in command, less alone: the room was filling up with old smells, churches flooded with sunlight, barefoot *jayipí* children with runny noses, flowered balconies, matted hair. She raised one hand snakelike above her head, while the other twisted behind her back. She was dancing for her life. She was dancing to avoid being returned to Matamoros in disgrace. Raoul, the *sale flic* with the clean face, sat on a white chair and stared at her, his mouth slightly open, a curious grin lighting his eyes. Pepe and Manola reappeared in the kitchen as if by magic.

They were cowards, but at least they had not totally abandoned her, she thought. Pepe started picking at his guitar ever so lightly and tenderly. She fixed her senses inward, serious and hard. Flamenco demanded every ounce of concentration she had. The guitar notes raced one after another and cascaded onto the floor. She could recognize in her *zapateado* Miura bulls, neighing horses, sour oranges, red-tiled roofs, and sweet thyme. These allies made her strong.

"What's going on here?" asked Tim, galloping in from school and taking his *cartable* off his back. Manola whispered in his ear. The boy immediately picked up the bottle of wine and poured Raoul another glass.

Mercedes reached beyond the kitchen to the mansard rooftops and the black chimneys of Paris. Her arms touched the Arc de Triomphe and the smoggy sky beyond it. In one flowing movement, so that Raoul could not interrupt, she got up on the round kitchen table. Her eyes caught Tim's as he was sneaking a sip of Bordeaux. Her hair flew around her face. She arched her back like a brood mare and turned her hips to the four winds. The boy banged time with two spoons and twirled his wrists in arabesques the way she had taught him.

The front doorbell rang. It rang three times before Timothy trotted impatiently down to answer it. A tall, immaculately dressed chauffeur stood in the hallway, leather elbow pads on his tweed driving coat, goggles perched atop his racing cap. Tim immediately recognized him as Rothschild's chauffeur, but pretended not to. The man clicked his heels in a military salute and said:

"I wish to speak to Mademoiselle de los Angeles."

"She's busy," said Tim, starting to close the door.

"Then kindly give her this."

The chauffeur handed him a small pale blue envelope with initials embossed on the back. Tim opened it and read the calling card out loud:

> "The Baron Isidore de Rothschild, Senior, would desire the pleasure of Mademoiselle's company tonight. Dress is casual-to-intimate. The chauffeur will await your response. Signed—Hébertot, Personal Secretary to His Excellency, the Baron.

A bubble of gas escaped from Timi's backside. If only he could control the blasting from his nether regions like Gerbi, he would really give this natty chauffeur the response of a lifetime!

"I doubt she's interested," said Tim, again starting to close the front door. "But if she is, she'll send one of her peons. And tell His Moneyed Highness that any further communications with the Señorita should be addressed to me personally, her social secretary. You see, she's extremely busy."

He quickly closed the door and waited for the chauffeur's footsteps to disappear. Then he tore up the invitation and flushed it down the toilet. Who did this Baron think he was, anyway? Tim imagined "casual-to-intimate" meant that Isidore would be sporting nothing but a riding crop and a monocle. He ran to the front balcony to make certain that the impudent chauffeur was indeed vacating the premises. Then he galloped back to the kitchen.

Benz was raising one leg, then the other up high as Pepe picked a thousand notelets on the guitar and chased them, like little mice feet, up one's spine and down one's nerve endings. Manola stood by the door, clapping.

"AIE! AAAAAAAIIIIIIIEEEEEEEEE!" (When Benz started aie-aieing, she could go on for hours!)

The wine was burning Tim's stomach. Pepe drummed his

shiny rosewood guitar with his right thumb, while picking the strings with his fourth and fifth fingers. Raoul burped and held out his glass for Tim to refill.

"AAAAAAAAAA! AAAAAAAAAAAIIIIIEEEE!"

Tim took two swigs from the bottle. He examined Benz's long earrings and shiny hair through the thick green of the wine bottle. She swirled and turned on herself, one leg after the other, with the energy of fifty women. Her lilac-and-rose beauty spots were pearled with sweat. The music threaded itself like a transforming mist in the pit of Tim's stomach, up his throat, and along the electrical current of the house. Her flamenco had that trancelike attraction for Tim; it was like standing at a precipice where the first urge was always to jump.

"AAAAAAAAAAAAAAAAAAAAAAAAAAAAAAA!"

Tim took off his shoes and climbed up on the table. His throat was on fire from the Bordeaux. He stamped his feet. Each vein echoed a hundred strings. Each heartbeat was another thump on the lacquered rosewood guitar. Tim was no longer an American, part Emperor, part liar *sans-pareil,* part *boulevardier exceptionel.* No, he was El Cid, Don Quixote de la Mancha, Cabeza de Vaca, and Manolete! He was the *numero uno* male dancer of Cádiz, Málaga and places south! He was sailing in the crow's nests of the *Pinta, Niña,* and *Santa Maria.* The whole kitchen moved with balletic arm movements and minute strumming. The dance critics of the future were already jamming the wings to get an interview.

Mercedes knew Timoté was there, twirling beside her on this kitchen table. Tim was perhaps the only other person in this city who understood that for her, dancing was not only freedom, but at this moment, survival. And so what if she was slightly overweight and had not danced in front of an audience in six years? Let those fashionable French skeletons on spaghetti legs go to hell, she thought; I know what men like and what they look at, as Raoul is looking right now, and it certainly is not whether I can win a hundred-meter dash. She saw the sweat flick off her hair and land on his lips. She was thinking of *ganaderos* with bull farms as large as the Bois de Boulogne who offered millions of pesetas to their favorite Salomes. She was being inseminated by a river-sky of notes. The music was changing, swallowing her and flowing between her thighs like a typhoon. She rode its leaping back, a hundred times higher than the Paris rooftops, lifted into the clouds, arms and legs pinned down to the mast of a galleon. She was flying, falling, surrendering to the plum-colored waves. For Benz, flamenco was a voyage of discovery, a trip to that from which there is no return, an attempt once again to find what lies naked and alone at the heart of one's soul.

"GITANA PURA, DA ME UN BESO!" she shouted hoarsely.

Manola waved for Benz to stop: Raoul was snoring. "Let's throw the bastard into the snake well before he wakes up," said Pepe, wiping his forehead with a handkerchief and putting his guitar aside.

Manola lifted one of Raoul's eyelids to make certain he was not feigning his condition. Master Tim continued to dance by himself on the table, without music. His head throbbing with red wine, he belched and made airplane noises:

"Benz, I'm strafing the German positions on the Normandy beaches."

"If we kill Raoul, the house will be crawling with police," said Mercedes.

Tim raised his arms at his sides like airplane wings. Climbing the sky, he banked on a cottony cloud, swooped low over an enemy position. He could not stop hiccuping.

Pepe, Manola, and Mercedes carried Raoul to Master Tim's bed, as it was the nearest to the kitchen. They loosened his tie and removed the jacket of his uniform. Tim felt his wine-soaked *goûter* coming up. Clutching at his throat, he made one last daring sweep around the room, batting his arms, opening his bomb-bay doors to drop his payload—on target—into Raoul's dress-blue *képi.* As he banked steeply out of the room and climbed the main house stairs, he heard Manola scream at him for ruining "*el Capitano*'s" hat. Master Tim flew low to conserve fuel lest he have to ditch his Spitfire in the Channel. Faint with battle fatigue and mad, unstoppable hiccups, he swooped below the clouds and made for a narrow landing strip.

Hearing a slight commotion, Phoebe put on her bifocals and

was surprised to make out Tim sleeping on Wonderdog's rug between her bed and Agatha's. The poor growing boy was so tired! She decided to let him sleep.

HE'S coming in half an hour and I have nothing to wear!" shrieked Mercedes, rushing to Madame's closet and adjusting the strap on her nose. Tim rushed after her:

"Benz, that nose strap doesn't make you look like Cleopatra. It makes you look ridiculous!"

"Be quiet, *niño!*"

Mercedes twisted her ankle and limped forward through a jungle in Madame's closet. The plumed hats made her sneeze, and the monkey skins and ostrich feathers made her sad. She found a pink evening gown with white lace trim and held it up to the light. She loved the fullness of the skirt and winked at Tim with both eyes, waiting for his professional assessment.

"Benz, that nose strap makes you look like a Chinaman!"

"What have I done to God to deserve you, Timi?"

"Benz, you're a beautiful woman. Why d'you think swivel-heads turn around in the street when you pass? You don't need that stupid strap—take it off!"

She dashed back to Manola and Pepe's room on the fourth floor, and found, carefully laid out on the bed, the stockings, blouse, and white shawl that Manola had painstakingly selected for her from her own wardrobe. She begged Manola to sew the missing button on the pink dress. Pepe buzzed the intercom from downstairs.

"Hey, the longest Citroën stretch limousine in living memory is waiting outside. It can't even fit in the driveway, so it's double-parked in the *contre-allée!*"

Mercedes called upon the Virgen de Guadalupe to intercede in her behalf and bit a hangnail on her left index finger. With a mouth full of bobby pins, Manola combed Benz's hair into an elegant chignon. Mercedes tried on the pink ball gown.

"You look like Doris Day in that," said Timi.

"And you, you brat, look like Pinocchio."

Mercedes threw open Manola's closet where she kept some of her more temperamental and audacious Sunday outfits and selected a turquoise skirt with a broad silver belt and a slit up the side.

"He wants to know how long you'll be," cackled Pepe over the intercom.

"I'm coming! I'm coming!" shouted Mercedes, turning in the full-length mirror.

Dying of curiosity, she ran, followed by Tim and Wonderdog, to the front balcony, where she saw a black limousine parked in front of the house. Pepe, for once, had not exaggerated: it was so long she could swear it needed hinges in the middle to turn corners. It was purring like some mysterious African panther, with tinted windows for eyes and a telephone antenna for a tail.

"I don't understand," said Tim. "How did the Baron invite you? Did he write you a note, did he telephone? I'm sure his chauffeur hasn't delivered a formal message or anything. I mean, isn't that the way it's supposed to be done?"

Mercedes, ignoring him, rushed back inside in a panic.

On this overcast evening, could she trust an elegant, perfumed baron who rode in a steel black leopard on wheels? What was he really like? Was he here out of genuine interest in her, the need to find a companion for his sunset years, or because of overwhelming passion, attraction, love?

"Nothing looks good on you tonight," said Tim, shaking his head and leaning against the wall.

"Timoté, you are thirteen. You should not be watching me undress like this!"

The boy sucked on the end of a licorice stick, blackening his lips and fingers.

"Maybe you should just cancel your date."

Mercedes screamed and chased him out of the room. She ripped off her turquoise skirt and put on a white wool minidress with a thin gold lamé belt. Manola tried sweeping her hair up over a comb. What if the Baron asked her about politics? What if they dined on a banquette and she sat on his right (displaying her better profile) and he asked her what she thought of de Gaulle's monetary policy?

"Oh that's real classy, Benz. You look like the bride of Frankenstein."

"Timoté, I am going to get Manola's Mauser and shoot you like I shot Sean."

"Rothschild will swallow his dentures when he sees you!"

"Por Dios! Shut up!" She slammed her foot so hard that the heel of her left patent-leather shoe broke off. Manola ran in with another of Madame's dresses, susurrating a million love words.

What if the Baron puts his hand on my knee, thought Benz, looks deep into my soul, and whispers as if in half-prayer that he loves me?

"Manola, what if he laughs at my lack of general culture and for not knowing who La Contessa de Gouligouza's first husband was?" Mercedes made the sign of the cross.

"Don't worry, darling. 'Saints never make miracles at home.' I promise you the Baron will find you very beautiful and intelligent."

"Hey," shouted Pepe over the intercom. "Traffic is backed up the side street almost to the Arc de Triomphe!"

"Well, tell them to back up all the way to Rouen while they're at it!" screamed Mercedes, hopping on one foot and trying to squeeze into a petticoat. Whimpering loudly, she teased her hair into a bouffant beehive.

"And you be quiet!" she shouted at Timoté, who was just standing there. The Baron was richer than God; so what? She was not scared. Never! She was an Andaluz Gypsy! Her forefathers had beaten Napoleon at the Battle of Bailén in 1806. A handful of barefoot knife throwers did what no one in Europe could do up until then.

Manola ran back down the long hallway with a pair of Madame's red spike-heeled shoes, open at the toe.

"My Princesita, you look beautiful!"

Manola helped Benz out of her petticoat and into a green African *booboo* of Madame's. Benz repeated to herself that she was not scared. The Andaluz were the bravest people in the world. After all, when he saw La División Azul, hadn't Hitler told Mussolini, "They're all out of step and they look like *merde*, but they are the best troops I have on the Russian front"?

"Men always like it when a woman laughs," said Manola. "Remember to giggle and to make him talk about himself and about what he likes."

"You look really great," said Tim.

"Oh, you shut up!"

This *booboo* made her look like a field of corn in July. Manola tried to flatten the top of Benz's spring-coiled hair into some sort of recognizable shape, but the full-length mirror left Mercedes in doubt.

"The police are questioning the Baron's chauffeur," shouted Pepe. "I think you better get down here fast!"

Half mad with terror, she ripped off the *booboo* and jumped out of her one black and her one red shoe. Manola pulled out another of Cascasia's evening gowns.

"Benz, if you want, I can tell him you're sick," offered Tim.

She tried to slap his face, but he ducked in time. Hearing Benz whimper, the dog pricked up his ears. Tim felt only impending doom and disaster. Her hands were trembling as she applied rouge to her cheeks. She was starting something irreversible; she was embarking on a journey that would make it impossible for him to say the million and one things he had been stacking up inside himself over the years waiting to say to her.

"Benz, just tell me why I can't go with you!"

"Do not start with me, Timoté."

"Just give me one good reason why I can't go!"

"Because you cannot."

"That isn't a reason. You have to have a reason why you won't let me accompany you!"

"Because I don't want you to."

"But that is not a reason!"

"Timi, if you continue I will slap your teeth into the middle of next month!"

"Just tell me, just give me one eentsy-teentsy good reason

why you can't take me with you, and I promise I'll let you alone."

Beams of terror skidded across Mercedes' face: What if the Baron were to discuss stocks and bonds all night? What if he rambled on like the senile old men in Matamoros?

"Benz, tell me the truth!"

She caught the boy with an expertly timed backhand, rings in just the right position to inflict maximum shock and send his glasses flying. He was not expecting it.

"Por Dios, Timoté, don't cry!"

"I can't help it!"

"The Baron's chauffeur says he'll drive around the block," announced Pepe over the intercom.

"Benz, I won't be a bother. And I won't make fun of the Baron. I won't even let out a peep. I'll just sit quietly in a corner, I promise!"

Benz tried on a flowered cotton dress. Manola came rushing in, wiped off Benz's pink lipstick, and applied a new shade of violent deep red gloss, Madame's favorite.

"Benz, are you ashamed of me—is that it?"

Mercedes pulled a tortoiseshell comb through her hair so hard some of the teeth broke off.

"Timi, be nice tonight to your Benz, I beg of you!"

Manola purred compliments at Benz and stuffed tissue paper into her bra.

"Benz, stay with me tonight. We'll have a good time. We'll play Beatles records if you want."

"Princesita, he will faint when he sees how beautiful you are!"

"Yeah," said Tim. "The fossil will take one look at you and have a heart attack. You better wear black."

Benz added powder to her cheeks and squeezed into Madame's dress shoes. Then, peering into the mirror, she tried to make her green almond eyes as mysterious and alluring as possible. The night smelled of love-taming mists and calico cats, she thought. Pearls of light glinted off the cloisonné earrings that Madame had given her.

"I don't know how much longer the Baron can wait." There

was real urgency in Pepe's voice. "His chauffeur is making rude Italian hand gestures from behind the tinted windshield."

Mercedes ran to the elevator trailing her silk Hermès scarf, whiffs of Ne Me Quitte Pas, and Timothy.

"Are you going to do something you don't want me to see? Is that why I can't come along?"

Mercedes did an about-face, rushed back to Manola's room, grabbed her handbag, and kissed Timoté on the lips.

"Be good, Timi. And pray very hard for me tonight!"

"You want to marry a corpse? Is that what you want, Benz?"

The shoes were too tight and caused her to run like a penguin, throwing her weight from side to side. Her hair was in a dark cone with bangs down the front. She wiped the tears from her left cheek. The Elevator from the Year One was, as usual, not working. Tim listened to Benz clatter down the main staircase, then flew to the front balcony and stood there barefoot, his striped cotton pajamas fluttering in the breeze.

The black behemoth of a limousine sat there waiting, blinking, with a long white tail of blocked traffic stretching behind it. Tim was really scared now. He imagined the Baron, lounging inside the car, to be of Transylvanian descent, a best friend to the Phantom of the Opera, attended by a retinue of vampire bats, one-eyed hunchbacks, and corpses from the Rue Morgue. Death was making its midnight call early tonight, for it was not yet eleven. The floodlights of the Arc de Triomphe had not yet been switched off, and it still glowed bright white like an enormous angel-food cake. The wind blew, and one of the shutters creaked behind him.

Manola and Pepe joined Tim on the balcony. He wished he had a sufficient supply of wine to drown this half-dead millionaire and his kilometer-long car. Manola and Pepe hooted and clapped like farmers when Benz appeared in the driveway below. Half-hidden by the linden-tree leaves, she turned to wave up at them.

"Benz, I'll never forgive you for this!" shouted Tim.

"Be good and pray like you mean it!" She laughed giddily.

Mercedes quickly inventoried the contents of her handbag. This baron may not be for me, she thought, but tonight, my first date since the explosion, I shall be like a rose that opens its buds after a long winter's hibernation. Tonight, I may hate the Baron's guts, or trip as I sashay past the maître d', but I don't care; I am alive again.

"Your nose strap! Take it off," shouted Manola as she threw down the white woolen shawl that Benz had forgotten.

Mercedes yanked off her 20-franc Cleopatra Special, purchased at the Prisunic beauty counter, blew them a kiss, and, pulling her shoulders up as high as they would go, swept toward the limousine. "And so a maid becomes a queen," muttered Pepe.

The cars lined up behind the Baron's limousine were honking like angry geese. Tim grasped the wrought-iron balcony and shouted at the top of his lungs:

"Benz, I'll telephone that old fossil tomorrow and tell him that your beautiful black hair is dyed!"

Manola covered the boy's mouth. The black car engulfed Benz and sped away, followed by an enormously long tail of red lights. And on this balmy, humid night in Paris with the cook's fat palm clamped over his mouth, he watched his accident-prone nanny be taken away, perhaps forever. Suddenly there was only death and loneliness gripping him.

THE big day had finally arrived: his Aunties had at last allowed him to wear long pants! His first pair were of gray corduroy, with a back pocket like the ones in which American gangsters kept their overstuffed wallets. Master Tim kicked his Arabian charger and gave him full rein. His imperial armies had all but disappeared. A group calling itself the Student Worker Alliance had taken over the courtyard. Today, they were screaming into a megaphone:

SMASH THE RICH! DOWN WITH THE PLUTOCRATS!

Tim didn't recognize Saint-Philippe. His troops had deserted him to become Socialists, Trotskyites, *Nouvelle Gauche* Maoists, and after so many brilliant victories, he now faced his own Waterloo alone. It was hard with these blaring slogans for

Tim to re-create his Imperial Mission. The grenadiers warming themselves at a campfire, the suicidal charges across the vast, daunting plains of Russia, these were difficult, almost impossible, given the current ambiance.

THE RICH HOARD THEIR GOLD AND LIVE OFF THE BLOOD OF THE WORKERS!

Gerbi waved from the telephone booth outside the Café Muette. Tim trotted debonairly out of Saint-Philippe, crossed Rue de la Pompe, and reined in his steed. Gerbi was bent in two, laughing. He gave Tim the receiver and explained that for 1 franc he could call anywhere in the world and the broken phone would give him 2 francs back. Having dialed Japan, he was now trying India.

"We'll ask what the weather is like in Calcutta," said Gerbi, pinching his nose so no one would recognize his voice.

How totally stupid, thought Tim as he climbed back on Pamplemousse and galloped to the schoolyard. On this wet Wednesday morning in April, with the new carrot-green leaves flicking in the wind, he burst through the fog, thinking of the rain-soaked hills of Waterloo. Of all the Napoleonic legends, this was the hardest for him to reenact, for deep down inside, he refused to believe it had ever actually happened.

DO YOU KNOW WHAT SLUMS OUR WORKERS LIVE IN?

"Hey, Tim, it's thirty-five degrees in Madagascar!" shouted Gerbi.

Tim paid no attention. His loyal followers had been misled, confused, bamboozled, swindled, betrayed, hornswoggled, and lemming-led into the supposedly real world of current events. Even poor Laval, his once-trusted enemy, was at the foot of the podium, listening to an older student shout into the megaphone:

DOWN WITH THE BOSSES! DOWN WITH CAPITALISM!

Tim's horse reared: A yellow-spotted butterfly opened and closed its delicate wings. How beautiful it was in the afternoon light with its iron-gray antennae and twin silver-blue tails! Someone pushed him from behind. There was a rush of older boys —thugs, rather, with chains and helmets. Tim fell off his horse and scraped his right knee.

ONLY THE PARTY TRULY UNDERSTANDS THE WORKERS!

His brand-new corduroy pants, his never-before-worn long pants, were ripped! Tim slowly rolled up his trouser leg. Blood was seeping through from his kneecap. With short pants, you could immediately see how bad a cut was, and you didn't worry about stains. Where had Pamplemousse bolted to? It was unlike him to gallop away by himself. Usually he remained, even untethered, by Tim's side. Still squatting, Tim looked around the hammer-and-sickle–painted walls of the courtyard for his horse. This really made him mad.

Suddenly the yellow, blue-tailed butterfly stopped with its mottled wings in mid-extension. The Waterloo fog rolling up the hill of Tim's imagination froze. The leftist students brawling with rightist hecklers dimmed. In this captured moment, as Tim squatted and examined his knee, a voice spoke inside him:

"We are fleeting, you and I, Tim. And when you are thirty, remember that you knelt here in this courtyard and stared at this bleeding bony knee of yours. Not even the bones remember. All is death and passing time. And when you go, you are gone. So remember, try to wedge this moment into your memory as hard as you can."

WORKERS AND STUDENTS OF PARIS, UNITE!

The spell was broken. Tim rushed to tell his best friend what had just happened.

"Roland, you'll never believe this! But just now, as I was kneeling, I heard voices!"

Roland was studying the political rally at the other end of the courtyard. Students they had never seen before were swinging steel chains above their heads and advancing onto the podium.

"All right," said Tim, "not voices. A voice. Maybe it was God; I don't know."

Roland shrugged:

"Everyone has religious epiphanies. Saul on the road to Damascus. Joan of Arc. What do you think I'm doing when I stare off in the distance and look bored, huh? Sooner or later, the Unknown contacts us."

Tim panted quietly. Roland was in permanent consultation with God? No wonder he was so smart! Through the megaphone, Laval shouted something unintelligible. Gerbi was talking to Tierra del Fuego and called Tim to help him speak Spanish.

YOU FASCIST PIGS DON'T SCARE US!

There was a scream. A boy ran by with blood streaming from his nose. Two others were punching Laval in the temples. Tim wanted to give his old enemy a hand, but Roland held him back:

"The Communists did the same to the Right last week."

"They did? I didn't notice."

"You were too busy galloping around, making stupid clicking noises with your tongue."

This reminded him of Pamplemousse. Tim looked desperately around the courtyard, his throat tightening and his vision becoming blurry. Where were his red Dragoon saddle and gold-embroidered Hussard field jacket? He searched in all his favorite hiding places. Where were his white standards and bicephalous eagles? This was what happened when you were careless: you misplaced all your loved ones! A loud explosion rocked the podium. It was engulfed in smoke. Hundreds of children poured out into Rue de la Pompe. Tim and Roland found themselves next to Gerbi's telephone booth listening to police sirens howl. A Peugeot ambulance drove along the sidewalk and into the schoolyard.

"You can't go back in there," said Roland, holding Tim's arm. "It's a full-scale riot. You want to get killed?"

Policemen and firemen cordoned off the area and prevented Tim from searching for Pamplemousse. On the way home, alone, he tried to gallop, but stopped. It was silly to make neighing and hoofing sounds without a horse—people looked at you in a funny way. For Tim, the world was suddenly a tiny place, and it was getting smaller all the time. To lose one's horse, just like that, between two sentences, without a trace—how incredibly stupid!

The walk home was tedious and slow. Tim looked into the fashionable Victor Hugo shopwindows without seeing anything. For almost ten years he had galloped to and from Saint-Philippe. Even when Benz used to accompany him, he would gallop; even in the fall, during the chestnut wars, when galloping made you an easy target.

Colin Delavaud, a boy two grades behind him, cantered by, making clicking sounds with his tongue. Tim thought of trying to ride with him, but felt embarrassed. The boy was gone, anyway. Tim pushed his way through a crowd of idiot shoppers, disgusted with himself, tired of life.

MERCEDES pulled open the red velvet curtain and entered the booth. She had not been to confession in years, but the faint dusty smell was familiar, as was the feel of the padded knee bench. She waited for the panel to slide open behind the wrought-iron grille. Because Monet was the Principal, he said Mass and heard confession only once every two weeks.

"Yes, my child, what have you to confess?"

The sonorous voice was very close, almost up against her ear. A voice like that could rape you, she thought. She mumbled. Father Monet asked her to speak up.

"Forgive me, Father, for I have sinned."

"Yes, my child? . . . How?"

What could she say? The facts sounded stupid, really.

"Father, I am in love. Well, in lust, actually."

"Wonderful! Are you dating someone, my child?"

"Well, an older man—a baron, actually. But I have come here concerning a boy. He is only fourteen."

Monet waited for her to continue.

"Nothing has happened. But his glands are developing rapidly. And he has the most beautiful long, soft hands in the world."

"Who is he, my child?"

"Father, I have come for your guidance, not to give names and addresses. Now, tell me, what should I do? We live in the same house. I see him every day."

There was silence.

"Is the boy not like your son? Think hard, now, because that may constitute incest, my child."

"I've taken care of him since he was eight. But he is becoming a man-boy, much different from the *tichno* runt I raised."

"Does the boy have desire for you?"

"I think so."

"How do you know? Has he said something to you?"

"Well, no. But I just know it."

"Has he done anything to you?"

"Well, not really. But I was serving the family Sunday brunch, and when I leaned over with a tray of *raie au beurre noire,* the boy squeezed my arm. He pretended to mistake my elbow for the serving spoon, and then looked up expectantly at me. Well, at that moment, I knew, knew as well as anything, that even if I airmailed the boy's head to Marseille, he would come back for me."

"Yes—go on."

"That's all."

"Has he any girlfriends of his own age?"

"He says I am his girlfriend. Father, tell me what to do."

"Jesus said we can love Him through each other. A Platonic relationship should not pose a problem."

"In my village, they say Platonic love is either 'too good' to be Platonic or 'too Platonic' to be good."

"Well, you have done nothing wrong as yet, child. Can you keep it unrequited? That is the purest kind of love."

"But my desires for the boy are sometimes carnal; I am often absolutely filthy in thought, word, and deed."

"At least you are honest, my child."

She did not know what to say next. She sensed that Monet too was at a loss. He stared straight ahead of him. She wanted him to turn and look at her. The silence in the confessional grew heavy. From this angle, his face looked soft and baby-like. How handsome and alone the Jesuit was behind the black grille. The school bell was ringing. Timi would be running out now. She made the sign of the cross quickly and promised to do her acts of contrition at home.

"But you must come back. We have not finished discussing this problem."

"Yes, yes, Father. I'm sorry, but I have to run."

Tim would kill her, or at least question her to death, if he knew she was confessing herself to Monet.

WHEN Mercedes left Manola and Pepe in the kitchen, they were screaming and breaking plates. Tonight Pepe was pummeling his wife harder than usual. Luckily for Manola, she had the biceps of a sailor. Mercedes kissed Timi good night, went up to her room, took off her makeup, brushed her teeth, and got into bed. Usually, when she lay down she did not so much fall asleep as faint with fatigue. But tonight the odor of long-stemmed roses kept her awake.

What is the matter? she thought. Why am I so picky? I will never find a man who meets all my standards. After all, Isidore was marvelously refined. Their first date had gone like clockwork. He had sent her enough roses to fill a small Rue de la Pompe funeral parlor. He had invited her to go on a two-week vacation to Sri Lanka! So what if the baron never grabbed her passionately in public or bit her ear in private? Their affair was not exactly a Hollywood exclusive. It was not the Indigo Zoom of Lana Turner staring at Cary Grant, the camera lens zooming forward into the sea, everything expanding blue, bluer, bluest, melting oceanward into a horizonless limbo. She had expected her dates with the Baron to shoot her out of a cannon toward a man, into a lifestyle so intoxicating that even the Paris sun would shine with excitement. But if Isidore was not at all the Indigo Zoom, he had other qualities. He was quiet, reserved, and sweet. Blue water trickled through his veins.

Mercedes smelled tobacco in her room and opened her eyes. Was she dreaming?

Someone was sitting by the window. The tip of a cigarette brightened red in the dark and subsided. She switched on her bedside lamp.

"Manola, vida mia, que te pasa?"

Her face was bruised and swollen like an old peach.

"My God! Has Pepe done this to you?"

Benz walked over to Manola and touched her big, red scrubbed hands. The knuckles were bruised. They smelled of chicken soup and soap when Benz kissed them. She opened her medicine cabinet and took out some peroxide and cotton.

"I'm all right," said Manola, struggling for breath and wiping her nose on her sleeve.

Knowing it was useless to argue, Benz closed her door, slipped on the chain lock she had just installed, and climbed back into bed.

"Maybe I cannot read or write, like Pepe," said Manola, blowing out a cloud of Gitane smoke. "But I learned more about fighting in the streets of Madrid than that peasant will ever forget!"

"Manola, it's two-thirty in the morning! Why don't you get in bed with me? We can talk about this in the morning."

Benz imagined that to an ant walking along Manola's upper lip, each black hair must appear as stout as a tree trunk. Manola's oversized chest rose and fell with great difficulty. Mercedes smelled a fragrance of zucchini and artichokes in the room—tomorrow's menu, no doubt.

"Pepe thinks I am only a pack mule that washes and cooks all day! But I fight three years with Julian Gorkin; Joaquín Maurín, the Secretary General of the POUM; and Indalezio Prieto—God bless them all!" Manola stubbed out her cigarette. "When I was seventeen, I run messages across enemy lines! They never catch me, never, *no, Señor!* And we pour burning olive oil on their tanks and cannon!"

"Manola, please, I've heard your stories a thousand times already."

Mercedes put a clean handkerchief over the lampshade on her nighttable so the light would not shine so brightly in her eyes and lay back on her side.

"Everyone I love die in the Civil War. In 1939, I meet Pepe. I am helping to hide the Spanish gold in the French banks to keep it out of Franco's hands. On a donkey, across the Pyrenees I go! And you think that 'it is only the scared face that the bee chooses to sting'? Well, Manola cannot be scared anymore. No, *Señora,* not since the Fascists bomb Madrid!"

Mercedes turned over on her side and tried to fall asleep without snoring.

"Benz, I am forty-seven. I am not young. Maybe Pepe one day hits me too hard and kills me. Maybe I slip on a banana peel. So I want you to know my secret, my search."

Mercedes did not want to encourage her by sitting up in bed, but she loved secrets and began to listen intently.

"Princesita, eyes of my life, breath of my days, you are the only other person in the world who will know this secret. I tell you this in case I die without finding it."

Mercedes was sitting up in bed, wide awake now, staring at Manola with eyes bright.

"Do not tell anyone. Not even Timoté."

Manola lit another Gitane. Benz brought her knees up to her chest. The number of secrets in this house! Just when she thought she knew them all, more tumbled out of the woodwork.

"Eyes of my soul, remember what I am going to tell you: That bandit-without-a-soul, Juan Negrín, *El Campesino*, and that terrible Dolores Ibarruri, La Pasionaria, take half the Spanish gold to Moscow, February five, 1937. Franco thinks they take all of it, but that is not true. The other half of the gold, we Loyalists try to send to Mexico to help our refugees. But Bilbao, our port, falls too quickly to the Falange. So we pack it on three donkeys and I bring it over the Pyrenees. I meet Pepe in Andorra. He is a small contrabandist and a big coward, avoiding the French and Spanish conscription. He follows me. We bring the bullion to Paris. It is 1939 and impossible to book a passage to Mexico. So what can I do? Your Baron, Isidore, approximately the best and most honest Jew I ever meet, he says the French government will confiscate our gold if it is deposited in his bank and inventoried. At the very least, the Franco regime will tie it up in litigation. So Roastchild, he helps us to bring the gold, unnoticed, all the way from his bank to the Cardozo house, where I find work. Here, with the Irish Embassy under the same roof, we have diplomatic immunity. It is 1940. I dig and hide the gold in the cellar. I do not tell anyone. Not even Pepe!" Manola took a deep puff on her Gitane. "There, now you know everything."

Mercedes waited for her to continue, but Manola was quiet, examining one of the many bruises on her arms. Then she looked around the room and mopped her brow with the cloth on Benz's table.

"Manola, don't tell me you've forgotten where you hid it? *Dios mío,* is that why the boy says there are so many holes in the basement?"

"During the war, we hide a million and one things down there. The cellar is very vast. Much larger than my memory!"

"But what if the gold isn't there anymore?"

"No, it is there! It must be there!" shouted Manola. She approached the bed and dug her short nails into Mercedes' forearms. "I tell you it *must* be there!"

"Yes, don't get upset. Of course it is there."

Benz waited for Manola to pull her face away. "How long have you been digging for it?"

"Many years."

Benz recalled that when she had arrived at the Cardozo house, Manola had told her and the Aunties that a new branch of the Métro was being constructed under the foundations of the house and not to worry about any digging sounds they might hear coming from the cellar.

Manola climbed into Mercedes' little bed. Her enormous weight caused the mattress to sag in the middle. Mercedes had to make herself as thin as possible up against the wall.

"Light of my years, many Loyalists die for this gold—my poor Andrés Nin, freedom fighter for Cataluña; Lezo de Urreiztieta the Basque; and thousands of heroes like my father and brothers, not famous but beloved of God. The gold belongs to their widows and children! I will use it to make certain Franco dies in the street like a dog, and then I will publish the truth about how Moscow betrayed us."

Mercedes leaned over Manola's whalelike body and switched off the bedside lamp. What was husband-hunting compared with a civil war? Benz felt sad for the POUM. She was a Babylonian willow, nostalgic for spices and silk. Who today in Paris cared one leek for the Loyalists? She loved hopeless causes. Her thoughts were filled with ancient light and the topaz-fickle sea. *Boom, boom* went the distant cannon inside Manola's chest. *Boom* responded Benz's, as her blood quickened.

Benz lay on her back in the dark and saw herself up on the barricades. Who needed a millionaire baron when she could be clutching a baby to her naked breast and fending off the assault troops? She was in the front lines with bare feet and gold-laden donkeys, fighting the whole world. She was defending Madrid from Fascist tanks and planes; she was blasting away at the Falange bastards. She would teach the loyal Timi how to tell a Moscow man from an anarchist hero, just by how ugly and short he was!

After a silence, Mercedes turned on her side and whispered:

"Do you think the Baron is too short for me?"

Manola opened one eye and said:

"No, not when he is standing on his wallet."

CHAPTER 8

Adolescent Tremors into Manhood's Puzzlements

THERE WAS a faceless woman in Tim's dreams. She came to him half-wrapped in gauze and blurry, like one of the statues on Notre Dame whose features are partly eaten away by the elements. He could see only a trace of her lip, the curve of her cheek, the roundness of her hips.

Tonight the faceless woman in his dream was wearing a pair of stockings. As she bent down to make his bed, he saw a tear in her nylons and there, curling up from under her panties, the blackest of pubic hairs. He could smell it, touch it, almost talk to it. The thick, muscular thighs, the curve of the panty line, the rip in the stockings: there was no possible doubt to whom these legs belonged. He woke up in a sweat, hard and wet. She was visiting him in his dreams!

When he returned from school, he raced to the fourth floor to tell Benz. She was serving the Aunties dinner. On his way up, he combed his hair with the five fingers on his left hand and tucked in his shirt. He knocked. Benz was seated on the bed spoon-feeding Agatha. Tim stood uneasily in the doorway. Who was this pale, bedridden stick of a woman with the brown splotches on her balding scalp? Agatha? Her face seemed to disappear like camouflage into the flower print of her pillow. She was so weak, Benz had to prop her head up off the pillow for each spoonful.

"What do you want, Timi?" asked Benz.

He approached Agatha's bed with his mouth wide open, embarrassed to mention his dreams. Benz was caressing the purple veins that bulged and twisted like copper wires down his Auntie's right temple. Her skin was like an ancient map, dry old leather stretched over sun-bleached stones.

"Doesn't your Auntie look better today?" asked Benz, catching the cream of oats slipping down Agatha's chin.

Better? Tim imagined the doctor drawing his old-fashioned gold-cased watch from his vest pocket and slowly shaking his head. He imagined the nurse in the waiting room and the soundless whispers in the hall as the watch fob clicked shut. Benz shouted into her ear:

"AGATHA, THIS IS TIMOTÉ! T-I-M-O-T-É! HE HAS COME TO VISIT YOU! HE IS OVER HERE, AT THE FOOT OF THE BED. SEE HIS DARK SHADOW?"

His aunt made the faintest motion to nod and turned her blue corpse eyes toward him. He never paid enough attention to his Aunties. It would be just like Pamplemousse all over again; he would lose them out of sheer negligence. You had to nail down your loved ones, keep them always within arm's reach, look in on them once a day.

"HE HAS COME TO TELL YOU HOW MUCH HE LOVES YOU! AND HOW MUCH BETTER YOU ARE GOING TO FEEL WHEN YOU GET OVER THIS HEAD COLD!"

Head cold? Tim had trouble swallowing. This was no ordinary catarrh; this was the cold of beyond, the cold off the coast of No Where. He could hear the thud of gravel being shoveled onto Agatha's casket. This was what he deserved for treating Agatha like a deaf old crow who never heard him when he forgot his key and had to bang on the locked door downstairs for what seemed like hours.

"Timoté, she can hear almost everything I say! Isn't that wonderful?"

The body in the bed managed to smile—a gaping hole in a white mass of wrinkles. Tim watched, with tears filling his eyes, in total awe as Benz massaged the clawlike fingers, then kissed Agatha's cheek.

"I just washed her this morning," whispered Benz. "Does she not smell fresh?"

"Benz, you deserve the Nobel Peace Prize for this," said Tim, resting his eyes on the vast stretch of clean ceiling plaster.

"OH, BUT FOR ME, IT IS A JOY TO LOOK AFTER AGATHA! YOU HEAR ME, AGATHE! YOU ARE MY LITTLE BRIOCHE, ARE YOU NOT? AND WE HAVE SO MUCH FUN TOGETHER. I TAKE GOOD CARE OF YOU, N'EST-CE PAS?"

Tim retreated to the door. He imagined his Benz kneeling in a cemetery, pulling skin and bones out of the mud and breathing life into them. He wanted to remember his Agatha gliding around the house, doing her smiling amoeba routine, wearing cherries in her pale blue hair and calling to the pigeons nesting in the chimney as if she had known each one of them since before the war.

Tim fled the room without turning around. Did Tim's love for Benz encompass kissing a bald scalp? If she lay dying in a hospital, would he be able to sit at her bedside and spoon-feed her corpse?

TIM turned onto his back. And again onto his side. It was night. He could hear Manola and Pepe still shouting and fighting in the kitchen. He couldn't sleep. Benz had not come to kiss him tonight. He could not get her out of his mind—he was pregnant with her! In math class yesterday, he had discussed her stupid Matamoros sayings. In Latin, he had reviewed her chances with the Baron. During lunch he had promised himself to yell at her for her makeup. He had never had insomnia before, and could not stand it any longer. He would sneak up to her room and sleep with her! Why not? The idea blossomed in his head like one of the Japanese water flowers Aunt Phoebe so loved. He put on his slippers, tiptoed to the hallway where the keys hung, took little XKE out of his cage for companionship, and hurried up the service staircase. She was out with the Baron, but he would wait in her bedroom forever—longer if he needed to.

When she returned from her date and found him asleep in her cave, she would at long last start accepting him as a man, no longer just a kid brother.

XKE seemed excited to be included in Tim's itinerary. His nose bumped inside Tim's cupped hands and worked overtime, gathering in all the new smells. Tim unlocked Benz's door. He was greeted by the unmistakable, beloved odor of her bear cave: Nivea cream, spools of damp wool stuck through with knitting needles, chocolate-bar wrappers, eau de cologne. On her little table was a half-finished shopping list in Benzese dialect:

Djurnal
tabako
peti trook poor la figoor
biftakos
Nibaya
tiketes de Loteria
Olivas
Orangas

Tim lay down on her bed, staring at her scrunched-up handwriting, then at the humid moldings that she herself contemplated when she lay here. XKE squeaked and tried to push his little nose through Tim's fingers. Tim went over to the washbasin. In her medicine chest, he counted thirteen ointments, seven lipsticks, four hair-removal pomades, a box of cotton swabs, suppositories for constipation and dizziness, and three types of homeopathic leaves. He undid the lid of a jar of white skin-cleansing cream, dipped his right forefinger into it and tasted its contents. He carefully picked up an empty Cri du Coeur perfume bottle from her wastebasket and put it in his bathrobe pocket. It was past midnight; he could not understand what was keeping her.

"*Squeeeeak! Squeak-squeak-squeak!*" went XKE.

Master Tim heard a scurrying of tiny feet and a frantic thumping. He peered under the bed. A rat that looked as big as Wonderdog was dragging his little white mouse toward a hole in the baseboard! Quickly, Tim grabbed one of Benz's furry slippers and hit the rat on the head. It scurried into the wall. He picked up his white furry escort, whose heart was racing like a runaway sewing machine, and stumbled back to his room on the third floor.

"Don't worry, XKE. I'll call the vet tomorrow," said Tim, running back to his room.

"Squeeeeeak!"

"I know exactly how you feel, XKE! First attempts rarely succeed."

He decided not to go through the kitchen and past Manola and Pepe's room because they might still be fighting. If they were awake, they would question him as to where he had been. So he took the long way around down through the cellar. But as he ran on toe-tips past the Gallo-Roman well, something caught his attention:

Two eyes glinted at him diamond-bright in the darkness. Slowly, he approached the Gallo-Roman well. Was this another of Pepe's practical jokes? A creature half-submerged in the water, a snouted voyager of the subterranean seas, was staring at Tim, beckoning him forward, hypnotizing him. Tim was too scared to move a muscle. He thought he saw two Ping-Pong balls at the end of the creature's long snout, but perhaps he was just imagining them. Mesmerized, he watched in silence as the beast's head slowly sank underwater, sending slow concentric ripples to the edges of the well. Why now? For years he had traveled down here with Roland and Gerbi, with Benz, with his dad to show them the crocodiles, and each time the calm, flat waters had left his guests unimpressed and impatient to leave the basement.

XKE squeaked again. Tim raced back to his room and poured his mouse a new dish of seeds, which XKE declined. Then he draped a towel over the cage. Now, as he lay in bed, his thoughts still roamed through Benz's sloping-roofed dream kingdom on the sixth floor. After several whiffs of her Cri du Coeur, redolent of underarms and bear-cave, he tucked the bottle under his pillow. He could reach for it whenever he felt lonely.

• • •

MERCEDES was in the greenhouse of the first-floor garden. Weeding and planting was Pepe's job, but he was so lazy that she had taken over these duties almost two years ago. Today she was pruning roses and cutting a bouquet for the dinner table. It was Timoté's last Latin exam, and the Aunties wanted to celebrate. Manola was preparing his favorite dish, duck with green olives.

Mercedes loved the light in this greenhouse, the prismatic greens and reds, the feeling of airiness and freshness, the snug coziness of the flowers. She loved to talk to them, to feel their roots, to dig her fingers into the dirt. Suddenly she felt the boy's hands on her haunches. Timi the brave, the loyal, Timi the at-last-grown-up, Timi of the sparkling squirrel eyes, was back from school.

"I smell *anis* on your breath, bad boy. Have you been drinking pastis? How were your final exams?"

A band of sunlight crossed his bare, hairless white arms. So clean-cut, so glossy-haired, he was becoming one of the handsomest man-boys in Paris.

"Benz, I waited for you in your bedroom the other night. You didn't come back."

"What were you doing in my room?" She could almost feel his glandular desire.

"I was worried about you. Where did you go?"

"After the discothèque closed, we had breakfast at Les Halles."

"Benz, you know what I keep seeing in my dreams? This hair right here! Only I see it through a rip in your stocking!"

"Stop! You are *répugnant,*" she said, pushing his hand away.

In this transparent glass house, with all the pigments of flowers draining into Timi's cheeks, he pulled her gently toward him. She tried to push him away, but slowly, inevitably, like the pigeon feather that Mercedes had seen falling gently to the surface of the goldfish pond, as if it had been created for the very purpose of that one free fall, their lips pressed together.

He closed his eyes, but she kissed without blinking. This is not happening, she thought, running her fingers through his recently cut hair. She fed her mouth to the boy (gleam of teeth, white pressed shirt, thin English tie), losing herself in the white nimbus of gardenias behind his head. Even the plants seemed to sigh.

"No, Timoté, no. Wait! Dinner will be ready soon. And there is too much light here."

Mercedes let out a sigh as she felt this man-boy hard and naked below the rhododendrons. No gooseflesh in this steamy greenhouse: just a young engorged blue-veined limb and a mouth tasting of first cigarette.

"No, no, this not possible. Not here."

What an appetite she had for his lips! Young boys definitely tasted better. And to be wanted like this in this splash of jagged sunlight! She looked over his shoulder, past the geraniums: the garden was walled off from the avenue and the wall covered with ivy, but could not the neighbors peek down from the windows above and see through the greenery?

"Benz, you are so beautiful."

She brushed the hair off his face. He nibbled on her left ear, his underlip glistening. Who was seducing whom here? she wondered.

"Benz, I hate the *payo* education. I want to become a Gypsy knife grinder, so you and I can go on the road and wander the world. We'd be merry-go-round owners, horse traders, clairvoyants. Don't say no. I'm serious."

She lay down in the forget-me-nots. He plucked a white lily and slipped it into her hair. On either side pansies and violets tilted their heads to watch. She put her mouth to his. The Japanese lanterns of her imagination swayed. The summer skies sailed blue overhead. The boy was finding his way through the green leaves and under her skirts. "O time, O life," she remembered an actress saying in one of those Indigo Zoom scenes. "Oh, raise me from the grass, oh, pluck me from the boughs!" Her hands were digging into the flower bed. He was fumbling with her bra. He was caressing her inner thigh up to her cotton underpants. He was licking her arms, her neck. She felt his lower lip twitch uncontrollably; he was a mass of tingling glands.

"Wait, Timoté, wait. I have no protection."

He was a vampire, sucking on her throat. He was vaporous air, sinuous muscle, and pale hairless skin.

"Espera, espera . . ."

She knew all his secrets—the color of his thoughts when the seasons changed, the smell of bread in the boy's mouth and the Bordeaux he drank on Sundays cut with water. She narrowed her amphibian eyes. What woman would break his heart and steal his laughter?

"Timi, just lie still. Let me get on top."

Benz kneeling over him now in the gardenias; a blue-black fly buzzing against the greenhouse windows. Benz wet with his saliva, now licking him. The boy lying quiet and still, his skin fresh like an apple. A musical bell sounding softly in the distance to indicate Manola had prepared a sumptuous end-of-exams repast. The Aunties would be scurrying around in their new pleated cotton dresses looking for him. Benz now taking his glasses off. Tasting him, taking him slowly and whole the way she liked to devour a dish of profiterolles.

"Shhh, Timi, don't move. Relax."

In this fragile light full of thyme and lilacs, Benz and the boy became one sweating body, shaking in the peonies. And Benz, riding her boy, galloped him into adulthood.

"Timi, oh, Timi, you make me crazy!"

Aunt Agatha called out their names from the balcony.

A furious shaking of leaves. The entire garden moving now. The smell of their lovemaking welling up from the newly mulched soil. Her hands, knees, and feet digging six little furrows, a new summer planting. Thank God Agatha is blind, and God forgive me for thinking this, thought Benz.

The two adjusting their clothes now. Tim smiling, with eyes like duck eggs. Benz combing his hair with her fingers. Rubbing the traces of lipstick off his cheeks with her thumbs. Fitting his bony protrusion back inside his pants and zipping him up. Brushing off all traces of dirt from her knees and elbows. And time now for dinner.

"Oh, there you are!" shouted Aunt Phoebe. "Tell us, Tim, how did it go? Do you think you passed your exam?"

TIM knocked on her door.

"Qui c'est?"

"Me."

"What do you want? I'm asleep."

"Benz, open up. It's me, Timi!"

She opened the door slowly, rubbing her eyes and closing her pale blue bathrobe.

"Darling, what are you doing up here barefoot? It's one fifteen in the morning! You must be freezing."

She wrapped him in the folds of her cotton bathrobe. The boy looked around the room and fingered an empty cigarette pack left on the night table.

"When did you start smoking again, Benz?"

"Oh, Manola left those here."

"Manola smokes Gitanes; these are Kools."

"Did you come up here to conduct an inquisition?"

"I just want to know. Tell me the truth, Benz."

"Well, if you must know, they're Raoul's cigarettes. He still visits me. Don't look at me like that. You know that a foreigner like me can't afford to offend a Raoul."

Tim curled up on her bed and stared at the crucifix on the green wall. Movie magazines were stacked by the bed, and the wrappers of Suchard chocolate bars lay balled up in a corner. Benz locked her door and pulled the peach-colored eiderdown up over his shoulders.

"Timi, this is very dangerous. You must promise not to visit at night ever again."

She put a Beatles record on, the same one she had made Tim translate for her, word for word, months before.

"Just in case someone is listening."

"Like who?"

"Well, Pepe; the Ambassador; Raoul."

"Tell them all to go to hell."

"I do, but even so, sometimes my room is like the Gare de Lyon ticket office!"

"Manola and Pepe took the Aunties to the thermal baths in Evian. We are alone, at least for two weeks."

"But there are neighbors. And the walls have eyes."

"I locked all the doors, turned off all the lights."

"Timi, you are a man: tell me why the Baron sends me roses, says he loves me, and then doesn't call for three weeks. Is this normal? Why are men like that?"

Benz selected a Sri Lankan tea given to her by the Baron, spooning it into the small silver strainer for her teapot, the kettle balanced precariously on the hot plate. Then she stuffed the Baron's Baccarat roses face down into the garbage.

"Timi, what happened in the greenhouse yesterday was beautiful, but it cannot become a habit. I could be your mother. I am your adoptive mother! I could go to jail for this!"

Her damp little room could be the coziest spot on earth during these balmy spring nights. The kettle began to whistle. She turned the record over on her small portable record player.

"Timi, you are nine years younger than me. I am twenty-four!"

"We won't do anything, I promise!"

"You liar. Your nose is growing longer."

It was not Tim's nose that grew under the eiderdown. He snuggled there remembering the greenhouse, and earlier tonight, waking up with milk on his palms, the running up the spiral staircase, stopping to catch his breath on the last landing and walking along the cold terra-cotta tiles with goose bumps rising on his arms, one voice telling him to turn back, another telling him he was a mamma's boy and not to be so scared.

"Benz, if I can't bear to be without you, does that mean that I'm in love with you?"

She laughed and shrugged:

"Maybe. Timi, do you want chamomile, mint, or Lapsang souchong?"

All the smells of Aragon and Andalusia were making it hard for him to breathe. Her incessant talk of men had in the past been of little concern; Tim was accustomed to it, and was used to treating it with little more thought than the weekend soccer scores. But now that he was with seed, these matters took on a new dimension. For he knew as well as he would ever know anything that she would make the perfect wife for him.

"The Baron wants to take me to Sri Lanka for a month's vacation."

"I thought it was only two weeks."

"He changed his mind."

Tim sipped his tea and curled up next to Benz as she opened a new issue of *Paris-Unveiled.* The streetlights cast a pale purplish tinge on the pastel green ceiling.

"Can you believe this, Timoté, a man in Lillie asked his wife for a linguine marinara. Instead, she gave it to him alla carbonara. The man got so angry he killed her!"

"Maybe it had liver in it, or Brussels sprouts?"

"Do not try to act stupid, Timi. It comes naturally enough to you without trying."

She turned a page of her newspaper. Tim's newfound member was flying at full mast. The night, the smells, Benz's voice were warm and rich like a big cow's udder all around him. He stared at the flesh on her arm: how many beauty spots were there? How perfectly smooth the skin stretched toward her underarm. The tiny hairs each in its follicle, the minute interconnecting cells, the pale blue rivers, these had a life all their own.

"Oh, no, here is a woman who was cut up into little pieces and eaten by her father-in-law!"

BENZ opened her eyes. What day was it? When would the Aunties be returning? The boy was snoring lightly. There was a pink brush of sunrise over the rooftop chimneys. Pigeons were swooping in and out of the chestnut tree in front of the house. She could feel the light blue air shimmering. Tim's little triangular face lay on her pillow. At a younger age, the sleeping Tim used to look like a drowned rat. But at fourteen, he was still growing into his face, a long-limbed dandy in dirty linen. She caressed his cheek.

She knew how his bones moved in their sockets and she knew the sound of his hair growing on his scalp. Her fingers lingered on his tight, flat abdomen. The breeze through the half-parted windows blew in the Napoleon curtains. She knew his sleep smells, his breakfast smells, his school smells. She loved to have him, dripping of sex and desire, sidle up to her from an angle and quiz her when she returned from one of her dates with the Baron. No man had ever been so completely her ally, a rock in the flood of her love, as constant and loyal as a dog.

Even in his sleep, Tim was hard. Had he remained in this ossified state all night? By fourteen, a Gypsy boy was already a Methuselah of the soul, proficient in the art of seducing tourists away from their money. If Tim were her brother, he would be waking up now in a field with smoke curling up from an open fire. He would be walking toward the bulls in the pasture, with sleep and sex still thick in his eyes. And he would be familiar with the loneliness of what it must be to be a man, like the vet in Matamoros whose job it was to guide the bull's penis into the cow.

"Will you live with me, Benz?" asked Tim, who had obviously been awake for some time.

She threw open her Napoleon-print curtains; bright sunlight reflecting off the mansard roof colored her face gold and orange. The boy wagged at half mast.

"Timi, we must be careful. They say, 'The shrimp that sleeps is taken away by the current.' And some people even say, 'The shrimp that sleeps is raped by the frog.' Are you listening? Timi, we must be more careful. The neighbors will talk."

The boy yawned and turned over on his side.

"Timoté, *calorrós* say, 'When a man and a woman are alone, the third person in the room is the Devil.' "

"Give me one good reason why we shouldn't live together."

"I have a fiancé."

"The Baron will never marry you. He says he will, but he won't."

"I have others."

"Who?"

"None of your business."

"Who? Raoul? Ambassador McLuck?"

"Timoté, when you are twenty, I will be twenty-nine. And when you are fifty, I will be an old dishrag."

"Yeah, but when you're thirty, Roastchild'll be a hundred and thirty!"

"That's different," said Mercedes looking at her face in her concave magnifying mirror.

"No, it isn't. It's exactly the same."

"Timoté, do not pull on it. Please, that's enough now. You will get sick if we keep doing this."

"Don't change the subject."

She counted the wrinkles around her mouth. Here she was, arguing with a teenager! She pulled off her nightgown and changed into her uniform.

"Just give me one good reason."

"Timi, you are a man now. You must get yourself a nice girlfriend."

She began to slip on her stockings.

"If you won't live with me, I'll kill myself."

She loved these absurd promises that she had taught him to throw out. He was a clinging jasmine vine of a boy with desire oozing out of his pores. What did it matter, Mercedes thought, that he exaggerated? If you exaggerate something long enough, it eventually becomes reality by affirmation.

"I'll do my best to catch syphilis and go blind and die in the gutter like a dog. And all because of you, Benz!"

She began to pin her hair up into a bun.

"There's no one in the house. Where are you going?"

She stopped. The boy was right. She could sleep in all day if she wanted to!

"I have to clean the chandeliers," she lied, and pulled a wide-tooth tortoiseshell comb through the storm tangle of her hair. In the mirror, she saw the boy lying on her eiderdown, primed, bursting with sap, clawing at the ground. How could she protect him? How could she ensure that the years would not leave him bitter and insensitive and distant, like most men when they grow old?

"Benz, look!"

"Don't touch it."

"I'm not! It's wagging by itself."

"How can you always be hard?"

"Is that bad?"

"No, just a little unusual. Now don't think about it."

"I'm not. I'm thinking about you."

"Think of something else, and it will go away."

"I can't."

"Try."

"I have, and I can't. I've decided not to go to New York for my vacation," said the boy, motionless on his back, staring at the ceiling. "I'll stay here with you. I'll say I'm sick. Benz, quick, help me. The juices are coming up."

"Shhh."

Slowly she knelt by the bed. She examined Tim carefully with the tips of her fingers. She knew that for the boy, at this moment, the entire universe was lodged in his groin. And she wanted to be there with him.

Oh, Tim, thought Benz, sliding under him, my *sustirí* pal, when you are inside me, it is the violins of the earth playing their oldest lament. And what can I tell you of your future, of your road? The angle of the morning sun today on your lips was beautiful. So were your long hands. And to feel you growing inside me was, I swear, like having a tree shooting a new green limb full of birds and transparent colors into me, what I believe your mother calls an "*apasionado* of swan necks." And I think of the prospect of being without you one day. Light of my hands, light of the sun falling on my garret at dusk, light of your mother practicing her arpeggios with Signor Cinquemani at the pianoforte, light of ten cheetahs crossing the Bois de Boulogne, light of my nights and of my tides when they turn. This will get us in trouble, Timi. They don't allow people to be happy like this. Light of my years and of this city, light of my rebirth, light of Claude Monet, who took my head in his hands and asked if I would like to play the Virgin Mary in the Christmas pageant, what can I tell you of what I did, except that I wanted to be with you there when it happened?

"Oh, oh, oh, Benz."

The boy clutched at her black hair, the blood draining in a rush from his head. He was sailing through Indian-infested waters, transported by the wind into the fog that engulfed the tip of the Eiffel Tower, the Palais de Chaillot, and the Champs de Mars. He groaned and bit into Benz's arm.

They both lay back, panting, more serene and calm than the thousands of dust particles that danced in the shaft of sunlight cutting through the round window. Her rumpled uniform lay half on the floor, half at the foot of the bed.

"Benz, do you love me?"

MERCEDES kneeled in the confessional. Father Monet was busy with a penitent on the other side, so she had some time to collect her thoughts. Two confessions in the space of six months; he would know this was serious.

"Yes, my child?"

"Father, forgive me, for I have sinned."

"How have you sinned?"

"It is not so much what I am doing, as the fact that I feel no guilt about doing it, Father."

"What do you mean?"

"With the boy, it is so natural, so beautiful. I feel I am doing nothing wrong."

"But you have come here to confess and be cleansed of your sins?"

"Yes, Father, I think, well, I feel guilty because I may be 'using' him. I always flirted with him. But what if I am using him the way men used to use me? He is a soul mate, or as much of one as a *payo* can be to a *gitana*. And I am not sure what to do anymore, or how to get out of it. Help me, Father."

"You must be very strong, very strict with yourself. No matter what your heart tells you, my child, you must stop."

• • •

IT was a beautiful day on the Faubourg Saint-Honoré. He had first thought of shopping on Victor Hugo, at Chez Jones or Céline, right around the corner. But the salesgirls were probably friends of his mother's; walking into a ladies' lingerie store in his own neighborhood was dangerous. Now he and Roland were in the Eighth Arrondissement, a safe distance from home, where American tourists bought ladies' silks by the kilo.

"Why fall in love?" asked Roland. "There are so many other things you should be concentrating on right now."

Tim jokingly passed the fingers of his right hand under his nose.

"Yes, I know. But Tim, in class you just sit there with your teeth in your mouth. The teachers think you're stupid."

They entered Miss Tinguette's, a boutique full of miniskirts and crushed velvet. A girl with paint on her face twice as thick as Benz's stepped forward and asked Tim what he was looking for.

"A *chemisette en soie,*" Tim whispered.

"What size chest?" asked the girl, with the trace of a smile.

Tim shrugged.

"Comme moi?" she asked, pushing her breasts toward him.

He shook his head and indicated that he needed a bigger size.

She laughed and took him to a long rack of silk chemises.

"One size fits all, pretty much. I just wanted to ask that to embarrass you," said the salesgirl, giggling.

He had in mind something beautiful, sensual, and expensive for Benz's birthday, perhaps even Oriental and hourilike. She usually wore only cotton close to her skin. He searched through the fuchsia chemises, peach, russet, luxuriant red, aqua blue, bordello mauve, shocking pink. A silk undershirt would not attract Pepe or Manola's attention and would avoid subjecting her to prying questions. He pointed to the only beige silk chemise on the rack and asked for it to be wrapped. While they watched the salesgirl do so, Roland said:

"Tim, you know the great irony of our old chestnut wars: Napoleon—actually Bonaparte, I should say—championed the ideals of the Revolution. That's why the Marxists today love him. You had it all wrong when you called yourself a Monarchist!"

Tim paid as quickly as he could.

"Roland, would you shut up? My groin is on fire. Now talk about something relevant. What should I do about Benz?"

"BENZ, open up."

Master Tim stood out in the hallway in front of her door, his bare feet freezing on the red tiles.

"Go back to bed."

"I can't."

"You promised you would never come up here again."

"But this is really important."

"What is it?"

"An emergency."

"What kind of an emergency?"

"I can't tell you."

"Whisper it to me through the keyhole."

"I love you."

"What? I can't hear you."

"Benz, open up, for God's sake!"

"It is too dangerous. Timi, you promised the last time that you would visit me only if it was a matter of life and death."

"I haven't been up here in two months, well okay, two weeks."

"Timoté, do not start with me."

"Benz, 'the orders of the King are forever obeyed and never carried out.' You taught me that saying. Come on. I can't sleep without you."

"Try counting sheep."

"I have."

"Try again."

"It doesn't work."

"You aren't trying hard enough."

"Hey, I'm freezing out here. You know it's snowing outside!"

"No, it isn't. It's twelve degrees."

"Don't be so literal, Benz. It's cold out here; it's November, you know."

"That is not an emergency."

"Oh, yeah? You come out here and stand for half an hour, see how you like it! Hey, Benz, where were you last night? With the Baron again?"

"None of your business."

"Open up!"

"Nobody is more hardheaded than a donkey except maybe a *gitana.*"

"Listen, the rats out here are the size of small ponies. One just walked by with blood on its fangs. Maybe the same one that almost ate XKE!"

"Then go back to bed."

"No fooling, I'm catching a cold."

"Timi, Manola would kill us if she knew. Now, go downstairs this instant."

"Benz, the glands in my throat are swelling up. I couldn't make it to my room in my weakened condition."

She heard him cough not too convincingly. There had to be an end to these impossible midnight rendezvous.

"The radio promises gales of North Atlantic sleet, frost, and ice."

"I don't care if the radio promises a typhoon."

There was a silence.

The wind scratched a plaintive little whine at her window. She heard him cough again and opened her door. Tim was wearing his most endearing Don't-kill-my-dog look.

"You will run back at six before Manola wakes up?"

He got into her bed without a word.

"Timoté, you must let me sleep. Okay? Behave yourself."

The bed was a frightful mess of potato chips, magazines, and nail-polish remover. He snuggled up to kiss her tuft of armpit, and discovered she was wearing his silk *chemisette.* She turned off the light. Under these humid sheets, gazing out through her open curtains at the Tour Eiffel, framed in her tiny window like a postcard, he could not help wondering which would attract more tourists, it or he himself, if he were to stand nude astride the Seine and charge admission.

Tim ran one hand gently down her hips and over her back. She was an ocean, the Sea of Tranquility, *Mare* Benz sprinkled with beauty spots like thousands of islands. He was a little river; a rivulet; a tributary, really.

She offered him a plate of fresh strawberries and cream, held one up to his lips, but he shook his head.

"Benz, rape me!"

"Shhh, *por Dios.*"

She kissed him and through her open teeth passed the whole strawberry, licking the juice that flowed down his chin. Then she squeezed him, blue-veined and distended, as hard as she could.

"Benz, that hurts!"

"It is the only way to get your attention! We must talk."

To distract her, he licked the edge of her vaccination scar. She loosened her grasp a little and he surged bigger than ever before. She quickly squeezed him back to manageable size again.

"Timoté, you live in the salon. I live in the kitchen."

"So what?"

"We have to stop."

"Benz, stop saying it can't work! You're so damned negative. A born pessimist. I don't care that you read stupid magazines or pick your teeth after dinner. Just love me, that's all I want. Benz, sometimes when I think I'm going to lose you, I can't breathe. I get these palpitations in my heart and everything starts swimming around."

"LOOK, Benz, if I pull it, it spurts milk."

"Timi, stop it. Stop it. *Por Dios!* Not in the bathroom. Someone may hear us. I have to do the windows."

• • •

TIM was running back to his room. He was scurrying down the steps, barefoot. He went the long way around, down through the cellar, so as to avoid Manola and Pepe's room. How many times since Christmas had he run up and down these freezing stairs, his breath curling in front of him like a horse's, terrified of bumping into an early riser. Today Benz was especially nervous and had sent him down at five, rather than an hour later, as usual. It was a wonder he was getting any sleep at all. His usual post-Benz washup was to bathe as little as possible, brush his teeth, comb his hair, and then spend most of the day in class redolent of her, half-supine, dreaming the afternoon away. Since he now sat next to Gerbi, no one commented on his odor.

Every morning he left her love-humid sheets and ran down these steep stairs, lovesick. After a night of pinch and bite, all he could think was that he should have insisted on taking her one more time, should have given her one additional kiss, licked her one last time. As he ran through the cellar, he saw Benz lying in bed: her arms bent back behind her head, tenderness and hot sleepy breath, telling him through closed eyes to get up.

"What are you doing here, at this hour?"

Surprised by the voice, Tim stopped in his tracks. In the shadows of the cellar, Manola boxed him on the ears.

"Now I catch you!" She glared at him.

What would he tell her? That he had been sleepwalking? That he was night-fishing for crocodiles? She had a shovel and a pickaxe. Was Manola the one who had dug these dozen and one holes?

"Are you spying on me again, Timi?"

Manola splashed well water on her face and washed black dirt off her hands and neck. With her index finger, she brushed her teeth and then switched off the electric water pump. At last she bent down, picked up a blue thermos bottle, and took a long drink.

"Are you up visiting Benz?"

"No no . . . I . . . I came here to see the zombies," mumbled Timi.

"You are lying!" shouted Manola.

"I'm not, I swear it," pleaded Tim. "Roland says that zombies' skin is pale, almost like cream, because they rarely see the sun. But they're not dangerous unless ordered to attack."

"You are spying on me–do not lie!"

Tim shook his head. Manola pinched his left ear and twisted it clockwise.

"Manola, please! I swear, I was going to bring down some Voodoo reliquaries, a gas mask, a saber, a crucifix, a wreath of garlic, and a candle. But now that I know it is you down here digging and not zombies—"

"It is not me! I am not here!" shouted Manola. She pulled his face up to hers. "Timoté, I come here only to get something from the freezer, that is all! *Comprendes, idiota?*"

"But this isn't the way to the freezers."

In this eerie light her mustache looked fuller, almost like a man's. She wiped some dirt off her pants and shirt and shook it out of her hair.

"Don't be impudent, *estúpido*. I tell you so many times not to come down here!"

A large bug with a polished fuselage cleaned its face. Its antennae waved in the semidarkness.

"You get me so angry, I want to throw you in the well! Then you can taste how sharp are the triple rows of razor-like piranha teeth."

Three times Master Tim promised not to say a word about seeing Manola on her way to the freezers at five in the morning. When Manola had sufficiently calmed down, she wiped her brow and said:

"You want to know why I am here? I tell you why! In 1942, your father, Pepe, and the Baron, we go to the Jardin d'Acclimatation, where the animals are dying because there is not enough food to feed them. So your father and the Baron, they buy all sorts of exotic marine life, snakes and piranhas and lizards, and we stock this Gallo-Roman well. During the war they use it to dispose of Gestapo or traitors. It is a very efficient disposal system, because it leaves no traces. After the war, the Aunties pay for a team of scientists to come and take away all the sea creatures. They send for Capitaine Cousteau's brother, Henri. They entrust the cleanup details to me. I say *'Oui, oui,* I take care of everything.' But I never call Capitaine Cousteau or his friends. Because I know the value of a good disposal system. So if you breathe a word that I am here, I throw you in!"

SHE watched his penis come to the surface of the soapy water.

"No, no, not here, Timi, *por Dios,* not here. There are cadaver ladies drinking tea with Aunt Phoebe downstairs. This is too dangerous."

Tim, in the bathtub, stared up at the ceiling as Mercedes bent over to wash him. She stopped, lifted her head like a scared animal and looked around the bathroom. Tim guided her hand down again.

"Timi, love is not just sex. Now, put that away—slam it in a drawer or in a closet; I don't care."

"Benz, get in, get in the bathtub, for God's sake."

Benz made the sign of the cross as she kicked off her shoes and climbed into the bath.

"Wait, wait, I must take off my blouse."

Timi felt up her legs and thighs while she stood with her black skirt and blouse caught covering her face. Yanking them over her head, Benz broke a button. Wonderdog scratched and whined at the door. Mercedes slowly lowered herself before Timi. The water started to splash as her big breasts floated up and down beguilingly before him.

"Timi, from now on, you must take a cold shower, or study longer hours at school, because this cannot continue. I get no work done around the house and neither do you."

She dug her fingers into his arms and stopped. The key was turning in the lock. She pinched his arms so hard he gasped.

"Anyone here?" said Aunt Agatha, toddling in with a bunch of keys in her right hand.

She's blind, but she has keys, thought Benz, terrified. Her heart had stopped. Here was Agatha feeling along the wall, touching the dressers, checking that the sink faucets were properly closed. And Timi, his head underwater, stifled a laugh, letting bubbles escape.

"Anybody here?" repeated Agatha.

Wonderdog scratched the side of the bathtub, trying inconclusively to bark at Benz's soapy breasts. This is it, she thought; we are dead. Virgin of the Poor and the Oppressed, I promise to be good. I will never do anything wrong, ever again. I will even go to confession if you make me disappear.

"Oh, it's you," said Agatha, bending down to pat the dog.

Then she looked straight at Benz with her milky stare, paused for a second, and walked to the door, carefully locking it behind her. Mercedes exhaled deeply. Timothy started to speak, but she covered the boy's mouth until she heard the Auntie's footsteps disappear down the hallway.

MERCEDES stood in line at the Prisunic checkout counter. Even the so-called "express lines" took hours. While she waited, she opened a copy of *Oui* magazine. When she'd discovered several issues of it in Tim's room, she had torn them up and yelled at him ("You want to see a *derrière*, here, take a bite of this one! You want some breast? Isn't this one big enough for you? Don't turn away when I am shouting at you!") But in fact, she found pornography somewhat arousing, in a perverse way.

She dreaded leaving the house; it had become a sort of pleasure palace. She never knew when or where Timi would take her. In the bathroom; under the piano. It was a wonder the boy had any stamina left for school or friends. He certainly had energy to spare! And for Benz Number 10½ was becoming synonymous with eroticism. Wiping windows, making beds, shining mirrors became an excuse for dangerous fooling around, and knee burns on the carpet. The housekeeping was suffering, but Manola and Pepe seemed not to notice. Certainly the Aunties didn't:

"Agatha and I want you to know, Mercedes, how happy we are with how Timothy is doing at school. His notebooks show all the signs of serious application and diligence. No more doodling, no more marriage lists. He appears to have finally made the distinction between what is important in life and what is a waste of time. And Benz, we believe that you are partially responsible for this turnaround. No, no, don't blush."

At times such as these, Benz found herself actually wondering whether Tim was the handsome dark-haired man foretold in the egg yolk she had consulted in the bathtub.

" . . . and she's corrupting minors."

Benz was not certain she had heard properly, but she instinctively reached for her sunglasses and raised the magazine over her face.

"Yes," said an old biddy two spaces ahead of her in the Prisunic line. "I've seen them holding hands, kissing, and God knows what else they do up there on the sixth floor."

Benz was not certain these were the same *concierges* who had maligned her once before in the Pharmacie de l'Etoile. These brittle, gray, rat-faced women all looked alike to her. And she knew by heart now all of their objections to her—those dour *paya* bitches!

"Yes, now that you mention it, the boy always looks so tired, so lazy. Yes, and she too seems quite pale."

Mercedes turned to face a display of ribbons and colored wrapping paper. The Child Welfare Department, the Morals Squad, the Division of Immigration and Alien Control, she saw them all converging on the Cardozo house, walkie-talkies blaring, pursued by photographers and tabloid journalists.

"And I'll tell you something else: I've never liked her, never trusted her. You see how she walks that dog? Swanking around like she was a professional! Trying to stop as many cars as she can."

Benz flushed red and wanted to slap these two stupid women she had never before seen in her life. But after the *pharmacie* episode of two years ago, she knew she had to control her temper. No, she would definitely have to break off everything with the boy. Rumors were like cockroaches: if one *concierge* knew about it, a thousand *concierges* in the neighborhood also knew about it!

She raced home without waiting for her lipsticks and beauty aids. As she rushed past the embassy, Raoul Delbosc accosted her.

"Yes, what is it, Raoul? I am very busy."

Wrenching himself out of his shyness, the policeman stammered:

"Mercedes, I'd like to have another chance with you. Please, I don't know what's gone wrong between us. I beg you, give me another try."

Raoul's persistence was flattering. The worse you treated men, the more they responded. She promised to consider his request but asked him to leave her alone for now. And wait, she thought, for me to whistle.

MERCEDES shushed the boy. She felt quite romantic tonight, but there was a noise coming from the stairs. She cocked her ear toward the door and listened. All Mercedes could hear was the pigeons cooing in the chimney and the dull hum of distant traffic. This had been meant to be their last night together, but she was becoming addicted. And what she wanted then, as she clasped Timi's tight fingers to her breasts, ah, what she wanted, on this chilly February night when Métros screamed under the Arc de Triomphe like electric giants zooming for points east and south, blazing furiously through the underground night, shaking these century-old foundations with voracious desire, was the landscape of this young man, unleashed.

"*Deutschland, Deutschland* . . . " sang a voice from the stairs.

She grabbed Timi by the hair, and motioned toward the hallway.

"Sounds like a drunken tourist," said the boy.

"No, it is Pepe! Quick, get under the bed!"

The singing was getting closer. When sober, Pepe kept it clear in his mind which side had won the war, but this was not so when he was inebriated for then his sympathies veered in many directions.

"DEUTSCHLAND UUUUBER AAAAAALLES!"

Mercedes pushed the boy onto the cold parquet floor and under the sagging bed. He sneezed.

"Benz, tell him your new boyfriend has a purple belt in Jujitsu and that I will make him lose ninety pounds in just under three and a half seconds flat."

She double-bolted the new locks on her door and stood in the sink light, wrapping her heavy pink bathrobe tightly around herself. The wind chimed through a crack in the window.

"Open this door, you stinking pile of dung!" shouted Pepe.

She threw her back against the door and whispered to Timi not to move. What exactly had this coward done during the war? she wondered. Pepe's fists pounded on the door. Mercedes stuffed Tim's bathrobe and slippers into her closet.

"Open up, woman! I saw you with the boy the other day. Don't lie, you were behind the rhododendron!"

The lock rattled and the door splintered. Except for Timi, the men in her life—Sean, Raoul, Marcel the butcher's son, Pepe—were basically, when she analyzed them, Cro-Magnon men, egos attached to penises. No wonder the palm reader had said she would be saved by a white horse, not a man! On her life line and in her tea leaves, the reader had predicted Mercedes clattering through Paris on a white horse with wings of gold! Suddenly the chain lock gave way. Pepe stood silhouetted under the naked bulb of the hallway, his drunken breath billowing into her face.

"If you're not good to me, Benz, I'll announce to the Aunts at breakfast tomorrow what's going on between you and the boy!"

With the toilet plunger, she pushed Pepe back into the hallway as hard as she could.

"I shall call the police, you pig."

"Go ahead," said Pepe, reentering the room and closing the door behind him. "They may go easy on you and just send you to a penitentiary or perhaps a psychiatric clinic. It won't be so bad. The boy will be allowed to come visit you once a month. Question is, will he want to when all your hair is shaved off?"

There was another knock on the door. From his vantage

point under the bed, Tim saw Pepe's brown espadrilles and Benz's bare martyr's feet stop doing the dance of Saint Vitus. Judging by its thickness, the layers of dust under her bed surely antedated even the Elevator from the Year One!

"Who's there?" asked Mercedes in a sweet, thin voice.

"It's Raoul. I just got off duty."

"Get in the closet, quick," whispered Mercedes to Pepe. And then, louder: "Well, I'm sleeping."

"I heard someone shouting. I thought you might be in trouble. Is everything all right?"

Slowly, Raoul pushed his meek weasel face into the room. Pepe roared and charged forward with one of his patented Basque head-jabs, which, when his guidance system was properly set, could kill a man. The bedside lamp toppled over. Benz yelled for them to stop. She kicked and slapped Pepe, but he was unstoppable. Mercedes knew that dealing with men was like bullfighting: you had to let them have their way until they became too tired or bored. Then you could befuddle them, taunt them, make them run in circles, and when they were finally exhausted, it was easy, almost a deliverance, to dispatch them with a wound like "I don't love you," or "I could never love you." Something lethal and straightforward thrust right into their hearts that they could understand without much difficulty.

Tim watched from his ringside seat. This was yet another Great Moment in History. Stars bloomed like diamonds up in the little round window. Little rats' feet scampered behind the walls. Now there was yet another knock on the door, followed by total silence. Raoul croaked into his walkie-talkie for reinforcements:

"S.O.S.! Au secours, tout de suite!"

Perhaps there was no knock at all, perhaps Manola just appeared, like the Curse of the Mummy. Perhaps she had watched the entire evening unfold from the beginning. But suddenly she stood in the doorway, in her hair curlers and nightgown. Tim imagined this silence was the terrifying sound one hears a millisecond before the end of the world.

"So the men of the house are all sharing you, are they?"

"I can explain everything, Manola," said Mercedes.

She might have, but Manola grabbed her by the hair and pulled her down, arching her like a classical dancer to the floor, giving Raoul the opportunity to sucker-punch Pepe in the throat. A chair broke. The porcelain washbasin crashed to the floor. The little crucifix flew from the wall and landed on the floor next to Tim.

"You floozy, of no shame, no education . . . when I think of all the money I give you for your abortion!" shouted Manola.

"Your husband is the pig! He is the one who has no shame. Why does he come up here and break down my door?"

Someone's dentures landed at Tim's feet. Judging by the size of the bicuspids, he figured they were Pepe's. A pillow ripped, and goose feathers began to blizzard around the room. How beautiful, thought Tim, scrunched up behind the armchair.

"Ever since we take you out of that breadline in church," shouted Manola, pulling a tuft of hair from Benz's head, "you drive Pepe *loco*. Now he drinks and gambles. You temptress, you!"

"Pepe is an animal! He should be kept on a leash!" shouted Benz, spitting in Manola's face.

Pillow feathers swirled around the room like a wonderful snowstorm. Pepe managed a left uppercut that sent the hapless Raoul sailing horizontally out into the hallway, hitting his head and slumping to the floor with a deep thud.

Down the hall, past the immobile Raoul, went Benz and Manola, biting, clawing, punching each other like those dog litters in which a twisted mass of little legs and noses fight each other for a teat. Tim followed, with a white feather floating on his shoulder. Rat eyes peeked from their little cubbyholes.

Pepe tried to separate the women, but they were entwined in a mortal, full-nelson, half-twist, over-the-shoulder death lock. All three fell. Down the narrow staircase they spiraled like one of Timi's Slinkies. The human punching ball bounced down the steep steps and off each landing, leaving curses, smears of blood and tufts of hair in its wake. At last they toppled into the garbage cans on the ground floor in the corner of the courtyard.

Tim followed quietly and, without a word, handed Pepe back his dentures.

"You are sleeping with the boy, you slut!" shouted Manola, the last to get up. "You have soiled him. You have ruined his life."

The lights went on in the fourth-floor Aunties' rooms. Benz did not answer. She was busy picking a strip of Manola's nightgown out of her mouth. Tim was quiet. What could he say to defend Benz? More neighbors' windows were being lit. It was always hot news when there was noise coming from Number 10½: it meant either an embassy bash or movie actors misbehaving! It had started snowing outside; the courtyard was a storm of swirling flakes.

"For shame!" hissed Manola. "*Puta, putana!* You corrupt him for your vicious pleasures, you sin seeker! *Zorra!*"

"*Taisez-vous! On essaie de dormir!*" shouted a neighbor.

"*Desgraciada, sin vergüenza! Puerca!*" continued Manola.

Tim said nothing. He did not move. He had caused all this. He wanted to stand up to all these grown-ups, tell them all to go away, shut them up. But he did nothing. It was very nearly a replay of the night when his mother had gotten into bed with him and his father had stood at the foot of the bed yelling coarsely about her money-spending habits. Then too he had wanted to take charge of the situation, tell his father to stop and his mother to go fight her own battles. But he had held absolutely still and absolutely silent, hating himself for his cowardice, rationalizing his inactivity with a variety of arguments, such as "My father is a fair man," "He knows what he is doing," or "This situation is beyond me." Many of the same arguments returned now: "Benz, you're twenty-four, you can get yourself out of this; I'm only fifteen, not even fifteen yet." Loathing everything about himself, Tim said nothing and retreated abjectly in the dark back to his room.

The Aunties peered down from their bedroom window. The February snow made it difficult for Phoebe to see. Pepe reinserted his dentures, but bent out of shape, they would not fit properly. The Ambassador opened his large bay windows and invited all to "Come in and have one last nightcap." Raoul slunk along the back wall to the driveway, his walkie-talkie pressed to his lips.

"If you are pregnant with the boy's child, *los ojos de Dios van a llorar!*" shouted Manola, waving her fists at the sky. *"Mar-ana, desgraciada, sin vergüenza!"*

"Taisez-vous!" shouted a neighbor.

"C'est un scandale! Allez au lit," shouted another.

The Ambassador commented on how beautiful the snow looked. He was followed by a butler who carried a tray of champagne glasses. Two leg ladies appeared out of the drive-way shadows to warn that the *flics* were on their way and tried to hide behind the Ambassador. The first policeman to enter the courtyard grabbed Raoul by the scruff of the neck and slapped handcuffs on his wrists.

A young lieutenant called for identification papers. The leg ladies retreated into the shadows, as did Manola and Benz. That left only Pepe; Raoul, tugging at his handcuffs; and the Ambas-sador. The Aunties decided to pull their woolen coats on over their nighties and see what this was all about. The entire neigh-borhood was lit up, and they could hear Mercedes sobbing in the staircase.

ON the morning which followed the night that was, no one came to wake Tim up. He neither showered nor breakfasted, but dressed quickly by himself. A centimeter of pale white snow covered the courtyard. In a corner, by the garbage cans, he found drops of blood and other vestiges of the evening. And there, purring by itself, was a black limousine, a rampant death leopard with tinted eyes. Was the Baron stalking his prey? Were they sending Benz away? He looked inside the night cat: it was empty. But the engine was still running. He started for school, then retraced his steps and waited in the driveway. There was something evil about these quiet cars that appeared, black and spotless, out of nowhere when you least expected them.

At last, he saw a tall blonde walk toward the car, followed by the studio chauffeur carrying matching suitcases. He looked at her pale river-blue eyes. No one had told him that Kim Novak was back, or that she was leaving today. (In the early days, when Benz was in charge of spying on movie actors, they would have known exactly when she had arrived and what she ate for breakfast every day.)

"Kim, do you remember me?" he asked.

"Yes, you're Timi. My God, how you've grown."

"We met when I was eight. Now I'm almost fifteen."

"We all get old, don't we?"

She offered him the widest movie screen smile he had ever seen. Her sweatshirt was pulled down over one shoulder, and her hair cut very short. He was finding it hard to get his tongue to move. An unmistakable current passed between her eyes and his.

"You had quite some party here last night, huh?"

Tim reddened.

"Yeah."

"I'm going back to Santa Monica. You wanna come?"

He nodded. What a strange sensation, to go mute like this. Where was Santa Monica? Her sunlight eyes were pouring down on him like honey. What would the Aunties say about last night? What would the Police Judiciaire say, or, for that matter, The Ladies of the Passy Literary, Knitting and Opera Society? Everyone in Passy must have heard Manola's screams. Perhaps this was the ideal time for Tim to visit Santa Monica, play the turtle, deny everything, and find a safer place for their future assignations?

"Will you write to me?" asked Kim, climbing into her black panther.

She was the most glamorous woman alive at that moment.

"Yes, of course."

"I want long, informative letters."

Mist spilled into his eyes like a silver waterfall. This must be what they called "love"; but then what was it that he felt for Benz?

He waved as the car glided away. Down the driveway and down the snowy avenue it purred. Sooner or later they all forsook him: Alec Guinness, Cary Grant, Sophia Loren, and now Kim Novak. They zapped him with high-voltage X-ray eyes, in what Benz had explained was the Indigo Zoom, then just drove off. He hadn't even asked for her address! How could he forget? They couldn't become pen pals—he would probably never see her again! He kicked the snow and walked slowly, horseless, Benz-less, to school.

CHAPTER 9

Master Tim and the Indigo Zoom

ROLAND AND TIM had a subscription to the Comédie Française. The classical matinee series was held every other Thursday at the theater built by Molière more than two centuries before. Tim could never get comfortable in the deep, red velvet seats, but the droning of these famous actors was one of the strongest nonprescription sedatives a boy of fifteen could find in Paris. Today they were playing *Bérénice* by Racine:

YES, THE HONOR OF THY FOREFATHERS IS AT STAKE!
O, WOMEN OF ROME, REND THY BREASTS AND CRY OUT FOR JUSTICE!

These classics were guaranteed to make one yawn in approximately two minutes, thirty seconds! The actors never moved; obviously, they were sleepwalking through their roles. Even the mamma's boys in the front rows with their neatly combed hair and their short pants nodded off to sleep by the second act. Only the jack-off artists in the balcony and the rear mezzanine stayed awake, thanks mostly to their strenuous and noisy extracurricular activity.

'TIS FAR BETTER TO DIE WITH HONOR AND DIGNITY
THAN TO LIVE THE LIFE OF A REGICIDE!
WOE TO US, WOE, O CITIZENS!

Master Tim tried to unscrew one of the bolts of his velvet chair. It was too tight. He pulled out his Swiss Army knife and selected the small screwdriver blade. Women in Greek robes entered and exited the stage to a chorus of snores from the audience. Bruising the thumb and index finger of his right hand, Tim managed to pry one large screw loose under his seat. By his careful reckoning, he judged there must be 139 other screws holding the seat together.

Benz, I love you
More than my life.
I beg of you,
Please be my wife.

The Aunties looked at each other and then back at the pages of a three-ring binder that Tim had hidden in the corner of his sock drawer under his strongbox. He would be at the theater all day.

"A rather plebeian rhyme scheme," said Phoebe, stirring a spoon in her tea.

"At least he keeps his meter regular," said Agatha, who always tried to see the bright side of things.

Phoebe continued to read. It was clear that these were drafts for longer poems that, when copied out longhand, were ripped out of the notebook and given to his loved one.

"I do believe," said Agatha, who was the blinder of the two, "that Mercedes is with child."

"Oh, no, not again!"

"Yes, she is starting to waddle."

Phoebe stared dumbfounded at her sister, for she knew that Agatha could see only the barest patterns of light and shadow.

"And what if our Timothy is the father?" said Agatha, continuing her train of thought. "Then we are in quite a piddle."

Phoebe coughed up her herbal tea and reached for a handkerchief. Her sister waited for her to compose herself.

WOE TO OUR CITY AND WOE TO THE GODS! HE WHO WOULD BETRAY
THE TRUST OF BLOOD MUST PAY
WITH HIS OWN BLOOD!

Thirteen down, 127 left to go. Tim did not have the slightest idea what this ridiculous play was about. A Messenger ran on stage, bleeding, and lay down to die. As this was the first actual event to occur within the proscenium in over an hour, Tim stopped unscrewing the bolts of his chair and waited to see if something else might happen. But the wounded man spoke for twenty minutes. Each time he stopped to catch his breath, Tim thought he would certainly die. But each time the actor jerked his head up in a state of high dudgeon and continued to declaim:

LET US NOW GRIEVE FOR THE EVENTS THAT HAVE BEFALLEN US!
O CITIZENS, THE UNEXPECTED IS ALWAYS UPON US
—IN OUR HOMES, IN THE STREETS, ON OUR STAGES!

The monotony of the play was relieved only by the cries of ecstasy from the boys in the balcony—the misnamed "Family Circle." Roland, who could fall asleep under a moving train, was sprawled out, his head thrown back, his left arm every now and then twitching. He snored ever so lightly, with his mouth open. Tim resumed work on the lug bolts.

Benz, you and I will have eight beautiful part gitano,
part Jewish children. We'll work at . . .

Phoebe reread this last line: It was all the proof needed that Tim was, or might be construed to be, the father of Benz's *in utero*. Phoebe held her forehead with her right hand and winced. She waited for a solution to come, as one waits for the electric selector at the dry cleaner's to turn the conveyor belt until the dress appears that matches the number on one's ticket. Obviously, the maid and the boy had to be separated. Benz must be married, but to whom? And Tim must be sent away, but where?

"Why not send him on vacation with his little friend Roland?"

Phoebe rejected this and various of her sister's other ideas as not addressing the real problem.

"Agatha, we are dealing with hidden structure here. It is not just Benz we have to eradicate from his life. It is the idea of her we must remove from his consciousness."

Agatha smiled and held her tongue. Sometimes her older sister could not see what was staring her right in the face:

"A summer vacation in the Caribbean: It will be very hot. He will see many native women with bare breasts. And he will do what comes naturally to teenagers on a beach under the stars."

"Non, je t'en prie!" Phoebe blushed. "Agatha, really. How do you think of such things?"

"One fights fire with fire, my dear."

THERE CAN BE NO GREAT TRUTH WITHOUT A CERTAIN PAIN; AND THUS,
VERY MUCH AS IT HAPPENS IN LIFE, O FAIR BÉRÉNICE,
ONE TRAGEDY COMES TO AN END AND ANOTHER BEGINS.

One hundred thirty-nine bolts. No small accomplishment in the dark in just under three hours forty minutes. Tim started to work on the last screw. The final curtain could not be more than one or two speeches away. A mere five thousand words—short by Racine's standards. The lug bolt was loose now. The entire row would collapse as soon as he dislodged it. Grimy tissues rained from the Ejaculation Kings in the upper balcony. The curtain at last came down. It rose again for the desultory applause of a few polite kiss-asses. The others slowly stirred, yawned, reached for their jackets.

Presto, voilà. All 140 bolts were on the floor now, a feat of teenage engineering. Tim folded up his Swiss Army knife and grabbed Roland just before the row gave way. His friend woke with a start. Several boys screamed, trapped in the collapsing row of chairs like clams in their shells. Masters Tim and Roland raced out. Bewildered ushers ran from the red-lit EXIT signs to help the boys screaming from inside their chairs.

"Timothy will never agree to leave Paris and leave Benz," said Agatha, fetching more cream from the sideboard. "He is more hardheaded than a she-camel in heat."

"Yes, it is a family trait," agreed Phoebe.

"One thing at least is clear," said Agatha. "We cannot continue to do all the housework ourselves."

For two weeks, Pepe and Manola and their head bandages, Mercedes and her cries and hysterics, had remained locked in their respective rooms.

"This is a fine state of affairs!" said Phoebe.

"At least Cascasia and Alphonse are away," said Agatha pressing a white lace handkerchief to her lips.

"Yes, thank God. Now let's get to work, my dear."

DIEUJUSTE, the Lapatte family retainer, handed Timothy a rum punch and said:

"Jérôme will be terrible, sir. Please, it is time to leave the swimming pool now, sir."

Tim nodded and paddled on his lie-low as a few drops of rain began to fall. The bay of Port-au-Prince was filling up with black clouds that tumbled low over the Voodoo-infested hills of Pétionville. If the Aunties thought they could make him forget Benz by sending him here, thought Master Tim, they were sadly mistaken. He had thought of nothing but her during his entire vacation. This was his first major trip out of Paris, but he noticed very little. Benz's night smells, her Nivea arms and large fleshy backside, these were the things he studied, categorized, reviewed every day. He did not want to be a fickle swivel-head who forgets.

"Monsieur, tonight very bad weather. Please come now."

Master Tim asked Dieujuste to fetch him another Barbancourt rum.

"Monsieur, we are worried you will fry in the *piscine*."

Tim swiveled in the water and looked at the kaleidoscope colors of the sky: sunset reds and purples mixed with flashes of lightning. Hummingbirds helicoptered in and out of the flame-tree blossoms. Green tree toads made tiny cymbal-like noises. But in Roland's hydrangea-stocked vista, overlooking the bay, Tim knew nothing in the world could replace Benz, not even a typhoon. Drops of rain splashed on the surface of the aquamarine pool.

"Madame Lapatte says this must definitely be your last drink for today. She says you have had enough."

Thunder boomed across Pétionville. Servants scurried around the house roping down furniture, placing mattresses up against the windows. Flowerpots on the patio were brought into the house. Forget-me-nots waved blue-and-white in the half-light. Tim paddled farther out into the pool. Papaya, rubber, avocado, bamboo, almond, palm, and lemon trees fretted and shook.

"Monsieur, vite. Vite!"

"Calm down, Dieujuste. People give these things too much importance."

Another clap of thunder. This time a white zipper of lightning cut the sky in two. The grenadine and laurel bent to the ground.

"Monsieur, the Lapattes do not have insurance to cover guests' safety in the *piscine.*"

Roland's family waved from the house for him to come inside. He pretended not to see them. What did they understand of heartbreak? Of despair? The wind sent a bunch of bananas slamming into the pool and bullied his little rubber raft around like a thimble. Roland shouted from the patio:

"Hey Captain Courageous, we're going to have a hurricane!"

"So what?"

"Well, the cats and dogs and the rest of us have crowded into our cellar. Just thought you'd like to know."

"I'm not scared of anything, except of a life without love!"

"You're an idiot!"

The clouds swirled and darkened and grew as thick as a shroud. The yolk of the sun broke and spread in streams over the harbor waters—a river-sky of blue-black. Poinsettias, orchids, camellias, and hibiscus filled the air with perfume. Bats swooped low to scoop water from the pool before zigzagging back to the trees. The mosquitoes and dragonflies grew quiet. Even the toads ceased their bell ringing.

"Jérôme is here, Monsieur," said Dieujuste raising his eyebrows for emphasis.

"Well, good. Invite him over, then."

The rain broke in the distance, and advanced up the hill, the drops growing fat, fatter, fattest. Rain gunned the pool, turning the road beyond the garden into a muddy torrent, half-drowning Tim in his inflated rubber lie-low. The power went off in the house. As Dieujuste escorted him back to the safety of the living room, Tim watched his beige lie-low sail over the trees and down toward the marketplace. Violette, the maid, handed him a towel. Roland's mulatto cousin Patricia wondered whether he was brave, crazy, or both. Thunder boomed. Lightning flashed on and off like a *son-et-lumière* show. The rain fell in diagonal gray sheets.

"So where is Jérôme? And who is he, anyway?"

"Jérôme is the hurricane, stupid," laughed the beautiful Patricia.

Coconuts flew past the house. The swings from the garden left the ground and clattered over the wall down the road. Rainwater sloshed ankle-deep through the house. Black faces and white eyes huddled in the dark. A portable radio emitted static.

"I'm so scared," said Patricia, clutching Tim's hand.

He didn't want any woman other than Benz to come close to him, and he pulled his hand away as if he had been burned.

The wind whistled through the cracks and the venerable old house groaned. Dieujuste mouthed Hail Marys. The last candle blew out. Above the mattressed windows, Tim could see the foul sky swirling around and around the house like a witch's brew.

What was Benz doing now? he wondered.

THE Baron excused himself and asked the waiter for the men's room. Mercedes watched him walk to the back through the crowded little Ile St.-Louis restaurant. The headwaiter of Chez

Hubert proposed various dessert specialties. She explained that they did not have enough time because they had to catch a flight to Sri Lanka.

Since leaving the Cardozo house, she had felt like soggy, overripe fruit, heavy and ready to burst. Her solution, for the time being, was to apply another layer of purple and vermilion to her eyes and a little powder and base on her cheeks. She needed all the camouflage she could get to keep her smile from falling off. Her life was beginning to sound dangerously like a headline in *Paris-Unveiled:*

PREGNANT SPANISH MAID TRICKS BARON
INTO SWEEPING HER OFF HER FEET

Isidore was taking a long time in the bathroom. She lit a cigarette and checked her watch. Smoking was bad for the baby, but she did not want to give Isi any reason to suspect her situation. The maître d' delivered the bill with utmost delicacy, with perhaps a touch too much solicitude. She let it lie, face down, in the middle of the table, and glanced at her watch. Past eleven already! Some waiters were counting up their tips. Others were changing into street clothes. What time did airplanes stop taking off? (She imagined them all rising into the dusk, one after another, like a flight of geese.) She could see an Algerian boy in a blue smock mopping the tiled floor.

The Baron had been gone twenty minutes! Maybe he had had a heart attack or a stroke? She gave him another five minutes, then walked to the telephone booth and dialed his automobile. There was no answer. Benz asked the Algerian to check the men's room.

No reason to panic. Maybe Isidore had been called away on some urgent political mission. She toyed with the idea of calling one of those women's-liberation groups that would recommend a hundred painful ways to castrate the Baron for doing what she thought he was in the process of doing to her.

"Y' a personne dans les toilettes," the Algerian busboy whispered in her ear. She handed him her last 10-franc note.

The *mato payo* bastard! No one treated Benz like a bread

crumb soaking at the bottom of a urinal! She lit another cigarette. What if she kept the baby this time? Alone, with no papers, no *carte de séjour,* no money! A baby was always good for begging, as her mother and her grandmother had found. A baby might force her to put down some roots. Benz never wanted to be alone again, never again so totally vulnerable, so transient.

Chez Hubert (formerly "Le Coq d'Or," said the menu) did not exist. Neither did the Air France plane she would take to Sri Lanka. She was not curious in the slightest about her destination, or even about the street outside the restaurant. Leaving the Cardozos was a sunset for her, one that would never recur. The Aunties, the ballroom, her tiny rooftop maid's room with its sitting-dog windows, the gutter machicolations, the spiral service staircase, all had ceased to exist.

The maître d' and two of the waiters stood smoking at the end of the bar. The bill sat in front of her like an insult. She was too proud to throw it in their damn faces! To whom would she turn now for absolute devotion and adoration, now that Timi had proved himself a total coward and allowed her, in effect, to be kicked out of the Cardozo house? Her friends Fufa and Dora worked in houses, but she could not impose on them. Nor could she go back to the Spanish Church—Manola and Pepe would find out, and she had too much pride for that. Where would she sleep tonight? She eyed the Algerian sweeping the floor.

It was almost midnight. She telephoned the Baron's home, taking care not to look the maître d' in the eye. Rothschild's butler answered that he did not know where Monsieur was or when he would be returning from his trip to Asia. Would she please leave her name, however, so that the Baron would be informed of her call when he returned, three months from now? "Tell the Baron that the only original thought he ever had died of solitary confinement, and that he is an impotent voyeur bastard!" She slammed down the phone and returned to the table. The restaurant was totally empty, and so was her wallet. The waiters were collecting ashtrays and putting the chairs up on the tables; the bartender was locking the cash register.

She sat back in the only chair left on the floor of the restaurant and lit a cigarette. If there were an atomic war and she could pick only one human to come with her on the last train to safety, who would that be? Until recently, she would have picked the one she had promised the Aunties never to see ever again. But the spoiled little brat could go to hell—he had not lifted a finger in her defense, not said anything at all when the neighborhood lynch mob came to call! Instead of chasing them away, Tim had gone on vacation, leaving her barricaded in her room with an ice pack on her head. And as for the rest of them, they had been so very friendly. "Please come see us again. We love you, Benz." "Oh, yes, you must come and see us often. Here, here's some cash to tide you over." "To us, you will always be family, Benz, but you understand . . ." She understood—oh, yes—that they could all go to hell.

One afternoon, Aunt Phoebe had knocked on the door and said:

"Agatha is still on the third-floor landing. She has insisted on bringing you something to eat herself. But I think she's dropped most of it on the way.

Mercedes could just see sweet, transparent Agatha toddling up the spiral steps at the rate of a centimeter a minute, dropping croissants along her path.

"We know who did this to you," said Phoebe. "He is such a ladies' man! But Raoul has promised his superiors and us that he will marry you."

Marry Raoul? Mercedes had never let that cop so much as touch her. To do so would have insulted entire generations of the Los Angeles family! She quickly opened a bottle of aspirin and swallowed two more. Phoebe's reedy little voice continued through the locked door:

"Agatha and I made it very clear to our good friend Martin Duchesne, the Minister of Justice, that if Raoul did not do the honorable thing by you, we would stop donating to the Police Benevolent Fund."

In the empty restaurant, two tears slipped down Mercedes' face. The Baron had obviously decamped, and all the remaining personnel—barman, maître d', busboys, waiters—were watching her. She could feel their stares. It made perfect sense: The Baron owned three-quarters of the world and had a majority share in the rest. He went through servants, horses, fortunes, roulette wheels, *millésimé* bottles, women—with absolutely no sense of shame. Why had she always been so mesmerized by the rich and powerful? They were *payo* shit! And these restaurateurs with their oily mouths had no doubt been in on it from the beginning! They had waited, nineteen to the dozen, for her to announce she did not have enough to pay, humiliating her right up until closing time before offering, with great *noblesse-oblige:*

"We will bill Monsieur le Baron at home. Do not trouble yourself, Mademoiselle."

The barman locked up his drawers and sealed the money bags; the lights were switched off one by one in the kitchen. The maître d' cleared his throat. She stubbed out her cigarette. Surrender was a most un-Gypsy-like act. Yet her father always said, "Better to flee than to fight badly." To think she had already had one abortion in order to play by *payo* rules! She had called it a miscarriage, but in actuality, it had been *une opération manquée.*

She stood up and slowly collected the change she had intended to leave as a *pourboire.* She made certain the maître d' noticed her picking up every centime. (See what a sense of humor I have, you overdressed pigs!) Then, lifting the heavy rope-tied cardboard suitcases left at the checkroom, she swept out of the restaurant, her head high, like Madame Cardozo when she was leading a train of a half-dozen servants.

Where to go? She stood on the sidewalk and stared at the vast city. The leaves of autumn that had colored her days with red and gold were gone. She was totally alone.

She would go immediately to the obstetrician. The bastards would not prevent her from having a family! She would have her baby alone, in a gutter if need be, wrapped in old copies of *Paris-Unveiled.* And he would be a fine *gitano* boy, a cutthroat and a purse snatcher; no snazzy suits or *payo* education for him! No Italian leather shoes. No phony British accent. The Baron, Pepe, Sean, McLuck, Marcel, Monsieur Henri—she would soar above these little piss-ants and would not bother wasting her precious hatred on them. Her suitcases were so heavy they seemed to be packed with rocks. But she felt invincible.

She would go to Claude Monet, S.J. He would put her up in one of the rooms at Saint-Philippe reserved for boarders. She could do chores around the school. Perhaps Monet would find her a place in a convent, at least until the last month of the pregnancy; there would be less risk of running into Timi there. Gone were her dreams of passion and of the Indigo Zoom. This was survival now; survival and progeny; daily life and procreation.

She passed a wino on the sidewalk and handed him the Baron's business card, on the back of which Isidore had drawn a heart pierced with an arrow and containing her initials.

THEY walked slowly out to the workout mats wearing their spotless white kimonos and purple belts, tied à la Dr. Feng. In the visitors' lounge, by the Coke machine, sat Patricia Lapatte. She attended the Lycée Montaigne, but Tim had not seen her since Port-au-Prince. With her jingling bracelets all up and down her thin arms, the narrow doelike nose, and the cream-colored eyelids which hung permanently half-closed, she had a dreamy, sensuous look. Her bored porphyry expression, so haughty and regal, might have excited him were he not already spoken for. He smiled at her, but Patricia stifled a yawn and stared right through him.

"Begin free style," said Dr. Feng in his clipped voice.

The honorable friends bowed deeply and grabbed each other's lapels. They took two steps forward, then two steps back. Three sideways. Kick, turn. Roland's legs were sequoia trees, and they shot out of nowhere. Tim held on to his friend's kimono as tightly as he could. Roland feinted left, swiveled his hip right, and threw Tim over his shoulder.

"Gud. Gud. Excellent falling-down technique. No hurt!"

Tim got up as nonchalantly as he could, while running two

fingers through his hair. Dr. Feng always assured Tim a fall did not hurt.

"Roland, please don't embarrass me in front of your cousin."

Sparring with Roland was always a mad *arpeggio-glissando, molto-vivace* around and around the Jujitsu exercise room, as Dr. Feng grunted monosyllabic advice and encouragement. Kick, turn, kick. Tim lunged, slipped, staggered, skidded, and pirouetted on the balls of his feet as if stepping on burning coals. For a split second, he saw his face—an open mouth full of terror, and two peaked eyebrows like caterpillars—in one of the full-length mirrors. Too late:

"No hurt! No hurt! Get up, quick."

Master Tim, the champion faller, lay dazed. His entire right side felt raw and red like *steak tartare*. Patricia yawned again. Why had she bothered coming, he wondered, if this bored her so much? Roland started to retie his belt. Tim jumped on his blind side, thrust his leg forward, and pulled Roland up over his shoulder as hard as he could. Now he had him! This would definitely impress Patricia and Dr. Feng. But first he had to flip Roland over.

"What are you carrying in your pockets?" whispered Tim as he tugged on his friend's kimono. Roland was as immovable as a high-rise building. If Patricia ever opened her eyes, she would laugh.

"Now floor exercises," said Dr. Feng.

At last Tim's chance to really shine. Tim licked his palms and applied his favorite tiger-cage death grip around Roland's larynx. From this position, he could asphyxiate a man in twenty seconds, tear out his Adam's apple, or punch a hole in his chest. Roland was not as wiry or eel-like as Tim and had difficulty getting out of headlocks. Dr. Feng counted out the seconds.

Patricia did not appear to be especially impressed, or even fully awake. There was a cracking sound like that of logs in a fireplace, perhaps bones breaking. But Tim was reevaluating the last days with Benz. The teenage passion of a fourteen-year-old had given way to the mature reflections of a fifteen-year-old. He was studying philosophy at Saint-Philippe; he could now analyze his Benz relationship with a certain objectivity.

Returning from Haiti, he had dropped his bags and run up the stairs to the sixth floor. Her room was empty. That was to be expected, really—he had been away at Roland's the whole summer. The silver crucifix no longer hung over the bed. Used Band-Aids and dust balls remained in one corner of the room. A faint odor of Nivea cream and hair lacquer clung to the walls. On a windowsill, a long line of ants filed past Tim's elbow to lift the corpse of a huge blue fly with see-through wings. Tim had planned, with some care and detail, how he and Benz would sail westward to that rhododendron-invaded island in the Caribbean where wise men sip Barbancourt all day and hurricanes terrorize the natives.

Tim's crossed wrists ached from pulling and digging viselike into Roland's bull neck. But he continued his daydream:

Where in this enormous, untamed city would he find Benz? And could he do so before she naturally gravitated into yet another disaster? He saw himself combing through the Luis Mariano concerts, the special-ladies'-night-discount dance halls, listening for the telltale goose hissing of maids; he saw himself pushing through the flower market at the Place des Ternes, sitting through High Mass at the Spanish Church on Rue de la Pompe, where he would certainly find her if she was looking for employment.

Tim did not hear his friend beating his left hand on the mat to signify surrender. He was wondering whether he could fly after his Benz, sweeping over the lost continents of the *gitano* empire, racing against the magnet of fate, landing in a screech of burning rubber and heartbeats just in time to be there when she had carried her bulging suitcases out of Number 10½ Avenue Foch for the last time. He imagined her in her Bordeaux raincoat, white handbag, and needle-thin high heels. And now that he would be preparing for a *baccalauréat* in philosophy, he could express all the reasons for his present predicament in Lockeian, Hegelian, and even Marxist terms.

"You idiot, you're killing him!" shouted Patricia, as she dashed from the visitors' area across the exercise mats.

Tim looked down at Roland. He had forgotten about his tiger-cage headlock and could not say how long he had been staring off into space. Roland's lungs were thumping up and down like a fish out of water.

"You imbecile, let go!" Patricia's gold bracelets jingled wildly.

Roland's face was ashen pale; his eyes had rolled up into his head. How could Tim be so scatterbrained? Dr. Feng performed mouth-to-mouth resuscitation. The blood slowly returned to Roland's cheeks, and his eyes flickered open.

Patricia massaged her cousin's neck and walked him up and down the length of the exercise room. When she passed Tim, she hissed, *"Espèce d'imbécile."* Roland blinked and stretched like a swimmer getting ready for a race. Patricia's skirt swished from side to side with a marvelous, rich Schweppes sound.

"One more round of free-form," said Dr. Feng, whose half-smile had not deserted him during this episode.

Tim tried to equivocate. But Dr. Feng insisted on it. They resumed their bouncing, slamming, spinning. This time the *molto-allegro* was more of a *furioso-vivace farandole diabolesque.* Master Tim whispered a hundred apologies to his friend. Benz's departure has made me absentminded. I won't do it again, ever. Roland, please go against your natural instinct, act like a decent guy, and don't make a fool of me in front of Patricia.

His all-purpose evade-and-tango technique now gave way to plain running. Then suddenly, on a purely spatial plane, Tim found himself airborne. The room was spinning: he was being twirled above Roland's head like a bullfighter's cape. He was passing in front of Patricia's shining brown eyes. He was mirrored in Dr. Feng's wire-rimmed glasses and in the windows. His physical being contoured the walls, flew over the Coke machine, the visitor's chair, skimmed the floor mats. He counted the seconds remaining in his biological presence on earth.

Roland let go of his friend's purple belt and allowed Master Tim to give an exhibition of his most daring and advanced falling-down technique. It was a masterly twisting Samurai double-Banzai, back-and-hip three-point landing which left even Dr. Feng speechless.

In the changing room, Tim could hardly lift his arms to undress.

"Do you realize you almost killed me out there?" asked Roland, shaking his head in the shower.

"I'm really sorry. I wasn't thinking," said Tim, stepping into the spray of warm water.

"You were going to sacrifice me to the memory of Benz, weren't you, Tim?"

Roland handed him the soap.

"Why not ask Patricia out on a date?" suggested Roland when they were getting dressed. "She's got her left eye on you."

"I'm not interested," said Tim, pulling on a sock.

"Just don't talk to her about Benz. You get exceedingly tiresome and repetitive on that topic. Even I'm bored with it. Take her out and see how it goes. It'll help you forget Benz."

"JESUIT PRINCIPAL WEDS CONCUBINE." Mercedes imagined the headline in *Paris-Unveiled,* which she seldom read anymore. She was too busy, growing fat and reclining on Monet's lumpy couch. After Sean and the Baron, who used to see her at such odd hours and on such little notice, it was heaven to have a man with hours as regular as a school bell. Monet was sweet, gentle, and happy to do nearly everything she asked. It was hard to imagine such a lamb chop ruling a student body of two thousand nose-dripping, spoiled, rebellious young *payos.* She was constantly urging him to be tougher in disciplining them.

When she had first arrived from Chez Hubert, having used her last centimes to pay for the taxi, Monet was already in bed. She had awakened the *concierge* and insisted, to the point of tears, that she see the Principal. When at last Monet appeared in his slippers and woolen bathrobe, he had said:

"Yes, of course. Come right in, of course."

Monet sent the *concierge* away and carried her cardboard

suitcases to his apartments, two rather severe rooms smelling of bachelorhood and student copybooks, in the northwest tower of the main school building.

"You look exhausted," he said. "Put your legs up on the couch, and I shall prepare you some hot tea."

She was tired, cold, lonely, embarrassed, scared, and nauseous. But all the rage pent up since the restaurant scene now flowed out of her, and she sobbed uncontrollably in his arms. She could still feel the stare of those waiters! And there was nothing she could do to get back at the Baron, that self-important pig; she could not even scratch the paint of his Rolls-Royce. Eventually, Benz dozed off in Monet's arms. He carried her over to his single bed. She woke with a start.

"You sleep here, child. I'll take the couch."

"Oh, no, Father, please, I do not want to put you out."

She threw some cushions on the floor and together they built a makeshift bed for her.

Her "just one night" had grown to almost two months. She had worked in the school kitchens, cleaning the floor and washing dishes. She had sewn new curtains for Claude, and from a cotton pattern of Provençal pink roses, she had made him an eiderdown and cushions. Each day his rooms became more feminine, more comfortable. She was now so round-bellied that it was difficult to do much more than think up names for the baby: "Cascasia, Cassandra, or Carmen" if it was a girl; "Ludowig, Balthazar, or Boris" if it was a boy.

When lonely, she would hoist herself up on the windowsill and peek down from her tower. Monet had asked her not to do this, but she could not resist. She sometimes saw Timoté in the school courtyard below after lunch. From this angle six stories up, he looked not like the fifteen-year-old he had become, but like the boy she had first shepherded home from here more than seven years before. Only now, he did not play or run, but walked around the courtyard by himself, hands deep in his pockets.

At night, when Monet came to her, it was not perspiring and full of wine, but quietly and with compassion. He liked to wash her feet, in an *imitatio Christi.* He would kneel at the side of the bed and slowly, methodically pass a washcloth between her toes, feeling her ankles, studying her bones.

One Saturday afternoon, they slept in each other's arms, though he never touched her below the waist, did not even brush up against her legs. She asked him if he ever had desire for a woman. He answered, as he usually did, obliquely:

"Mercedes, what makes Catholicism so different from the other religions is how Christ dealt with the physical. He promised to resurrect us in the flesh. The whole meaning of the New Testament is surely that."

"Will I be resurrected with or without my gray hairs?" asked Benz.

"Without," said Monet, smiling so broadly his lips almost touched his ears. "Jesus said that we would build the Kingdom of Heaven on earth. He did not mean we would build it in Jerusalem, or in Passy or in New York, but within each of us, within ourselves."

She felt an emotional closeness to this man, who laughed so easily and lived so quietly, even though she found a strange insecurity beneath his calm.

They did not make love. But sometimes Mercedes dreamed of him returning from High Mass, goatish and primed, and taking her on the floor, or kneeling at the foot of the couch and having her prehistorically wet and naked. She knew this was fantasy, since the obstetrician had said it was not possible after the seventh month.

One Sunday morning, as she lay on the floor timing her contractions, there was a knock on Monet's door followed by a scratching sound. No one was supposed to know she was there! The *concierge*, wheezing for breath, whispered through the keyhole:

"If you care about him, leave! Everyone knows you are here. Take your baby and run! There are rumors that Rome is sending an inspector general. Do not do this to him! They will fire him if you stay here."

• • •

GERBI was standing shirtless and sweating in the back of the sculpture room of Saint-Philippe de Passy. Roland and Tim watched him feeding papers into an enormous antiquated printing press. Since no one kept birth certificates in Sidi-bel-Abbès, it was a matter of much conjecture in class exactly how old Gerbi was. Judging by his chest hair, he could easily be twenty, thought Tim.

SCHLOOP, SHTACK, VLING, went the press as it produced each new flyer.

Gerbi smiled with his good eye, while his bad one pointed west. Smoke was curling from the black oily gears of the oversized machine, as it whistled and knocked. Wreathed in its blue smoke, Roland bent down and picked up one of the tracts. In big bold letters, it read:

THE STUDENT/WORKER ALLIANCE FOR A MARXIST TAKEOVER!

Gerbi dripped with sweat, gobs of grease smearing his arms and face. The overheated press creaked and rattled.

VLOOP, SHTACK, VLING. SCHLOOP, VLOOP!

"Gerbi, do you even know what this pamphlet says?"

New copies were shooting out, one every four and a half seconds, as the ponderous old flatbed press slammed down on a brass plate to engrave another sheet. Master Tim felt drops of sweat run from his armpits down his rib cage.

SMASH PHALLOCRACY AND HETEROSEXISM!
SMASH BOURGEOIS MORALITY
THAT STRANGLES THE WORKERS AND STUDENTS!

Gerbi had a meter-high stack of tracts piled up against the wall. Who had taught Gerbi such words? wondered Tim. They stared at the bolts rattling and the steam rushing out from the mouth of the press as it slammed down. Gerbi and correct French usage were almost total strangers; when they met at all, it was usually a chance and unhappy encounter. The pamphlet's vocabulary belonged more to the Hall of Mirrors in Versailles than to Gerbi's street-wise argot. Tim placed an arm on his friend's wet shoulder and shouted above the din:

"Gerbi, who's putting you up to this?"

SCHLOOP, SHTACK, VLING! BANG! answered the machine.

"Whatever they're paying you isn't worth risking jail. If you need money, I'd be glad to help you out."

Gerbi looked up for a split second. Tim felt all the racist jokes about North Africans, all the sly put-downs, the not-so-private insults, reflected in Gerbi's grease-smeared glasses and frozen expression.

VLOOP, SCHLOOP, SHTACK!

"Oh, no! Watch oooooout, Gerbiiiiii!"

The press, the full two tons of it, descended as if in slow motion, steel and steam hissing like a dry cleaner's iron, on Gerbi's hand. When Tim and Roland opened their eyes, the cover of the machine had lifted up and Gerbi was smiling a mouth full of teeth at them, trying to insert another sheet of paper. His right hand was intact, but his left was flattened out like an extra-thin sheet of see-through tissue paper. It looked like a big catcher's mitt! Roland turned pale and fainted. The fingers were webbed together, serrated in a fine, clear, toasty-warm, still-smoking membrane. Gerbi tried to pick his nose, felt the rubberlike fin brush against his cheek and shrieked. As the realization sank in, tears of fear sprouted from Gerbi's eyes. Unplugged, the machine snorted and chugged to a halt. Tim led his friend, shirtless, toward the infirmary.

On that wet April day, with the cumuli low and gray over the city roofs, Mademoiselle Savonex and the doctor were flirting to pass the time, comparing vacations in Morocco and the Greek isles. Tim knocked on the dispensary door and, without waiting, led his friend in by the elbow:

"My buddy here just fell down a staircase."

Gerbi carried his hand straight out in front of him like some futuristic tray. Mademoiselle Savonex turned and ran to the *toilettes* to vomit up her croissant and *café-crème*. The good doctor, remembering Gerbi's eyeball prank from several years before, quickly dialed the Principal's office. Tim tried his best to explain that the affair was serious, but he could not prevent the doctor from fleeing down the hall or the nurse from remaining locked in the bathroom.

"Savonex, come out this instant!" shouted Tim.

Gerbi and Tim were alone. They surveyed the infirmary: Cotton swabs, needles in sterile plastic bags. Prescription drugs under lock and key. A large rubber bag for administering enemas. The good doctor was charging back now with two healthy Jesuit acolytes and an injection so large it seemed to have been prepared for a horse. Gerbi had seen enough Three Musketeers movies to perform a good imitation. And so, to Tim's shouts of encouragement, he extended his avant-garde baseball-glove hand, and thrust and parried *à la* d'Artagnan with the hypodermic-toting doctor. For a while, Gerbi managed to keep the authorities at bay.

Mademoiselle Savonex opened the toilet door ever so quietly. Before Tim could warn his friend, she stabbed him through his brown corduroy pants, the ones donated to him by The Ladies of Passy Literary, Knitting and Opera Society. The heavy sedative set in immediately. Gerbi twisted, hopped, spiraled around the room as if his *derrière* were on fire, and fell headfirst accidentally on purpose, onto the large white bosom of Mademoiselle Savonex.

MAY 1968. Mercedes sat in dappled sunlight on a bench on Boulevard Saint-Michel. The newspapers were full of headlines about student riots and strikes—and not just *Paris-Unveiled,* either! On May 24, she was reading how De Gaulle flew to visit the French Army of the Rhine to make certain that General Massu was behind him and would retake Paris, if need be. On page 3 was an article quoting the Baron Isidore de Rothschild, ex of the Resistance group "the Chameleons," stating that he who controlled the bridges controlled Paris.

She did not care about the *payo* student revolt, nor did she care that she did not care. Monet had reassured her on the subject of her disinterest with a single vignette: One day during the revolution of 1848, Balzac heard some noise, leaned out his window, saw the barricades going up in the streets, then returned to his writing desk, and declared, "And now back to the real world."

Today she was Balzac, only with a baby instead of a novel. Her real world was this boy gurgling in her arms, gulping down the fresh May air. She noticed, but did not much care about, the long line of blue vans full of riot police forming at the end of the avenue. She did not think about the lone cobblestone that fell in front of a group of helmeted *flics* as they formed a phalanx of clear plastic shields. Her boy would learn to dance flamenco! In the troupe, they would call him "Señor Three Palms" because he was so short. She would dress him in white spangles like Luis Mariano.

The air where Mercedes was sitting suddenly became foggy. A canister of tear gas had exploded near the entrance to the Métro. The police charged. Students retreated behind their barricades, hurling rocks.

The avenue was littered with the skeletons of burned-out cars and buses. The baby started to cry. How empty the city looked devoid of tourists, mimeographed sheets glued to the walls and all the stores closed! On reflection, she was much better off without a lover. She had never met a man to whom the need for affection and loyalty was as absolute as it was for her. Perhaps Claude Monet's sympathy and tenderness were sufficient companionship. Sharing life with a Jesuit and a healthy blue-eyed baby would be enough. Benz's life was not especially romantic, but she was content. If along the road, some handsome picker of lavender with lips as sweet as sparrow's sperm chose to make his life with her, fine. But if not, *tant pis!*

The students counterattacked. She ran toward the Métro, but a water cannon rolled down the avenue. Cut off from all possible retreat, she rushed into the first available doorway. In a large amphitheater (the Théâtre de l'Odéon had become the center of the new provisional student government), a bearded man ladled out bowls of soup. She sat in aisle seat 103 of Row PP and ate her first Anarcho-Syndicalist meal: greasy water with a few dingy leeks at the bottom and a stale piece of *pain de mie*, which the baby spat up. Judging by this gastronomic fare, she did not hold out much hope for the new regime.

On stage, newsmen pressed around a central figure who was giving an impromptu press conference. She recognized Anatole Gerbi and waved. Gerbi looked surprised and, with a bandaged hand, waved back as he told the reporter:

"First, we must destroy our bourgeois past. Then, the Student-Worker Alliance will rebuild an equitable system based not on status, but on social justice!"

The bearded youth who was lighting a pipe was a far cry from the boy who used to eat his own snot. Cameras clicked. More questions. Gerbi's cockeyed glass eye pointed ineffectually westward, giving him a certain Old World charm, adding weight to what he said. Minutes later, he was offering Benz a cot to sleep on near his command post and, promising her, with a wink of his good eye, that when the revolution was successful, he would name her Minister of Culture for Dancing and Singing. Mercedes immediately accepted this honor.

"How's Tim?" asked Gerbi.

"I haven't seen Timoté in a long time," said Benz. "We don't talk anymore. And if he asks about me, and if you have any real respect for liberation, you will say you have not seen me for a hundred years!"

Before leaving, she pointed at the stumps of the chestnut and plane trees that had been cut down to make barricades and told Gerbi:

"The trees are gentle witnesses and do not belong to you. Tell your friends to stop cutting them down."

Then she hurried back to Father Monet, recalling the sound of his voice as a drop of cool water on her fevered lips.

MASTER Tim returned to the Spanish Church on Rue de la Pompe. He had watched the faithful file in for eleven o'clock Mass. Now, staring through the squid-cloud pattern cast by a dark stained-glass window, camouflaged in the back by the holy-water font, he watched as all the maids of Portugal and

Spain filed out of three-o'clock Mass. As they passed with bowed heads, he examined the color of their skin; but the pink and apricot-colored limbs were all too pale to belong to Benz.

It did not take him long to decide to place a personal in *Paris-Unveiled.* The clerk who took the order assured Tim the newspaper was sold throughout France, Belgium, Switzerland, Andorra, Luxembourg, North Africa, Guadeloupe, Martinique, New Caledonia, and the Territoires d'Outremer. He prayed she had not returned to Matamoros, although the clerk also reassured him that vacationers often took the newspaper to Spain with them. One of the ads he placed read simply:

> Benz, where the hell are you?
> I need you. Tim.

The other promised financial reward for information leading to the whereabouts of a certain young Spanish Gypsy woman, age approximately 24, shoulder-length black hair, 65 kilos, 171 centimeters tall. He provided a photograph. Master Tim waited impatiently for answers to his ad, which seemed to arrive only very slowly.

Where would a pregnant half-Gypsy with no education go? Fufa and Dora had not heard from Benz since the "event." Master Tim walked to Place Blanche and Pigalle. For the first time, he noticed the cruelty of everyday life in the streets. Cripples sat propped in café windows. *"Tu viens avec moi, petit?"* asked a cheap leg lady with more gold in her mouth than Benz. He kept walking. Would he enter every *hotel de passe?* He felt the humid smear of a tear down his cheek. Dutch tourists flowed out of a large silver bus.

He was not an urban scientist. He had not quadrisected every area of the city and gone door to door looking for Benz. But he had visited more strange neighborhoods than he had ever known existed and had stood, waiting, in the noncommittal shadows for closed doors to open. He pulled out a handful of letters and reread one at random:

> Cher Monsieur X: I am half-Nubian, half-Bedouin,
> both are closely related to the Gypsies of Middle and

Southern Europe. Size 95-63-93. I am pregnant. I can come to you with or without my children. I am poor, but of good breeding stock and would make you a devoted and loyal companion.

Dear Mr. X—Etablissements Gaston & Delfeil, private investigators since 1764, would be glad to pursue the matter related in your *petite annonce* of Tuesday the 25th. Please return to us the enclosed contract. It obligates you to nothing. We humbly guarantee results within fourteen days.

Timothy went to the *toilettes* in a *café-tabac,* ripped these letters to pieces, and threw them into the gaping hole with the two molded porcelain feet for the uninitiated.

Back, for the hundredth time, to Wagram, he pushed his way into the Spanish Theater, where advance tickets were on sale for the Ballet Histérico de Córdoba. The woman in the little ticket kiosk blinked and shook her head when Tim questioned her about the possible whereabouts of a beautiful half-Gypsy.

"Ah, Monsieur, we see so many bronze-skinned girls here. And they almost all wear long earrings. How am I supposed to know if they are made of gold and coral? And as to which of them is a half or a quadroon Gypsy—ah, there you really have me! But we still have some cheap second-balcony matinée tickets if you want to investigate yourself. You could do very well here, Monsieur, especially on Saturday afternoon, if you are partial to such things."

Tim said *"Non, merci"* ever so politely and walked home. At Place des Ternes, he opened yet another letter, whose envelope bore an odd, cuneiform handwriting:

Cher Monsieur X—I have traveled for years through Transylvania, Moldavia, the Balkan states, Eastern Tyrol, the Carpathians, and as a result, have an excellent collection of photographs of Romanichal women, in the flower of youth, which I believe will be of interest to a man of such discerning taste as

> yourself. If any of these specimens catch your eye, it would eventually be possible to invite the young girl in question to France for a trial period, your identity being kept entirely confidential, of course."

He walked slowly back up the Rue Rude. Helga was on duty today. She smiled as he approached:

"*Alors, Monsieur Tim, vous êtes bien triste aujourd'hui.* Still no news of Mercedes?"

He shook his head and praised Helga for her accent—her "customer English," as she called it.

"If you don't mind my saying so, Monsieur, that Mercedes was nothing but trouble and disorder. More than once I had to chase her away. Whenever she walked the dog, she ruined our business! Much too young and too exotic for a high-quality, high-turnover sidewalk like Avenue Foch. She confused the customer. And what's worse, she did it on purpose!"

Tim nodded and stopped in the driveway of Number 10½ to read another response from a man who had started a club to study Tsigani folklore:

> We meet in one of the classrooms of the Lycée Charlemagne, once a month, to hear lectures and discuss preselected themes, such as the Sanskrit roots of the Romani language, patterns of Rom persecution throughout the ages, Gypsy migration routes from India through the Balkans, north to England and south to Spain. Membership is only 100 francs a year, plus a small contribution for our Christmas party held at Issy-les-Moulineaux.

"Monsieur, I feel sorry for you, so I will tell you what I know."

Helga was positive that Ambassador McLuck had told her the Baron was taking Mercedes somewhere. This was the first lead Tim had gotten in months! He questioned her closely, already smelling Benz's Ne Me Quitte Pas. But Helga couldn't remember the details. Tim thanked her and began to walk down the street toward the new chancery gate. The policeman on duty,

Raoul's replacement, watched from behind his bulletproof vest and machine gun as Helga ran after Tim, grabbed his lapels, and said:

"What the Ambassador may or may not have said to me is a professional secret. *Compris?* If you go ruining my business, you'll pay for it!"

He swore on his mother's and father's heads to keep out of her private business and not to mention this to the Ambassador. Helga set his tie straight and patted down his ruffled hair. It was clear that Tim would have to confront the Baron himself.

CHAPTER 10

"Soy Puri, Soy Pureta"

BENZ LOVED COMING here in the summer months with Anwar (so named at Gerbi's suggestion) in her arms. After the baby was born, Claude Monet had moved her to the Couvent des Ursulines, where she had been cared for by kind, discreet women; but she could not live forever surrounded by crucifixes and missals, scared of being discovered. So she had come to visit Gerbi in his kingdom of horse dung and manicured green fields. She did not feel so lonely here among stableboys currying, rubbing, scrubbing. All *gitanos* were horse traders at heart. There was a lazy ripple of wind. The yellow, turquoise, and fuchsia of the jockeys' clean jerseys hanging up to dry swayed and glowed, full of sun. It was important, after the revolution of May '68, that Gerbi lie low and work at a job where neither the authorities nor his anarchist friends were likely to find him. The Aunties, in conjunction with the Passy Literary, Knitting and Opera Society, had hired him back to his old job of sweeping out the stables at the Bagatelle gardens.

In the far paddock, where Gerbi was shoveling manure, stood a sickly mare named "Edithe de Mon Coeur." Gerbi stopped and showed Benz the horse's fact sheet: She had finished second to last in the Longchamps Prix des Orteilles and had three scratches due to colds or angina. At the Romeo Invitational in Monaco earlier in the year, the mare had pulled a tendon.

"A human could run faster than Edithe de Mon Coeur," said Gerbi, smiling.

Perhaps Edithe is just getting old, thought Benz. As I am. *Soy puri, soy pureta*—"I am old, I am ancient"—as they said in *caló*. She was twenty-five. When would she ever get the courage to declare herself a flamenco dancer and live by what she loved most in life? Among Gypsies, strong feelings, like deep roots, demand darkness. Americans showed their feelings to almost anyone who happened along. Madame Cascasia, for example, advertised hers to the world. But how long could Benz go on—unmarried, dreams broken, memories fading? Could she survive the struggle, living only for Anwar? Could she enjoy a vicarious crypto-existence through his fledgling dreams? Would her heart one day be cauterized by ennui and the slow, hard realization that life was not as it should be?

In the past the men who visited her in dreams were taller, stronger, handsomer than any men she knew. But not more so than Monet. He really was perfect in almost all respects, except one: when, oh, when, would Claude take her in the night-sweet scent of his strong arms and love her?

"Edithe de Mon Coeur," Gerbi was saying, "is a daughter of Joly Boy IV and Edithe aux Camélias, granddaughter of Pepe le Moko III and Edithe aux Groseilles, begat of Edithe aux Hortensias, begat of . . ." To Mercedes, this genealogy sounded frighteningly like the Old Testament.

Gerbi explained that his father owned a three-year-old filly in Sidi-bel-Abbès called "Grand Bidet." Grand Bidet had finished first in the Baghdad National Grand Prix, and in two Marrakesh Dish-Dash cups. Then Gerbi became excited and began to expound upon social injustice, the French government's education policy, the housing conditions which made it impossible for North African immigrants to compete on an equal footing. Somehow, all of this added up to the fact that he and his father were going to rig the Grand Prix de Longchamps and switch Grand Bidet for Edithe. Benz did not follow the logic, but the enthusiasm was contagious. And she did not want to hurt the feelings of a boy whose eyes pointed in opposite directions by questioning the legality of his plan.

"Benz, after the last race of the season, if everything goes according to plan, you and I will be millionaires," declared Gerbi, squeezing her arm.

Mercedes was partial to this kind of grandiloquent plan: The world, and by this she really meant herself, was too timid. Ever since her decision to have the baby, she had decided to live on a higher plane of possibility.

"Gerbi, do it; risk everything. It is the only way to be. All my life, I have played it safe, hidden, kept quiet. But it is a big mistake to be too polite, too careful."

She looked down at her baby as proof of this last statement. Anwar slept peacefully. Bidding Gerbi goodbye, she rolled the pram toward the rose garden.

"See this carmine Baccarat, Anwar? You are just as intricate and delicate as this rose. You and I have the true blood, *tacho rati*. We will show the bastards. *Maman* had you, and that, my little man, was only the beginning. Now, when *Maman* finally takes to the dance floor, dressed in her white sequins with a black shawl and a carnation pinned behind her ear, audiences will fall to their knees and cry out for mercy! Men will weep and gnash their teeth; thousands will shake and pray to God. Their bowels will turn to soup. They will offer us snakes that spit fire and palaces made of tigereye and lapis lazuli. They will dress me in angel's hair and diadems. They will bow low and say: 'Princess, the prisoners awaiting execution beg for the honor of being put to death by your hand.' And all the greats—Alec Guinness; Gregory Peck; Yves Montand, who winked at me once when he passed me in the first-floor hallway—will ply us with nectar and ambrosia. And the women—ah, the women—they will scream with jealousy and try to flatter me and befriend me, or buy, use, and betray me. But Anwar, what do I care if those fat bourgeois criticize me with their turned-up noses? Let the pariah jackals in the village judge me too! I live for love."

Mercedes pushed the pram in and out of dappled light. She loved Claude Monet. There were worse fates, she supposed, than to be an undiscovered flamenco star in love with an incorruptible Jesuit. "What is yours you cannot lose," she recalled her mother saying when she dealt the cards; "what is not yours, even the good God will take away!"

A white-haired footman led Tim across a marble atrium, past a row of tellers to a hallway and a bank of elevators. They glided over a deep green plain of carpet emblazoned with the letter "R" in gold curlicues. Tim sniffed at the lemon-waxed paneling and moved uneasily inside his dark pin-striped suit. All around him, hushed tones of secretaries mixed with the beat of their shiny electric typewriters.

"Monsieur, this way please."

The elevator stopped on the fourth floor. Deep beige carpets and rows of prim secretaries behind spotless desks lay before him. Messengers in gray-and-gold jackets plied the halls with bundles of mail. Tim glided quietly past the gold-framed Honoré Daumier prints. The white-haired footman nodded to a secretary who had a room all to herself:

"Fleur, Monsieur has an appointment with the Baron."

"Oh, yes: the young Cardozo, for a summer position. We'll squeeze you in as soon as the Baron is free."

Mademoiselle Fleur was a faded specimen with reading glasses on a chain around her neck. Her voice had the same patented pearl shape that Tim had heard floating about the hallways. She offered him a cup of espresso. Tim, who for nearly seventeen years now, had been drinking only hot cocoa in the morning, felt it incumbent on him to accept. He sat in a red leather chair, burning his lips on the disgusting stuff, sipping the acrid potion as slowly as possible without appearing rude. Coffee would probably give him zits, he thought.

Through the wall, Tim could hear the Baron's muffled shouting. He stared out the window at the Place Vendôme and prepared all his answers very carefully. "So you want a summer job here, *mon petit?*"—"Oh, yes, Monsieur. But first a few specifics, *s'il vous plaît,* concerning my nanny: Date last seen? Time? Place? Color of dress worn? Type of earrings? Width of belly? Was she standing nose to window at a bakery? Or is she perhaps in this very bank, at the center of this corporate maze, a prisoner, an offering for the exotic tastes of your Middle Eastern clientele?"

The telephones rang ceaselessly. Memoranda piled up in Mademoiselle Fleur's In tray. Pink telephone messages appeared and disappeared on her desk. Tim picked a bit of lint off his sleeve. He stared at the bronze column in the middle of the Place Vendôme. The monument had been built from Napoleon's melted-down cannon to please the fat British and German bankers. (The new French merchant class made rich by Napoleon had been the first to turn on him when his battle fortunes changed.) He was starting to sweat.

What if the Baron had killed Benz and was at this very moment ordering his henchmen to chop her into little *fondue bourguignonne* pieces? Or worse yet, what if he had placed her in his middle-echelon-executive training program? What if she were at this minute running around in a gray suit and white silk blouse, frantically buying and selling stocks?

Tim was ushered into a vast office in which the Baron sat talking to two younger men who stood before him:

"This has to be done immediately!"

It was hard for Tim to hate the round, soft-looking little man tapping his fist on his desk.

Mademoiselle Fleur, standing protectively at Tim's side, coughed politely. The Baron's gaze came to rest on Tim; Fleur explained the purpose of his visit. The Baron nodded, offered one word—"Junot"—and turned to pick up a telephone. Tim was not sure he had said "Junot." He could have said, "Don't know," or "Go now." He was led out of the office, to an elevator, down to the second floor, to a tiny office where a nondescript man called Juneaut began filling in a form. Name, age, ("seventeen years and six months," but Tim was lying: he was not yet seventeen), school, hobbies, awards, prizes ("first in Religious Instruction, before the Jesuits told me not to take any more religion"). Tim answered this all in a daze. He had not said a word to the Baron! While Juneaut explained what an honor it was to be in the bank's summer internship program, Tim asked the way to the men's room.

Would Mademoiselle Fleur allow him back in to see The Great Man? "Dare," Napoleon had said. But dare what? The Baron had clearly not been overjoyed to see him. Tim found the men's room on the fourth floor and locked himself in the far stall. This was ridiculous: to have to spy on the snorts and washings and expectorations of international bankers!

Dollops of sweat ran down his underarms. How, exactly, would he confront the Baron? What form of address should he use? "Give me back my nanny, you *salop*"? Or perhaps more graciously: "Sir, my Aunties have begged me to ask you if you might still be roguering our little Spanish maid"? His nerves were tingling. He felt his heart racing. Loud flushings were followed by the running of water in the sink. What if the cleaning lady came? Dear Baron, when I was nine, Benz and I entered the Pan-Am offices on the Champs-Elysées and signed our names to the reservation list for a trip to the moon. The 10,432 people ahead of us on that list have either died or changed their minds, so would you please hand Benz over so we can take our lunar voyage together. Thank you in advance.

A stately slow walk. Tim strained to see through the crack of the door. A pair of shiny shoes and baggy trousers: it was he, The Great Man, pissing into the closest urinal. Tim ran trembling fingers through his hair and emerged from his stall.

"Bonjour, Monsieur."

Tim's throat had constricted and his words came out in a high-pitched warble. The Baron turned slowly:

"Ah, young Cardozo—everything work out all right?"

"Yes, sir. I wanted to ask you something; do you have a minute?"

"Of course."

The Baron zipped himself back into his pants and moved quickly to wash his chubby fingers. Tim followed him out the door and down the hallway.

"Sir, I am looking for Mercedes de los Angeles, whom I believe you knew well."

The espresso coursed through Tim's veins and thumped in his temples.

"Mercedes . . . Benz. She used to work at our house."

The Baron shook his head, stopped to look over Tim's shoulder at a young associate:

"Get me the Suez file, will you, Jean-François?"

Tim followed the Baron into his office, but it became evident that the Baron had totally forgotten his existence. Tim walked up to his desk:

"Don't you remember? I was there at the polo match when you picked her up."

The Baron cast a steely eye in Tim's direction, pointing an index finger at Mademoiselle Fleur. The thought suddenly crept into Tim's mind that maybe Helga was lying; maybe the Baron was an innocuous old fossil; maybe when Benz called him impotent, she had been telling the truth. How reliable a source was Helga, anyway?

"Baron, I know full well what you've done with Señorita de los Angeles."

Tim hadn't spoken loudly enough. He was a coward. He tried again, this time tugging on the Baron's arm. But The Great Man was deep in conversation about profit ratios east of Suez.

"Don't deny you know her!"

Tim noticed two private guards moving quickly down the hallway. The Baron slipped behind a paneled door and vanished without a trace. Tim could hear the guards' voices buzzing in their walkie-talkies, and he ran without turning around. He felt like Tolstoy's Nicholas Rostov, charging the French rear guard at the Berezina river in *War and Peace*. Why were the guards chasing him? He was only trying to save a pregnant Gypsy from being sold into white slavery. Remembering Nicholas Rostov's fate, Tim sprinted past the craning secretaries.

Back in the lobby, the white-haired doorman tipped his hat and asked if Monsieur would be needing a taxi.

"Yes, please. I'm in a hurry," said Tim as he ran out of the bank and down the street.

• • •

MERCEDES fidgeted. It was a polka-dot *sevillana* fiesta dress with bouffant arms and seven layers of billowing petticoats. Claude Monet, that man of many talents, was sewing the very last stitch to her orange-and-green waist. Her stomach felt as if composed of a thousand electric eels (jellied and live) twisting and short-circuiting. She had danced in the crowded bars of Andalusia; she had been dancing the late show at La Venta restaurant when the manager of the Folies Bergères saw her and offered her this job—but to do so now, before hundreds of American tourists who came here mostly for nude girls and understood nothing of the soul of Andalusia, that was quite different!

At least, she was not alone: Monet was dressing her, and Anwar was entertaining them both from his stroller. The backstage changing rooms were full of tall, sluttish women chewing gum and eyeing her Jesuit with oily grins. Monet was so sweet in his plain black suit, with his clerical collar; so strong, so confident! Some of the dancers came up and played with Anwar, while others smoked and knitted. Claude was shy when surrounded by these Amazons who wore nothing but a feather in their backsides and another in their hair. He looked out of place, like a brave dandelion she had once seen growing between the cracks on the sidewalk of the Champs-Elysées.

"Claude, the audience will be salesmen, corporate managers, Americans; they want backsides and chests, not flamenco. No, I am not going out there!" Panic was taking over.

"You dance more beguilingly than Salome in her dance of the seven veils," said Monet, eyeing his emergency needlework on her dress. "And you look beautiful."

"No, this is not right. I feel it in my bones. The cards are against it."

Claude Monet picked Anwar up in his arms and kissed the boy on the forehead.

"Benz, you will not be alone. You will be with me and with Anwar. Dance for us, Benz."

"No, no, no! I am not a masochist."

"Benz, I have never even once asked you for anything. Now I am asking you to go out there and dance for me. This is a small thing, but it is all I want."

She looked at him, startled. He stared fixedly at her. It was true: this was the first favor Monet had ever asked. She felt his strength, his dignity, his command. She pressed her sticky red lips to his warm mouth.

The stagehands moved the set. Machinery turned, pulleys tightened, walls slipped into place. The lake of mirrors with ice skaters in purple see-through halter tops, the waterfall, the swings with the naked mermaids, these gave way to a light blue gauze curtain drawn by a hundred white pigeons and behind it, *le Bateau de Rêves.* Out of black velvet walls, bare arms suddenly appeared holding torches. A man in overalls with a Gitane glued to his lower lip whispered to Benz that she was *"sur scène."* Benz took a minute to pray for calm and luck, for courage, insight, timing, and guidance, and for Monet and Anwar. Then she slipped a holy picture of Saint Agatha into her bra and walked out onto the pitch-black stage.

The first guitar note struck. The pale blue spot turned icy mauve. Benz stood with her back to the audience, slowly unfolding one finger, then a hand, then an arm. The guitar notes leapt out faster. She stepped off the Ship of Dreams and stamped one heel, turning slowly with a double-arm arabesque. She was in absolute control. So what if they did not ask her to dance here again? Men, with a few important exceptions such as Monet, were dissembling, lying frauds. But dance did not lie. She had rehearsed this so often, despaired so utterly that she would spend her whole life cleaning crystals and ironing shirts, that she could not stop laughing, laughing inside herself. And so, after years of struggling and fighting for this tiny moment, she let flamenco flow out of her like a river seeking the sea. And she danced as she had never danced before.

• • •

TIM visited the Manitas de Plata ensemble, then the Rita Dolores Dance School at the Place Clichy. He watched row upon row of dancers, from beginners to advanced classes; but none of the teachers knew of Benz, and most of the girls he questioned were not interested in helping him.

Several times he returned to the Spanish Church on Rue de la Pompe. The vestry was full of recently arrived girls waiting to find work; they sat around the courtyard talking and laughing in groups, wearing heavy makeup on their cheeks, now and then hurling out a French word in the same thick, peasant accent he remembered Benz having had when she first arrived. None of the priests remembered Benz.

Having given up on *Paris-Unveiled,* Tim decided to direct his search at a religious audience. He visited the offices of *La Voix Chrétienne* on Rue de Grenelle. As he arrived at the building, he saw Claude Monet entering—it was too late to hide. He debated whether he should tell the truth or make up a story. Could Monet help? Could the old curmudgeon possibly understand what he was searching for and why? Would Monet respond by piling more homework on Tim in order to keep him off the streets? It was, after all, a school day, and Tim was skipping chemistry class.

At the elevator, the two looked each other in the eye and smiled.

"*Alors,* Cardozo, is everything all right with you? We haven't spoken in a long time."

Without his beard, Monet looked to Tim like a young chicken, not nearly so formidable or fierce. But he did not trust or understand Monet's continual attempts to court him.

"Everything's fine, thank you."

"Is the family all right? Your Aunts Agatha and Phoebe?"

"Fine, thanks," said Tim, eyes glued to the elevator floor. They both got off on the fifth floor, walking with a certain embarrassment to the same office, until Tim stopped at the information window.

"I should like to take out an ad for a missing person," he said as Monet passed through to the Director's office. Surprisingly, the Principal had not even inquired what he was doing here.

• • •

Tim now stood at the Place de la Concorde, hands deep in his pockets, watching the sparrows bathing in pools of dust. Where in this crush of tourists and strollers and taxis might Benz be? Had she returned to Matamoros? How could a person disappear so totally without a trace? He watched the green bronze porpoises and large-breasted mermaids spouting water around the Obelisk. It would not have surprised him at all to see Benz emerge nude from the foaming water, rising in the middle of the fountain with a bronze porpoise on her head to ask him, annoyed, why he had taken so long to find her.

Thinking that Benz might have moved to a street whose name appealed to her sense of the dramatic and to her admiration for martyred saints, he had walked the Rue Saint-Blaise, in the Twentieth Arrondissement, and Rue Saint-Bon, a street with only six houses, off Rue de Rivoli. And in quick succession, with Roland driving him on his Vespa, they had visited the Impasse Saint-Charles, Rue Saint-Christophe, Saint-Claude, Saint-Denis (was Benz now living near the Cimetière des Innocents?), Rue Saint-Dominique, Saint-Eleuthère, Saint-Elois, Saint-Etienne-de-Mont, Saint-Eustache, Saint-Exupéry (who wasn't a saint at all, but who had died under mysterious circumstances), Rue des Saints-Pères, Rue des Martyres. It was hopeless!

The world was a big place. Tim looked up all the Delboscs listed in the telephone book. He finally found Raoul and his mother living on a leafy street in Les Lilas beyond Belleville. And he stayed all day and into the night, watching from the street to make certain Raoul's mother had been telling the truth, before taking the last Métro home. Knowing Benz's pride and her penchant for calling herself a queen of the Gypsies, he visited Cours de la Reine, Place de la Reine Astrid, Rue de la Reine Blanche, Passage de la Reine de Hongrie. But that too was in vain. He walked down to the Sunday market at the Place des Ternes. Marcel, the butcher's son, now sported a mustache and sideburns. Over the course of three hours, there was no sign of Benz.

• • •

Perhaps if Timothy just took root here on the sidewalk of the Etoile, became one of the Dadaist lampposts, or a neoclassical facade, Benz would eventually appear, when least expected, doing her Countess of Wiggle Waggle. He stopped to look in a travel-agency window; overhead, the plane and chestnut trees stood out in all their summer splendor. Tim entered the offices of the Citirama Tour Company, owned by Laval's family. The night before, he had agreed to do his school friend a favor and stand in for one of the company's sick tour guides. Tim had no interest or training in this, but Laval's father had been desperate for someone able to explicate in three languages the glories of Paris. A woman with a clipboard approached him:

"You speak English? How about Spanish and Japanese? Well, Japanese doesn't matter. We can't be too picky. And above all, remember to be polite."

For Tim, it was one more way to search for Benz. If he did not investigate every possible nook and cranny of this city, the ghost of Benz would never give him any peace. The woman extended a hundred-franc bill and said he would get another hundred plus tips at the end of the day.

It was an enormous two-decker, futuristic behemoth painted red, with speakerphones, a toilet, and gray-tinted windows. He was handed a map, a microphone, and an official guide's cap. The tourists piled on: Japanese bowing at the waist, Germans comparing suntans and wristwatches, Americans talking about professional football and exchange rates.

The doors closed with a great "*whoosh,*" and off they went. Tim had never taken a tour of his native city. He sat in the front seat of the air-conditioned whisper-jet bus with his little cap and mike. All day he could sweep up and down the Seine, examining the sidewalks for traces of the elusive Benz. He scrutinized the first sentence of his guidebook, "The beautiful architecture of this jewel of a city," then closed it and put it under his seat. The American and Japanese tourists switched their buttons on and off. The Germans complained to the driver that the audio system was not working. Tim picked up the microphone:

"*Welcome to our superdeluxe whizbang three-hour tour of*

the City of Lights. We will be cruising through the major points of interest marked with red dots on the maps in front of you."

As they circled the Etoile, Tim noticed a new leg lady on the corner of Rue de Tilsitt. Had Helga been forced into retirement? That sidewalk got handed down from one generation to another like a land title. He saw the Algerian cheese man, the newsstand of Monsieur Roy, the baker, the pharmacist.

"We are now traveling down the Champs-Elysées. Russian troops stationed here after Waterloo coined the word 'bistro,' *which in Russian means 'quick,' as they shouted at the café waiters, 'Quick, double-bistro!' "*

Cameras clicked. Not even the driver seemed to notice that the official Citirama text had been discarded. The city passed behind the tinted glass, a distant television show. This was a trip through Tim's mind, a chance to get acquainted with his idea of the city, with his memory.

"German troops in 1815 taught us the word 'vasistas.' In French it now means 'transom.' But what did Frenchmen call transoms before the Germans asked 'Was ist das?' I have no bloody idea! Do you?"

No reactions from the sheep seated behind him. The bus stopped at la Madeleine and let out another "*whoosh*" as its doors opened. Without Tim's having to tell them what to do, the tourists left their deep-cushioned seats. Click-click-click—the sheep were out to pasture, using up their film on a church with absolutely no grace or significance to Tim, other than the fact that Hitler had driven around it once.

Back on the bus, they rewound their film and chatted. More farting issued from the doors of this two-tone luxury vehicle, and off they went in smooth glide-o-rama comfort. So many layers of lubrified shock absorbers and padding to protect one's derrière from the rough cobblestones! L'Opéra, Rue des Dames, Pigalle, Place Blanche, Sacré-Coeur, La Bourse, La Bibliothèque Nationale, Rue de Rivoli, le Louvre, le Châtelet, Les Halles, the Marais passed by Tim's window like gauzy apparitions. He sank back in his seat. How he loved this painted whore of a city!

"We are now on the 'grands boulevards,' the first set of

circular avenues around the heart of the city. To your left is the Porte Saint-Denis, world headquarters of the gonococcus bacterium."

One elderly gentleman, switching off his channel, turned to his wife and asked whether she had heard that. A middle-aged woman wearing a T-shirt from the University of Wyoming removed her sunglasses and studied Tim attentively. But Tim was lost in thoughts of Benz and didn't mind if Citirama lost all its customers.

"And now we are crossing over to the Ile de la Cité. I'll give you three guesses as to what this church is to your left. Who can tell me?"

The Japanese raised their hands: "Me, me, I know! It is Notedam. Bootiful Notedam."

"You will now have time to get out and—"

"No, they won't," grunted the driver. "We can save a full half-hour by going straight across."

The *bateaux-mouches* sparkled, all glass and white on the Seine, booksellers lined the quais, and old men fished in the green slime below the Pont Neuf. (Should he bother informing his sheep that the oldest bridge in Paris was called the Pont Neuf? No need, they had already passed it.) With approximately 22.5 seconds alloted to each monument and vista, you had to be damn quick.

The bus raced over to the left bank and veered up Boulevard Saint-Michel toward the Luxembourg Gardens.

"But gee whiz—not to visit Notre-Dame. That's pretty extreme, isn't it?" said Tim, searching for Benz through the surging crowds.

"They got postcards of it, don't they?" retorted the driver.

"This is the Panthéon. Here are buried France's most illustrious dead, save our emperor, of course. And that was the Luxembourg Gardens. Now a little farther down, by the Champs de Mars, is your basic phallic symbol, rising three hundred meters straight up."

"Hey, bud, some of us good Christians from Tennessee don't take to your blue language very much."

Tim ignored the objection; Jesus never answered Pilate. The

bus stopped again, the Germans leading the way out. Tim stood under this giant metal Christmas tree with its neat elevators zipping up and down, its cantilevered legs like some toy Erector Set. It was not their fault he could not find Benz, but they were not exactly helping him, either.

This city had such inviolable virginity: The barbarians down through the ages had sacked her, starting with the Visigoths attacking Lutetia, but also the Jacobins, the SS, and now battalions of credit-card-carrying tourists. They all came to gape, get drunk, write postcards home. Through lack of care or mere stupidity, he had allowed the bastards to snatch his Benz away from him. And now they were going to steal his city from him as well? Never! Tim could not understand why the neoclassical buildings stood by so serenely and forgave the barbarian invaders their many sins. The old tourists, the decrepit ones who panted like dogs, sat with their noses pressed against the window, too tired to leave the bus.

The driver finished his Coke and called everyone back.

"Don't you think," said Tim. "We're sort of giving them the quick one-two?"

"Today, I'm being generous," grunted the driver. "Usually we'd be finished by now."

The bus closed its doors as tight as an oyster and raced back across the Seine, along the Quai de l'Alma, back to the Etoile. Tim did not even bother looking for Benz on the crowded sidewalks. Something about tourists, happy and taking photographs, made him sick to his stomach. The city didn't need foreigners to come and fill its already bemerded waters with cans, cigarettes, Styrofoam cups. If you want to visit us, thought Tim, you must come on your knees, as befits lesser beings without a beautiful city of your own."

"Hey, no more comintawy?" asked a Japanese man.

"Fini," Tim said, waving his arms.

The bus swerved up George V and back to its starting point. Tim rode with tears streaming down his face.

"Hey, are you all right, little fella?" said the woman in the University of Wyoming T-shirt.

The bus opened its flatulent doors. The Germans tipped Tim

and so did most of the Japanese, who bowed and thanked him. The francs piled up in his palms, burning a hole in his hand and pockets. Thirty pieces of silver for selling the city. He had kissed Paris on the cheek in the garden of Gethsemane. But Tim was an American, too; what made him so different from these tourists—that he had spent seventeen years here instead of seventeen days? The large T-shirted woman asked him:

"Are you sad because of all the Burger Kings invading Paris? Hey, it's not you who's Americanizing the culture. It's not your fault, little fella. You're just a little cog in a huge machine. Don't cry. Come on. I mean foreigners want to see Paris. What's so awful about that? We didn't come to destroy it. We just want to love it and admire it."

Tim stood on the sidewalk, the wind blowing in his hair. He said goodbye to his last tourist and walked back home. Paris, the city of eternal love, might survive, might not be raped after all if at the last moment, as she had historically, she consented to the act. No matter how many times they bought and sold you, thought Tim, the important thing for a city, as well as for a human, was not to act like a whore.

THE Aunties had turned to Ambassador McLuck for help in how best to eradicate Benz from their grandnephew's psyche. The Ambassador had responded generously with tickets to his private box at certain evening establishments.

"Of course he's depressed. He's in love," said Phoebe. "I recognize all the symptoms."

"Well, one does see splendid, inspiring Nordic women at the Lido and the Crazy Horse," said the Ambassador.

"But he is underage."

"Don't worry yourselves," said the Ambassador with a wave of his left fingers. "The maître d' is a friend of mine. And on Thursday we shall introduce him to the new revue at the Folies Bergères."

The Aunties looked at each other as if to say, Do you think we're doing the right thing?

"Now, if this doesn't ease the mind of our troubled young friend," said the Ambassador, "*A chacun son goût.* I can easily arrange for a personal introduction to certain mature lady friends of mine."

"No—no, thank you," interrupted Phoebe. "That will not be necessary. After all, there are limits to what we can engineer."

"Now, Ambassador," whispered Agatha, who always paid attention to details, "when you give Timothy your tickets, please do not breathe a word about this conversation."

Tim and Roland went to the Crazy Horse Saloon. Tim had been appalled not so much by the idea of barbarians, heavy with dollar wallets, watching a herd of statuesque women as by the sudden possibility that one of the girls might be Benz! It wasn't Paris that needed protecting, it was Mercedes. For in spite of everything the government did to boost tourism, Parisians continued to mistreat foreigners with a vengeance. And the latter didn't seem to mind. On the contrary.

WRAPPED in guitar notes and thickly padded dreams, Mercedes was dancing a four-week engagement, two shows a night except Mondays, and every evening the "bravas" cascaded down as if for the first time. Yet how quiet and lamblike they were when she danced!

The *Bateau de Rèves* was starting to creak and lose some of its shine, but Benz's dancing became stronger and more self-assured. This Thursday night, in the changing room just before going on, she noticed that Claude was not concentrating. He had misplaced her tortoiseshell comb and didn't know what time it was. As he helped her into her shoes and adjusted her fishnet stockings, she asked him if anything was wrong. He tried to smile, but he was not a very good actor. At last he said:

"You don't think I am going to lose you to your success, do you?"

She bent down next to him. Anwar was crying in his crib, but she put her hands on both sides of this sad priest's face and, touching the deep dark circles under his eyes, said:

"Claude, you never have to worry about me. I am more loyal than the trees and the mountains, more loyal than the ocean! Even if one day *payos* kiss the hem of my skirt like blind men stopping to listen to the song of a nightingale, even if they try to lick my clam-cut feet, or beg to become Benz touchers, they will never *ever* replace you in my affections. Nothing will ever separate us. You, Anwar, and me."

Only that morning, after prayers, Claude had turned to her and said:

"You and Anwar have filled up a void I didn't even know existed. I pray that God will forgive me."

Tonight, as she completed her Cartagena Number 3 turn and pulled out the pins from her black hair so that it crashed down over her face like a curtain, she saw Claude and the baby standing in the wings, four dark eyes in a Goya painting. How happy they made her!

She was only 1.71 meters tall. But on stage she felt endless, without borders. Her arms were swan necks and her legs pink flamingos. She was on fire. The music stopped and she froze as if dead, with one hand above her head. One minute, Monet was clapping and hugging her; the next, he and Anwar were gone. The "bravas" swelled as nude feathered ladies lined up in the pink floodlights. Suddenly Timoté and Roland were pushing their way past the security guard at the artists' entrance.

"Benz, that was absolutely wonderful," gasped Tim.

"Let go of me," she said coldly, and turned away.

"Benz, I can't believe this! I've finally found you!"

Tim laughed and tried to kiss her, but she pushed him away.

"Don't touch me."

"Benz, what's the matter?"

"My great loyal defender! You know very well what is the matter."

"No, I don't."

"Where is he?"

Mercedes looked around for Monet, S.J. One of the stagehands handed her Anwar and said that the priest had run out as soon as he had seen the two boys racing toward her loge.

"Benz, wait. I'm sorry. What could I do?" said Tim.

She ran for the exit, the boy at her heels.

A beautiful Thursday afternoon at the Arc de Triomphe. Master Tim, Wonderdog, and little Anwar, pushing his stroller ahead of him, stopped in front of a *bar-tabac*. It was not clear who in this trio exactly was leading whom. Chantal, the new girl on the corner of Rue Presbourg, stopped and cooed at the baby.

"Anwar, this is your Tante Chantal."

"Oh, he looks so much like you!" said Chantal, who was starting her afternoon shift in front of the Café Tilsitt.

"Anwar is in fact my adopted nephew."

"But the family resemblance is definitely there, Monsieur."

Tim tried to disentangle his dog from Chantal's legs. Chantal called over to Helga and her half-sister Nicole. The leg ladies smothered Anwar with their cheap perfume and heavy lipstick.

"This is Mercedes' baby."

"Oh, she is back in the house with you?" asked Helga.

"Yes. My Aunt Agatha insisted that Benz come and live with us again. Pepe and Manola weren't too happy about it. But so far, no problems."

On the corner of Wagram, Helga shouted to Evelyne, who brought with her Nastasia and Zaza. Anwar looked quite the little gentleman standing among these painted courtesans as they fussed over his little shorts, pale knee socks, and neatly combed hair.

"Anwar, I bet you never knew you had so many aunts," said Tim.

"He is so handsome!"

"—hey, did you hear? He just called you 'Papa'!"

"Oh, ha-ha-ha. No, that is only a joke."

The ladies asked Anwar a thousand questions. Tim was growing drunk on the fumes of their cheap cologne. Anwar gave the stroller a shove, kicked Wonderdog, and looked up at

Timothy defiantly, as if to say: "There, I've been a bad boy. Now will you lock me in my room?"

"Ah, the 'terrible twos,'" said Myrtille. "He is learning to assert his independence."

Anwar boxed Wonderdog's ears and reaffirmed his desire for punishment.

In his prime, Wonderdog would have bitten back; but now he only waited mournfully for Master Tim to assert his authority. After many a false start, Tim wished the ladies a good day and headed home with Anwar and Wonderdog.

Tim carried Anwar straight to Benz's room on the second floor. The Aunties (with the special consent of Alphonse Cardozo, obtained by telex) had insisted that Benz stay in a guest room, waited on by Manola and Pepe, at least until she finished her engagement at the Folies Bergères.

Benz was subject to fits of depression. She could not explain why or how: they just came, moments when everything was black and hopeless. She had her baby and her dancing, but from time to time, she would just sit in her bathtub with no interest in living. She missed Claude terribly.

Perhaps she should travel. Perhaps it was the lack of a man. *Paris Unveiled* ran an article on page 4 titled:

ENFORCED SEXUAL ABSTINENCE KILLS BEAUTY QUEEN!

The article, with quotes from acknowledged authorities and professors, told of a Miss Europe who, because of abstinence, had suffered terrible mood shifts, nervousness, laziness, loss of appetite, and anorexia and who had ultimately died, an apparent suicide. A psychiatrist at l'Hôpital Sainte-Anne was quoted as saying:

> "It's a life choice which an increasing number of young women today are making, fully conscious of what they are doing."

I am not one of those, thought Benz, who had made a different life choice; and yet when she counted the months, stretching back to before Anwar's birth, the weight of her involuntary abstinence became heavy on her shoulders.

"You're always laughing," said the girl who dressed next to her at the Folies. "You must be in love."

"In love?" said Benz, surprised.

"Yes, you're the happiest girl in the show. Always giggling, always talking."

Benz *was* in love. She loved Monet; he made all other men seem insignificant. She knew that if she were ever to consider life with another male, she would first have to forget Monet's enormous generosity and kindness, and this did not seem possible. The ones you want don't want you, and the ones you don't want forever chase after you, thought Benz, reading a stupid advertisement in *Paris Unveiled* that made her nauseous:

> Benz, please forgive me. I am a hopeless coward.
> How can I ever make it up to you? Tim

Tim found Mercedes in the pink bathroom, smoking, in a bubble bath. A splash of white light cutting through the lace curtains spread across her face. When the curtain moved, the play of shadow gave her face a strange otherworldly appearance.

"Benz, Anwar is being a brat. If I punish him as he expects me to, then it's not a punishment, it's more of a reward, right?"

She did not answer, but traced patterns with her hand through the bubbles.

"Benz, why are you taking a bath fully dressed?"

There was a wine bottle on the floor. Next to it, Tim noticed an electric wire running from the wall socket and two exposed copper filaments.

"Leave me alone," said Benz, staring at the smoke rings that curled up to the white-tiled ceiling and extending her dripping left hand toward the wires.

Tim grabbed and quickly unplugged the electric wire. There was Spanish guitar music playing on her cassette recorder. She had taken the intercom off the hook.

"Are you crazy, Benz?"

Little Anwar screamed from the potty, wanting to show how well he could wipe himself.

"Benz, are you trying to commit suicide?" Tim shouted.

She turned her face to the wall. Tim replaced the intercom on the hook and opened the windows wide. He knew she hated rock-and-roll, so he switched on Radio Luxembourg. Let her hate him! Let her chase him around the house. Anything was better for her than to lie here motionless, wrapped in her silence, floating in the blue-white water, her pearl-studded dress swaying indolently among the bubbles.

"I can't kill myself," she sighed, her breath heavy with wine. "You have ruined the moment!"

Tim collected all the razor blades and vials of prescription drugs he could find.

"My suicide attempt took so much effort to prepare," said Mercedes, closing her eyes. "I do not know when I will be this inspired again."

Tim unplugged the fuses for the entire second floor, and turned off the gas in the water heater. He put the boy to bed for his afternoon nap and returned to Benz's bathtub. He wished he could take all his energy and transplant it into her chest: You're depressed? Who isn't, these days? He brought her a bath towel and made her stand up.

"Timi, why can I never hold on to a man? What is my problem?" She had an unforgettable expression which the human countenance registers perhaps only once.

"Benz, you're an artist. Who ever heard of a happy artist?"

He wrapped a terry-cloth bathrobe around her.

"Timi, I am so tired of starting over and over. I do not have the energy to begin anew. I have become an *immobiliste.* I want to give up."

Had he ever known her, Tim wondered, this shivering Mercedes Pilar de Los Angeles del Rosario? How many death urges did she have hidden under that Gypsy will to survive? What was she thinking, for instance, as she closed her eyes and strained like a symphony conductor to catch some faraway sound?

"It's worse than falling for a married man."

"What is?"

"A priest."

"You're in love with a priest?"

She was silent. Flat tears were slowly spreading down her cheeks.

Was it conceivable that he didn't know her at all? How many times had Benz—Madonna of the high cheeks, flamenco child and husband hunter—attempted suicide? How often had she, while walking Wonderdog in her high heels along the dirty Paris streets or feeding soup to the sick Aunties, wanted to float away into an archipelago of ice and purity?

"I cannot be passive and quiet, Timi; I cannot tell him, '*Cheri*, stay with the Church.' This goes against every instinct in my body. I have hair, teeth, nails, and throat. I am not a saint; I cannot suppress my real feelings forever!"

"Please stop crying, Benz."

Tim pulled a strand of wet hair from her mouth. The tears were flooding her face. Benz the hot, Benz the gold-earringed, Benz the woman who had cured Tim of his first hangover with an Andaluz potion of raw egg, salt, garlic, red pepper, nutmeg, crushed basil, ginger, celery seeds, and rum (though the rum was only to give it taste), she was not what she seemed.

"All my life I am a young shoot. And I bend and bend in the wind. But now I am a tree and I snap."

Tim sat on the floor and massaged the calluses on the soles of her feet.

"If this priest loves you, he'll come for you, Benz."

"No, he won't."

"Why not?"

"He asked me to help him make his decision because he knows I am a Catholic and will answer him like a good parishioner. Ah, the Jesuits—my father used to say they could get into a revolving door behind you and come out in front! But I am not a '*Oui-oui-oui, mon père.*' I am not a dish towel, quiet, and passive—no! Without him, I have no interest in dancing."

Tim wrapped another towel around her.

"Benz, there hasn't been a night when I went to bed without thinking of you."

"Oh, shut up."

"Sometimes I'd look in a shopwindow at the Place des Ternes and every carrot, every cheese reminded me of you. At the MacMahon cinématheque, every seat, every ticket taker was you."

"Timi, I left your house like a whore, like a *dix-centime salope,* with two suitcases tied with string and a taxi waiting outside. And you were off somewhere on a vacation, chasing young girls around the swimming pool. If you'd been here then, I promise you, you'd have a very high-pitched voice today, Tim."

"Benz, I love you."

"You love me like you love ice cream or *steak pommes frites* —when things are easy. But what about when the wolf is at the door? When there was blood in the courtyard, then where were you?"

"Benz, I want to make it up to you."

"Yes, of course, because you feel guilty."

"No, because I care about you."

"Care all you want. And when you have finished growing up, then give me a call and we will talk again."

Tim's eyes filled with water.

"I'm sorry, Benz. I didn't know what to do. I'm a coward. I panicked."

Mercedes touched his cheek and put out her cigarette.

"Benz, please forgive me. I can't go on feeling like this. Please, I can't stand myself when I think about what I did."

He could not hold back his tears any longer.

"Stop it, Tim. Now you are being melodramatic and sloppy."

Benz of the brightly painted eyes with a memory bigger than all the attics of Avenue Foch and the *boulevards périphériques* put together, Benz the generous, Benz the pincher and slapper, Benz his soul mate of the easy laugh brushed her wet hair back from her forehead.

"Timi, it was also my fault. I should have been more careful.

I told people at the marketplace and in church that I was in love with a boy. I was happy. I talked too much."

"Benz, who is this new man of yours?"

"Timi, we are too sweet, we lack vigilance; that is why we get hurt. 'Protect your happiness like a bitch,' they say, 'and keep strangers away from it.' That is why today I am careful. I have learned my lesson."

"So that's why you won't tell me his name?"

"Yes, that and other reasons. Now fetch me a cup of coffee. I'm all right now. I feel better. The crying has helped me. Don't worry, I won't do anything stupid."

Tim's feelings for her were like all the notes on Pepe's guitar: there was no one chord he could pick out that he loved above the rest; they all formed a background hum of loyalty. When he leaned over to caress her cheek, he was really caressing the years he had lived with her in this big house. Her lips were swollen from crying.

"It's okay, Timi," she said. "I know you love me."

When she looked at him like this, he became a lonely trombone full of anxiety. What could he answer? As recently as three months before, he had wanted to live with her as man and wife; but now she was more like a sister, a mother, or both. What had happened to that unconditional, bottomless surrender, with an unlimited view on all sides?

ANWAR went in search of his Mister Slinky down the spiral service staircase. Mercedes gave chase and found him examining the mushrooms on the medieval cellar masonry.

"Anwar, *mon cheri,* this is a bad and dangerous place!"

In the furnace room, as orange-and-black shadows flew across the ceiling of the crypt, Anwar fingered a piece of bone and asked what it was. Mercedes did not answer, for as she bent down to pick him up, she saw an enormous menacing shadow on the wall—she saw Manola! The sparks and crush of the fire were so loud that Benz, carrying the child, could approach unheard. Manola wore a pair of wraparound sunglasses, rubber Wellingtons, the breastplate of a fourteenth-century suit of armor, ski mittens, and an oily gabardine that Pepe once used for gardening. Holding a fire poker in her right hand and a pair of tongs in the left, she was muttering to herself:

"Manola, hurry yourself and do not go crazy! This is for León and Murcia, for Madrid and Cartagena . . ."

Next to her on the ground was a metal crate full of gold coins, and behind, another crate full of solid-gold bars. Manola picked one up now with her tongs and thrust it into the fire. The gold crackled and melted. On the floor below the furnace was a very large silver mold which reminded Benz of the fenders of Pepe's highly temperamental Peugeot 203.

"Valencia, Albacete, Badajoz," continued Manola to herself. "For Valladollid, Burgos and Cáceres! For Salamanca, San Sebastián, Zaragoza, Bilbao, Barcelona . . ."

Mercedes kissed Anwar's cheek, but the noise of the furnace scared him and he began to cry. Manola turned quickly, brandishing the red-hot poker. Soot covered her face and neck. Her little ruby eyes flickered as she removed her sunglasses, and she growled:

"Benz, I have *find* the Loyalist gold! You must swear on all that is most *holy* to you, on Anwar, never to mention this to anyone! They ask you what you see here and you answer: *'Nada! Nada! Nada!' Comprendes?* Absolutely *nada!*"

Because Manola could not read or write in any language, Mercedes read the inscription on the box out loud and translated it into Spanish for her:

OR MASSIF PUR DE LA BANQUE DE FRANCE

"Never mind what it says," shouted Manola, baring her teeth. "This gold is mislabeled! We do this in 1939 to trick the Fascists. But every ounce is paid for in Loyalist blood. The soul of Spain has the receipt!" Manola made a fist with her right hand and bit her first knuckle. "This fist I have clenched for almost thirty years. I am not going to unclench it now! Each one of my memories is like a star nailed in the sky, and it whispers to me: 'Manola, this is for Jaén. This is for Santander. This is for Pamplona.' And Benz, I tell you, they shall not pass! *No Pasarán!* Not the Falange. Not the Trotskyites. And not the Moscow bastards of Negrín!" She wiped away the tears that rolled down her cheeks. "After the war, they take away my papa and two brothers and four hundred thousand other innocents. And these children of God never return!"

She dipped her hands deep into the gold coins and was quiet. Benz and Anwar stared in silence at this fat little woman dressed in an oily gabardine and armor:

"Manola if this is stolen gold, you could be in a lot of trouble."

"Trouble?" Manola slammed the red-hot poker into the furnace. "Benz, I do not give three whistles for what they may do to me! As Delegate Urreiztieta says at our last POUM General Assembly: 'Honored colleagues, I copiously defecate on the misbegotten ancestors of this bastardized world! *E dicho!*' In Madrid, we die like moths, by the thousands. We are so hungry, we eat flies. We eat the bark off trees; cats; flowers. We boil horse carcasses and shoes. And finally we eat the cowards who want to surrender. I do not let policemen like Raoul and his French laws scare me."

She spat on the ground.

"There are Moors on the coast," whispered Mercedes.

"What?" said Manola. "Benz, your Andaluz indirects don't work with us Basques."

"Someone is coming," explained Mercedes.

They were quiet for a moment. A man carrying a flashlight stumbled in the dark. After much swearing, Pepe climbed out of a hole at the bottom of the staircase and dusted himself off. He approached the two women shading his eyes with his left hand:

"The Aunties and the *señorito* are screaming for dinner. You two birds have any idea what time it is?" Noticing the shiny gold, Pepe knelt down by the first crate and caressed the bullion. "What the hell is this? Hey, I could use some of this to bet on Grand Bidet in the ninth."

Manola pulled out her Mauser and pointed it at her husband's head.

"Manola, my peach, you are the smartest, most intelligent woman I know. Let me tell you about this Algerian miracle horse that Anatole Gerbi is going to ride in the Grand Prix de Longchamps."

His wife pressed the barrel of her gun to his temple and said:

"Darling Pepe, because you say I am so intelligent, you are to drive me to Switzerland. And we are the most adoring, calm couple ever seen on the Autoroute du Sud. No arguing, no drinking, no fighting, no slapping. You agree?"

Pepe tried to kiss his wife, but she pulled his head back by the hair and said:

"I make new fenders for your car. With this strategem in 1937 we sneak gold out of Badajoz from under the nose of the Fascists. Now we do the same and deposit it in Geneva. But first you make certain the Peugeot is in perfect working order, *non?"*

Pepe nodded slowly at the ceiling, his head held back at a 45-degree angle by his wife's strong hands.

"Maman, are they fighting?" asked Anwar in a whisper.

"Non, mon petit chéri, Pepe and Manola love each other," Mercedes explained, and carried her child upstairs.

CHAPTER 11

Grand Bidet in the Ninth

MERCEDES HAD TRIED to live her life in big luminous drops of hope. She kept her desires and achievements limpid and private like the dome of the sky just before sunrise. But how many eons had she twisted and turned in her bed, and sighed for a happiness that seemed as unattainable as the horizon? Gypsies were not supposed to be in a hurry. But she was exhausted with waiting, and her suffering seemed to benefit no one.

She had achieved almost everything she set her mind to. But men were so stupid! How much more time, energy, and effort would she waste on them? Answer: none. Not one more milligram of moth-sperm of her energy would she spend in looking for the love of her life. "It will be Raoul, and bring on the wild horses," she told Manola.

Manola threw her arms around her and showered her with kisses and began to make plans for the wedding.

"You will be so happy, Benz. I know it."

To herself Benz said: Every night Raoul and I shall watch Antenne Deux on the tele; on weekends we'll have very married sex; we'll grow fat and ugly together. But at least Anwar will have a father.

She could not continue to live like a sewer rat without a *carte de séjour,* always scared of the police. She wanted Anwar to grow up a regular little Parisian boy with proper identification papers, his *cartable* on his back, gray knee socks, and his hair combed from right to left just like Timoté's. She no longer wanted to be an independent woman, strong, full of imagination, and lonely in bed on Saturday night. If later on some Errol Flynn or Cary Grant were to throw pebbles at her window at midnight, she would consider it. But until then she would be a policeman's wife, a law-abiding citizen of France.

IT was Tim's first date with a girl other than Benz. He had invited Patricia to the Jardin d'Acclimatation—an obvious choice, considering that he knew no square kilometer of Paris better.

They walked in through the gardens. He counted her hundreds of long thin braids intertwined like snakes and examined the space between her two front teeth. Tim loved her ready laugh, her chocolate skin, darker around the knuckles and the joints of her fingers. He counted the turquoise-and-gold spangles at her neck. Patricia's were not the thick Suchard and Nivea smells of Benz's bear cave, but a light, almost imperceptible vanilla.

Licking their ice cream cones, Patricia and Tim stopped to watch Monsieur Henri's gas-fired speedsters. Tim bought five laps' worth of tickets, but she declined to join him. (The possibility that someone might pass up a ride on one of these modified speedsters had never crossed Tim's mind.) He promised to be quick and strapped himself into his old blue Number 7. Monsieur Henri had not changed much in the four years since he'd last seen him—a few more wrinkles around the eyes, but the same grease on the arms, the same shy smile.

Tim accelerated. The blue speedster roared off, sputtering and skidding around the track. It was not as fast, or as dangerous, as he remembered. In fact, it felt stupid. Maybe Benz had been just as bored as Patricia, but at least with her newspaper she had managed not to show it, not to make him feel silly.

Tim stopped in the pits and offered the balance of his unused tickets to a boy waiting in line. He felt sheepish. Patricia looked up from her reverie and said, "Oh, you're done already," as one might to someone returning from a public *pissoir.* Tim left without talking to Monsieur Henri, embarrassed to be so much older than the other boys on the track today.

They walked from stand to stand. Patricia was not interested in any of the games Tim suggested. With regret he had to forgo shooting the cardboard clowns in the eye to win a chocolate Carambar. Nor was she in the mood to fish in the duck pond for magic prizes. The phony, frozen smile that Patricia gave him when he asked whether she might be interested in firing a machine gun reminded him of the smiles his mother used to flash into the void as she spoke on the telephone to people she couldn't stand. In desperation, Tim suggested the baby merry-go-round, but Patricia declined.

She stopped by a cage of peacocks and Java roosters. In all his years of coming to the Jardin d'Acclimatation, Tim had not once paid attention to these birds, or to any of the wild animals here, for that matter. Patricia knelt and poked her little finger through the fence:

"Aren't they beautiful?"

Tim nodded. He waited patiently while she talked to the birds in chirps and kisses.

"Too bad the Fratellini circus isn't in town," said Tim. "You would have laughed your head off at some of their gags."

Patricia ran forward to see a bear stand up for peanuts. Tim stood very near her now. He examined the henna in her hair. The strap of her brassiere showed through her cream-colored blouse. He thought perhaps he ought to kiss her, as any one of his schoolmates would have traded in his aviator sunglasses to do. But he felt awkward in the extreme. The bear sniffed the air. Tim's lips brushed against Patricia's cheekbone.

"Don't," she said, and started running down the main footpath toward the exit on her long gazelle legs.

For a moment he watched her. Then he raced after her. Past the candy-apple vendor, the *crêpes bretonnes* salesman, past the Corsican machine-gun man with his ancient three-legged dog sleeping on the counter, past the Arab fortune-teller. Tim's red face reddened even more as Monsieur Henri emerged from behind a sputtering engine and gave him a knowing wave of the hand. He had never come here with a girl before! They were all watching him: the *guimauve* salesman, the old woman who ran the bumper cars, even Zangaro, the lion tamer, and Zangaro's young audience who waited for him to start his act. Tim would never be able to come here again, in the same way he used to; no more cheating or bending the score to get a bigger Napoleon statuette or a bird whistle. After today, he would always be "the boy who had chased after a mulatto girl."

Why had he brought Patricia here, of all places, he wondered: to his holy of holies? He wasn't only running past the flying saucer where he had pedaled so fast Gerbi vomited out of the porthole, past the monkey and bird houses, past the herbarium and distorting mirrors; he was running out of the playground in his mind. Each stride he took made him older. He was running out of youth and into middle age!

What destruction he was leaving in his wake! Only seventeen and already he had lost Benz, lost his Jardin d'Acclimatation, lost his horse. He was losing his hair, teeth, and eyesight. He was becoming a man with a past! Only Anwar gave him some sense of permanence, and even he was growing at an alarming rate.

Patricia was hailing a taxi when he caught up with her by the front gate on the Rue de la Porte de Sablons. The wooden train was filling up with children and their nannies for its short run through the Bois de Boulogne. Patricia was crying.

"What's the matter?" he asked, breathing hard.

"All you can think about is that stupid Benz—don't lie! You are so distant, it makes me sick! Well, go marry her if you love her so much! She's got a huge chest and a big ass. So what if she doesn't know who Franz Kafka is or how to conjugate a verb? Don't touch me."

Tim knew the entire playground was watching him. Two eyes from behind every little booth stared at this beautiful mulatto girl who was crying. And what could he say? She was right. But how did Patricia know? (He hadn't uttered a word all afternoon about Mercedes.) Maybe she sensed she was not a part of the marrow of his bones or the architecture of his soul, as Benz was.

Tim watched Patricia get into a taxi and waved goodbye. He held his palm inward toward his face, the way Benz had taught him, so as not to cast an evil spell.

GRAND Bidet was so high-strung that it took both Mohammed and Ismaël to hold her still while Anatole Gerbi mounted her. Gerbi's left hand had not regained its full strength, and so he wrapped the reins around his wrist as tightly as he could.

Benz sat in the Cardozo box at Longchamps with Anwar next to her, dressed in a little suit and hat. The Aunties had set the date for her wedding to Raoul. He was there by her side, long-nosed, emanating Métro odors, his uniform askew and various neck hairs, missed while shaving, sticking out of his shirt collar. Benz had not heard from Monet since he had been visited by a Jesuit envoy from Rome about five months earlier. Ah, Claude, Claude, you will become another chimera in my life—like Sean, like the Baron, these rabbit-footed lovers who ran at the first smell of trouble. Cowards all, thought Benz, fanning herself with a race program.

On the track, Grand Bidet bucked and reared. Gerbi, wearing the candy-pink-and-turquoise colors of the Cardozo racing stable, was trembling like a leaf. Tim worried that Grand Bidet, alias Edithe de Mon Coeur, would not make it past the reviewing stands, much less all the way to the starting gate, without throwing Gerbi to the ground. The thoroughbred, naturally excitable, appeared not to have taken at all well to the boat trip from Algiers, or to the stabling in the garage shared by the Irish Embassy and the Cardozos, or to her new surroundings.

Through his field glasses, the Baron Isidore noticed that the jockey of the white Number 3 filly had one eye pointing east and the other floating westward. In spite of what McLuck counseled, Rothschild changed his bet to the favorites, Fils de Personne and Tappepassifort. No matter how reliable a tip, the

Baron insisted on the jockey at least being sober, although he elected not to tell his good friend the Ambassador about the rider's condition.

Race officials waited patiently for the Cardozo entry to side-step and rear her way down to the start. Master Tim secretly prayed that a flood or other natural disaster might force the cancellation of this race and thus avoid the scandal that would ensue when the judges discovered Gerbi's horse-switching deal, and banned the Cardozo stable from Longchamps forever!

Benz named the riders' colors—"pink, baby green, blue-black, canary yellow, Bordeaux, aquamarine"—one by one to Anwar. The odds against the Cardozo-stable entry were getting worse by the minute. A hundred to one. A hundred and twenty-five to one. A hundred and forty-eight to one. Pepe had bet every centime he could borrow, including Agatha's charity-ball money which she kept in a sewing box behind her hats. The French flag fluttered in the center of the racecourse. The crowd waited tensely.

Suddenly the horses were off. All except Grand Bidet, that is, who had somehow gotten turned around in the starting gate and was trotting in the opposite direction. Yellow, turquoise, orange-striped, mauve, white-checked, and royal blue came thundering down the straightaway. The jockeys seesawed for the lead, and the crowd cheered. Monsieur Gerbi *père* sat with his head in his hands, not daring to look.

"What is he doing?" screamed Raoul, who had taken his entire savings out from under his mattress to bet on this race. Raoul Delbose had a real aversion to spending money and generally subscribed to the school of thought that said you should never buy sugar, salt, pepper, or napkins if you could steal these from the police force cantine.

At long last Gerbi got his mount turned in the proper direction and shouted the magic words:

"AAAALLLAHHH AKKKHHHBBBAAARRRR!"

The mare had been owned by a muezzin crier in Sidi-bel-Abbès and, according to Gerbi, had a great desire to get into heaven first, before any other horse. Grand Bidet had proved this in Abu Dhabi, Baghdad, and Algiers. At the words "Allah

Akhbar," her ears shot back and her beautifully thin legs pistoned so hard Gerbi was held airborne on the tiny saddle. Grand Bidet was catching up fast.

Her competition was bunched together at the far end of the track, with the white horse bringing up the rear. The jockeys bent over their mounts, faces replaced by goggles. Black, maroon, dappled, the horses blended into one another. At the back of the pack, one madman bounced up and down, howling the name of the Lord of Islam:

"AAALLLAAAHHH AAAAKKKKHHHHBBBBAAARRR!!"

"That's enough! Be quiet now!" screamed Pepe.

There was nothing *per se* illegal about a jockey shouting at his horse during a race; but Pepe had cautioned Gerbi that this might be sufficient cause for disqualification if the judges determined that it hindered the other riders.

"Vas-y, Fils de Personne!" shouted the Baron.

"Allez, Tappepassifort!" chimed his chauffeur.

The favorites were neck-and-neck in the lead. Algerian street cleaners and waiters who filled the first rows of the cheapest General Admissions section began to press forward. Having placed their 5-franc bets for themselves and their friends at home, they suddenly took up Gerbi's muezzin call and howled:

"ALLAH AKHBAR!"

Out of the last turn, Grand Bidet was fourth. Down the stretch they thundered. It was hard to see. The jockeys' racing colors left a trail of blurred rainbow: Hooves kicking up dirt. Whips on the flanks and on the hindquarters. Horses nosing one another out of the way. Saliva flung backward over the bridles. Sweat down the legs and foam slipping from the bit. Speed and clattering dust. With the Algerian waiters in the stands giving a rousing call to the beneficence of the Almighty and His prophet, Grand Bidet heaved into third place.

"Maman, this is boring," said Anwar.

"Be patient. Maman will take you home in five minutes."

Gerbi slipped, bounced, caught himself, lunged forward, and grabbed Grand Bidet's mane with his good hand. Suddenly the white filly was only two heads behind the leader and gaining. Only one head behind. On his hands and knees, Pepe was picking up the betting stubs he had thrown to the ground. The horses thundered toward a photo finish.

It was over! Mercedes cried and hugged her son. Pepe leaped into the air waving his beloved tickets and kissed McLuck on the cheeks three times. Press photographers crowded around the Cardozo box. In the winner's circle, the President of the Association Hippique de Longchamps prepared to award the prize. Anwar asked if they could go home now. The Baron lodged a protest, for there was nothing else he quite disliked so much as losing money.

The judges pored over the televised replay of the race and checked Edithe de Mon Coeur's vital statistics against those of the Number 3 horse that had run. They checked her urine and her eyes, and after a tense half-hour, unanimously declared the white Number 3 horse the winner. Gerbi, his father, and Ismaël hurried to help Grand Bidet back into her trailer. The animal's general disposition toward humanity had not changed or softened with the race—she started kicking as soon as she was inside the trailer. Instead of stabling her at Bagatelle with the other Cardozo horses where prying eyes might come and investigate, Gerbi drove directly to Number 10½. Tim had agreed that Gerbi could hide the horse in the converted carriage house that now served as a garage until it was safe to ship her back to Algeria, incognito.

That afternoon the collection line was extremely short: Raoul, Pepe, Tim, McLuck, Benz; two leg ladies from the Rue Rude who had taken the afternoon off; three Algerians who were members of the same neo-Trotskyite wing of the Party as Gerbi *père*, and who asked for their money in crisp new 100-franc notes.

AUNT Agatha took her chamber pot out from under the bed, made sure it was clean, and asked Mercedes to hang it from her balcony. As in all Bastille Day celebrations, she did this in memory of her Aristo admirer, le Marquis de Prévost. Around the Arc de Triomphe, tricolored Republican flags fluttered in the breeze. Pepe still had the same red Médoc glow in his cheeks he had acquired when Grand Bidet rode into the Grand Prix de Longchamps record books.

On the avenue below, Foreign Legionnaires, firemen, Boy Scouts, and armored divisions gathered to begin their annual parade down the Champs-Elysées. Mercedes watched them form in neat little uniformed rows and march off toward the Arc, their legs moving in perfect unison. Two squadrons of close-formation jets roared down the axis of the avenue, skimming over the rooftops, rattling the windows and trailing thick red-white-and-blue smoke. The cloud cover broke and two or three rays of sunlight shone down, touching the balconies of Number 10½ ever so gently.

Mercedes headed to the kitchen in her snow-white dress and lit a cigarette. Aunt Phoebe, who saw Benz's unenthusiastic acquiescence to this marriage as the crowning achievement of a three-year campaign, rushed around the house frantically, ordering the caterers about. She and Agatha were so happy with this wedding—the first the Cardozo house had seen since Cascasia and Alphonse had married in 1950. The rooms were filled with young men in long white aprons shining the crystal and silverware, arranging bouquets and wreaths, stocking the bar with swizzle sticks and coasters, counting the tureens and sauces on the sideboard.

Sitting in the kitchen, her head in a cloud of steam, Benz felt the same resignation she imagined Mary must have felt when she settled for an ox, an ass, and a bed of hay. Joseph may have been no better than Raoul, a pale stand-in for her real lover. But he would do, "*faute de mieux,*" as they say. Prepared to officiate, Claude Monet entered the kitchen dressed in a black habit and a yellow-and-purple sash around his waist. In Benz's many recent *penaṛ a baji,* the man (or transvestite) she was to marry had appeared in the floating egg yolk, dressed in a black dress! Now she had the occasion for a private goodbye.

"Claude, can you not save me from a life without love?"

It was a cruel thing to say, but if she did not do so now, when would she?

"Mercedes, I cannot do what you want me to do."

"Why not?"

"If it were only a matter of my desires and my career, this would be easily resolved, Mercedes. But it creates too many conflicts for others. It would hurt Raoul terribly and the school and the Order. It would upset the Cardozos, and it would not be proper to ask you to bear this burden."

"We don't have to get married. I can say I'm your cook."

"That's not what I mean," he said, smiling.

"Claude, I don't care if I have to live in a nunnery, just give me a child. If you don't I shall become a hard, nail-bitten, nail-spitting liberated woman. A woman without love. Is that what you want?"

Why not use blackmail to inflict guilt? God tugged on Claude's conscience every minute of every day. She had to get her say in as well.

The doorbell rang. Gerbi and his dad arrived, both wearing gray suits and white shirts buttoned at the collar, without ties. Ambassador McLuck and his charming wife, Fiona, followed, as did Signor Cinquemani. Roland, with his parents and cousin Patricia, came next. The doorbell rang to announce the bridegroom and his friends from the police force. Many new arrivals. From the kitchen, Mercedes could hear Manola addressing them all—the sergeant, the lieutenant, and the other garlic-breathing flatfoots—as *"mi capitán,"* but she did not get up and greet any of them. The Ladies of the Passy Literary, Knitting and Opera Society floated in. A film crew sent by Mr. Cardozo's studio to do a documentary on the house stalked the halls with sound boom and bright lights.

Mercedes poured herself a glass of red wine and collected the train of her gown, a hand-me-down of Madame's. From behind the white veil, she could hear the guests crowd into the Grand Ballroom. Her isolation, her faith in her *baraka* were still formidable. It struck her that she should be called not just "Benz," but "Lioness Benz"—she hunted alone, raised her young alone, fought the whole world alone.

There was a muffled noise in the hallway. Manola suddenly pushed Pepe into the kitchen, kicking and slapping him with a folded-up newspaper:

"You worse-than-imbecile, you are not even smart enough to be a cretin! The car and solid-gold fenders are disappeared!"

"Who should want," mumbled Pepe, "to steal my old Peugeot rattletrap?"

"God forgive me," shouted Manola, "for marrying a worse-than-moron!"

Pepe fetched his keys and wallet. Manola extinguished a cigarette and lit another without noticing that two more of hers burned in the ashtray on the counter:

"Pepe, you are seventy-three! You should learn something by now! At first, I try to civilize you. But you never get better. You get worse! I must have rocks in my head to marry you! My family, they beg me: 'Get rid of the bum.' But oh, no, I defend you! I try to say it is Benz who leads you astray, poor Benz who is as pure as the driven snow. But you are a pig! Do not return to the house until you find the Peugeot!"

More guests stood at the door. Mercedes filled her glass and swept toward the front of the house. It is never too late to make your entrance, she thought, especially on the day you finally discard your dreams. The Baron entered with a tall, stiff-looking blond model on his arm. Isidore smiled at her with an oily mouth and said:

"*Mercedes chérie, ça fait tellement longtemps . . .*"

She recalled the shame of waiting at Chez Hubert as if it had happened this morning. She heard every guffaw, every grotesque whisper of the maître d' and of the waiters, and she began, squinting at the Baron:

"Pardon—you have aged so terribly since we last met, I fear I cannot remember your name. But I heard the operation was not successful. Do the doctors let you out on weekends now?"

It was not easy to embarrass an old bastard like the Baron. He smiled with charming aplomb and, unruffled, introduced his companion, a *danseuse* called Myrna. Mercedes slowly picked lint off the Baron's lapel, turned toward Myrna, and said:

"He really is very short, even when he stands on his wallet. How do you not lose him in a crowd?"

• • •

Gerbi was at the wheel of Pepe's Peugeot 203. They had taken it from the garage, next to where Grand Bidet was stabled. The sputtering car made Monsieur Henri's old speedsters feel like magic carpets by comparison. The 203 banged and backfired, then jolted forward. Gerbi pretended to close his good eye and drive only with his glass eye. The gears caught, and the car zoomed straight up Rue Rude, then along the sidewalk of Avenue de la Grande Armée. Gerbi swerved to avoid two nuns and bumped along with the right wheels up on the curb.

Usually when they went for joyrides, Tim, Roland, and Gerbi borrowed the Cardozo Citroën. This was the first time they had borrowed Pepe's ancient air-injected Peugeot and the first time they had let Gerbi drive. But worse, because of the Bastille day parade, the police had cordoned off vast sections of the city.

"You idiot," shouted Timothy. "That was a red light you missed!"

"It's a question of averages—just like grades," said Gerbi, pumping the rather tired accelerator, whooping and yahooing. "I stop for most of them."

The car sputtered, lunged forward, careened into five lanes of merging traffic, and skidded to a stop. Gerbi closed both eyes as he maneuvered the heavy old car. Roland tapped Tim on the shoulder:

"Tim, remember my observation that the rich live on the west side of Paris? Well, studies have shown that cities develop—"

Tim leaned over and grabbed the wheel to avoid a car coming off Avenue Marceau on the right:

"Gerbi, it's '*priorité à droite.*' Ever hear of that?"

They hiccuped every three meters and slammed into a bus in front of them. Swerving again *à droite,* they sped toward the Seine.

"New wealth tends to grow on the west side," said Roland, seemingly unaffected by Gerbi's driving technique, "but when they rehabilitate the older east side of a city, then the center moves east again, and the rich remain—"

"Roland, would you shut up!"

Dizzy and shaken, Timothy again lunged for the wheel. Twelve lanes of traffic were converging into one, all demanding the right of way. Gerbi opened his good eye and put his foot on Pepe's famous air brakes.

Mercedes stood on the balcony. She could see lovers parading down Avenue Foch arm in arm, staring up at the fireworks; blue and red, yellow and pink, silver and gold sparkles lit up the night sky in massive drooping orchids. Below, her guests continued to arrive at the door. From behind, Pepe whispered to Benz:

"I am leaving the old witch tonight!"

"You can't leave Manola at your age!" said Mercedes, trying to hold him upright, for he was quite drunk by now.

"The hell I can't. Just watch," said Pepe, staggering off.

Whoosh-whoosh—the firework rockets flew skyward, enveloping the base of the Eiffel Tower in thick smoke. Below on the avenue, firemen, Foreign Legionnaires, and neighborhood girls stopped dancing and stared up at the sky. Manola's Spanish girlfriends oohed and aahed along with the *capitáns*. Even The Ladies of the Passy Literary, Knitting and Opera Society who had seen almost a century of annual fireworks displays fell quiet and stared in amazement.

Manola, meanwhile, began throwing cabbages and other old vegetables off the balcony at Pepe. He was on the corner of Rue Rude, talking to Chantal and Helga, who never took days off, not even for national holidays. Helga yelled up at Manola: "Stop that, you stupid cow." Pepe began to return her cabbages.

The fireworks boomed. Guests on the balconies gasped and clapped as blue-and-pink irises cascaded into reds and turquoises and floated lazily to the ground. Silver-and-blue sparkles banged and, rushing earthward, burned bright orange. When the fireworks subsided, the crowd on Avenue Foch began to disperse. Ambassador McLuck leaned from the Cardozo balcony and invited his footmen and maids standing in the driveway below to join the celebration at Number 10½. Flashbulbs exploded in the lobby. Martin Duchesne, now Minister of the Interior, arrived and kissed the Aunties on both cheeks:

"ON BEHALF OF THE REPUBLIC AND IN RESPECT OF THE POWERS VESTED IN ME BY THE PRESIDENT AND BY THE NATIONAL ASSEMBLY, IT IS MY GREAT HONOR AND PLEASURE TO . . ."

Agatha smiled. Phoebe pinched her cheeks so as not to look too pale in the next day's press photographs. The minister draped a red-ribboned medal around each Auntie's neck. Benz could hear Grand Bidet, locked up in the garage, kicking and rearing in her makeshift stable. The minister stopped to sip some champagne and continued:

". . . TO PERSONALLY DECORATE THESE CHARMING LADIES WITH THE ORDER OF THE GRAND MERIT AND HEREBY DESIGNATE THIS EXQUISITE MANSION AN HISTORICAL MONUMENT."

Tim, Roland, and Gerbi returned more dead than alive from their automobile ride, just as Wagner's wedding march began playing on the phonograph. They joined the guests climbing to the private chapel on the fourth floor of the Irish Embassy. First went the Aunties, then Master Tim with Benz on his arm, then the Minister and his bodyguards, then The Ladies of the Passy Literary, Knitting and Opera Society. A cabbage crashed through one of the staircase windows as the leg ladies and Pepe continued to return Manola's fire.

Raoul waited at the altar, wearing a blue tuxedo with white lapels and looking uncommonly like Luis Mariano.

"Am I really going to marry this stupid man?" Benz whispered to Tim as they walked down the aisle.

Tim was blinded by the gold teeth of the Spanish girls lining the bride's side of the chapel, which seemed to reflect the waxed mustaches of the *mi capitáns*. The Aunties sat in the first row with flowered dresses and cherries in their white hats.

"Don't let me do this, Tim."

He squeezed Benz's hand. During the organ prelude, Claude Monet, S.J., appeared at the altar. He looked terribly handsome and yet gaunt in his black-and-white vestments. He bade them all stand.

• • •

In the converted garage, Grand Bidet, terrified by the sounds of the fireworks, the guests, and now the honking of horns in the street, was rearing and kicking. With eyes rolling and ears straight back, the white Algerian thoroughbred landed a direct kick on the wooden carriage-house door. It splintered open. Hearing the sound of the wedding music, the winner of the most recent Longchamps Grand Prix ripped her halter and, slipping on the flagstones and kicking wildly, exploded into the central courtyard of the Cardozo home. Chauffeurs and embassy personnel guards tried to subdue her, but Grand Bidet reared and bucked mercilessly.

After the invocation, Claude Monet spread his arms wide and said in a slow calm voice:

"Mercedes Pilar de los Angeles del Rosario, do you take Raoul—" the rest of the sentence was inaudible. Even Raoul did not hear the "to be your lawful wedded husband to have and to hold, for better or for worse?" The priest had stopped in mid-sentence and was staring at Mercedes.

In the silence that followed, Raoul looked around at his best man and his friends to see if this was a practical joke of some sort. His fellow *capitáns* were advancing on the altar. Monet and Benz were running away! The lieutenant tried to grab Monet, but already he and Benz had locked the sacristy door and were running down the main staircase. A Lady of Passy fainted. Martin Duchesne and Ambassador McLuck cheered Mercedes on from the back of the chapel.

"What ever is going on?" Agatha asked Phoebe.

"I don't know," said Phoebe, "but you can't say our Benz is not a determined young woman."

"Defrocker of priests!" shouted Raoul, but his intended bride was not listening. She was gripping her Jesuit. They ran, followed by uniformed policemen, with lipstick on their white service collars, and screaming maids. (Fufa, Dora, and Manola were kicking shins and swinging their handbags.) Monet had never looked handsomer—his hair disheveled, his vestments blowing like a cape behind him, as he rushed down the main staircase.

They stopped on the third-floor landing. The *capitáns* were closing in on them from all sides, as the official chauffeurs and embassy guards rushed up the stairs to see what was happening. Benz remembered the trapdoor behind the Gobelin tapestry that Sean used to use, and they managed to break free and run down to the second floor. But more policemen appeared there. Monet opened a French window. Below them was a rearing white horse, just as Benz's *baji* had always predicted. Raoul grabbed Benz's left arm, but Tim, lunging forward, bit Raoul's right earlobe and managed to get him to let go of Benz. Roland caught the first charging lieutenant with a patented Dr. Feng roundhouse kick to the larynx. Gerbi asked Raoul's best man and sergeant for a match and then kneed him in the groin. It was magical for Benz to watch her men fighting the *payo* police force in the finest *gitano* tradition! Casting off his chasuble, Monet leapt from the first-floor window onto Grand Bidet. Without saddle or bridle, the tall, strong priest managed to stay on the bucking mare by grabbing her white mane as tightly as he had ever grabbed anything. Just at that moment, an explosion and a flash of light from a lone firework silhouetted Monet against the night. Grand Bidet reared. The police and the chauffeurs cowered before the animal's wildly stamping hooves. Realizing that the prophecy was being fulfilled, Benz kissed Timi on the lips, jumped out after her Jesuit, locked her arms around his waist, and screamed up:

"Take care of Anwar for me, Timi. I will send for my *churumbel* when all is clear."

The police in the courtyard were trying to pull the Jesuit off his mount, but Grand Bidet kicked up such a fuss that they were unable to approach. Gerbi issued his familiar Islamic call to prayer. The filly's ears shot back; with all four hooves springing in the air at once, she clattered loudly out of the courtyard, under the front portal, and down the driveway. Tim ran to the front balcony and saw Benz's long black hair trailing over the horse's white back as it galloped down the Avenue.

"Go, Benz! Go!"

Holding Monet tightly around the middle, Mercedes, who was an expert rider, turned her face into the wind and breathed in the smell of freedom. Police cars raced after them, but already Grand Bidet was past Place Malakoff and Porte Dauphine, heading into the protective foliage of the Bois de Boulogne. The midnight streets were full of Bastille Day revelers. Her Jesuit was throwing everything away for her, and she would love him madly. She would be as loyal as his dog, or the shadow of his dog. They would start a new religion together, better than the old one. But first they would stay in bed for a week.

"What excitement!" said Phoebe, who did not want this disturbance to ruin the Cardozo festivities.

The guests, minus Raoul and his fellow *capitáns,* slowly reconvened in the Grand Ballroom. Ambassador McLuck sidled up to the bar and said to the Baron:

"We really must visit Seville one day, or wherever that Gypsy lass is from. Who knows? We may get lucky and find another one just like her!"

One Lady of Passy asked Agatha:

"McLuck has diplomatic immunity and a very undiplomatic desire for Scotch and French women. I wonder if he is not the father of Mercedes' little boy."

"Oh, no, I know who the father is," replied Agatha. "I even know his two great grandaunts."

Two Ladies of Passy gasped. Agatha offered them each another flute glass of champagne.

Pepe and Manola were carrying their small suitcases to their recently returned Peugeot, past the ministerial chauffeur and bodyguards. It was convenient that most of Raoul's friends on the force, as well as the minister's uniformed police escort, had chased after the runaway horse—they had even forgotten about Pepe's cabbage throwing and dropped the charges against him for "illicit mopery with intent to loiter."

Waving goodbye to the Aunties and honking the horn, Pepe and Manola set off on their short vacation to Switzerland. From the front balcony, Tim watched the heavy gold fenders cause the exhaust pipe to scrape along the ground, igniting a large spark every now and then.

"Papa, what are you doing?" asked Anwar, rubbing sleep

from his puffy eyes and standing in his little striped pajamas on the balcony of the Grand Ballroom.

"I am *not* your papa. I am your—well, your uncle," said Tim, who, slightly drunk, was inserting his *zizi* through the wrought-iron flowers of the balcony and yellowing off the third floor into the garden below.

"But Auntie Agatha and Auntie Phoebe say you are my papa."

"They are only joking."

"Maman also says you are."

"She does?"

Tim's testicles suddenly retreated up into his belly, and the vocal cords tightened in his throat.

"Yes. And tell me, Papa, why are you not potty-trained?"

"When I was your age, I used to be a dead shot for the azaleas down there. Sometimes I even managed to hit a Hollywood actor on the head, if I was lucky."

Anwar made no reply.

How could Mercedes be so certain he was the papa? What a surprise, to become a parent at eighteen—just like that, as you were urinating into the azaleas. It was a little off-putting. Still, it was better than becoming a papa at fifteen, the year that Benz had been dismissed. It was like playing a game of cards: For months, years, perhaps even decades, you never knew why a certain person acted a certain way, did a certain thing. But years later, when you least expected it, *à propos* of nothing, you turned over the card that explained all that had gone on before. "Everything eventually falls into place," Pepe liked to say.

Tim looked down into the first-floor garden. There was someone there; a woman in white was sitting in the shadows of the greenhouse. As far as he knew, no one had used the first-floor studio since Sophia Loren two months ago. He made his way downstairs, past couples kissing in doorways and the minister's chauffeur sharing a bottle of wine with Helga and Chantal. Laughter and music wafted out from the ballroom.

Stealing through the driveway, he quietly opened the ivy-covered gate and looked into the garden. In the semidarkness, he picked his way past the impatiens and roses. Upstairs, the phonograph poured forth his Aunties' favorite Strauss waltz.

Far in the back, under the purple wisteria of the gazebo, he could see a tall blond figure sitting alone. Tim approached her quietly. She was lost in thought, her sky-blue eyes floating in the darkness amid the pungent smell of honeysuckle and mint.

"Hello, Kim."

"Oh. Hi, Tim."

"You remember *me*, your pen pal who never writes?"

"Of course; have a seat. What is all the festivity about?"

"Oh, Mercedes just got married. She married her priest."

Was he dreaming, or had it started to snow on Bastille Day? The entire landscape was turning white. Kim Novak sat quietly in her snowbound garden looking dreamily at him. He dared not touch her or even speak. She seemed so delicate and evanescent, a sudden gesture or a cough might make her disappear. Not since he had run barefoot up the service staircase to see Benz at fifteen had he felt this sensation of water running inside him.

"I had to come back," said Kim.

All the stars were out on this July 14, but still snow continued to fall in big dry flakes! There was such a perfume-laden intimacy between them, such a conspiracy of the heart, that it was difficult for Tim to think of anything to say.

"When I lived here I was so sad," said Kim. "I felt so alone, almost suicidal."

"I know," said Tim. "I used to watch you sit here by yourself for hours at a time."

In this dark, wisteria-covered gazebo where snow lay in a blanket and more fell from God knows where, Tim sensed that he and Kim had lived prior lives together.

"Isn't it strange what nostalgia we have for places, even the ones that made us feel miserable? We love them because they're part of us."

Tim nodded.

"I told the director that I remember sitting here alone in winter, here in the most secluded and intimate corner of the whole globe. And so for the shoot tomorrow, the film crew is giving us man-made snow."

"Help!"

Aunt Agatha had opened the gate to the garden and stumbled in. Tim ran to the bed of impatiens where she had slipped and helped her to her feet. The two or three sips of champagne she had allowed herself had gone straight to her head.

"Everything is all right, Auntie," said Tim. "That was only a horse, a white horse. Mercedes eloped with Claude Monet, my school Principal."

"Oh, really, that girl!" said Agatha, her face broadening into a smile.

Tim introduced Kim Novak to his Aunt and led them both upstairs to the ballroom. A late-night fog descended on the Tour Eiffel. Time was slowing down. Firecrackers and waltzes faded in the distance. The guests blurred into the background. Auntie Agatha floated away. The Chinese paper lanterns on the Irish Embassy balcony played red, pink, and blue in the wind. Nothing remained in the rooms but these pale Hollywood eyes, staring tirelessly at him.

He gave Kim the full tour of the house, starting, of course, in his little room with the Napoleon curtains and the dangling Messerschmitts, and ending up in his father's study on the fifth floor, where Kim studied Alphonse's collection of fertility dolls and fetishes and Tim pointed out her autographed picture among those framed on the wall.

Waiters collected the silverware, piling dirty dishes on trays, gathering empty bottles. Tablecloths were shaken out off the courtyard balconies, and napkins were tossed into laundry bags. The kitchen filled up with dishes. Snow continued to fall outside the window, courtesy of the Cardozo movie studio, amassing on the balcony and spilling into the street, while the rest of Avenue Foch remained green and lush. Guests rejoined their limousines as the Cardozo party wound to an end.

On the *boulevards périphériques*, leading south toward the Porte d'Orléans, newsmen were fighting to get the latest details on a mysterious black Peugeot that was throwing off sparks and leaving a trail of 24-karat-gold nuggets, causing enormous traffic jams in its wake. Treasure hunters, Bastille Day partiers, and ne'er-do-wells were fighting each other for specimens. A reporter for *Paris Unveiled* noted that the "suspicious black sedan" was being driven by "hit men for a mass racketeering syndicate."

Tim and Kim Novak danced alone. Every now and then, looming out of the gauze of the night, floating on a riverbed of fog, a building appeared. Next door, the Ambassador shouted increasingly drunken orders to his uniformed soubrettes. Tim gripped his mythical Kim Novak. There would be time to begin again, to look back and examine all that was or could have been, to analyze and reaffirm. But for now, he was quite at peace with the world, in the arms of this mythical being he had known for so many years.

They danced silently. In the distance, Notre-Dame appeared out of the mists and floated by, bathed in floodlights.

MASTER Tim accompanied his son to his first day of school. He was only three and a half, but the Jesuits liked to start them young. Abbé Picabia was the new Principal of Saint-Philippe de Passy. Master Tim stood in the courtyard, shaking hands with his old professors: Fathers Brouette, Marcellin, LeClerc, Roquebrune. Anwar, at his side, rolled a ball of snot between thumb and forefinger like a regular little gentleman. The oculist had prescribed corrective lenses, and Anwar wore new round wire-rimmed glasses that made him look very earnest indeed, not unlike Tim at the same age.

"How long did you say Maman was going to stay on vacation?"

"Oh, not too long. She called to say she loves you very much. And that she wants you to study very hard."

Tim remembered the first day he had come here, death and terror pounding in his heart. He recalled standing in this very spot, holding on to Pepe's corduroy jacket and realizing for the first time that the world consisted of nothing but a bunch of bastards waiting to beat you into a pulp. Pepe had stood reading his horse-racing sheets, oblivious to Tim's entreaties and arguments for going home. In his day, Tim had searched desperately for a friendly face in the crowd of nasty *payos*.

But little Anwar was much different. Brave and resolute, he let go of Tim's hand and walked alone into the sea of tear-stained, maudlin, punchy faces. (They all looked shabby and ill-fed at this age, even the rich ones who dined on *canard à l'orange* every night.) Somehow Anwar had already managed to get ink on his fingers. But he was making the rounds like a politician, perhaps a future inspector of finished works, surveying the terrain, shaking hands with unknown colleagues, even smiling politely.

Tim walked to his old classroom. He entered it quietly, as if entering a chapel. The room was crowded with voices, smells, ghosts. How could he have fitted his knees under such a small desk? There it was, in the middle of the last row, with his name carved in letters eight centimeters high: TIM CARDOZO. The O.A.S. signs and de Gaulle's *Croix de Lorraine* etched into his old desktop had almost entirely disappeared. Superimposed were Marxist slogans, Mitterand's name, and the *Nouvelle Droite* symbol of a circle with a cross through it.

Yes, this was where he had once vomited so effectively into a paper cone, up to the brim. And this was the path the cone had traveled as his Royalists troops passed it to the front of the class. This was where that King of Kiss-asses, Laval, had crunched the cone, splattered himself, screamed, and been slapped by the Abbé for disturbing a geography class. This was the door out which Laval had run, crying, to the general merriment of everyone except his Republican followers. And this was where, years earlier, Tim had peed in his pants rather than raise his hand to ask to go to the bathroom and risk incurring the ire of Père Buchner, a math teacher reputed to be a Nazi camp commandant. This was where they had lined up to pay their condolences the day after Kennedy was shot.

"Come on, Papa."

"Anwar, is this going to be your classroom?"

"Papa, it's time for you to go. All the other parents are leaving."

"Have you found new little friends, then?"

"No. Not yet."

"Don't worry. The first day is the worst. It gets better. See this desk? It belonged to Uncle Gerbi. Notice the chewing gum and the snot stuck under the chair here? If they assign you this desk, ask to be transferred. That was my desk over here, with Uncle Roland."

"Papa, my classroom is at the other end of the courtyard, one of the new ones they've just built. Now you have to leave."

"And don't give away any of your bread-and-chocolate *goûter*—unless, of course, it's absolutely crucial to win over a new ally."

"Papa, you can't stay here."

"I used to give mine away regularly to make them think I was a big shot, and I was a fool. Your little comrades will like you regardless of that. *Compris?*"

"Oui, Papa."

"And try to pay attention to what's being said in class by the teacher. I never listened. But I was an idiot. I didn't know then what I know now."

"Papa, you talk like an old man. But you're not, you're still in *lycée!*"

"I just don't want you to get into trouble by trying to copy me, that's all."

"Don't worry. Maman told me never to do anything the way you did it."

"Your mother said that?"

"Oui."

Master Tim was silent for a moment.

"Well . . . she's right. Of course."

"Come on, Papa. The other boys are going to laugh if they see you staying behind with me."

"Well, goodbye, Anwar. Don't cry. Be a brave little fellow."

"And you too, Papa."

Little Anwar, with his big eyes looking so serious behind his round wire-rims, caressed his father's cheek. Then he led Tim out of the classroom and through the courtyard, where the priests were lining up the students alphabetically and by age, and where the names of the many alumni who had fallen in the Great War of 1914–1918 were engraved in gold on white marble plaques.

"Okay. Go home now, Papa."